PRAISE FOR KATE FURNIVALL'S

The Russian Concubine

"I read it in one sitting! Not only a gripping love story, but a novel which captures the sights, smells, hopes, and desires of Russia at the dawn of the twentieth century, and pre–Revolutionary China, so skillfully that readers will feel they are there."   —Kate Mosse

"The kaleidoscopic intensity of British writer Kate Furnivall's debut novel, *The Russian Concubine*, compellingly transports us back to 1928 and across the globe to the city of Junchow in northern China. . . . Lydia is an endearing character, a young woman with pluck and determination. . . . With artistry, Furnivall weaves a main plot that hinges on Lydia's love affair with Chang An Lo, a Chinese youth who is a dedicated Communist at a time when Chiang Kai-shek's Nationalists are gaining ground. . . . Furnivall's novel is an admirable work of historical fiction."   —*Minneapolis Star Tribune*

"Furnivall vividly evokes Lydia's character and personal struggles against a backdrop of depravity and corruption."   —*Publishers Weekly*

"The wonderfully drawn and all-too-human characters struggle to survive in a world of danger and bewildering change . . . caught between cultures, ideologies—and the growing realization that only the frail reed of love is strong enough to withstand the destroying winds of time."   —Diana Gabaldon

"This stunning debut brings the atmosphere of 1920s China vividly to life. . . . Furnivall draws an excellent portrait of this distant time and place."   —*Historical Novels Review*

Also by the Author

THE RUSSIAN CONCUBINE

THE

Red Scarf

KATE FURNIVALL

BERKLEY BOOKS, NEW YORK

THE BERKLEY PUBLISHING GROUP
Published by the Penguin Group
Penguin Group (USA) Inc.
375 Hudson Street, New York, New York 10014, USA
Penguin Group (Canada), 90 Eglinton Avenue East, Suite 700, Toronto, Ontario M4P 2Y3, Canada
(a division of Pearson Penguin Canada Inc.)
Penguin Books Ltd., 80 Strand, London WC2R 0RL, England
Penguin Group Ireland, 25 St. Stephen's Green, Dublin 2, Ireland (a division of Penguin Books Ltd.)
Penguin Group (Australia), 250 Camberwell Road, Camberwell, Victoria 3124, Australia
(a division of Pearson Australia Group Pty. Ltd.)
Penguin Books India Pvt. Ltd., 11 Community Centre, Panchsheel Park, New Delhi—110 017, India
Penguin Group (NZ), 67 Apollo Drive, Rosedale, North Shore, 0632, New Zealand
(a division of Pearson New Zealand Ltd.)
Penguin Books (South Africa) (Pty.) Ltd., 24 Sturdee Avenue, Rosebank, Johannesburg 2196,
South Africa

Penguin Books Ltd., Registered Offices: 80 Strand, London WC2R 0RL, England

This is a work of fiction. Names, characters, places, and incidents either are the product of the author's imagination or are used fictitiously, and any resemblance to actual persons, living or dead, business establishments, events, or locales is entirely coincidental. The publisher does not have any control over and does not assume any responsibility for author or third-party websites or their content.

First edition: July 2008

Library of Congress Cataloging-in-Publication Data

Furnivall, Kate.
   The red scarf / Kate Furnivall.—Berkley trade paperback ed.
      p. cm.
   ISBN 978-0-425-22164-8
   1. Women prisoners—Fiction.   2. Russia (Federation)—Fiction.   I. Title.
   PR6116.U76R43 2008
   823'.92—dc22

                                                        2007040037

PRINTED IN THE UNITED STATES OF AMERICA

10 9 8 7 6 5 4 3 2 1

For Norman
With my love

ACKNOWLEDGMENTS

I would like to thank Jackie Cantor for her guidance and all at Berkley for their wonderful enthusiasm and beautiful artwork. Special thanks to my agent, Teresa Chris, for wisely curbing my excesses and for her invaluable insight into the heart of the book.

Thanks also to Alla Sashniluc, for providing me with not only the Russian language but also a greater understanding of the Russian way of life in a Urals village, and for correcting my blunders.

I am grateful to Amy Schneider for casting her eagle eye over the manuscript with such expertise and to Patty Moosbrugger for her generous support.

Finally to Norman, with my love and thanks for your constant encouragement and advice. It means everything to me.

ONE

Davinsky Labor Camp, Siberia
February 1933

THE Zone. That was what the compound was called.

A double barrier of dense barbed wire encircled it, backed by a high fence and watchtowers that never slept. In Sofia Morozova's mind it merged with all the other hated lice-ridden camps she'd been in. Transit camps were the worst. They ate up your soul, then spat you out into cattle trucks to move you on to the next transit camp. *Etap* it was called, this shifting of prisoners from one camp to another until you had no friends, no possessions, and no self left. You became nothing. That was what they wanted.

WORK IS AN ACT OF HONOR, COURAGE, AND HEROISM

Those words were emblazoned in letters of iron a meter high over the gates of Davinsky prison labor camp, and every time Sofia was marched in and out to work in the depths of the taiga forest she read Stalin's words above her head. Twice a day for the ten years that were her sentence. That would add up to over seven thousand times, if she lived that long, that is, which was unlikely. Would she come to believe that hard labor was an ACT OF HEROISM after reading those words seven thousand times? Would she care any more whether she believed it?

As she trudged out into the snow in the five o'clock darkness of an Arctic morning, six hundred prisoners, two abreast in a long silent shuffling crocodile, she spat as she passed under Stalin's words. The spittle froze before it hit the ground.

*T*HERE'S going to be a whiteout," Sofia said.

She had an uncanny knack for smelling out the weather half a day before it arrived. It wasn't something she'd been aware of in the days when she lived near Petrograd, but there the skies were nowhere near as high, nor as alarmingly empty. Out here, where the forests swallowed you whole, it came easily to her. She turned to the young woman sitting at her side.

"Go on, Anna, you'd better go over and tell the guards to get the ropes out."

"A good excuse for me to warm my hands on their fire, anyway," Anna smiled. She was a fragile figure, always quick to find a smile, but the shadows under her blue eyes had grown so dark they looked bruised, as though she'd been in a fight.

Sofia was more worried about her friend than she was willing to admit even to herself. Just watching Anna stamping her feet to keep the blood flowing made her anxious.

"Make sure the brainless bastards take note of it," grimaced Nina, a wide-hipped Ukrainian who knew how to swing a sledgehammer better than any of them. "I don't want our brigade to lose any of you in the whiteout. We need every single pair of hands if we're ever going to get this blasted road built."

When visibility dropped to absolute zero in blizzard conditions, the prisoners were roped together on the long trek back to the camp. Not to stop them from escaping, but to prevent them from blundering out of line and freezing to death in the snow.

"Fuck the ropes," snorted Tasha, the woman on the other side of Sofia. Tasha tucked her greasy dark hair back under her headscarf. She had small narrow features and a prim mouth that was surprisingly adept at swearing. "If they've got any bloody sense, we'll finish early today and get back to the stinking huts ahead of it."

"That would be better for you, Anna," Sofia nodded. "A shorter day. You could rest."

"Don't worry about me."

"But I do worry."

"No, I'm doing well today. I'll soon be catching up with your work rate, Nina. You'd better watch out."

Anna gave a mischievous smile to the three other women and they laughed outright, but Sofia noticed that she didn't miss the quick glance that passed between them. Anna struggled against another spasm of coughing and sipped her midday *chai* to soothe her raw throat. Not that the drink deserved the name of tea. It was a bitter brew made from pine needles and moss that was said to fight scurvy. Whether that was true or just a rumor spread around to make them drink the brown muck was uncertain, but it fooled the stomach into thinking it was being fed and that was all they cared about.

The four women were seated on a felled pine tree, huddled together for warmth, kicking bald patches in the snow with their *lapti*, boots shaped from soft birch bark. They were making the most of their half-hour midday break from perpetual labor. Sofia tipped her head back to ease the ache in her shoulders and stared up at the blank white sky that today lay like a lid on them, shutting them in, pressing them down, stealing their freedom from them. She felt a familiar ball of anger burn in her chest. This was no life. Not even fit for an animal. But anger was not the answer because all it did was drain the few pathetic scraps of energy you possess from your veins. She knew that. She'd struggled to rid herself of it, but it wouldn't go away. It trailed in her footsteps like a sick dog.

All around as far as the eye could see, and the mind could imagine, stretched dense forests of pine trees, great seas of them that swept in endless waves across the whole of northern Russia, packed tight under snow, and through it all they were attempting to carve a road. It was like trying to dig a coal mine with a teaspoon. Dear God, but road building was wretched. Brutal at the best of times, but with inadequate tools and temperatures of twenty and even thirty degrees below freezing it became a living nightmare. Your shovels cracked, your hands turned black, your breath froze in your lungs.

"*Davay!* Hurry! Back to work!"

The guards crowded around the brazier and shouted orders but didn't leave their circle of precious warmth. Along the length of the arrow-straight scar that sliced through the trees to make space for the new road, hunched bodies pulled their padded coats and ragged gloves over any patch of exposed skin. A collective sigh of resignation rose like smoke in the air as the brigades of women took up their hammers and spades once more.

Anna was the first on her feet, eager to prove she could meet the required norm, the work quota for each day.

"Come on, you lazy . . ."

She didn't finish the sentence. She swayed, her blue eyes glazed, and she would have fallen if she hadn't been clutching her shovel. Sofia reached her first and held her safe. The frail body started to shake as coughs raked her lungs and she jammed a rag over her mouth.

"She won't last," Tasha whispered. "Her fucking lungs are . . ."

"Ssh." Sofia frowned at her.

Nina patted Anna's shoulder and said nothing. Sofia walked Anna back to her patch of the road, helped her scramble up onto its raised surface and gently placed the shovel in her hand. Not once had Anna come even close to meeting the norm in the last month, and that meant less food each day in her ration. Sofia shifted a few shovels of rock for her.

"Thanks," Anna said and wiped her mouth. "Get on with your own work." She managed a convincing smile. "We'll be home early today. Before the whiteout hits."

Sofia stared at her with amazement. *Home.* How could she bear to call that place *home*?

"I'll be fine now," Anna assured her.

You're not fine, Sofia wanted to shout, *and you're not going to be fine.* Instead she gazed hard into her friend's sunken eyes, and what she saw there made her chest tighten. *Oh Anna.* A frail wisp of a thing, twenty-eight years old. Too soon to die, much too soon. And that moment, on an ice-bound patch of rock in an empty Siberian wilderness, was when Sofia made the decision. *I swear to God, Anna, I'll get you out of here. If it kills me.*

TWO

_T_HE whiteout came just as Sofia said it would. But this time the guards paid heed to her warning, and before it hit they roped together the gray crocodile of ragged figures and set off on the long mindless trudge back to camp.

The track threaded its way through unremitting taiga forest, so dark it was like night inside, the slender columns of the pine trees standing like Stalin's sentinels overseeing the march. The breath of hundreds of women created a strange and disturbing sound in the silence, while their feet shuffled and stumbled over snow-caked ruts.

Sofia hated the forest. Which was odd, because she had spent most of her life on a farm and was used to rural living, whereas Anna, who loved the forest and declared it magical, had been brought up in cities. But maybe that was why. Sofia knew too well what a forest was capable of; she could feel it breathing down her neck like a huge unwelcome presence, so that when sudden soft sounds escaped from the trees as layers of snow slid from the branches to the forest floor, it made her shiver. It was as though the forest were sighing.

The wind picked up, stealing the last remnants of heat from their bodies. As the prisoners made their way through the trees, Sofia and Anna ducked their faces out of the icy blast, pulled their scarves tighter around their heads. They pushed one exhausted foot in front of the other and huddled their bodies close to each other. This was an attempt to share their remaining wisps of warmth, but it was also something else, something more important to both of them. More important even than warmth.

They talked to each other. Not just the usual moans about aching backs or broken spades or which brigade was falling behind on its norm, but real words that wove real pictures. The harsh scenes that made up the daily brutal existence of Davinsky camp were difficult to escape; even in your head they clamored at you. Their grip on the mind, as well as on the body, was so intractable that no other thoughts could squeeze their way in.

Early on, Sofia had worked out that in a labor camp you exist from minute to minute, from mouthful to mouthful. You divide every piece of time into tiny portions and you tell yourself, *I can survive just this small portion*. That's how you get through a day. No past, no future. Just this moment. Sofia had been certain that it was the only way to survive here, a slow and painful starvation of the soul.

But Anna had other ideas. She had broken all Sofia's self-imposed rules and made each day bearable. With words. Each morning on the two-hour trek out to the Work Zone and each evening on the weary trudge back to the camp, they put their heads close and created pictures, each word a colorful stitch in the tapestry, until the delicately crafted scenes were all their eyes could see. The guards, the rifles, the dank forest and the unrelenting savagery of the place faded, as dreams fade, so that you're left with no more than faint snatches of something dimly remembered.

Anna was better at it. She could make the words dance. She would tell her stories and then laugh with an expression of pure pleasure. And the sound of it was so rare and so unfettered that other heads would turn and whimper with envy. The stories were all about Anna's childhood in Petrograd before the Revolution, and day by day, month by month, year by year, Sofia felt the words and the stories build up inside her own bones. They packed tight and dense in there when the marrow was long gone, and kept her limbs firm and solid as she swung an ax or dug a ditch.

But now things had changed. As the snow began to fall and whiten the shoulders of the prisoners in front, Sofia turned her face away from them to Anna. It had taken her a long time to get used to the howling of a Siberian wind, but now she could switch it off in her ears, along with the growls of the guard dogs and the sobs of the girl behind.

"Anna," she urged, holding on to the rope that bound them together, "tell me about Vasily again."

Anna smiled; she couldn't help it. Just the mention of the name *Vasily* turned a light on inside her and her blue eyes blazed, however wet or tired or sick she was. Vasily Dyuzheyev—Sofia had already learned a lot about him. He was Anna's childhood friend in Petrograd, two years older but the companion of her every waking thought and of many of her nighttime dreams. He was the son of Svetlana and Grigori Dyuzheyev, aristocratic friends of Anna's father, and right now Sofia needed to know everything about him. *Everything.* Not just for pleasure this time—though she didn't like to admit even to herself how much pleasure Anna's talk of Vasily gave her—now it was serious.

Sofia had decided to get Anna out of this hellhole before it was too late, and her only hope of succeeding was with help. Vasily was the only one she could turn to. But would he help? And could she find him?

The day was as colorless as today. It was winter and the new year of 1917 had just started. All around me the white sky and the white ground merged to become one crisp shell, frozen in a silent world, for there was no wind, just the sound of a swan stamping on the ice of the lake with its big flat feet. Vasily and I had come out for a walk together, just the two of us, wrapped up well against the cold. Our fur boots crunched satisfyingly in the snow as we ran across the lawn to keep warm.

"Vasily, I can see St. Isaac's Cathedral dome from here. It looks like a big shiny snowball," I shouted from high up in the sycamore tree.

I'd always loved to climb trees and this was a particularly tempting one down by the lake on his father's estate.

"I'll build you a snow sleigh fit for a Snow Queen," he promised.

You should have seen him, Sofia. His eyes were bright and sparkling like the icicle fingers that trailed from the tree's branches, and he watched me climb high up among its huge naked limbs that spread out over the lawn like a skeleton. He didn't once say "Be careful" or "It's not ladylike," like my governess, Maria, would have.

"You'll keep dry up there," he laughed, "and it'll stop you leaping over the sleigh with your big feet before it's finished."

I threw a snowball at him, then took pleasure in studying the way he carefully carved runners out of the deep snow and set about creating the body of the sleigh with long sweeping sides. At first I sang "Gaida Troika" to him, swinging my feet in rhythm, but eventually I couldn't hold back the question that was sitting on my tongue burning a hole.

"Will you tell me what you've been doing, Vasily? You're hardly ever here anymore. I . . . hear things."

"What kind of things?"

"The servants are saying it's getting dangerous on the streets."

"You should always listen to the servants, Annochka," he laughed. "They know everything."

But I wasn't going to be put off so easily. "Tell me, Vasily."

He looked up at me, his gaze suddenly solemn, his soft brown hair falling off his face so that the bones of his forehead and his cheeks stood out sharply. It occurred to me that he was thinner, and my stomach swooped when I realized why. He was giving away his food.

"Do you really want to know?"

"Yes, I'm twelve now, old enough to hear what's going on. Tell me, Vasily. Please."

He nodded pensively, and then proceeded to tell me about the crowds that had gathered noisily in the Winter Palace Square the previous day and how a shot had been fired. The cavalry had come barging in on their horses and flashed their sabers to keep order.

"But it won't be long, Anna. It's like a firework. The taper is lit. It's just a question of when it will explode."

"Explosions cause damage." I was frightened for him.

From my high perch I dropped a snowball at his feet and watched it vanish in a puff of white.

"Exactly. That's why I'm telling you, Anna, to warn you. My parents refuse to listen to me, but if they don't change their way of living right now, it'll be . . ." He paused.

"It'll be what, Vasily?"

"It'll be too late."

I wasn't cold in my beaver hat and cape, but nevertheless a shiver skittered up my spine. I could see the sorrow in his upturned face. Quickly I started to climb down, swinging easily between branches, and when I neared the bottom, Vasily held out his arms and I jumped down into them. He caught me safely and I inhaled the scent of his hair, all crisp and cool and masculine. A foreign territory that I loved to explore. I kissed his cheek and he held me close, then swung me in an arc through the air and dropped me inside the snow sleigh on the seat he'd carved. He bowed to me.

"Your carriage, Princess Anna."

My heart wasn't in it now, but to please him I picked up the imaginary reins with a flourish. Flick, flick. A click of my tongue to the make-believe horse and I was flying along a forest track in my silver sleigh, the trees leaning in on me, whispering. But then I looked around suddenly, swivelling on the cold seat. Where was Vasily? I spotted him leaning against the dark trunk of the sycamore, smoking a cigarette and wearing his sad face.

"Vasily," I called.

He dropped the cigarette in the snow where it hissed.

"What is it, Princess?"

He came over, but he didn't smile. His gray eyes were staring at his father's house, three stories of elegant windows and tall chimneys.

"Do you know," he asked, "how many families could live in a house like ours?"

"One. Yours."

"No. Twelve families. Probably more, with children sharing rooms. Things are going to change, Anna. The tsarina's evil old sorcerer, Rasputin, was murdered last month and that's just the start. You must be prepared."

I tapped a glove on his cheek and lifted one corner of his mouth. "I like change."

"I know you do. But there are people out there, millions of them, who will demand change not because they like it but because they need it."

"Are they the ones on strike?"

"Yes. They're desperately poor, Anna, with their rights stolen from them.

You don't realize what it's like because you've lived all your life in a golden cage. You don't know what it is to be cold and hungry."

We'd had arguments before about this, and I knew better now than to mention Vasily's own golden cage. "They can have my other coat," I offered. "It's in the car."

At that the smile he gave me made my heart lurch. It was worth the loss of my coat. "Come on, let's go and get it," I laughed.

He set off in long galloping strides across the lawn, leaving a trail of deep black holes in the snow behind them. I stretched my legs as wide as I could to place my fur boots directly in each of his footsteps, and all the way I could still hear the wind tinkling in the frozen trees. It sounded like a warning.

$\int$OFIA sat cross-legged on the dirty floorboards without moving. The night was dark and bitterly cold as the temperature plummeted, but her muscles had learned control. She had taught herself patience. So that when the inquisitive gray mouse pushed its nose through the rotten planks of the hut wall, its eyes bright and whiskers twitching, she was ready for it.

She didn't breathe. She saw it sense danger, but the lure of the single crumb of bread placed on the floor was too great in the food-less world of the labor camp, and the little creature made its fatal mistake. It scurried toward the crumb. Sofia's hand shot out. One squeak and it was over. She added the miniature body to the three already in her lap, carefully broke the tiny crumb of bread in two, popped one half of it into her own mouth, replaced the other on the floor, and settled down again into an immobile silence.

"You're very good at that," Anna's quiet voice said.

Sofia looked up, surprised. In the dim light she could just make out the restless blond head on one of the bunks and the delicate pale face.

"Can't you sleep, Anna?" Sofia asked softly.

"I like watching you. I don't know how you move so fast. It takes my mind off"—she gestured about her with a loose flick of her hand—"off this."

Sofia glanced around. The darkness was cut into slices by a bright trickle of moonlight through the narrow gaps between the planking of the walls. The long wooden hut was crammed with a hundred and fifty undernourished women on their hard communal bunks, all dreaming of food and filling the chill air with their snores and coughs and moans. But only one was sitting with a precious pile of meat in her lap. Though only twenty-six, Sofia had spent enough years in a labor camp to know the secrets of survival.

"Hungry?" Sofia asked with a crooked smile.

"Not really."

"Don't fancy roast rodent?"

"*Nyet*. No, not tonight. You eat them all."

Sofia jumped up, bent over Anna's bunk, and breathed in the stale smell of the five unwashed bodies and unfilled bellies that lay on the bedboard.

She said fiercely, "Don't, Anna. Don't give up." She took hold of her arm and squeezed it hard. "You're just a bundle of bird bones under this coat. Listen to me, you've come too far to give up now. You've got to eat whatever I catch for you, even if it tastes foul. You hear me? If you don't eat, how are you going to work tomorrow?"

Anna closed her large blue eyes and turned her face away into the darkness.

"Don't you dare shut me out, Anna Fedorina. Don't do that. Talk to me."

Only silence. And the quick shallow breathing. Outside, the wind rattled the wooden planks of the roof, and Sofia heard the faint screech of something metal. One of the guard dogs at the perimeter fence barked a challenge.

"Anna," Sofia said angrily, "what would Vasily say?"

She held her breath. Never before had she spoken those words or used Vasily's name as a lever. Slowly the tousled blond head rolled back and a smile curved the corners of her pale lips, a faint smudge in the darkness that couldn't hide the fresh spark of energy that flickered in the blue eyes.

"Go and cook your wretched mice then," Anna muttered.

"You promise to eat them?"

"Yes."

"I'll catch one more first."

"You should be sleeping." Anna's hand gripped Sofia's. "Why are you doing this for me?"

"Because you saved my life."

Sofia felt rather than saw Anna's shrug.

"That's forgotten," Anna whispered.

"Not by me. Whatever it takes, Anna, I won't let you die." She stroked the mittened fingers, then pulled her own coat tighter and returned to her spot by the hole and the crumb. She leaned her back against the wall, letting the trembling in her limbs subside until she was absolutely still once more.

"Sofia." Anna's whisper rippled inside a gentle laugh. "You have the persistence of the devil."

Sofia smiled. "He and I are well acquainted."

THREE

SOFIA leaned against the hut wall, shutting her mind to the icy drafts, and let Anna's words echo quietly in her head.

That's forgotten.

Two years, eight months ago. Sofia pulled off the makeshift mitten on her right hand, stitched out of blanket threads and mattress ticking, and lifted the two scarred fingers right up to her face. She could just make out the twisted flesh, a reminder every single day of her life. So no, not *forgotten*.

It had started when they were taken off axing the boughs from felled trees and put to work on the road instead. It was progressing fast. The prison labor brigades were not told where it had come from nor where it was headed, but the pressure was hard and unrelenting and it showed in the attitude of the guards, who grew more demanding and less forgiving of any delays. People started making mistakes.

Sofia reached such a state of exhaustion that her mind became foggy and the skin on her hands was shredded despite the makeshift gloves. Her world became nothing but stones and rocks and gravel, and then more stones and rocks and gravel. She piled them in her sleep, shoveled grit in her dreams. Hammered piles of granite into smooth flat surfaces till the muscles in her back forgot what it was like not to ache with that dull grinding pain that saps your willpower because you know it's never going away. Even worse was the ditch digging. Feet in slime and filthy water all day and spine fixed in a permanent twist that wouldn't unscrew. Sleep became a luxury, and eating became the only aim in life.

"Can any of you scarecrows sing?"

The surprising request came from a new guard. He was tall and as lean as the prisoners themselves, only in his twenties and with a bright, intelligent face. What was he doing as a guard, Sofia wondered? Most likely he'd slipped up somewhere in his career and was paying for it now.

"Well, which one can sing?"

Singing used up precious energy. No one ever sang. Anyway, work was supposed to be conducted in silence.

"Well? Come on. I fancy a serenade to brighten my day. I'm sick of the sound of your fucking hammers."

Anna was up on the raised road crushing stones into place, but Sofia noticed her lift her head and could see the thought start to form. A song? Yes, why not? She could manage a song, yes, an old love ballad would . . .

Sofia tossed a pebble and it clipped Anna's ankle. She winced and looked over to where Sofia was standing three meters away knee-deep in ditch water, scooping out mud and stones. Her face was filthy, streaked with slime and covered in bites and sweat. The summer day was overcast but warm, and the need to keep limbs completely wrapped up in rags against the mosquitoes made everyone hot and morose. Sofia shook her head at Anna, her lips tight in warning. *Don't*, she mouthed.

"I can sing."

It was a small dark-haired woman in her thirties who'd spoken. She was usually quiet and uncommunicative.

"I am an . . ." She corrected herself. "I *was* an opera singer. I've performed in Moscow and in Paris and Milan and . . ."

"Excellent! *Otlichno!* Warble something sweet for me, little song-bird." The guard folded his arms around his rifle and smiled expectantly.

The woman didn't hesitate. She threw down her hammer with disdain, drew herself up to her full height, took two deep breaths, and started to sing. The sound soared out of her, pure and heart-wrenching in its astonishing beauty. Heads lifted as smiles and tears altered faces.

"Un bel di, vedremo levarsi un fil di fumo dall'estremo confin del mare. E poi . . ."

"It's *Madame Butterfly*," murmured a woman who was hauling a wheelbarrow piled high with rocks into position on the road.

As the music filled the air with golden enchantment, a warning shout tore through it. Heads turned. They all saw it happen. The woman with the barrow had dropped it carelessly to the ground as she stopped to listen to the singing and it had started to topple. It was the accident all feared, a barrow load of rocks plunging down over the edge of the raised road surface on top of you in the ditch. You didn't stand a chance.

"Sofia," Anna screamed.

Sofia was fast. Water up to her knees hampered her escape, but her reflexes had her spinning out of the path of the rocks. A great jet of water leaped out of the ditch as the rocks crashed down behind her. Except for one. It ricocheted off the rubble that layered the side of the new road and came crunching down on Sofia's right hand just where her fingers were clinging to the bank of stones.

She made no sound.

"Get back to work," the guard yelled at everyone, disturbed by what he'd caused.

Anna leaped into the water beside Sofia and seized her hand. The tips of two fingers were crushed to a pulp, blood spurting out in a deep crimson flow that spilled into the water.

"Bind it up," the guard called out and threw her a rag from his own pocket.

Anna took it. It was dirty and she cursed loudly. "Everything is always dirty in this godforsaken hole."

"It'll be all right," Sofia said as Anna quickly bound the scrap of cloth around the two damaged fingers, strapping them together as a splint for each other and stemming the blood. "Here, take my glove as well."

Sofia could feel the blood draining from her face as well as her fingers, and there was an odd chalky taste inside her mouth.

"Thank you," she muttered.

Her eyes stared into Anna's and though she kept them steady, she knew Anna could see something shadowy move deep down in them, like the first flutter of the wing of death.

"Sofia," she said as she thrust the hand first into her own glove and then into Sofia's wet one for greater protection against knocks, "don't you dare."

Sofia reclaimed her hand and looked at the bulky object as though it didn't belong to her anymore. They both knew it was inevitable that it would become infected and both knew that her body lacked sufficient nutrition to fight the infection.

"Back to work, you two," the guard shouted. "No talking."

"Don't dare what?" Sofia asked under her breath.

"Don't you dare even think that you won't come through this. Now get on that road in my place and haul stones. At least they're dry." Anna seized the shovel from where it had fallen and set to work in the water.

Sofia scrambled up onto the road and for a second stared down at Anna's blond head, as if she were memorizing every hair of it. "One day, Anna, I'll repay you for this."

AFTER that, Sofia became ill. They both knew she would, but the speed of it shocked them.

"Tell me something happy, Anna," Sofia had said. "Make me smile."

It was past midnight and they were sitting on the floor of the barrack hut, backs to the wall in their usual place, only four days after the accident. Sofia could sense Anna's concern like something solid in her lap. Neither said much, but they weren't fooling each other. The injured hand was worse, much worse, and her skin had grown dry and feverish. Her cheeks were so flushed that Anna told her she looked almost healthy, which made Sofia laugh, but what little flesh she possessed was melting away, leaving just bones and sharp angles behind. Her work rate was too slow to earn anywhere near the norm and even though Anna fed her pieces of her own meager *paiok*, Sofia couldn't always keep it down. The fever made her vomit.

Sofia cradled her throbbing hand against her breast and said once more in a low whispery voice, "Tell me something happy, Anna."

From somewhere nearby came the popping sound of thumbnails crushing the plump gray bodies of lice, but Anna started to weave her words and the pain began to drift away into the darkness. That was the time that Anna told her about when Vasily taught her to ice-skate on the frozen lake. At the end of it Sofia had laid her head on Anna's shoulder and chuckled.

"I believe," she said softly, "I am falling in love with your Vasily."

T'M going to lose my hand."

"No."

"You've seen it, Anna."

"Go to the medical hut when we get back to the Zone."

They looked at each other. Both knew that was a stupid statement. The *feldshers* wouldn't bother with a bandaged hand. Anyway infections were so rife in the medical hut that if you were well when you went in there, you would certainly be dead by the time you came out. TB was endemic in the camp, bloody lungs eaten up with it and spreading the disease with every cough.

"I was thinking," Sofia said calmly, "of getting hold of Nina's saw and asking you to cut off my hand."

Anna stared hard at her. The punishment for self-mutilation was a bullet in the brain. "I think," she said sharply, "we must think of something better than that."

*A*NNA did think of something else, but it wasn't something better. At the time the hut was full of uneasy rumors. They rustled in the air like the wind in the forest as the ragged prisoners huddled on their bunks and told each other it was the woman's own fault. *That stupid woman.* They meant the opera singer.

She'd been shot. A quick bullet in the back of the brain. You don't break rules, not where everyone can see. The guard learned the same

lesson, but his was a harder one because he was forced to face an exe-
cution squad made up of his own colleagues. That way they all
learned the lesson. Sofia shuddered when she recalled how close Anna
had come to bursting into song that day on the road.

"Here, this will help." Cradling the hand gently, Anna had started
to unwind the slimy piece of rag that bound it.

Sofia didn't even open her eyes. She was lying on the bedboard,
her breath fast and shallow, her skin splitting wherever it was touched.
She felt that she had already sunk beyond reach. She hadn't worked
for days and in this camp if you didn't work, you didn't eat.

"Sofia," Anna said harshly, "open your eyes. Come on, show me
you're alive."

The blond eyelashes fluttered, but not enough to open her eyes.

"Try harder," Anna insisted. "Please."

With a huge effort, Sofia opened her eyes.

The sight of the hand was almost too much to bear. It was a black
and swollen piece of rotten meat with great splits between the fingers
that oozed a foul smelling pus. Each time Anna bathed it, strips of
flesh floated away.

"My poor Sofia," Anna breathed. She brushed a hand over Sofia's
burning forehead, sweeping the hair off her face. It was soaked in
sweat. "This will help," she murmured again, "it'll make you well."

She wrapped a poultice of green and orange lichen around the
hand, working it in between the fingers and up the skeletal wrist. As
she did so, though she was gentle, Sofia shuddered and a trail of bile
trickled from her mouth. Anna slipped a strip of shredded leaves
mixed with butter between Sofia's cracked lips.

"Chew," she ordered. "It'll help the pain."

She watched like a hawk as Sofia's jaw slowly attempted to chew.

"Anna." A raw whisper.

"I'm here."

"Tell me . . . where did this come from?"

"It doesn't matter, just swallow it. There'll be more tomorrow, I
promise."

It was followed by a nugget of pork fat. Sofia's cloudy blue eyes
had fixed on Anna's face with an expression of confusion, and then as
understanding abruptly dawned on her sluggish mind, it changed to

one of despair. She moaned, a deep bone-aching sound that made Anna flinch. There was only one way a woman prisoner could lay her hands on the guards' pork fat in this camp, and they both knew what it was. Sofia felt dirty. Inside her body and under her skin she could feel the dirt, gritty and hard. Her good hand reached across and clung to Anna's wrist.

"Don't," Sofia hissed. A tear slid out and crept down to her ear. "Don't do it anymore, I beg you. I won't eat the food."

"Sofia, I want a friend who is alive. Not one rotting in the stinking pit of corpses they dump in the forest."

"I can't bear it."

"If I can, you can," Anna shouted at her in an outburst of anger.

Sofia stared at Anna for a long time, and then slowly her fingers uncurled from Anna's wrist and with gentle soothing strokes they caressed her arm as a mother would a child.

"Now," Anna said fiercely, "eat this."

Sofia opened her mouth.

*T*WO years and eight months had passed since that day. Yet the memory of it still had the power to rip something open inside her and make her want to shake Anna till her teeth rattled. And hug her, hug her to death. From where Sofia was sitting on the floor waiting for the next overadventurous mouse to venture into the hut, she could see the blond head tossing from side to side on the crowded bedboard. She could hear the coughs despite the cloth jammed over the mouth.

"Anna," she whispered, too low for anyone's ears, "I haven't forgotten."

She dipped her forehead to her knees. *Whatever it takes, Anna.* Vasily was the key. Anna had no family and she was far too weak to make the journey of a thousand miles through the taiga, even if she could escape from this hellhole, so there was only one answer. Sofia would have to find Vasily and hope he would help. *Hope.* No, that was far too weak a word. *Believe.* That was it. She had to believe, first that she could find him, second that he would be willing to help Anna even though he hadn't seen her for sixteen years—but to be brutally honest with herself, was it likely he'd risk his life?—and third, that he had the means to do so.

She lifted her head and grimaced. Put like that, it sounded absurd. It was an insane and impossible idea, but it was all she had to cling to. She nodded firmly.

"Vasily," she breathed, "I'm trusting you."

The risks were huge. And of course there was the small matter of how she herself could escape under the malevolent but watchful gaze of the guards. Hundreds tried it every year, but few made it more than a verst or two. The trackers' dogs, the lack of food, the wolves, the cold in the winter, or in the summer the heat and swarms of black mosquitoes that ate you alive, they all defeated the most determined spirit.

She shivered, but it wasn't from the cold. A part of her tired brain had just caught a glimpse of something that she'd almost forgotten about because all her thoughts had been directed at Anna and Vasily. It was something bright and breathing, and it shimmered just on the far edge of her vision where it flickered, tempting her.

It was freedom.

FOUR

Davinsky Camp
March 1933

THE sky was a vast and vivid lake of blue above Anna's head. She smiled up at the sun climbing slowly over the treeline and into the freedom of the wide open sky. She envied it its space.

She was lying on her back thinking the day was a good day. She wasn't cold because around her neck lay a thick wool scarf that Nina had won in a poker game, and it kept her warm. Her boots were dry and she wasn't walking. She was riding in the back of an open truck and it felt like being on holiday. Yes, today was definitely a good day.

"Anna! Are you all right?"

The question came from Sofia. Anna smiled at her and nodded. They were packed together with eighteen others, all sitting on the floor of the truck, their bodies keeping each other warm, and everyone was so relieved not to be making the two-hour trek on foot along snow-covered trails to the usual Work Zone that there was a sense of delight in the small work gang. It briefly eased the permanent lines of tension across the women's foreheads and the tightness around their mouths. Roll call in camp had been fast and efficient for once, and then a truck had backed up into the compound and dropped its tailgate. A group of twenty prisoners was selected at random to climb into the back. Puffing smoke from its exhaust pipe like a bad-tempered old man, the truck rolled through the double set of gates and out into the forest.

"Where are we going?" asked a small Tartar woman with a heavy accent.

"Who cares? Wherever it is, this beats walking."

"I think they're going to shoot us and dump our bodies in the forest."

It was a young girl who spoke. On her first day as a teacher in Novgorod she was denounced by a pupil for mentioning that she thought that, as an artistic form, the Romanov symbol of the double-headed eagle was more attractive than the stark hammer and sickle. Now an inmate of Davinsky camp, every day she voiced the same fear. *Shot and dumped.* Anna felt sorry for her.

"No, it's obvious," Sofia said. "They're short of labor somewhere, so they're trucking us in to do some dirty job, I expect."

But no one seemed to worry about what lay ahead. There was really no point, so they all chose to enjoy this moment. There was even raucous laughter when Nina suggested they were being taken to set up a *publichniy dom*, a brothel in one of the men's camps.

"I used to have beautiful tits," Tasha grinned. "Great big fleshy melons you could stand a teacup on. I'd have been the star of any brothel." She patted her flat chest. "Thin as a stick I am now, just look at me. They're nothing but scrawny pancakes, but I could still give any man his money's worth." She rippled her body in a parody of seduction, and everyone laughed.

"Are you all right, Anna?"

It was Sofia again.

"I'm fine. I'm watching the birds, a flock of them over there above the trees. See how they swoop and swirl. Don't you wish you were a bird?"

Sofia's hand rested for a moment on Anna's forehead. "Try to sleep," she said gently.

"No," Anna smiled, "I'm content to watch the birds."

The truck's engine growled its way across the flat marshy waste-land and jolted them over the slippery ice as Anna squinted at the flock in the distance. It occurred to her that they were moving strangely.

"Are they hawks?" she asked. She lifted a hand to point but it was too heavy, so she let it fall.

"Anna," Sofia whispered in her ear, "it's smoke."

Anna smiled. "I know it's smoke. I was teasing you."

Sofia laughed oddly. "Of course you were."

*T*HE work was quite bearable. For one thing it was indoors inside a long well-lit shed, so the north wind that greeted their arrival in a desolate and ravaged landscape was not the usual problem. Anna tried not to breathe too deeply, but the dust and the grit in the air made her cough worse and she had to wrap her scarf tightly around her mouth.

"It looks like we've come to a party in hell," she muttered as they clambered from the truck.

"No talking," the guard shouted.

"It's a fucking gold mine," Tasha said under her breath and made a furtive sign of the cross in front of her.

Ugly black craters stretched out before their eyes as though some alien monster had bitten vast chunks out of the land and stripped it of all vegetation. It was how Anna imagined the moon to be, but here, unlike the moon, ants scurried all over the craters. Except they weren't ants, they were men, working at depths of thirty or forty meters with barrows and pickaxes and shovels, and raising the rocks out of the huge craters via an intricate network of planks that looked like a spider's web. The never-ending, earsplitting sound of the hammering and the speed with which they raced up the precipitous planks behind their overladen barrows to fulfill their brigade's norms set Anna's head spinning. It made road building look like child's play.

"In there. *Davay, davay!* Let's go!" the guard shouted, aiming the women in the direction of the wooden shed.

The work was simple, sorting rocks. At one end of the long shed was a large metal maw that tumbled the rocks from the barrows down a chute and onto a conveyor belt. It rattled noisily the thirty-meter length to the other end, and the women had to sort the rocks, either to be hammered into smaller sizes or to be crushed under a giant steam hammer that ripped through the eardrums like a blowtorch. The air was so thick with rock dust that it was impossible to see clearly across to the thin line of windows, and Anna could feel the pain in her chest worsen as she worked. Her head throbbed in time to the steam hammer.

Somebody was laughing, she could hear them, but for some reason she couldn't see them. The rocks on the conveyor belt started to retreat inside gray shadows that looked like ash tipped into the air, and she began to wonder if the problem was in her eyes rather than in the shed. She hesitated and slowly raised her hand in front of her face. She saw nothing but ash.

"Back to work, *bistro!*" yelled a guard.

Her lungs were shutting down, she could feel it happening, starving her brain of oxygen. She dragged at the air in a last desperate gasp, but it was far too late. She felt herself fall.

WHAT she needs is injections of calcium chlorate. That's what they'd use to cure her."

"Anna, talk to me."

Anna could hear Sofia's voice. It drifted down to her where she lay flat on her back, though for the moment she had no idea where that was.

"Come on, Anna. You're scaring me."

With an effort of will that left her quivering, Anna clambered up from the dark toward the voice but instantly regretted it when the raw agony in her lungs returned. The jolting under her body told her exactly where she was, back in the truck. She thought about opening her eyes, but they had lead weights on them, so she gave up. But still, voices curled around her.

"She's too sick to work anymore."

"Keep your voice down. If the guards hear, they'll just dump her over the side of the truck to freeze to death."

"What she needs is proper treatment."

"And proper food."

A harsh laugh. "Don't we all?"

Sofia's voice again, warm on Anna's skin. "Wake up, Anna. *Bistro,*

quickly, you lazy toad. I'm not fooled you know. I can tell you're"—
the words sounded tight in her throat—"you're just pretending."

Anna pushed off the weights and forced open her eyes. The world
jumped sharply into focus and she could smell the moldy odor of
damp earth as it emerged from its winter freeze in the forest. She was
lying flat on her back, and the sky was black and sequined above her,
while much closer Sofia's face swayed into view.

"So you've bothered to wake up at last. How are you feeling?"

"I'm fine."

"I know you are." Sofia's voice was bright and cheerful. "So stop
pretending."

Anna laughed.

I'VE decided," Sofia announced. "I'm leaving."

"What?"

"Leaving."

"Leaving where?"

"Leaving Davinsky camp. I've had enough of it, so I'm going to
escape."

"No," Anna cried out, then looked quickly about her and lowered
her voice to a small whisper. "You're insane, you mustn't even try.
Nearly everyone who tries it ends up dead. They'll set the dogs on
your trail and when they catch you they'll put you in the isolator and
we both know that's worse than any coffin. You'll die slowly in there."

"No, I won't because I won't let the bastards catch me."

"That's what everyone says."

"But I mean it."

"So did they, and they're dead."

*I*F you're so hell-bent on going, I'm coming too."

Anna couldn't believe that she'd said the words. She must be out of
her mind. Her presence on the escape attempt would be a death sentence for both of them, but she was in such despair over what Sofia
was planning that she just wasn't thinking straight.

"I'm coming too," she insisted. She was leaning against a tree
trunk in as casual a way as she could, pretending she didn't really need
it to hold her upright.

"No, you're not," Sofia said calmly. "You wouldn't get ten miles with your lungs, never mind a thousand. Don't look at me like that, you know it's true."

"Everyone says that if you try to escape through the taiga, you must take someone with you, someone you can kill for food when there's nothing but starvation left. So take me. I know I'm ill, so I won't mind. You can eat me."

Sofia hit her. She swung back her arm and gave Anna a hard slap that left a mark on the cheek. "Don't you ever say that to me again."

So Anna hugged her. Held her tight.

ANNA was terrified. Terrified of losing Sofia. Terrified that Sofia would die out there. Terrified she would be caught and brought back and shut in the isolator until she either dropped dead or went insane.

"Please, Sofia, stay. It doesn't make sense. Why leave now? You've done five years already, so it's only another five and you'll be released."

Only another five. Who was she fooling?

She tried tears and she tried begging. But nothing worked. Sofia was hell-bent on going. For Anna it felt as though her heart were being cut out. Of course she couldn't blame her friend for choosing to make a break for freedom, to find a life worth living. No one could deny her that. Thousands tried escape every year, though very few actually made it to safety, but . . . it still felt like . . . No. *Nyet.* Anna wouldn't think it, refused to let the word into her head. But at night when she lay awake racked by coughs and by fears for Sofia's survival, the word slithered in, dark and silent as a snake. *Desertion.* It felt like desertion, like being abandoned yet again. No one Anna loved ever stayed.

ANNA started counting. She counted the planks of wood in the wall and the nails in each plank and which type of nail, flat-headed or round-headed. It meant she didn't have to think.

"Stop it," Sofia snapped at her.

"Stop what?"

"Counting."

"What makes you think I'm counting?"

"Because you're sitting there staring with the blank eyes of an owl at the opposite wall, and I know you're counting. Stop it, I hate it."

"I'm not counting."

"You are. Your lips are moving."

"I'm praying for you."

"Don't lie."

"I'll count if I want. Like you'll escape if you want."

They stared at each other, then looked away and said no more.

*T*HEY planned it carefully. Sofia would follow the railway track, travel by night and hide up in the forest by day. It was safer that way and meant she wouldn't suffer from the cold overnight because she'd be walking. It was March now and the temperatures were rising each day, the snow and ice melting, the floor of the pine forests turning into a soft damp carpet of needles. She should travel fast.

"You must head for the River Ob," Anna urged her, "and once you've found it, follow it south. But even on foot and in the dark, traveling will be hard without identity papers."

"I'll manage."

Anna said nothing more. The likelihood of Sofia getting even as far as the River Ob was almost nil. Nevertheless they continued with their preparations and took to stealing, not only from the guards, but also from other prisoners. They stole matches and string and pins for fishhooks and a pair of extra leggings. They wanted a knife, but nothing went right for it despite several attempts. By the eve of the day planned for the escape, they still had no blade for Sofia, but Anna made one last foray.

"Look," she said as she came into the barrack hut, her scarf wound tight over her mouth.

She hunched down beside Sofia in their usual place on the wooden floor, backs to the wall near the door where the air was cleaner, to avoid the kerosene fumes that always set off Anna's coughing spasms. From under a protective fold of her jacket she drew her final haul: a sharp-edged skinning knife, a small tin of *tushonka*, stewed beef, two thick slices of black bread, and a pair of half-decent canvas gloves.

Sofia's eyes widened.

"I stole them," Anna said. "From the toolshed and the kitchens, so don't worry, I paid nothing for them."

They both knew what she meant.

"Anna, you shouldn't. If a guard had caught you, you'd be shot, and I don't want you dead."

"I don't want you dead either."

Both spoke coolly, an edge to their voices. That was how it was between them now, cool and practical. Sofia took the items from Anna's cold hands and tucked them away in the secret pocket they had stitched inside her padded jacket.

"*Spasibo.*"

For a while they didn't speak because there was nothing left to say that hadn't been said. Anna coughed into her scarf, wiped her mouth, leaned her head back against the wall, and concentrated on the spot where their shoulders touched. It was the only place of warmth between them now and she cherished it.

"I'm fearful for you, Sofia."

"Don't be."

"Fear is a filthy stain rotting the heart out of this country, like it's rotting my lungs." Anna struggled for breath. For a while they said nothing more, but the silences hurt, so Anna asked, "Where will you go?"

"I'll do as you say and follow the River Ob, then head west to Sverdlovsk and the Ural Mountains. To Tivil."

That came as a shock. "Why Tivil?"

"Because Vasily is there."

The blood drained from Anna's brain, and she felt the sick hand of jealousy squeeze her guts.

"Are you all right, Anna?"

Sofia's blue eyes were gazing at her with concern, and that was when the red haze hit. It made her want to strike out, to shout and scream *Nyet* into that sweetly anxious face. How dare Sofia go to Tivil? She thrust her hands tight between her knees and clamped them there.

"Vasily?"

"Yes, I want to find him."

"Is he the reason you're escaping?"

"Yes."

"I see."

"No, you don't."

But she did. Anna saw only too well. Sofia wanted Vasily for herself.

Sofia looked at Anna intently and then sighed. "Listen to me, you idiot. You said that your governess, Maria, told you about Svetlana Dyuzheyeva's jewelry."

Anna frowned. "Yes. Vasily's mother possessed beautiful jewels."

"Maria told you," Sofia continued slowly as though speaking to a child, "that Vasily said that his father had buried some of the jewels in their garden at the start of nineteen seventeen for fear of what might happen."

"Yes."

"And that after the civil war, Vasily went back for them and later hid them in the church in Tivil."

"So it's just the jewels you're going for."

"No, not just the jewels."

"Vasily too?"

"Yes, for Vasily too."

Anna shuddered. She couldn't stop it, a cold spiky tremor that crept through her bones, and again she said, "I see."

Sofia's shoulder gave a little shove that took Anna by surprise and started her coughing again. She hunched over her scarf, pressing it to her mouth, and fought for breath, but when it was over, she looked flat-eyed at Sofia.

"Take good care of him," she whispered.

Sofia tilted her head to one side. For a while she said nothing, and then she reached out and pulled back the scarf from Anna's mouth. In silence they both studied the blood stains on the cloth, and then Sofia spoke very clearly and deliberately.

"There's only one reason I'm leaving here. Using the jewels and with Vasily's help, I will come back."

"Why in God's name would you want to return to this stink-hole?"

"To fetch you."

Three words, only three. But they changed Anna's world.

"You won't survive another winter here," Sofia said quietly. "You know you won't, but you're too weak to walk hundreds of miles through this bloody taiga, even if you could escape. If I don't go to fetch help for you, you'll die."

Anna couldn't look at Sofia. She turned her head away and fought the onrush of tears. She felt the sickening weight of fear and knew it would be there inside her for every second that Sofia was gone.

"Sofia," she said in a voice that she barely recognized, "don't get yourself eaten by a wolf."

Sofia laughed. "A wolf wouldn't stand a chance."

FIVE

The Ural Mountains
July 1933

THE dog. That was what Sofia heard first. The dog. Then the men.

The sound of them carried to her through the quivering breath of the forest as the hound's paws splashed through a gully and scrabbled up the other side. Coming closer, too close, with belly-deep whines, teeth bared, and tongue loose, thirsting for the taste of blood. It set Sofia's own hackles rising into sharp spikes of fury. Her hand reached out, her scarred fingertips clutching at the air in front of her, as if for one last second she could capture its placid warmth and cradle it to her chest.

But how could she be angry with a dog? The animal was only doing what it did best, what it was bred to do. Tracking its prey.

And she was its prey. So they'd come for her at last. She shivered.

Had they come by accident? Or design?

It didn't matter. She was prepared.

★   ★   ★

*S*OFIA had been watching the evening sun slide away from her along the curving line of the trees, transforming the greens to amber and then to a fierce painful red. A *komar* landed on her bare arm. She didn't move, but watched the insect's tiny body turn into a ruby tear as it drank its fill of her blood, and it made her think of the way the labor camp had tried to suck the lifeblood out of her. She struck hard and the mosquito was transformed into no more than a pink smear on her skin.

She was standing in the doorway of a cabin. She'd found it in a small clearing that was hidden way up on the northern slope of the forest, deep in the Ural Mountains, except it wasn't really a clearing, more a ragged scar where lightning had decapitated a tall birch, which had brought down a handful of young pine trees as it fell. The cabin was skillfully built to withstand the merciless Ural winters, but now it was old and patched with moss, with a tilt to the right like an old man with cramp.

The cabin looked as if its bones ached just the way hers did. It had taken four never-ending, hard, grinding months as a fugitive to reach this point. She'd scuttled and scrambled and fought her way halfway across Russia, traveling always southwest by the stars, and the odd thing was that it had taken her a long time—far too long—to get used to being on her own. That had startled her.

The nights were the worst. So big and empty. Five years of sleeping packed five to a bedboard and you'd think she'd relish the sudden relief of solitary living, but no. She could hardly bear to be on her own at first because the space around her was too huge and she found sleep hard, but gradually her mind and her body adapted. Then she traveled faster.

*T*HE actual escape from Davinsky had proved even more dangerous than she'd expected. It was a dull, damp day in March with a lingering mist that swirled among the trees like ghosts drifting from trunk to trunk. Visibility was poor. A perfect day to join the ghosts.

She and Anna had planned it carefully.

They waited until the *perekur*, the smoke break, which gave her five minutes, that was all. Sofia stood in a huddle with the other women from her brigade and saw Anna watching her, taking in every last detail, saying nothing. The idea of leaving Anna behind felt absurdly like treachery, but she had no choice, and even alone her own chances of survival were . . . She stopped her thoughts right there. Minute by minute, that was how she would survive. Adrenaline was pumping through her veins and her throat felt dry each time she swallowed.

She stepped closer to Anna and said quietly, "I promise I'll come back for you. Anna, wait for me."

Anna nodded to her. That was all. Just a nod and a look they gave each other. A moment frozen in time with no beginning and no end. A nod. A look. Then Anna left the huddle of women and hurried over to where four guards were standing around a brazier and smoking, stamping their feet and laughing at each other's crude jokes. One guard was holding a dog on a chain, a German shepherd that lay like a black shadow on a patch of icy grass and its eyes were narrow slits. Anna skirted it warily.

She was to create the distraction, so with a shriek of alarm she started to make a fuss, waving her arms about to draw attention.

"Look!" she shouted loudly, and heads turned toward her. "Look there!" she shouted again, and this time pointed urgently at the line of pine trees behind the guards.

A ribbon of space had been hacked out of the forest itself for the new road they were building, but beyond that lay a dense and gloomy world where little light penetrated and power was wielded by claws and teeth instead of guns.

"What?"

All four guards jumped uneasily and swung around, raising their rifles.

"Wolves!" she warned.

"Fuck."

"How many?"

"*Tri*. Three. I saw three," Anna lied. "It could have been more."

"Where?"

"I can't spot any."

"There's one," Anna screamed. "Over there. See that pale shape behind—" Her voice was rising in panic. "No, it's moved, but I saw it, I swear I did."

A rifle shot rang out. Just in case. The dog and its handler were running closer to the trees. The prisoners all watched nervously. Sofia seized that moment, when everyone's attention was focused on the forest to the north of the road, to turn and move in the opposite direction to the south. The trees were fifteen meters away. Her heart was hammering in her chest. *Don't hurry, walk slowly.* She cursed the ice that crunched noisily under her boots. Ten meters now, and she could see the tall·slender trunks coming closer.

"There," Sofia heard Anna cry out again. "Quick, off to your right, look, one of the wolves is over that way."

The guard dog whined as it strained at its leash, but the handler uttered a single word of command and the animal dropped to the ground in silence. The hairs on the back of Sofia's neck rose and she didn't dare breathe. Six meters between her and the beckoning darkness of the forest, that was all. So close she could taste it. She made herself keep to a steady walk and resisted the urge to look behind her.

A rifle shot rang out in the still air and Sofia instinctively ducked, but it wasn't aimed at her. It was followed by a string of bullets that ripped through the undergrowth on the north side of the road, but no howls lifted into the mist.

"That'll scare the shit out of the creatures," one guard declared with satisfaction, and he lit himself a cigarette.

"Okay, *davay*, back to work, you lazy scum."

There was a murmur of voices, and quickly Sofia lengthened her stride. Three more steps and . . .

"Stop right there."

Sofia stopped.

"Where the hell do you think you're sneaking off to?"

Sofia turned. Thank God it wasn't one of the guards. It was the leader of one of the other brigades, a woman with hard eyes and harder fists. Sofia breathed again.

"I'm just going to the latrine pit, Olga."

"Get back to your work or I'll call a guard."

"Leave it, Olga, I'm desperate to—"

"Don't fuck around, we both know the nearest latrine is in the opposite direction."

"That one's overflowing, too disgusting to use, so I—"

"Did a guard give you permission?"

Sofia sighed. "Are you blind, Olga? Of course not, they're all busy watching out for the wolves."

"You know the rules. You can't leave your work post without permission from a guard." The woman's mouth clamped shut with an audible snap of her false teeth.

"What's it to you, anyway?"

"I am a brigade leader. I make sure the rules are obeyed. That," she said with smug satisfaction, "is why I have bigger food rations and a better bed than you do. So—"

"Look, I really am desperate, so please just this once—"

"Guard!"

"Olga, no."

"Guard! This prisoner is running away."

*T*HE ground was still packed tight with the last of the winter ice. Every thrust of the spade made Sofia's bones crunch against each other and she muttered under her breath at the guard who stood watching her with a rifle draped over his arm and a grin let loose on his face.

She had been ordered to dig out a new latrine pit as punishment and it was like digging into iron, so it took her the rest of that day. It could have been worse, she kept telling herself. It could have been much worse. This punishment was for not requesting permission before stepping away from the road, because, thankfully, none of the guards believed the brigade leader's story that she was trying to escape. The punishment for an escape attempt? A bullet in the brain.

Damn it, though. Sofia cursed her luck for running into Olga. She'd been so close. She'd snatched a brief glimpse of the freedom that crouched out there in the deepening shadows of the forest, and now kept casting glances into its depths as she hacked at the frozen earth. She tried to draw into her mind some of its stubborn strength.

The latrine, which had to be three meters long and one meter deep, was set no more than two paces beyond the edge of the trees, where the pines were sparse and offered only token privacy. Near the end of the day when the mists were stealing the branches from the trees, a young dark-haired girl was made to come and help her as punishment for swearing at a guard. As they worked side by side in silence, except for the metal ring of spades, Sofia attempted to catch sight of Anna on the road, but already her brigade had moved on, so she was left alone with the girl and the guard.

Oddly, she didn't feel sick with disappointment at her failure, even though she knew she had let both Anna and herself down badly. It was as if she knew in that strange clear space inside her head that her brush with freedom was not yet over. So when the actual moment came, she was expecting it and didn't hesitate. The sky was beginning to darken and the rustlings on the forest floor were growing louder, when the girl suddenly pulled down her underpants, straddled the new latrine pit they'd dug, and promptly christened it. The guard's grin widened, and he ambled over to watch the steam rise from the yellow trickle between her legs.

That was the moment. Sofia knew it as clearly as she knew her own name. She stepped up behind him in the gloom, raised her spade, and with all the strength that remained in her exhausted limbs she slammed its metal blade onto the back of his head.

There was no going back now.

With no more than a muffled grunt, he folded neatly to the ground and slumped with his head and one arm hanging down into the pit. She didn't wait to find out if he was alive or dead. Before the girl had pulled up her underpants and screamed out in alarm, Sofia was gone.

*T*HEY came after her with dogs, of course. She knew they would. So she'd stuck to the marshes, where at this time of year the land was waterlogged and it was harder for the hounds to track down her scent. She raced through the boggy wastes with long bounding strides, water spraying out behind her, heart pounding and skin prickling with fear.

Time and again she heard the dogs come close and threw herself down on her back in the stagnant water with her eyes closed tight and only her nose and mouth above the surface. She lay immobile like that for hours in the slime while the guards searched, telling herself it was better to be eaten alive by biting insects than by dogs.

At first she had the stash of food scraps in her secret pockets that Anna had sewn inside her jacket but it didn't last long. After that she'd existed on worms and tree bark and thin air. Once she was lucky. She stumbled on an emaciated moose dying from a broken jaw. She'd used her knife to finish off the poor creature, and for two whole days she'd remained beside the carcass filling her belly with meat, until a wolf drove her to abandon it.

As she traveled farther through the taiga, mile after mile over brittle brown pine needles, seeking out the railway track that would lead her south, at times the loneliness was so bad that she shouted out at the top of her lungs, great whooping yells of sound, just to hear a human voice in the vast wilderness of pine trees. Nothing much lived there, barely any animals other than the occasional lumbering moose or solitary wolf, because there was almost nothing for them to eat. But in some odd kind of way the yelling and the shouting just made her feel worse because it left a hole in the world that she couldn't fill.

Eventually she found the railway track that she and Anna had talked about, its silver lines snaking into the distance, and followed it day and night, even sleeping beside it because she was afraid of getting lost, till she came to a river. Was this the Ob? How was she to know? She knew the River Ob headed south toward the Ural Mountains, but was this it? She felt a wave of panic. She was weak with hunger and couldn't think straight. The gray coils of water appeared horribly inviting.

She lost track of time. How long had she been wandering out here in this godforsaken wilderness? With an effort of will she made her mind focus and worked out that weeks must have passed because the sun was higher in the sky now than when she set out. As she tugged out her precious bent pin and twine that was wrapped in her pocket and started to trawl clumsily through the waves with it, it occurred to her that spring was turning into early summer, that the shoots on the birch trees had grown into full-size leaves and the warmth of the sun on her back made her skin come alive.

The first time she came across habitation she almost wept with pleasure. It was a farm, a scrawny subsistence scrap of worthless land, and she crouched behind a birch trunk all day, observing the comings and goings of the peasant couple who worked the place. An emaciated black-and-white cow was tethered to a fence next to a shed, and she watched with savage envy as the farmer's wife coaxed milk from the animal.

Could she go over there and beg a bowlful?

She stood up and took one step toward it.

Her mouth filled with saliva and she felt her whole body ache with desire for it, not just her stomach but the marrow in her bones and the few red cells left in her blood, and even the small sacs inside her lungs. They all whimpered for one mouthful of that white liquid.

But to come so far and risk everything?

She forced herself to sit again. To wait until dark. There was no moon, no stars, just another chill damp night inhabited only by bats, but Sofia was well used to it and moved easily through the darkness to the barn where the cow had been tucked away at the end of the day. She opened the lichen-covered door a crack, listened carefully. No sound, except the soft moist snoring of the cow. She slipped through the crack and felt a shiver of delight at being inside somewhere warm and protective at last after so long outside facing the elements. Even the old cow was obliging despite Sofia's cold fingers and allowed a few squirts of milk directly into her mouth. Never in her life had anything tasted so exquisite. That was when she made her mistake. The warmth, the smell of straw, the remnants of milk on her tongue, the sweet odor of the cow's hide, it all melted the shield of ice she'd built for herself. Without stopping to think, she bundled the straw into a cozy nest, curled up in it, and was instantly asleep. The night enveloped the barn.

SOMETHING sharp in her ribs woke her. She opened her eyes. It was a finger, thick-knuckled and full of strength. Attached to it was a hand with a spider's web of blue veins. Sofia leaped to her feet.

The farmer's wife was just visible standing in front of her in the first wisps of early morning light. The woman said nothing but pressed a cloth bundle into Sofia's hands and quickly led the cow out of the barn, but not before she'd given Sofia a sharp shake of her gray head in warning. Outside, her husband could be heard whistling and stacking logs onto a cart.

The barn door shut.

"*Spasibo*," Sofia whispered into the emptiness.

She longed to call the woman back and wrap her arms around her, but she knew better. Instead she ate the food in the bundle, kept an eye to a knothole in the door, and, when the farmer had finished with his logs, she vanished back into the lonely forest.

After that, things went wrong. Badly wrong. It was her own fault. She almost drowned when she was stupid enough to take a shortcut by swimming across a tributary of the river where the currents were lethal, and five times she came close to being caught with her hand in a chicken coop or stealing from a washing line. She lived on her wits, but as the villages started to appear with more regularity, it grew too dangerous to move by day without identity papers, so she traveled only at night, which slowed her progress.

Then disaster. For one whole insane week she headed in the wrong direction under starless skies, not realizing the Ob had swung west.

"*Dura!* Stupid fool!"

She cursed her idiocy and slumped down in a slice of moonlight on the riverbank, her blistered feet dangling in the dark waters, closed her eyes, and forced her mind to picture the place she was aiming for. *Tivil*, it was called. She'd never been there. But she conjured up a picture of it with ease. It was no more than a small distant speck in a vast land, a sleepy village somewhere in a fold of the ancient Ural Mountains.

But how the hell was she going to find it?

*Y*ET now, at last, she was here. In the clearing among the silver birches, the mossy cabin with its crooked roof warm at her back, the last of the sun's rays on her face. Here right in the heart of the Ural Mountains, but it seemed that just when she'd reached her goal, the dogs were coming for her again. The hound so close she could hear its whines.

She darted back into the cabin, snatched up her knife, and ran. Seconds later two men with rifles and a dog burst out of the tree line, but by then she had put the hut between them and herself as she raced for the back of the clearing, hunched low, breathing hard. The dark trunks opened up and she fell into their cool protection, but that was when she saw the boy. In a hollow not three paces away from him crouched a wolf.

SIX

PYOTR Pashin felt his heart curl up in his chest. He didn't move a muscle, didn't even blink, just stared at the creature. Its mean yellow eyes were fixed on him and he didn't dare breathe. Never before in his young life had he stood so close to a wolf.

Dead ones, yes, he'd seen plenty of those outside Boris's *izba* down in the village where their pelts were hung out on drying racks. Pyotr and his friend Yuri liked to trail the backs of their hands through the dense silky fur and even stuff a finger between the razor-edged teeth, but this was different. This wolf's black lips were pulled back in a silent snarl, and the last thing in the whole world that Pyotr wanted to do now was stick a finger in its mouth.

He'd jumped at the chance to come hunting when Boris asked him.

"You're a skinny runt," Boris had pointed out. "But you're good with the hound."

Which meant he wanted Pyotr to do all the running. But it hadn't turned out a good day. Game was scarce and his other fellow hunting companion, Igor, was tight-lipped as a lizard, so Boris had started in on the flask in his pocket, which only sent the day tumbling from bad to worse. It ended up with Boris giving Pyotr a clout with his rifle for not keeping a tight enough hold on the leash, which made Pyotr scoot off among the trees in a sulk.

"Pyotr, come back here, you skinny little bastard," Boris yelled into the twilit world of forest shadows, "or I'll skin the hide off you."

Pyotr ignored him. He knew that what he was doing was wrong because it broke the first rule of forest lore, which is that you never lose contact with your companions. Children of the *raion* grew up bombarded with bedtime stories of how you must never—never—roam alone in the forest, where you will be instantly devoured by goblins or wolves or even a fierce-eyed ax man who eats children for breakfast. The forest has a huge and hungry mouth of its own, and it will swallow you without a trace if you give it even half a chance.

But he was eleven now, and he reckoned he was able to look out for himself. Anyway, he was angry at Boris for the clout with the rifle butt and also, he wasn't sure exactly why, but . . . he felt stupid even thinking this . . . but in this part of the forest the air seemed to lick his cheek as the daylight began to fade and somehow drew him to this quiet circle of light that was the small clearing in the trees.

He caught sight of the back of the cabin, covered in bright green moss, and the fallen mess of branches sprawled lazily in the sun on the soft earth. His interest was roused. He took one more step and immediately heard a low-throated sound at his feet that made the hairs rise on the back of his neck. He swung around, and that was when he saw the wolf and his heart curled up.

He didn't dare breathe. Slowly, so slowly he wasn't sure it was happening at all, he started to move his left hand toward the whistle that hung on a green cord around his neck. Abruptly a blur of moonlight-pale hair and long golden limbs hurtled into this stillness. A young woman was churning up the air around him, her breath so loud he wanted to shout at her, to warn her, but he could feel a wild pulse thudding in his throat that prevented it. She stopped, blue eyes wide with surprise, but instead of screaming at the sight of the wolf, she gave it no more than a quick glance and smiled at Pyotr instead. It was a slow, slanting smile, small at first, then broadening into a wide conspiratorial grin.

"Hello," she mouthed. "*Privet.*"

She raised a finger to her lips and held it there as a signal to him to stay quiet, her mouth twitching as if in fun, but when he looked into her eyes, they weren't laughing. There was something in them that Pyotr recognized. A quivering. A sort of drawing down deep into herself, the same as he'd seen in the eyes of one of the boys at school when the bigger boys started picking on him. She was scared.

At that moment it dawned on Pyotr what she was. She was a fugitive. An enemy of the state on the run. They'd been warned about them in the weekly meetings in the hall. A sudden confusion tightened his chest. Definitely a saboteur or even a spy in hiding, some kind of socially dangerous element, because no normal person behaved so oddly—did they? So he made his decision. He raised the whistle to his mouth. Later he would recall the feel of the cold hard metal on his lips and remember the hammering in his chest as the two of them stood in front of those mean yellow eyes in the shade of the big pine, saying nothing.

She shook her head, urgent and forceful, and her eyes grew darker, their pale summer blue changing as if someone had spilled a droplet of ink into each one. Just as the whistle touched his lips, she gave a strange little shudder and moved her hand quickly. He thought at first it was to snatch the whistle from him, but instead it went to the blouse buttons at her throat and started to undo them. Pyotr watched. As each button revealed more, he felt his blood rush to his face, burning his cheeks.

Her skin was like milk. White and unused below the golden triangle at her neck where the sun had crept in. The blouse was shapeless, collarless, with short embroidered sleeves and though it may once have possessed color, now it was bleached to the gray of ash. As she slid the blouse open, he caught the flash of a knife at her waistband and that gave him a shock. Underneath the blouse she was wearing only a flimsy garment of threadbare material that clung to her thin body. The sight of her fragile collarbones made him forget the whistle, but it was her breasts he stared at, where the cloth outlined them clearly. His brain told him he should look away, but his eyes took no notice.

Then once more she pressed a finger to her lips and gave him a smile that, in a strange way he didn't understand, felt as if it stole something from inside him. It left a hole in a secret place inside him that previously only his mother had ever touched—and that was when he was just a little boy. His chest stung so badly he had to crush his hand against his ribs to stop the hurt, and by the time he looked back, she was gone. A faint movement of the branches and a shimmer of leaves, that was all that remained. Even the wolf had disappeared.

He stayed there with the whistle in his hand for what felt like forever but must have been no more than a minute, and gradually the sounds returned to him. The dog whining, the hunters calling and cursing him. A magpie rattled out its annoyance. He knew he should shout to them, it was his duty as a Soviet citizen to alert them. *Quick, there's a fugitive running down to the river. Bring your rifle.* But something stubborn hardened inside his young chest when he thought of the moonlight hair, and the words wouldn't come to his lips.

SEVEN

SOFIA stood without moving, concentrating on the sounds of the night, the rustle of some small creature as it skittered over a tree stump, a faint plop in the water, most likely a toad. Above her the sky was as black as she could wish, a warm summer night with the air moist on her skin, and no sign of the wolf. She'd seen the animal skulking around yesterday with its festering paw thick with summer flies, so knew the animal posed no threat to her or the boy. It just wanted somewhere to hide and lick its wound. No sign of the dog or the men either.

Were they listening for her, as silently as she was listening for them? Here among the trees. The silence a trap for her?

But no, OGPU troops didn't possess that kind of patience. They liked to storm in at night and yank you from your bed when you were soft and vulnerable and at your weakest. Not this silent soulless stalking. No. Whoever the men with the rifles were, they weren't the secret police.

She felt her pulse drop a notch and breathed more

easily. Her feet made no sound as she wove between the trees heading for the cabin, the pine needles releasing their fragrance under her feet. Hunters, that was what they must have been, with their hound on the scent of . . . what? The wolf probably. Already back in their village with a glass of *kvass* and a hand groping the skirts of a willing wife while . . .

Someone was in the clearing. A dim light spilled from the hut, cutting a yellow wedge out of the darkness that revealed a horse tethered outside. Sofia's heart stopped. She shrank back into the trees and merged with one of the black pine trunks, the length of her body tight against its rough bark. It smelled strongly of resin. She wanted to smell of resin too, to hide her scent in that of the tree. The light went out and instantly the cabin door opened and figures emerged. The horse whinnied a welcome and she heard two male voices speak in low whispers, but then came the excited bark of a hound and the creak of saddle leather as one of the men swung up on the horse. There was the shake of a bridle, the impatient stamp of hooves.

"Thank you, my friend," one man said, his voice unsteady with some strong emotion. "I . . . can say no more . . . but *spasibo*. Thank you."

Sofia caught the flat sound of two hands being clasped, and then the horse cantered away across the clearing, heading west. It was in a hurry. She listened for the other man and his dog, but he seemed to have vanished into the night itself. She told herself that whoever he was, he was nothing to her, just a temporary disturbance of her night's plans. She could still make it down to Tivil village before dawn.

She released her hold on the tree and felt a tremor of anticipation tighten her skin. With a stealth and sureness that was gained from months of traveling by night, she slid away into the blackness.

SHE had picked her time well. Still a couple of hours till dawn, so the villagers had not begun to stir from the warmth of their beds. The village of Tivil lay silent in the darkness. It looked crumpled and lifeless, yet Sofia's heart lifted at the sight of it. This was the place she'd spent months driving herself toward, and she'd pictured it a thousand times in her mind, sometimes bigger, sometimes smaller, but always with one person standing at the heart of it with open arms.

Vasily. She'd found his home. Now she had to find him.

Her pulse quickened as she stared down into the valley from the forest ridge, and again into her mind sprang the question that had plagued her steps each time she'd risked her life sneaking into barns or thieving chicken eggs to survive. Was Tivil the right place? Or had she come all this way for nothing? She shivered at the thought and pushed it away out of reach, because she had staked everything on one woman's word. That woman was Anna's childhood governess, Maria.

How good was her word?

Maria had whispered to Anna when she was arrested that Vasily had fled from Petrograd after the 1917 Revolution and turned up on the other side of Russia in Tivil, living under the name of Mikhail Pashin.

But how good was her word?

She had to believe he was here, had to know he was close.

"Vasily," she whispered aloud into the wind so that it would carry her words down to the houses below, "I need your help."

*S*HE slid down from the ridge with a soundless tread. The only movements along Tivil's dirt road were the brief flickers of shadow as clouds traced a path across the face of the moon, which had emerged from its sleep. She had observed the *izbas* carefully, the rough single-story houses that clung to the edge of the road, with their intricate shutters and precious patches of land staked out at the back in long rectangles. She watched till her eyes ached, trying to prize dark shapes out of a dark landscape. But nothing ruffled the stillness.

That was when she drew the knife from the rawhide pouch on her hip and finally, after so many months of effort, set foot in Tivil. It gave her a quick and unexpected surge of joy, and she felt her damaged fingertips tingle. The village was made up of a straggle of houses on each side of a single central street, mixed up with an untidy jumble of barns and stables and patched fences. It lay at the head of the Tiva Valley, which, farther down, shook itself loose and broadened into a wide plain protected by steep wooded ridges where hawks cruised by day.

At the center of the village stood the church. Now that in itself was strange. Throughout Russia most village churches had been blown up by order of the Politburo or were being used as storage for grain or manure, the ultimate insult. This one had escaped such shame, but judging by the abundance of notices pinned outside, it had been turned into a general assembly hall for the compulsory political meetings. The brick building loomed deeper black against the black sky, almost as much a presence as the forest itself, and it gave Sofia hope.

Maybe Maria was as good as her word. It could be true—all of it. But just because the church was here, she told herself, that didn't mean Vasily was, or that he'd be crazy enough to want to risk his life on the word of a stranger.

She moved with the shadows into the doorway of the church. *Chyort!* The lock was a big old-fashioned iron contraption that would shrug off any attempts of her knife. With another muttered oath she skirted around the side of the building, all the time scanning for any movement in the darkness, and at the back where the fields crept close to a scrubby yard, she found a small door, its lock flimsier. Immediately she set about it with the tip of her blade.

Sofia worked quickly, concentrating hard and careful to keep the sound low, but her pulse missed a beat when the shadows abruptly grew paler around her. A light must have been turned on somewhere close. She edged stealthily back to the corner of the building, her body becoming part of its solid mass, and holding her breath she peered around into the street.

The solitary light gleamed out at her like a warning. It came from the window of a nearby *izba*. And as she watched, a man crossed inside the rectangle of yellow lamplight from one side to the other, a tall figure moving in a hurry, and then he was gone. A moment later the *izba* was plunged once more into darkness and the sound of a front door shutting reached her ears.

What was he doing out so early? She hadn't bargained on the village coming to life before dawn. Didn't he sleep? A bat darted across her line of vision, making her jerk away awkwardly, and her hair felt slick on the back of her neck. In the street, footfalls sounded as clear as her own heartbeat in her ears, and she saw the figure pass. His determined stride and speed of movement made Sofia nervous, but still she crept forward to see more.

He was heading away from her down the street, picked out in detail by a brief trick of the moon. It allowed her to make out that his hair was clipped short and he was wearing a rough workman's shirt, which struck her as odd because he moved with the easy assurance and confidence of someone who was used to a position of command. Sofia breathed again and her hand relaxed on the knife.

Could it be Vasily?

She almost stepped out into the street and called his name. Except of course it would be *Mikhail Pashin*, the name Anna had said he was using. "Mikhail Pashin," she whispered, but too softly for anything but the moon to hear. She struggled to subdue a wave of excitement and to rein in an unruly surge of hope. Surely she couldn't be so lucky? She'd learned too well that nothing was ever this easy, and yet after all she'd been through in the last months, maybe it was time for a bit of luck. She scuttled along the front of the church, and as she peered out into the shadows that were wrapped around the village, her luck held and the moon gave up flirting behind the clouds and bathed the street in solid silver.

He was there, in front of her, clearly outlined, moonlight robbing him of color, so that he could have been a ghost. A ghost from the past. Is that what you are, Mikhail Pashin?

She saw him turn off the street up a steep rutted track that led uphill to the vague outline of a long dark building that she could only just make out. She was tempted to follow his footsteps, but something about him made her certain she would be discovered. There was an alertness that even in the dim light came off him like sparks.

She sank to the ground, waiting, invisible in the black overhang of the church, her back pressed firmly against the wall to keep her still, and her patience was rewarded ten minutes later when she heard the sound of a horse descending the track, its hooves lively on the dry earth. She exhaled with relief because the rider was the same man. He'd obviously been up to a stable and saddled his horse for an early morning start, his cropped hair and broad shoulders painted silver by the moonlight once again.

But to her surprise, behind him a man on foot was also trotting down the track, a small, slight figure, middle-aged but very light on his feet. They were talking in low voices, but there was a certain curtness in their manner toward each other that spoke of ill feeling. Sofia's gaze remained fixed on the rider.

Anna. Her lips didn't move but the words sounded sharp as ice in her head. *I think I've found Mikhail Pashin.* Her hand touched her face, and she was shocked to discover her cheeks burning.

Just then the two men reached the point where the rutted track joined the road, and the rider turned abruptly to the left without a word. The second man, the small one, turned right, but not before he had run the palm of his hand lovingly down the massive curve of the horse's rump as it swung away from him. Then, with his shoulders lifting and falling repeatedly, as if he were trying to uncage a painful tension in his neck, he stood staring after the horse and man.

The only sound in the night was the clink of a bridle and the soft shuffle of hooves in the dirt.

"Comrade Chairman Fomenko," the small man called out sharply, "don't push the horse too hard today. His leg is still sore and needs . . ."

In response the rider shortened the reins and pushed the animal into a canter and then a gallop. Steadily, man and horse disappeared toward the far end of the village until their outline merged with the night and they were gone.

"Comrade Chairman Fomenko," the small man growled once more, and he spat fiercely into the dust. Alone in the street and with the lightness stolen from his step, he headed up the road.

Sofia was shaking. She stumbled again into the blackness behind the church and rested her burning cheek against its cool bricks. The rider wasn't Vasily, he wasn't Mikhail Pashin after all, but someone called Fomenko. Fomenko! Damn the man! And damn her own stupidity! She'd gotten it wrong. As she wrapped her arms around herself, disappointment lay like a cold lead coffin in her stomach.

What else had she gotten wrong?

EIGHT

*T*HE stranger is here. I can feel it. She's close."

The words vibrated in the dark room and stirred the night air inside the small *izba* at the far end of Tivil, where two dark-haired figures leaned close across a table within an uncertain circle of light. A measured sprinkle of aromatic powder sent a spiral of flashes swirling out from the single candle flame that burned before them. Together they inhaled its delicate fragrance.

"I've drawn her close," Rafik murmured. "So close I can hear her heartbeat in Tivil."

His hand hovered over a black cloth on which lay a heavy crystal sphere. It gleamed, shimmered, and seemed to pulse in the darkness as the gypsy's hand circled above it, slow and attentive, listening to its voice.

"What do you hear?" whispered the olive-skinned girl.

"I hear her heart tearing. I hear blood spilling, drop by drop, and yet . . . I hear her laughing." The sound was sweet as birdsong in his ears. "Now tell me, Zenia, what you see."

The girl swirled the copper goblet that stood in front of her, so that the dark damp leaves inside it caught a glimmer of the uncertain light. Rafik loved to watch his daughter at work, to observe the passion for it that burned in her black eyes as she bent close. Though her gypsy skills differed greatly from his own, they seemed to bring her greater joy than his ever brought to him. He could feel her excitement burst forth, filling the drab little room with life, yet at the same time as fragile as blossom in springtime. It pleased his soul, and he gave thanks once more to the spirit of her long-dead mother. His own skills lay more like a heavy weight in his mind, like a meal that was too rich for the stomach and has left it feeling glutted and uncomfortable, churning over on itself on the edge of pain. That was how his mind felt now.

"Zenia, what do you see?"

"I see danger, a dark gray coat of danger that she is trailing behind her to Tivil."

Silence, cold as moonlight, settled in the room.

"More?" Rafik demanded.

The girl shook her tangle of wild black curls and shifted the goblet. She touched her lips to its rim and closed her eyes.

"It's wreathed in smoke," she breathed, but her eyelids fluttered, fast and fretful. "Behind the veil of smoke I see something else, something that sparkles brighter than the sun itself." She pursed her full red lips and shook her head to clear the image. "She seeks it, but it carries a shadow on it. It is the shadow of death."

"Does she understand why she is here?"

"She understands so little . . ."

Her hand was starting to tremble, and Rafik could sense the layers of darkness descending on her mind. Quickly he reached out, removed the warm goblet from her fingers, and silently touched a finger to his daughter's wide forehead. Her eyes brightened.

"She must choose," he said. "A fork in the road. One path to life, one path to death."

NINE

SOFIA was standing outside the *kuznitsa*, the smithy.

Nerves were prickling on her neck as though the darkness itself were running fingers down it. She ducked out of the way of a thin wavering strip of moonlight that rippled up the street like water. The old weather-beaten door was locked and she worked fast, digging the point of her blade into the dried-out wood around the lock. In less than two minutes she was inside the *kuznitsa*.

It was a long time since she'd been in any kind of smithy, but instantly the smell of scorched iron enveloped her, stinging her mind with childhood memories as it crept out of the heavy beams. She fumbled in the rawhide pouch that hung from her waist—damn it, what was wrong with her tonight? She was still shaken by what had happened, by her unguarded eagerness to claim any man—who looked roughly the right age—as Vasily. It had shocked her. She wouldn't make the same mistake again. *More caution.* She pushed a strand of fair hair out of her eyes and at last found her precious box of matches, took one out, and struck it.

In the sudden flare, the darkness edged backward and Sofia felt better. She licked her dry lips and looked around. The smithy was narrow. Above her she could just make out that the roof was made of sods of turf packed down on blackened laths and one wall was hung neatly with the tools of the trade: tongs and hammers, bellows and pincers, all kinds of blades and chisels. This smith, whoever he might be, was a tidy man. Just as the flame burned down to her fingers, Sofia reached out into the darkness that descended and her hand closed around the haft of a small ax. The church lock wouldn't stand a chance against it.

Moving fast, she emerged into the street and retraced her steps to the church, or assembly hall as it now was. But as she approached it, she was aware of feeling light-headed. She hadn't eaten all day, and only a handful of berries yesterday. This was her opportunity to fill her stomach. As the night breeze drifted up from the river that threaded through the valley and brought her the warning scent of wood smoke, she crept on past the church and chose the last *izba* before the tangle of rocks and forest. From there, escape into the trees would be easy if she was disturbed; she ducked low and slipped around to its vegetable plot at the back.

She peered through the blackness at the shabby wooden walls, patched in places with rough timber, a big fat water butt and a roof line as knobbly as a goat's back, but everything looked quiet. Searching among the rows of vegetables, she yanked up a couple of cabbages and thrust them into her pouch, then dug down with the ax and scrabbled from the earth whatever came to hand: a young beetroot, an onion, a radish. She glanced in the direction of the house, nerves taut, but the black shape of the *izba* remained solid and silent. Her stomach growled at the prospect of food, so she rubbed the radish against her sleeve and opened her mouth to bite off the end.

But before her teeth could close, a blow to the back of her head lifted her off her knees and sent her spiraling into blackness.

SOFIA shuddered. Where the hell was she? For one appalling moment she believed she was back in the iron grip of the labor camp. Maybe a crack on her head from one of the bastard guards amusing himself with a rifle butt. But no, she could hear a young goat bleating and stamping its feet somewhere nearby, and she knew for a fact there were no goats in the Zone. Anyway, she was lying on a bed, not a bunk. Her hands brushed against soft cotton sheets under her, and she knew the camp commandant would not be so obliging. So. Not Davinsky camp then.

But where?

She tried opening her eyes, surprised she hadn't thought of it before. But the light stabbed spear points straight into her brain, and she heard a voice cry out in pain. Instantly a spoon touched her lips, a male voice murmured soft words she couldn't understand, and a sickly sweet liquid trickled down her throat. Seconds later, she felt herself sliding backward, skimming over fields as agile as a dipping swallow, and coming to rest in the warm black pool of the Neva at low tide.

She slept.

*S*OFIA struggled to the surface.

Time. It floated from her grasp.

Faces drifted in and out.

Once, a voice cursed, a female voice. Sofia found herself telling her all about the wolf and the boy with the tawny eyes in the forest and about the long dangerous journey from the northern taiga all the way to Tivil. She told how her feet bled until she stole a pair of *valenki* and how at one time when she was starving in the forest, she could actually hear music in the form of bright flashes of a Rachmaninov symphony, like lights in the dark green world that had devoured her.

It was only when she'd finished that she realized she'd forgotten to open her mouth to say any of these things aloud, but by then she was too tired. So she slept.

A noise. A scratchy sound that scraped on the empty cavern of her mind. Remembrance came quickly. She lay still and opened her eyes just the faintest of cracks. The effort it took astonished her, but the thin strip of light that flickered between her lashes brought reality tumbling into focus and it didn't look so bad. She began to hope.

A mass of wild dark hair, that was what she saw first, around a young female face. A wide forehead and strong red lips. She was sitting in a stiff-backed chair beside Sofia's bed, bent over something on her lap, and that was where the noise was coming from. Without moving her head, Sofia tried to take in her surroundings, raising her eyelids a fraction more, but the sight of the room set her sluggish heart racing.

It was like no room she'd ever seen. The low ceiling was plastered and painted midnight blue with a hundred stars glittering and shimmering across it and a pale ethereal moon in each corner. Strange colored planets with rings of white ice seemed to swirl among them, creating a blur that Sofia felt was not just in her unsteady head. And at the center of this strange ceiling lay a huge painted eye at least a meter across. It was shaped like a diamond, its pupil as black as tar, and it stared down at her on the bed. It gave her the shudders. She looked away. The movement was slight, but instantly the dark head lifted and large black eyes fixed on hers. They were suspicious.

"You're awake." It wasn't a question.

Sofia tried to nod, but the thundering pain at the back of her skull burrowed deeper, so instead she blinked. Her mouth was bone dry and her tongue too heavy to use.

"You must sleep."

Her guardian stood up, and Sofia could see the objects in her hand. They were a pestle and mortar. She caught a glimpse of small shiny black seeds, some ground to a powder.

"No," Sofia mouthed.

The faintest of smiles touched the full red lips but not her eyes. "Yes."

Sofia felt a sharpening of her senses. She'd been wrong in thinking this person a full-grown woman. Despite the abundant curves of her breasts and hips, which were clothed in a black dress delicately embroidered with colorful stitching so that glossy birds and butterflies peeped out between the folds of her skirt, she was little more than a girl, sixteen or seventeen years old. With a young girl's translucent skin and long unruly curls that sprang into life at every turn of her head.

Across the room she started to pour liquid out of a dark brown bottle into a spoon. It smelled of musty earth and damp forests. Wary of what was going on here, Sofia took a deep breath and sat up.

Instantly the room and the girl cartwheeled in a spinning blaze of color that set Sofia's teeth on edge, but slowly she forced everything back into place. Even so, she leaned over the edge of the bed and vomited, nothing more than a dribble of saliva onto the hessian matting that covered the floor.

"Who are you?" she managed to ask the girl.

"I am Zenia Ilyan." Her voice was low and full of a kind of heat, as if her blood flowed fast.

"Why am I here?"

The girl came over to the bed, reached out a hand, and touched the nape of Sofia's neck. Gently the fingers started to massage it.

"You're here because you needed help. Now lie back."

The girl eased Sofia's shoulders down onto the pillow, and with one hand she wiped the sweat from Sofia's forehead while the other nudged a spoon against her lips.

"No," Sofia whispered.

"Yes. It will help you."

"No, I'm not sick."

"You don't know what you are." Then very slowly, as if speaking to a particularly stupid child, she said, "You will heal faster if you sleep. When you are well, we will wake you."

Sofia's eyelids started to grow heavy, but she jerked them wide open when she noticed a row of candles burning on a shelf, sending shadows and the smell of tallow swirling through the air. Only then did it occur to Sofia that the room possessed no window. Like a cellar. Or a prison. The pain in her head ricocheted around her skull.

"Sleep," the girl murmured.

"Sleep," Sofia echoed and opened her mouth.

TEN

"Run, Pyotr, run."

Pyotr Pashin tore down the dusty track, legs pumping, arms driving him on into the lead. Hot on his tail, nine other boys panted and scrabbled after him. And he felt a kick of joy as sweet as molasses in his stomach at the sight of nobody between him and the winning post. It was nothing more than a rusty stake hammered into the hard ground, but right now in the bright sunshine it gleamed a burnished gold.

Suddenly he felt breath moist on his bare shoulder and turned his head just enough to catch a glimpse of its owner. One final burst was all it would take to beat Yuri and a quick dip of his chest, like a waterfowl pulling weed, to get over the line in first place, but instead Pyotr put on the brakes—not hard enough to show, of course, but enough to do damage. In ten strides Yuri had outpaced him and was hurtling past the winning post. He watched the other boys crowd around Yuri, tumbling over themselves like puppies to be his best friend.

"Well done, Pyotr." It was his class teacher, Elizaveta Lishnikova, who had come to stand beside him. "*Molodiets!* Congratulations."

He looked up quickly. She was smiling, the wrinkles in her face rearranging themselves. Not often did he make her smile, so he dared to hope that he'd earn one of her red stars today. She was extremely tall and stiffly erect like one of the new telephone poles that were beginning to march across the landscape, with thick gray hair and a long thin nose that could sniff out a lie at a hundred paces.

"You ran well, Pyotr," she said.

"*Spasibo.* Thank you."

Instantly a flying body hurtled onto his back, choking the life out of him and sending him sprawling into the dirt in a tumble of arms and legs.

"Yuri, get off me, *durachok.*"

"You were brilliant, Pyotr. Fantastic. But I knew I could beat you, I knew it." Yuri thumped Pyotr on the chest, making his ribs ache, and raised his own arm in victory.

"Shut up, Yuri." But he couldn't help grinning.

There was something about Yuri Gamerov that made you want to please him. He was tall and strong with thick ginger hair and an easy way of always being the boss, which Pyotr envied. Pyotr was small and shy, but around Yuri he felt more . . . well, more colorful. And for some odd reason he couldn't quite understand, they were good friends. The grind of school term had finished for the summer and they were now into Young Pioneer Summer Camp, which Pyotr loved. But it was still held in the schoolyard each day and still organized by the headmistress, Elizaveta Lishnikova, with her assistant, so standards of behavior were not allowed to slip, despite the fact it wasn't actually school.

"Boys, take yourselves off the running track immediately. I am about to start the next race."

They scuttled off, their naked backs above their shorts tinged by the sun, and threw themselves down on the grass. It prickled their bare legs. Anastasia came trotting over at once.

Yuri groaned, "Here comes the mouse."

"She's not a mouse," Pyotr defended the girl.

Yuri was right, of course, Anastasia Tushkova did look like a mouse. Little pointed nose and chin, and a dull mouse color all over. Mousy hair that hung down her back in a skinny plait like a mouse-tail, and shorts that were much too big for her and made her legs look like pink pins. But Pyotr didn't mind her really, though he wouldn't admit that to Yuri. She plopped herself down on the grass in front of them and held out a hand. It was very grubby and on it lay a cookie.

"It's your prize for winning," she said to Yuri. "Teacher sent me over with it." She turned to Pyotr and gave him a sweet smile. She was eleven, the same age as Pyotr, but she looked younger, especially when she smiled like that. "You should have one too, Pyotr. You almost won."

"Almost is never good enough." Yuri grinned and took the *pechenka* from her. Very precisely he broke it into three equal parts and handed one to each of them.

"No," Pyotr said, pushing it away. "You won it, you eat it."

"I insist," Yuri said. "Equal shares for everyone. It's what we believe in."

That was the trouble with Yuri. He believed in applying Communism to every corner of his life—and everyone else's life too. Even cookies. Anastasia had no such problem.

"Mmm," she mewed, "*miod*. Honey."

Before Pyotr could blink, her share of the cookie had vanished into her mouth. Something about the speed of it embarrassed him, and he collapsed back on the dusty grass, feeling it dig shallow grooves in the delicate skin of his back. He loved the sky, the high blue arch of it over Tivil, with the sun a ball of gold, hovering and waiting to be caught. He lifted his arm straight up to see if he could touch it, but all he caught was a passing insect. He squashed it between his fingers and wiped it on his shorts. Yuri was sitting up watching the next race, but Anastasia was licking her fingers with the thoroughness of a cat licking its fur.

Through narrowed eyelashes Pyotr looked out at the dense jumble of greens that made up the forest as it marched up the steep ridges of the valley and over the mountains beyond. She was up there, some-where, the woman with the moonlight hair. Living in the forest.

"Pyotr." It was Anastasia.

"Yes?"

"Look."

Her little bony hand was pointing beyond the broad cedar tree that marked the start of the village to a spot in the distance where a ball of dust was rolling its way along the unpaved road toward them, slicing through the flat fields of cabbage on either side. Traffic on the road was always slight, usually no more than a few carts a day and, on rare occasions, a car or truck. Pyotr forgot the woman in the forest when he saw who was driving the cart that was trundling up the valley.

It was Chairman Aleksei Fomenko.

THE cart stopped outside the schoolyard. The piebald horse in the shafts tipped its back foot on edge to rest it and snorted loudly. Yuri leaped to his feet, dragging Anastasia with him.

"It's Comrade Fomenko. Come on, let's wave to him."

"No."

Pyotr stood up beside her. "Why not? What's wrong?"

"He took Masha last week." Anastasia's face had gone blank, but the mouse freckles on her skin stood out like warning spots. "He just drove that cart of his right up to our backyard and took her."

"No, Anastasia."

Pyotr didn't know what to say. Masha was the Tushkov family's last sow. All they had left. Without her . . .

"Here," he said, thrusting his share of the cookie into her hand.

She crammed it into her mouth.

"The pig was beautiful," Pyotr said, and he saw a spark of pleasure brighten her pale eyes, but her pointed chin gave a brief quiver. She put both her hands on top of her head and turned away, her elbows hiding her face.

Pyotr's chest hurt, though not from the running. He grasped Anastasia's wrist because he didn't know what else to do and squeezed it. He was shocked to find it no thicker than a *spichka*, a matchstick in his hand, just pale see-though skin stretched tight over a bundle of mouse bones.

"It's Comrade Fomenko's job," Pyotr whispered.

"To take our only pig?"

"Yes, of course it is," Yuri said with determination. "We're a *kolkhoz*, a collective farm. It's his duty to do his job properly."

"Then his job is wrong."

Yuri shook his head fiercely at her. "You mustn't say things like that, Anastasia. You could be put in prison for that."

"Maybe it was a mistake," Pyotr suggested.

"Do you think it might be?"

Anastasia's eyes gleamed with hope, and Pyotr was furious with himself for putting it there, but he couldn't bear to let her down now. He straightened his shoulders and ran a damp palm over his rumpled hair. He swallowed hard.

"I'll go and ask him."

*A*LEKSEI Fomenko was the chairman of Tivil's *kolkhoz*, the valley's collective farm, which was called *Krasnaya Strela*, the Red Arrow. He controlled it all. Though still in his early thirties, he was the one who decided the work rosters, allotted the rate of labor-days, made certain the workforce was in place each day, and ensured that the fulfilled quotas were sent off to the *raion* center on time. He had arrived from the *oblast* Central Office four years ago and brought order to a haphazard farm system that was so behind on taxes and quotas that the whole village was in danger of being labeled saboteurs and put in prison. Fomenko had set them straight. Pyotr worshipped him.

He was busy talking with the teacher, Elizaveta Lishnikova, in front of the schoolhouse, a neat whitewashed building with a newly tiled roof. Pyotr walked along the side of the cart, but it was too high for him to see inside, so he slunk around to the back where a young liver-colored filly was tethered to the hinge of the rear flap. She was long-backed and skittish, eager to barge her way to freedom. Pyotr tried to soothe her, but she would have none of it and attempted to nip him with her big yellow teeth but the halter was too tight.

"Comrade Chairman."

This was the first time Pyotr had ever spoken to Aleksei Fomenko, though he'd seen and heard him often enough at the political meetings in the assembly hall. He felt his cheeks flood scarlet, and his gaze found refuge on Fomenko's boots. They were good boots. Strong.

Proper factory-made ones. Not like the ones Papa wore, hand-stitched by a half-blind old cobbler in Dagorsk.

"Not now, Pyotr," his teacher said firmly.

"No, Elizaveta, let's hear our young comrade. He has the look of someone with something to say."

Elizaveta Lishnikova touched the elaborate knot of gray hair at the back of her head, a gesture of annoyance, but she said no more. Pyotr looked up at Aleksei Fomenko, grateful for the warmth of his words. Deep-set gray eyes were watching him with interest. The face was strong, like his boots. Straight thick eyebrows. And despite wearing a loose work shirt he looked lean and authoritative, exactly the way Pyotr longed to be.

"Well, what is it, young comrade? Speak up."

"Comrade Chairman, I . . . er . . ." His palms were hot. He brushed them on his shorts. "I have two things I wish to say."

"Which are?"

"Comrade Chairman, last week you took a pig from the Tushkov family."

The eyes narrowed. "Go on."

"It's just that . . . you see, I thought that perhaps it was a mis-take . . . and if I explained to you that . . ."

"It was no mistake."

"But they can't survive without Masha. Really they can't." The words came out in a rush. "The Tushkovs have eight children, Com-rade Chairman. They need the pig. To sell her litters. How else will they eat? And Anastasia is so . . ." He saw Chairman Fomenko's eyes change, somehow sink deeper in his head, but he didn't know what it meant. ". . . So thin," he finished weakly.

"Listen to me closely." The chairman placed a hand on Pyotr's bare shoulder, and Pyotr could feel the strength in it as his gaze fixed on Pyotr's. "Who do you think feeds the workers in our factories? In the towns and cities, all the people making our clothes and our machines and our medical supplies, all the men and women in the shipyards and down the mines? Who feeds them?"

"We do, Comrade Chairman."

"That's right. Each *kolkhoz*, each collective farm must fulfill its quota. It supplies the *raion*, the district, and each district supplies the *oblast*, the province. That's how the great proletariat of this vast country is fed and clothed. So which is more important, young comrade? The individual? Or the Soviet State?"

"The Soviet State." Pyotr said it passionately.

Fomenko smiled approval. "Well spoken. So which one matters more, the Tushkov family or the state?"

Pyotr was caught unawares by this sudden twist and felt the inside of his stomach burn. How had he come to this choice? He dropped his gaze, scuffed his feet on the brown grass, and stared again at the strong boots. Their owner was waiting for an answer.

"The state." It came out as a whisper.

"That is why I took the sow." The voice was gentle. "Do you understand?"

"Yes, Comrade Chairman."

"You agree it was right to take the sow?"

"Yes, Comrade Chairman."

"Good." He released Pyotr's shoulder. "And what was the second thing you wanted to talk to me about?"

Pyotr hated himself. He no longer cared about the second thing.

"Well?" Fomenko urged.

"It's the filly," Pyotr muttered. "The tether rope is too short and the halter too tight."

"You have good eyes, young comrade. The filly has thrown a shoe." He reached into his pocket, pulled out a fifty-kopeck coin, and tossed it into the air. The sunshine snatched at it. "Here, catch. You're obviously a bright lad and know something about horses; take her up to the blacksmith for me."

Pyotr caught the coin and glanced at Elizaveta Lishnikova. She nodded.

"Take Anastasia with you," she said, and there was a surprising softness in her voice that was usually reserved only for the younger children.

It made his shame worse, knowing she'd heard every word. His cheeks burned. He ran from the adults and unhitched the filly, and as he trudged up the street in the dust with Anastasia in tow, he threw her the fifty-kopeck coin. "You can have it."

"Thanks, Pyotr. You're the best friend in the world."

ELEVEN

SOFIA'S eyes opened to darkness. Her brain stuttered and almost slid back into the soft safe blankets of sleep, but she caught it just in time.

Where were the candles? What had happened to the girl?

She sat up. Mistake. The room splintered and lights flashed inside her eyeballs. She waited until the pieces slotted back together. She was on a bed, fully clothed, her fingertips told her that much. So far, so clear. She took a deep breath.

What else?

She was frightened. A tight ball of barbed wire was rolling around in her chest, but that was nothing new.

What else?

Her head hurt.

What else?

The darkness. It was changing, breaking down, as her eyes grew accustomed to it, into different shades of black and gray. She swung her feet to the floor, aware for the first time that she was not wearing shoes, and stood up. Not good, but not as bad as she expected. She took another breath and headed for a patch of gray. It was a door, held shut by a wooden latch on a string, and around the edge of it crept a whisper of daylight. Sofia put her ear to it and listened. No sounds. Just more silence and her own heartbeat battering her eardrums.

She lifted the latch. It opened onto a low-beamed living room with rough split-timber walls, unpainted, a carved chest in one corner, and in the center a home-built table with two upright chairs. At one end stood the *pechka*, a large stove, and, more surprisingly, a big maroon armchair turned to face the stove. The rough floor was covered with woven rushes and the air smelt heavily of herbs, which was hardly surprising, as bunches of all kinds of dried leaves were pinned around the walls in a fragrant frieze.

More to the point, the room was empty. No girl and no brown spoon. Over to her left was a window that revealed a dusty patch of road outside, and beside the window was the door. She ran for it and breathed a sigh of relief as her fingers lifted the metal latch and she stepped over the threshold.

"You'll need shoes."

She stopped dead. The voice had come from behind her, a man's voice. Dimly, like a muted echo from a dream, she recalled hearing the same voice before, murmuring to her with strange unfathomable words while she was unconscious. Slowly she turned. At first, after the scorching brightness of outside, she could make out nothing different in the room, but then a movement drew her attention to the faded maroon chair. There was a face, an upward curve of a gentle mouth, a shock of dense black hair swept straight back and an even blacker pair of eyes in a narrow face. He was watching her.

How had she not noticed him?

"Don't you want shoes?"

He spoke quietly. He was leaning around the edge of the armchair, most of him still hidden from view by the upright back of it, though his legs in scuffed brown leather trousers stuck out clearly and his bright yellow sleeve lay along the armrest.

"Don't you want shoes?" he asked again.

She had forgotten her feet were bare. She glanced over her shoulder at the sunlit slope, a tumble of honey-colored rocks that led up to the forest edge where secrecy and safety beckoned. *Run*, she told herself, *just run*. She'd come too far and worked too hard to risk losing her precious freedom now.

"Yes, I want my shoes."

"I'll fetch them for you."

He stood and moved away from the chair. He was shorter than she'd realized, not even as tall as herself, and older than his eyes and his hair indicated. Probably fifty, with the kind of skin that was swarthy and lined from years of living outdoors in the eye of the wind, like the traders who traveled up from Kazakhstan with their mountain horses. There was little flesh on his spare frame, but his arms looked muscular. He smiled, the gentle mouth curving more, and he walked over to the oak chest by the wall.

"Don't worry," he said. "I have no weapon hidden here."

He lifted the lid and extracted a pair of shoes. Slowly, so as not to startle her, he came forward and placed them on the table, and then he backed off and stood next to the stove. He was tempting her back in, as you tempt a horse into a stall with an apple. She shivered, made her choice, and walked back into the *izba*.

In some subtle way that she couldn't quite explain, the feel of the room had changed, and it struck her as odd. The smell of herbs was no longer suffocating but refreshing, and the place seemed to possess a kind of peace that was enticing. Sofia gave her head a sharp shake to clear it and cursed her confusion. Was it the result of the bang on the head or the residue of all that brown liquid still swilling through her veins? She looked at the shoes. Next to them on the table a bunch of purple wildflowers sat in a small pewter pot.

"Those aren't my shoes," she said.

"Yours are worn through. Holes in both soles and held together with string. I thought you might prefer these."

He spoke about them as if they were a pack of cheap *makhorka* tobacco instead of possessions that some would kill for. Well-softened pigskin stitched onto double-thickness rubber soles. New shoes. Who on earth could find new shoes these days? And then give them away. But she wasn't going to argue with him and instead strode over to the center of the room, snatched up the shoes, and slipped them on her feet. They fit perfectly.

"Thank you," she said.

He gave her a warm smile. "Enjoy them."

"I will."

"May they keep you safe."

"What?"

"It seems to me you need help, that's all." His tone was mild.

Sofia blinked, nervous of this gentle-mannered little man and nervous of the uncertainty that had settled on her mind. She couldn't afford uncertainty.

"How long have I been here?"

"Two days."

"Two days? It feels more like two weeks."

"No. It's only two days."

"I was attacked."

"Yes, that's right. My daughter found you stealing our vegetables." It wasn't an accusation, just a comment on how things were. "And you'd stolen an ax too."

"You kept me prisoner."

There was a silence. The smile had gone, and a kind of stiffness altered the way he held his shoulders, so that Sofia knew she had offended him.

"I tried to heal you," he pointed out quietly.

"Thank you. I'm grateful." She recalled once more the voice murmuring the strange words and the touch of cool hands on her burning forehead. "Is it your bedroom I've been sleeping in?"

"Yes."

"It has no windows."

"I don't need windows to see."

She wasn't sure what to make of that. "Thank you again for the use of it, but now I must leave."

She turned toward the open door, but behind her she heard his soft voice, so low she could easily have missed it.

"You don't have to leave."

She chose to ignore his words and kept heading straight for freedom.

"You can stay here. You'll be safe," he said, and this time his voice rumbled around the room and echoed inside her skull.

You'll be safe.

Sofia was desperately tired of being frightened, of having her innards permanently twisted into knots, awake or asleep. If she was going to reach Anna in time, she needed to be on the inside of Tivil, not struggling on the outside in the dead of night. Her thoughts became blurred, frayed around the edges.

"Sit down."

For the first time he came closer and stood with one hand on the table edge. She didn't move.

"Why? Why would you take me in? Without even asking why or how I came here. You must have realized that I'm . . . that it could make serious trouble for you and your daughter. So why take such a risk?"

His small wiry frame hardened, and the gentle mouth lost its curve. He placed both hands flat on the table and leaned forward, his eyes deep black tunnels. And that was when she recognized him. He was the man on the track, the one she'd seen talking to Fomenko on the dark road.

"If the people of this country do not help each other," he said fiercely, "soon there will be no Russia. No people. They will all be in labor camps. A whole nation condemned to a slow death. The only ones left will be the sleek Politburo in Moscow, because power makes pride grow in the human heart like fat in a pig. I curse their rotten godforsaken souls. May they starve as we have starved. May they lose their wives and their children as we lose ours. May they choke on their own committees and *cominterns*. Let the devil take the lot of them."

Sofia sat down on one of the chairs. She looked up into the intense eyes that missed nothing, and the world became a smaller place, as though just the two of them in this room existed. There was something extraordinary about this man.

She had survived this far because she'd learned that trust was as fragile as a moth's wings and you didn't give it lightly. But she gave him a smile anyway.

He laughed, a warm fluid sound, and held out his hand. "My name is Rafik Ilyan. But they call me the gypsy. You and I, we can help each other."

"My name is Sofia," she said.

TWELVE

*H*AVE you seen her?"

Elizaveta Lishnikova narrowed her gaze against the sun as she glanced up through the village toward the gypsy's *izba*.

"*Nyet*. No," Pokrovsky replied as he hammered the last nail into the well-oiled hoof and snipped off its metal tip with pincers.

The liver-coated filly kept turning her head, pulling at the halter to inspect what he was doing back there, but otherwise she'd surprised him for once and behaved herself. Her wide nostrils released a long chesty sigh as though thankful the ordeal was over.

"No," Pokrovsky said again. "The gypsy claims she's his niece by marriage."

"Do you believe him?"

"No."

The blacksmith had been busy in the yard at the side of the smithy when the schoolteacher strode in with her usual bluntness. He always enjoyed one of her visits, even though she did demand answers from him as if he were one of her scrawny pupils. The day was hot and humid and he'd been content at his work, but now he was suddenly aware of the sweat on his shaven head and the stink of horses on his leather apron. She always had that effect on him, making him feel big and clumsy instead of broad and powerful.

Elizaveta was tall in her long black dress nipped in tight at her tiny waist, but everything else about her was dainty and ladylike, the little white lace collar at her neck and the way her delicate handkerchief just peeped out from her sleeve, too shy to venture farther. He sneaked a glance at her elegant fingernails as she tucked a tortoiseshell hairpin back into her gray hair, then compared them with his own, which were hard and black and caked in grease.

"Neither do I believe him," she said.

"So why is she here?" He picked up a long file.

"Why do you think?"

His eyes met hers. She always made him do the thinking for himself, as if she didn't already know the answers. He ran the file back and forth over the filly's rear hoof, tidying the edges, and said the words he was sure were already in her mind.

"She's an informer, here to spy on us."

"But why would Rafik, who loves our village so strongly, take in someone like that?"

"Because . . ." He paused, ran one of his big hands along the fine muscles of the horse's leg, and released his hold on her hoof. She bounced up on her toes and nearly kicked over his stool. Pokrovsky stood up straight and rubbed his hands on a dirty rag at his waist. "Elizaveta, I'm only a simple blacksmith; you're the one with the brains."

She laughed at that, a girlish laugh, and poked her furled parasol into his ribs. "Simple you are not!"

With a deep chuckle he led her farther into the smithy, where he poured her a glass of vodka without asking and another for himself. He knocked back his drink in one, but she sipped hers as if it were tea.

"She stole my ax," he told her. "Zenia returned it to me."

Her brown eyes widened. "Why would this stranger do a thing like that, I wonder?"

"To chop wood?" He raised one burly eyebrow.

"Very funny," she said dismissively. "The question is whether Deputy Stirkhov has sent her here to watch us."

"Rafik would never take in one of that bastard's spies."

"He would if he wanted to keep an eye on her."

"You think that's it?"

"It could be." She finished her drink with a dainty flourish and let her eyes roam around the tools and forge. She gave a little nod of her head as though the orderliness satisfied her. Without turning to look at him, she said, "There's another package due in tonight, my friend."

Pokrovsky poured himself another glass. "I'll be there. You can rely on that." He drank it down.

*S*OMEONE is coming. A woman."

Sofia said the words calmly, but she felt a hint of alarm at the sight of a female figure heading toward the gypsy's house through the last traces of dusk. The habit of fear was hard to break. She was seated on the bleached wooden doorstep, her cheek resting on her hand, her gaze fixed firmly on the village. She was watching the cows being led in from the fields, weary and heavy footed, and the group of men heading for the meeting in the old church.

The evening had not been easy in the gypsy *izba*. Conversation was impossible. How could you talk in these bewildering circumstances without asking questions? But if you asked questions, someone was forced to give answers, and that meant lies. And who wanted lies?

"Who is it?" Rafik asked.

Zenia left her seat at the table where she was shredding a pile of dusky leaves, came over to where Sofia was sitting, and squinted into the gloom that had settled like dust on the street.

"It's Lilya Dimentieva."

"Does she have the child with her?" Rafik asked.

"Yes."

Sofia tensed as the woman and child came close, but she needn't have worried because Lilya Dimentieva showed no more interest in her than she did in the carving of the birds on the door lintel above her head. She was a woman in her twenties, small and slender with an impatient face and long brown hair bound up carelessly in a scarf. Her navy dress was neat and tidy, unlike Sofia's ragged skirt and blouse, but the little boy whose hand clutched tightly to hers was a different matter. He was barefoot and in need of a wash.

"Zenia, I want . . ."

"Hush, Lilya," the gypsy girl said sharply. "Come inside." She gestured to the stranger sitting silent on the step. "This is my cousin and she'll look after Misha. Won't you, Sofia?"

"Happily."

His mother disentangled him from her skirts and disappeared inside the house with Zenia. Sofia and the boy studied each other solemnly. He was no more than three or four, dressed in what looked like a cast-off army shirt cut down into a tunic that was far too big for him.

"Would you like to share my seat?" she asked, patting the warm step beside her.

He hesitated, fingering a shaggy blond curl.

She edged over to make room. "Shall I tell you a story?"

"Is it about soldiers?"

"No, it's about a fox and a crow. I think you'll like it."

He put out a tentative hand. She took it, soft and dusty, inside her own and drew him to share her doorstep, where he plopped down like a kitten, keeping a small safe gap of evening air between his own body and hers. Already he'd learned to be cautious.

"I don't like this house," he whispered, his pupils huge in the semidark. "It's full of . . . black," he blurted out. And then, as if he'd said something wicked, he clapped a hand over his own mouth.

Sofia gave a soft laugh, and the boy instantly pressed his other hand tight over her lips. She could taste onions on his fingers. Gently she removed his hand and held it between hers.

"No," she reassured the boy, "Rafik is a kind man, and it's just like any other house here in Tivil." She didn't mention the ceiling with the whirling planets and the staring eye. "No need to be frightened of it."

His hand patted her knee. "Tell the story."

She closed her eyes and leaned against the wooden doorpost, feeling the solidity of it all the way down her spine, and was surprised to find that Misha leaned with her, his shoulder nestling against her ribs.

Behind them in the room she could hear the murmur of low voices. She opened her eyes and smiled at the boy.

"There was once a fox called Rasta and he lived in a dark green forest up in the mountains among the clouds."

"A forest like ours?"

"Just like ours." The high ridge above the valley had been swallowed by the evening darkness, but they could both still see it in their heads. Somewhere a fox barked.

"There," she said, "there's Rasta calling for his story."

With the air around them so still it seemed to be listening, Sofia began to tell Misha the tale of the Reynard who made friends with the Crow, but before she was even halfway through it, the boy placed his head on her lap, his breathing heavy and slow. She picked a barley husk from his hair. As she stroked his cheek with her fingertips, aware of the child's warm body on her knee and the glow of the kerosene lamp flickering behind her among the voices, she could almost fool herself she'd found a home.

THIRTEEN

Davinsky Camp
July 1933

"ANNA, wait for me," Nina called out as she bent to stuff fresh moss into her shoes to keep the water out.

Anna lifted her head. Her heart raced.

Anna, wait for me. Those were the last words she had heard from Sofia. Anna heard them again as clearly as if Sofia were standing next to her now. They hung in the air, insistent. *Wait for me.* All these months Anna had worried and fretted, and tortured herself with nightmares imagining hideous fates for her friend. A slow and painful starvation in the steppes or pitchforked to death by a farmer or raped by a soldier. Torn to shreds by a bear or savaged by a wolf. Recaptured and sent to slave in a coal mine or, worst of all, recaptured with a bullet in the head. Recaptured. Recaptured. Recaptured. They had whirled around her brain.

Wait for me.

Anna looked around her at the women lining up for the exhausting trek back to the camp. It was the end of a long workday, a two-hour march ahead of them, feet sore and blistered, backs aching, and stomachs clenched with hunger. But it was a brief moment of time that Anna always enjoyed. Heads came up instead of drooping between shoulders, scarves were retied, and leggings that protected against insect bites in the slimy ditches were stripped off. Work had to be performed in strict silence, but for these brief few minutes the women broke into conversation with each other, and to Anna it was as sweet as if they'd broken into song. It wasn't important whether they discussed that day's moans or laughed at stupid jokes that set her chest aching; what mattered was that they talked to each other.

"How's your cranky knee today?"

"Much the same, you know what it's like. What about your leg ulcers?"

"A bloody pain."

"Has anyone got a length of cotton? Look, I've torn my shirt."

"Have you heard about Natalie?"

"No." A cluster of voices. "What news?"

"She's had the baby."

"Boy or girl?"

"A boy." A pause. "Born dead."

Two women crossed themselves discreetly, so guards wouldn't notice.

"Lucky fucking bastard," Tasha snapped. "Dead is better than . . ."

"Shut up," Nina scolded and took her place with a shrug of her broad shoulders beside Anna in the crocodile line. It used to be Sofia's place. Whenever Anna stumbled or fell behind, Nina's strong hand was there. "There's a rumor going around," Nina said under her breath.

"About what?" Anna asked.

"That we're soon to be put to work constructing a stretch of railway." She picked off a fat scab on her arm and slipped it into her mouth for something to chew on.

"The northern railway?"

Nina nodded and they exchanged a look.

"They say," Anna murmured as they started marching, "that the railtrack has killed forty thousand this year already."

Yet always more came, an unending river of prisoners carted across the country in cattle wagons. Each new arrival in the hut raised Anna's hopes, but each time she drew a blank.

"Have you spoken to anyone called Sofia Morozova? In a transit camp? On a train? In a prison cell?"

"*Nyet.*" Always the answer was "*Nyet.*"

Anna's eyes traveled to the dense wall of copper-colored tree trunks on either side of the raw scar that was the road that raked its way through the forest to another godforsaken camp and then another and another. Was Sofia out there? Somewhere? She raised her face to the silvery summer sky. She tried to hear the words again, *Anna, wait for me*, but they had gone. She felt cold, and the pain in her lungs sharpened. She coughed, wiped away the blood with her sleeve.

"Sofia, I can't wait," she murmured.

ONE foot. Then the other. And the first one again, left, right, left, right, keep them moving. A brief summer storm had passed, leaving the evening sky pale and drained of energy, while the pine trees stood like stiff green sentinels along the track as if in league with the guards.

One foot. Then the other. Don't let them stop.

The ground was soft with pine needles, the path worn into deep ruts by the daily tramp of hundreds of feet as they marched to and from the Work Zone. It was during the hours that Anna spent walking—or shuffling, if she was honest—that her mind skidded out of control. It slid from her grasp as a dog slips its collar and runs wild. Without Sofia to laugh at her stories, she no longer had the strength to keep her thoughts together, and they raced around in places she didn't always want to visit, colliding with each other.

At first, just separate moments started to skip into her mind, warm and vivid, like riding Papa's high-stepping black horse whose coat shone like polished metal and crowing with delight as her childish hands wrapped tight in the coarse black mane. Or her governess, Maria, standing in her second-best silk dress, the one that was the color of red wine, and telling Papa that Anna couldn't go out riding on his rounds with him today because of a sore throat. Papa's face had fallen and he'd tickled her under her chin, telling her to get well quickly, and he'd called her his sweet angel. He'd kissed her good-bye, his whiskers all prickly and smelling of fat cigars. When she was very young Anna had once stolen one from the humidor in his study and shredded it to pieces in secret up in the attic to see if she could find whatever it was that made it smell so wonderful, but all she ended up with was a lap full of crinkly brown dust.

"You're smiling," Nina muttered beside her, pleased.

"Tell me, Nina, do you ever think about your past?"

"Not if I can help it."

"So what do you think about?"

Nina's heavy features spread into a grin. "I think about sex. And when I'm too exhausted for that, I think about winning at cards."

"Last night I won that grimy piece of mirror off Tasha."

"Why on earth do you want a mirror? We all look awful."

Anna nodded a time or two and watched a bright orange lizard, a *yasheritsa*, dart out of the path of the marching feet and flash up a tree with an angry flick of its tail.

"I'm thinking of using it to burn the camp down one sunny day," she said.

Nina laughed so hard that a guard came over and stuck his rifle in her face.

$\mathcal{B}$UT the images and memories crowded in on top of each other while Anna concentrated on pushing each foot forward, leaving her with no strength for defenses against them. She forgot the dim forest trail and the blisters on her feet, and inside the unpredictable labyrinth of her head she was riding in the back of a luxurious black car.

It was a Daimler and it belonged to the Dyuzheyevs, bigger and shinier than Papa's Oakland, and with a glass partition between them and the chauffeur that didn't squeak. Svetlana and Grigori Dyuzheyev were Papa's dearest friends, wealthy aristocrats who lived in a magnificent villa in Petrograd.

"Your pearls are beautiful."

Svetlana Dyuzheyeva, a stylish and elegant woman, was delighted by the compliment and ran a finger along the triple strand of matched pearls at her creamy throat.

"Thank you, Anna. They used to belong to my mother and to her mother before that. Here"—she lifted one of Anna's fingers—"touch them."

They felt like silk, warm and alive, but smoother than her own skin. She couldn't imagine how such beauty could come out of something as ugly as an oyster.

"They're wonderful," she murmured. "And one day Vasily will own them." She was thinking aloud, already afraid that he'd be stupid and use them to feed his fellow demonstrators. She couldn't bear the idea of them going to waste.

Svetlana grinned mischievously, raised one eyebrow, and leaned close to Anna's ear. "Vasily . . . or his wife," she whispered.

To Anna's horror she felt her cheeks start to burn. She turned away to hide her quiver of excitement and looked out the other window. Maria, Anna's governess, was seated on the jump seat opposite Papa, in her very best dress of green watered silk and wearing her very best smile. Anna loved her governess, especially today because there had been no frowns, no scolding, and no schoolwork. Instead Maria had played the piano for them all when Grigori tired of doing so and danced with Papa until even her nose glowed pink.

Afterward there had been singing and champagne and wafer-thin squares of soft white bread piled high with glistening heaps of *osyotr* caviar that to Anna smelled of mermaids. Now Papa was accompanying Svetlana and Grigori to the theater, and the chauffeur would drive Anna and Maria home. Anna was perched between her father and Svetlana on the broad leather seat of the car. She had enjoyed the excitement of the day but was disappointed now that Vasily had vanished. He'd whispered to her that he had to meet a friend, but when she demanded, "To do what?" his face had closed down and he'd given no answer.

"Nikolai," Svetlana said, as though aware of Anna's thoughts, "it was very naughty of my Vasily not to escort your daughter home tonight. I hope you're not offended. He's a bad boy." But she said it with a mother's indulgent smile.

"Don't worry about that," Papa said. "With his snow sleighs and dancing, your Vasily knows exactly how to please my daughter and therefore how to please me,"

He glanced out of the side window as they crawled nose to tail behind a line of evening theater traffic along Bolshaya Morskaya, the lights in the shops twinkling invitingly, reflecting off the black silk of the top hats. After a moment he looked back at Svetlana.

"Where are they tonight?"

She gave an elegant shrug. "I don't know. There's an eight o'clock curfew."

"They're in Palace Square," Maria said quietly. "Thousands of them. With placards and banners."

"Damn Leninists!" Grigori growled.

Svetlana sighed. "What are they on strike for this time?"

"They're demanding bread, madam."

Svetlana touched the pearls at her throat and made no comment, but the words had caused an abrupt change of mood in the car. Anna had the feeling that her feet were suddenly in ice water.

She hated to see Papa's face so worried, and to cheer him up she said, "Vasily says that everything will get better for the workers soon." She stuck out her arm to point to one of the shops they were just passing. "Vasily says that jewelry shops like that one will close because they are criminals."

"Criminals?" Papa queried.

"Yes, he says they are criminals to make fifty-two eggs of gold for the tsarina and the dowager empress while the working man doesn't even—"

"Ah, I think Carl Fabergé may not agree with my son there," Grigori muttered grimly.

"And Vasily says there are machine guns on rooftops to—"

"Annochka," Svetlana said firmly, "you must not listen to everything my son tells you."

"Why not?" Anna felt chill.

"Because . . . he is like you." She wrapped an arm around Anna. "He still believes the world can be mended."

"Papa," Anna said seriously, "I believe we should do more to help some of these people Vasily says are without food or warm clothes. You and I have more than we need of both, you must admit. So we should share with them."

Papa patted her knee in a forgiving sort of way that was extremely annoying. Grigori grunted and Maria smiled. But Svetlana laughed out loud and tightened her arm around Anna's shoulders, so that the ostrich feathers that trimmed her midnight-blue velvet cloak tickled Anna's nose, making her sneeze.

"*Bud zdorova!*" the adults chorused. "Bless you."

Papa kissed her cheek. "Bless you, my dearest child. Bless you today, tomorrow, and all the tomorrows to come."

She stared out the window at the chauffeured cars, nose to tail like polished elephants. "Will the tsar be there tonight, Papa? Will it be very grand?"

Papa took a cigar from his silver case and rolled it between his fingers. "*Grand* is not a big enough word, my angel. Tonight the Alexandriinsky Theater will drip with grand dukes and gold roubles and imperial magnificence just so that people like us can see a silly melodrama about love and death called *Masquerade*."

"Nikolai," Svetlana murmured in faint rebuke.

Silently Papa lit his cigar, watched the first tendril of smoke swirl around the interior of the car, then fixed his gaze on Svetlana and Grigori.

"My dearest friends," he said earnestly, "if anything should ever happen to me, will you take care of Anna?"

Anna's mouth dropped open. Happen? What was going to happen to Papa?

"Nikolai, my dear, don't—"

"Svetlana, please. Now that my brother is dead of diphtheria there is no one else. And in these uncertain times one never knows, so . . ."

Svetlana reached behind Anna and squeezed Papa's shoulder. "It would be an honor. Rest easy, my friend. We love her dearly and would care for her as our own."

"*Spasibo*. Thank you." His voice was gruff.

Anna breathed carefully, unable to work out what was going on. She had a horrid fear that she had just been given away and didn't like the sound of it. But Papa hadn't finished. He turned to the governess.

"And you, Maria. If anything should . . . happen, will you also care for my daughter?"

Anna stared in astonishment at her governess. There were sudden tears in her large brown eyes. She tried to blink them away, but the streetlamp trickled its yellow light down her face.

"I will, *Doktor* Fedorin. I love the child."

"Promise me."

"*Ya keyanus.* I swear it, *Doktor.*"

Papa swallowed hard, then reached up and removed the pin he always wore in his tie. For no more than a second he gazed at it, at the exquisite pair of diamonds set in gold, then brushed his lips lightly over them.

Anna watched with wide eyes.

He leaned forward toward the governess on the opposite seat, lifted the lapel of her coat, and slid the point of the tie pin into the soft wool. But on the *underside* of the lapel. When he sat back once more, the tie pin was no longer visible.

"Nikolai," Svetlana said, so softly it was barely a word, "that pin was from Anna's mother. Her wedding gift to you."

"What better protection can I offer?"

Whatever was going on here, Anna was determined to put a stop to it.

"Papa, *ne boysya*, don't be afraid." She made her voice resolutely cheerful. "Nothing is going to happen to you. Don't worry, I'll take care of you." She gave him a wide grin and patted his strong arm. "You can rely on me. And Vasily."

THE streetlamps flicked past the car, painting bright stripes on the darkness. *Odeen . . . dva . . . tri . . .* Anna started to count them— one . . . two . . . three—but her eyes grew heavy and the lights too bright, so she let her eyelids slide shut and leaned her head against the warmth of Maria's shoulder. The familiar smell of lavender and mothballs that drifted from Maria's shawl was comforting.

The Dyuzheyev chauffeur was driving them home now that Papa, Grigori, and Svetlana were gone. The Daimler turned left off Nevsky past the wide steps of St. Isaac's Cathedral and under the lime trees. Anna drifted further into the billowing darkness that marks the edge of sleep. When the car slowed down she barely noticed, but she felt Maria stiffen and heard the shout of alarm from the chauffeur. She opened her eyes and suddenly there were faces all around them, looming out of the black street. Noses jammed like porridge against the glass, hands drumming a threat on the metalwork, mouths snarling, teeth bared.

Wolves. They were wolves. Wolves in cloth caps and thick scarves. Wolves howling words she couldn't understand, but she did know they wanted to tear her limb from limb. The car rocked on its wheels and beside her Maria screamed, and then the big car lurched forward, the engine growling, and the faces were gone. The tall houses whipped past as if in a race. Anna felt her heart on fire in her chest. Maria was breathing hard.

Anna took her governess's trembling hand in her own and crooned the way she used to do to her kitten when it was frightened by Grigori's borzoi hound. "You're safe now, you're safe now."

But Maria's eyes were huge in her plump round face, her lips still quivering. She pulled Anna close to her and whispered, "Try to sleep again."

Obediently Anna shut her eyes and breathed evenly, sleep breaths. But she was only pretending. Her bones felt stiff, the skin on her cheeks hard. She wouldn't tell what she'd seen, not to Maria, not to Papa. And certainly not to Svetlana or Grigori. She'd keep the secret safe, but very cautiously, bit by bit, she let the faces of the wolves loose inside her head. She shivered and made herself examine them, one by one, till she found it, the face she was looking for. Yes, he was there, behind the one pressed against the window on Maria's side of the car, a face she knew, a face she loved. Vasily.

He was wearing the thick red scarf she'd given him for Christmas, and a gray jacket she'd never seen before, but it looked old and shabby like the ones around him. It was definitely Vasily, but he had grown wolf teeth and wolf eyes.

Thin tears made tracks down her cheeks.

FOURTEEN

SOFIA woke with a jerk. The world was dark. A ferocious banging on the front door of the *izba* yanked her out of a nightmare she was glad to leave, but before she could even begin to think straight, her body reacted instinctively. It rolled out of the makeshift bed at the back of the stove in one fast fluid movement, ducked low, and raced across the living room, flattening against the wall behind the door.

Her knife. Where was her knife?

"Rafik! Open up, damn you," a man shouted outside. Its owner delivered a hefty kick that rattled the wooden planks on their hinges and made Sofia's heart jump.

The door to Rafik's bedroom opened abruptly, and a candle advanced across the room. Above the flickering flame the gypsy's face shifted in and out of the shadows as though still a part of Sofia's dream, but his movements were solid and steady enough. His black eyes took in her position of ambush and he spoke softly.

"It's all right, Sofia, calm down. It's only Mikhail Pashin, not the Blue Caps come to seize you. He is the *direktor* who runs the Levitsky factory in Dagorsk where Zenia works."

Mikhail Pashin. Vasily. He had come to her.

"Gypsy!" Another rap at the door. "For God's sake, you're wanted."

Sofia held her breath and reached out to lift the latch, but as she did so, Rafik's hand seized her wrist. Instantly she felt her panic subside.

"You're safe here," he said evenly.

"Am I?"

"Yes, so don't let your mind drown in your fear."

"I'll remember that."

"Good."

Rafik released her wrist and opened the door to a blast of cold air that made the candle gutter and spit. He curved his hand around the wick, and it managed to struggle back to life.

"What is it?"

"It's the bay mare," the voice outside replied. It was impatient.

"Foaling so early?"

"She's having a wretched time of it. Priest Logvinov is frightened we might lose her."

Rafik's expression showed a spasm of pain, as if the thought of losing a horse wounded him physically. Sofia took the candleholder from his fingers to steady it.

"Wait here, Pilot," the gypsy said to the voice at the door and disappeared back into the darkness of his room.

Mikhail Pashin stepped over the threshold and closed the door behind him, firmly shutting out the wind and the night. In the sudden silence that followed, Sofia saw in the wavering light a pair of intelligent eyes, gray and private with thoughts, an impression of soft brown hair tumbling over a high forehead. Two lines ran from his nose to the corners of his mouth in deep furrows, though she knew he was no more than thirty. They told of things kept unsaid. But in Russia now, who did not have words hidden behind their lips?

"I apologize for disturbing your sleep," he said.

He treated her to a courteous bow of his head. She was aware that he was studying her with interest, and she became conscious that she was wearing only a nightdress. It was one of fine white cotton that Rafik had given her. She lifted the candle higher to see more clearly what it was about Mikhail Pashin that brought such energy into the house, and she noticed the way his long limbs kept flexing as though eager to be on the move. On his feet were black shoes, highly polished, and he was wearing a charcoal suit with crisp white shirt and black tie, all oddly incongruous in this rough and informal setting. He seemed indifferent to it until he noticed her curious stare, and then he reached up, loosened his tie, and gave a slight shrug.

"Why does Rafik call you Pilot?" Sofia asked.

"It's his private joke. I'm not a pilot of anything."

"Except the Levitsky factory?"

He laughed, but there was an edge to it that made it clear he was anything but amused. "That's not piloting. That's crash landing."

"Is it wise?"

"What?"

"To say such things."

She hadn't meant to startle him. But she saw one eyebrow rise and felt a subtle shift of air between them. He took a step away from her into the deeper shadows that hovered beyond the candle flame's circle and bowed his head to her again, but this time there was no mistaking the hint of mockery in it.

"Thank you for the warning," he said smoothly.

"It wasn't a warning, it was . . ."

At that moment Rafik hurried into the room, fully dressed in a warm wool jacket, with a coarse blanket over one shoulder and a large leather satchel slung from the other.

"Come, Mikhail," he ordered. "We must be quick."

Mikhail Pashin spun around and opened the door, and without even a farewell to her, the two men hurried away into what remained of the night. Sofia watched them go, one figure short and scurrying, the other tall and lean with the long easy stride of a wolfhound. Neither carried a light, as if their feet knew these paths too well.

"It wasn't a warning, it was a question," she finished.

So he was real. Real flesh. Real blood. Not just a character in Anna's stories. He was solid, so solid she could have touched him had she chosen to, and her fingers would not have slipped straight through his body the way they did in her dreams. In Anna's dreams.

She'd found him.

He'd come to her, coalescing out of the darkness just as he'd done a thousand times before when she'd summoned him, but never before had he been made of body and bone. Never before did he have a voice. A tongue. Skin that had seen the sun. A long hard throat. Hair that smelled of early morning mists and stable straw. His jaw was more angular than in her imaginings and his gray eyes more guarded, but it was him. Vasily.

Mikhail Pashin.

Here in the gypsy's house she had breathed the same air he breathed. Her heart was pounding and she could still hear his voice. *I'm not a pilot of anything.*

"But you're wrong, Mikhail Pashin," she whispered, and she brushed her hand through the air where he had stood, as if she could hold on to his shadow. "You brought me here. You guided my footsteps to this village of Tivil as surely as if you had laid a trail for me."

And what had she done with the precious moment? Wasted it. Her foolish tongue had frightened him off with a question that sounded to his ears too much like a threat. Damn it, damn it. Where were the soft words she'd planned for him?

"Next time," she murmured, angry with herself, "next time I swear I'll touch you. I'll place my fingers on the muscles of your arm and feel the hard bone underneath your skin." Abruptly she slumped down at the table and stared blindly into the shimmering flame. "He's Anna's," she whispered to the night.

ELIZAVETA Lishnikova felt sorry for the man in the chamber. She was the one who had started calling the dark and dingy underground room a *chamber* to give it a degree of dignity, rather than a *hole*, which was how it had been referred to before. It was only three meters square, its earthen walls lined with planking, and a single candle on a shelf threw out strange-angled shadows that Elizaveta had often noticed made the occupant even more jumpy. Only one hard-backed chair stood against the wall, smelling of mildew, and there was a bundle of blankets folded on top of some sacking on the floor. A Bible lay on the shelf next to the candle. Elizaveta had placed it there, but tonight it was obvious it had not been touched.

The man's hand was shaking, but otherwise he was putting up a good show of confidence. His fair hair was combed into a neat parting, his shirt collar was clean, and he was managing to keep his shoulders straight. She didn't like it when they arrived out of the darkness in crumpled rags, their bodies hunched and boneless with fear. But that was just a quirk of hers. She liked to see a bit of backbone on display. Though God only knew how desperately each package had good reason to be fearful.

"Now, Comrade Gorkin—that's your new name by the way, Andrei Gorkin. Start getting used to it."

He blinked, as if to seal the name into his mind. "I won't forget," he said.

Elizaveta registered the refinement of his speech. Another intellectual, maybe a university lecturer who'd said one word too many in praise of the wrong kind of book or the wrong kind of music. She pulled her gray woolen shawl around her bony shoulders to keep out the chill of such thoughts.

"Here." She offered a small bundle wrapped in muslin. "Something to eat now. And something more for the journey. It's only black bread and a cone of sunflower seeds, but it'll start you on your way."

"*Spasibo.*" His voice was shaky, and he wiped a hand across his eyes.

"None of that," she said gently, in the tone she would use to one of the little girls in her class. "This is a time when you must be . . ." She was going to say *strong*, but one look into his nervous eyes and she changed it. "You must be prepared for a little hardship. Keep your wits about you and do exactly as you're told and you'll get through it safely."

"I can't thank you enough for—"

"Hush. Eat up. You'll be moving on any moment now."

She rested a hand on the ancient iron latch of the door, ready to open it the second she heard the coded knock, and watched him force himself to eat to please her. Clearly he had no stomach for food tonight. She didn't blame him. Nights like this set her own innards churning and she sighed at the thought of a whole generation of intellectuals being wiped out, anyone with a thought of his own. Who was going to teach the next generation to think?

"You must regard me as wretched," he said, and he smoothed his pale hair in an attempt to appear anything but wretched.

"No."

"I had a good job in Moscow in the—"

"Don't tell me. I don't want to know."

He sat down on the chair as suddenly as if she'd slapped him. Dear God, sometimes these packages expected too much from her.

"It's safer," she explained. "The less I know, the better for both of us."

"Yes, I understand."

The candle hissed as a draft took the flame, and she heard the rap of knuckles on old wood.

"Your guide is here," she whispered.

She unlocked the door, and the large figure of Pokrovsky slipped into the gloomy chamber. Not for the first time, she thought how light on his feet the blacksmith was for a big man. He seemed to take up half of the available space and she couldn't resist a smile at the black bear-fur hat on his head. He'd told her before that it was to hide any telltale gleam of moonlight off his shaven scalp in the darkness of the forest, but it always amused her nonetheless.

"Ready?" Pokrovsky demanded of the man.

"Yes."

"Do you have your new identity papers?"

"Yes, here in my pocket." He patted his jacket.

"Then let's go."

Elizaveta opened the door quietly, and the man stepped out into the fresh night air. She saw him hesitate. Everything was black under a thin cloud layer, and she could almost hear his heart rate pick up.

"I wish there were a moon tonight," he muttered.

"Then you're a fool," Pokrovsky growled.

A wind rustled through the nearby stand of poplars, and it could as easily have been boots creeping over dead leaves on the ground. Elizaveta swallowed the acid that rose in her throat and laid a hand on Pokrovsky's massive arm.

"My friend," she said softly, "take care."

"Don't worry, I'll deliver your package safely."

His expression was hidden from her in the darkness, but he

grunted, blew out through his nostrils like a horse does at water, and swung away from her, so that her arm fell to her side. He set off at speed, and the package had to scurry to keep up.

*Y*OU'RE not in bed."

"No, Zenia. I've made you tea," Sofia said. She tried a smile, but it got her nowhere.

The gypsy girl had just emerged from the tiny closet that was her bedroom and yawned loudly, her body still soft with sleep. She stretched, arching her supple spine, hitched her nightdress up to her knees, and stepped onto one of the chairs at the table.

"I like juniper in my tea," Zenia said ungraciously.

She pulled down a hank of dried berries from one of the hooks on the rafters and crouched on the chair, knees up under her chin. One by one she dropped half a dozen of the shriveled berries into the cup of tea Sofia had pushed in front of her.

"Smells good," Sofia said. She was treading carefully. The girl clearly did not want her here.

"Yes," Zenia muttered, shutting her eyes and inhaling the steam.

Sofia sat opposite, silently studying the girl's neatly trimmed nails, and waited for her to open her eyes. Minutes passed.

Finally the black lashes lifted. "What's the matter, couldn't you sleep? It's barely light yet."

"Here, have some *kasha*."

"Where's Rafik?"

"He left a couple of hours ago. To see to a horse that's foaling."

"Oh yes, he mentioned one of the mares was close to term."

"Is that what he does? Care for the horses here?"

Zenia took a mouthful of the semolina porridge Sofia had made for her. "Yes, my father is half horse himself. This whole *kolkhoz* would be on its knees if they didn't have him, though I don't think even Comrade Fomenko, our revered chairman of the *kolkhoz*, realizes it." She flicked her tongue along her lips, scooping up a stray speck of *kasha*.

"Tell me, Zenia, what is your boss at the factory like? Mikhail Pashin, I mean." Just saying his name aloud made Sofia's chest tighten with pleasure.

"Why?"

"I want him to give me a job."

"Without identity papers? You're crazy. You can't do anything without them, you must know that." The black eyes grew worried. "You do know that, don't you?"

"Of course."

"Sofia, let me eat in peace, will you?" She sank her spoon into the bowl once more.

"Of course. I'm sorry."

Sofia stood up. She didn't want to crowd the girl, so she opened the front door and leaned against the doorpost, breathing in the apple-scented tang of wood smoke. The smell of it set memories skittering through her mind.

"You can get chucked into one of the Gulag labor camps for stealing, you know." Zenia's voice behind her was casual.

Sofia slowly turned. Was it intended as a threat?

"It's anti-Soviet behavior," Zenia added, but she didn't meet Sofia's gaze.

"I know."

"So why take the risk of stealing our vegetables?"

"In a Soviet state, surely everything belongs to the proletariat. Well, I'm one of the proletariat."

Zenia laughed, a startlingly lovely sound, and wagged a finger in Sofia's direction. "I must tell that one to Boris Zakarov," she said. "He's the Party spy around these parts."

"I'd rather you didn't."

"I bet you would."

Zenia put her cup down on the table rather harder than was necessary, swept her hair into a black coil on top of her head, and walked out of the room. Sofia's head was pounding. A risk? Of course it was. Everything was a damn risk. She took a small step onto the colorless road outside. She could see movement in the village, figures silhouetted against the thin band of gold on the eastern horizon, lights flickering on in the houses. A goat bleated plaintively somewhere close; a cockerel crowed as if he owned the world.

Today. Today would be the beginning.

FIFTEEN

RAFIK held the stone in the palm of his hand. No larger than a duck egg, and white as a swan's throat. He stood in the strict privacy of his own room, and he'd brought out the white pebble from its bed of scarlet because he could sense danger gathering, sabers rattling, like troops lining up for battle.

It grieved him deep in his heart to know that his beloved Tivil was under threat once more tonight, and each time he closed his eyes he could see the blond-haired one, Sofia, tall and slender. She appeared to him like a blade, shining and well honed. He could see the fine edge of her slicing through the dark dense mass that was the danger. Behind his eyes a pinpoint of pain began to throb. With a sudden urgent need, he rested his thumb on the smooth white pebble and felt its coolness against his skin. It brought to mind the ancient strength of his ancestors, and it soothed the throbbing, cleared his mind. Now the Sight came to him more readily.

The stone had been passed down through his gypsy line for generations, father to son, and was said to have come originally from the stone that was rolled aside from the tomb of Jesus Christ in the Holy Land. Each time it lay in the center of his palm he was acutely aware that each one who owned it had imparted a sliver of his strength to its tightly packed crystals. He could sense the vibration of white life inside them.

A flame burned on the shelf. It rose out of a bowl of fragrant oil, and a slender cord of smoke twisted up from the tip of the flame to the ceiling, where it settled and gathered around the large black eye painted there. Solidified like a shield. His thumb lingered over the pebble. Caressed its smooth carapace, traced a circle around it, a circle of protection. Once more around the stone.

Rafik stared intently.

A third time around the circle, his thumb anointing the pebble, and he could almost hear it breathing. He circled again. Again. Again.

Then he uttered a long intricate curse in a language so strange and brittle that it rattled against the shield of smoke above his head. From the table he lifted a knife with a handle carved in ivory in the shape of a serpent and laid the tip of the blade on the inside skin of his own forearm. He drew a fine line until a trickle of red ran down to his wrist, where it formed a shallow pool. He let it gather. Then tipped it.

Three drips on the stone.

ZENIA."

His daughter came into the room at once, her body sheathed in a flowing red dress with a wide gypsy waistband and a woven plait of fresh tendrils of forest greenery around her neck. He thought how beautiful she looked, how like her dear dead mother. She gazed at the stone in his hand with alert eyes, bright and black and curious. Yet for her it possessed no resonance. Whenever she handled it and turned it over and over on her palm, it was nothing but a white pebble with a faint web of silvery veins threaded through it, an ordinary stone. He knew it frustrated her that she could gain no sense of her ancestors within it, and though he would never breathe a word of it aloud to her, his own disappointment was even greater than hers.

"Go with her tonight, my Zenia. But don't let her know you are my sight."

"Yes, Rafik." She paused. "Is she in danger so soon?"

"It comes from two directions. Make sure you guard her well."

"And you?"

Rafik closed his fist over the stone and swept it briefly through the candle flame. "Darkness is coming to Tivil tonight. Fire and darkness. The fire will burn the one she loves, and the darkness will quench the furnace in her."

"You are prepared?" Zenia asked, her voice unsteady.

He lifted the stone and laid it against his temple, held it there, listening to something inside his head. His brow furrowed, and a pulse beat strongly in his neck.

"I am prepared."

"But will you fall ill?"

He smiled, a deep and tender smile. "Don't be frightened, daughter. She is here."

SIXTEEN

PYOTR liked the meetings. He loved to sit right at the front of the assembly hall, under the nose of the speaker. Every week he arrived early with his Young Pioneer shirt freshly ironed by himself, knees and hands scrubbed clean, hair slicked down into temporary submission. His eyes, like his cheeks, were shining.

"*Dobriy vecher.* Good evening, Pyotr."

A large figure with a smooth shaven head and a spade-shaped black beard took the place next to him. The boy felt the bench sag beneath the man's weight and heard its groan of protest.

"*Dobriy vecher*, Comrade Pokrovsky."

The blacksmith also invariably selected the front bench at these weekly meetings, but for quite different reasons from Pyotr's. Pokrovsky liked to question the speaker.

"Your father not here again, Pyotr?"

"*Nyet.* He's working late. At the factory."

"Hah! Tell me an evening that he's not working late when there's a meeting going on here."

Pyotr felt his cheeks flush red. "No, honestly he's busy. Producing army uniforms, an important order. Directly from Moscow. He's been told to keep the factory working twenty-four hours a day if necessary because what he does is so important. Clothing our brave soldiers."

"Proudly spoken, boy."

Pokrovsky grinned at him. The black bush parted to reveal large white teeth, and it seemed to Pyotr that the blacksmith looked impressed. That made him feel less sick about his father's absence.

"It's important work," he said again, and then he feared he was insisting too much, so he shut up.

But his mood was spoiled. He slumped back on the bench and wished his friend Yuri would arrive. He stared moodily around at the plain walls where all the religious images had been whitewashed into a clean and bland uniformity. This pleased Pyotr. As did the metal table set up on the low platform in front of him where the gilt altar had once stood and the two sturdy chairs waiting for the speakers under the poster of the Great Leader himself. Beside it hung a bright red poster declaring, *"Smert Vragam Sovietskogo Naroda."* Death to the Enemies of Soviet People.

He looked behind him, where the benches were filling up. Most of the villagers were still in their work clothes of coarse blue cotton, though some of the younger women had discarded their dusty head-scarves and changed into bright pretty blouses that stood out in the drab crowd. The gypsy girl was one. Her scarlet blouse with little puff sleeves looked dramatic against her long black curls, but she kept her eyes lowered and her hands quiet in her lap, as if she were still in a church. Pyotr always felt she didn't quite belong in the village, though he wasn't sure why.

"Privet, Pyotr. Hello."

It was Yuri. He arrived in a scramble of long limbs and squeezed himself in next to Pyotr at the end of the bench, immaculate in his white Young Pioneer shirt and red neckerchief. Only then did Pyotr notice that his own ironing efforts weren't nearly as effective as Yuri's mother's. He shuffled up the seat a little toward Pokrovsky, so that their shirts wouldn't touch.

"Have you heard?" Yuri bent his ginger head to Pyotr's. He was always one to know the latest news.

"Heard what?"

Yuri grinned, his freckles dancing. "That Stirkhov is coming to address us tonight."

Pyotr's chest tightened just for a second. "Why? What have we done?"

"Don't be stupid. It's an honor for us to have the deputy chairman of the whole district here."

"No, Yuri, Stirkhov only ever comes to Tivil to complain."

The bulky figure of Pokrovsky leaned close, so close Pyotr could see where the black bristly hairs of his neatly trimmed beard were beginning to turn white in places.

"This time," the blacksmith said, fixing them with his dark eyes and pushing out his heavy jaw at them, "the bastard is probably checking up on people who don't attend these meetings."

Pyotr thought of his own father and felt that horrible tightness in his chest again.

"You wait and see, Comrade Pokrovsky," he blurted out. "Papa is soon to be awarded the decoration Hero of Labor First Class for his work for the Soviet State."

Pokrovsky slapped a hand down on Pyotr's fragile shoulder and roared with laughter, so loud that others turned and stared.

"May God forgive you, boy, for telling such lies in his church."

*I*T was the hands. That was what Pyotr decided. The way they moved through the air, strong and controlling. Wide slicing gestures to underline words, sharp jabs to force a point home. Even the flat palm to silence a rowdy voice from the floor. The hands held the power. Aleksei Fomenko, as *Predsedatel Kolkhoza*, chairman of the collective farm, had been speaking for an hour and a half, and yet Pyotr still couldn't take his eyes off him. He was seated behind the table, broad-chested and so full of energy that his lightweight brown jacket didn't look strong enough to contain him.

So far he had been listing the recent quotas set by the Central Control Commission, naming the shirkers who had fallen behind on their labor-days and urging them all to greater achievements. Fomenko leaned forward as he spoke, fixing his audience with his sharp gaze and scanning each villager in the hall. No one escaped.

"Beware of complacency," he urged. "We are nearly at the end of Stalin's First Five-Year Plan, which is building our country into the leading industrialized nation in the world. We have swept aside the superstitions of the past"—here his eyes turned to a tall bony man who possessed fierce eyes, with a lion's mane of chestnut hair and a straggly red beard, but his open shirt revealed the tip of a large wooden cross hanging around his neck—"and the concept of servitude has been replaced by the doctrine of freedom."

He clenched both fists.

"A new world is emerging. One that will sweep away the mistakes of past centuries, and we are the engine that drives it. Yes, you and I. And collectivism. Never forget that. The grip of the *kulaks*, those rich bourgeois farmers, class enemies who laughed at the tears of the poor and exploited you all, lashing your backs with their tyranny and their knout, their grip is broken thanks to the inspired vision of our Great Leader."

Fomenko turned to the giant poster of Stalin's all-powerful face that hung swathed in red banners behind him. "Our Great Leader," he repeated.

A murmur ran around the gathering. But nobody picked up the invitation, so it was Yuri who leaped to his feet.

"Long live our Great Leader," he shouted.

"Fine words," Fomenko said solemnly. "It takes a boy to show the rest of you the way. This young *tovarishch*, this comrade is a true proletarian, a man of the future."

A woman in the row behind Pyotr rose and echoed, "Long live our Great Leader."

"Josef Stalin, the Father of our Nation"—Fomenko's voice filled the hall right to the rafters, where the debased remains of the saints stared down on them—"is the one who is carrying throughout this great Union of Soviets the torch that Vladimir Ilyich Lenin lit for us. Stalin is the one who is ridding us of the saboteurs and subversives, the wreckers and the spoilers who would destroy the drive forward of the great Five-Year Plan." The chairman linked his hands together, fingers firmly entwined. "We must unite in the great fight toward the victory of Communism."

"What about some great bread to eat instead of a great fight?" the blacksmith demanded roughly.

Yuri scowled at him. Pyotr felt himself caught between the two of them. Hesitantly he rose to his feet and in a quiet voice he declared, "Comrade Stalin will feed us."

Beside him he heard the blacksmith groan and felt himself yanked back down onto the bench. Black fingernails like cockroaches sank into his freshly scrubbed flesh, but Pyotr was determined now and started to sing the words of the *Internationale*, "Arise you workers from your slumber . . ."

"Comrades."

The man who spoke was seated next to Fomenko at the table, a stocky figure with a smooth well-fed face, wiry hair, and oddly colorless eyes. He wore a sleek leather jacket that even Pyotr could see would have fed Anastasia's family for a month. He was the district party deputy chairman, sent by the *Raikom*, and however much Yuri insisted it was an honor to have him at their meeting, it didn't feel like that to Pyotr. It felt more like a rebuke.

"Comrades." The man paused. Waited for absolute quiet.

Fomenko eased back in his chair, instantly yielding control to his superior, but Pyotr saw the heel of his boot grind down on the floor. The hall fell silent.

"Comrades, I am proud to be here. With you, my brothers, the workers of Red Arrow *kolkhoz*. You all know me. I am Deputy Chairman Aleksandr Stirkhov from the *Raion* Committee. I am, always have been, and always will be a man of the people. I bring a message from our committee. We praise what you have achieved so far in this difficult year and urge you to greater efforts. The failure of the harvest last autumn was the work of wreckers and saboteurs, funded by foreign powers and their spies who plot to destroy our great new surge forward in technology. Throughout parts of Russia it meant we had to tighten our belts a notch or two . . ."

"Or three," a man called out from somewhere in the hall.

"Your own belt doesn't look so tight, Deputy Stirkhov." Another voice.

"Listen to me, Comrade Deputy, I lost my youngest child to starvation." This time Pyotr recognized the voice. It was Anastasia's mother. He would never forget the morning he'd seen her rocking the dead baby in her arms. Anastasia had missed school that day.

Stirkhov pursed his mouth. "Admittedly some shortages have occurred."

"It's a famine," Pokrovsky declared at Pyotr's side. "A fucking famine. People dying throughout—"

"Comrade Deputy Stirkhov is a busy man," Fomenko interrupted quickly. "He is not here to waste time listening to your accusations, Pokrovsky. There is no famine. That is a rumor spread about by the wreckers who have caused the shortages through their sabotage of our crops."

"That's a lie."

Stirkhov rounded on the blacksmith. "I remember you. You were a troublemaker when I was here before. Don't make me note you down as a propagator of negative statements, or . . ." He left the threat unsaid.

Everyone knew what happened to agitators.

Pokrovsky hunched his massive shoulders as though preparing to swing his hammer on his anvil, but he said nothing that the deputy's ears could pick up.

"Blacksmith." Stirkhov spoke quietly. He lifted a sheet of paper from the pile on the table. "I have here a list of items you made and services you performed in this village that were not strictly for the *kolkhoz*, not for the collective farm at all, in fact."

Pokrovsky ran a hand over his shaven head in a gesture of indifference. "So?"

"So you made a metal trough for Lenko's chickens, you repaired a stove chimney for Elizaveta Lishnikova, you mended the wheel on Vlasov's barrow, a pan handle for Zakarov . . ." He raised his reptilian eyes and studied Pokrovsky. "Need I go on?"

"No. What is your point?"

"My point is whether you were paid for these items."

"Not paid, exactly. But they thanked me with vegetables or a chicken, yes. And Elizaveta Lishnikova darned my shirts for me. I'm not much good with a needle." He held up his thick muscular fingers. There was a gentle titter among the benches. "As I said, not paid, exactly."

"Without your services, those gifts—and I have a long list of them here—would not have been given to you, so I believe we can class them as payment."

"Possibly."

"Which makes you a private speculator."

There was a hush. An intake of breath.

Pyotr wasn't watching Deputy Stirkhov anymore. His eyes were on Chairman Fomenko, and he saw the stiffening of the sinews in his strong neck. Everyone knew what happened to speculators. Pyotr felt a moment's panic and glanced swiftly around him.

That was when he saw her, the figure at the back near the door, standing as motionless as a deer. It was the young woman from the forest, the one with the moonlight hair, and her blue eyes were fixed on him. He felt his throat tighten, and he looked away quickly. Why was she here, the fugitive? A wrecker and a saboteur come to make trouble? Should he speak out? Could he? If only he possessed Yuri's absolute certainty of action in a black-and-white world. He dragged in a deep breath and jumped to his feet again.

"Comrade Chairman, I have something to say."

SEVENTEEN

SOFIA could see what was coming. Quickly she stepped into the aisle between the rows of benches.

"Comrade Deputy Chairman."

She spoke out clearly, overriding the boy's thin voice. Instantly all eyes swung away from him and focused on the newcomer. A murmur trickled around the hall. "Who is she? *Kto eto?*"

"State your name, Comrade," ordered Stirkhov.

"My name is Sofia Morozova." Her heart was kicking like a mule. "I've traveled down from Garinzov, near Lesosibirsk in the north, after the death of my aunt. I am the niece by marriage of Rafik Ilyan, who cares for your horses."

Heads turned to Zenia, who was seated next to the tall man with the lion's mane. She nodded, but kept her eyes fixed firmly on the bench in front and said nothing. Sofia wanted to shake her.

"What is it you wish to say, Comrade Morozova?" Stirkhov asked.

He had one of those oily half-smiles on his face, the kind she knew too well, the kind that made her want to spit.

"Comrade Deputy, I have come to this meeting to offer my labor for the harvest."

It was Chairman Aleksei Fomenko who responded. "We welcome laborers at harvest time when the hours are long and the work is hard. Have you done fieldwork before?"

She stared straight back at him, at the strong lines of his face. His observant gray gaze made her palms sweat.

"Yes," she said. "I've done fieldwork."

"Where?"

"On my aunt's farm."

Voices erupted along the benches.

"I could use her in my brigade."

"We need her in the potato fields," a woman shouted out. "It's hard, mind."

"She doesn't look as if she's up to it, Olga. All straw limbs."

"I'm strong," Sofia insisted.

A woman in a flowered headscarf and rubber boots reached out from the nearest bench and prodded Sofia's narrow thigh with a callused finger. "Good muscle."

"I'm not a horse," Sofia objected, but good-naturedly.

The women laughed. Aleksei Fomenko rapped on the table.

"Enough! Very well, Sofia Morozova, we will find you work. And I presume Rafik will speak for you."

"Yes, my uncle will speak for me."

"Have you registered at the *kolkhoz* office as a resident?"

"Not yet."

For the first time he paused. She saw the muscles around his eyes tighten and knew he had started to doubt her. "You must do so first thing tomorrow morning."

"Of course."

The boy's brown eyes were dark with fury as he prepared to speak again, and that was when she played her trump card.

She smiled straight at the boy and said, "I am a qualified tractor driver."

★ ★ ★

*P*YOTR felt his fear of her melt. One moment it was like acid in his throat, burning his flesh, and the next it tasted like honey, all sweet and cloying. He was confused. What had she done to him? She was an enemy of the people, he was convinced of it. Why else would she be a fugitive in the forest? But when he looked around at the faces, he couldn't understand why they couldn't see it too. What was she? A *vedma*? A witch?

"Pokrovsky," he whispered.

"What is it, boy?"

"I still have something to say."

"Just sit still and shut up," Pokrovsky growled with irritation. His attention was on the stranger.

Pyotr knew that tractor drivers were worth more than the finest black pearls of caviar from the Caspian Sea. The state ran tractor courses at every Machine and Tractor Station throughout the country, and a tractor driver was paid more in labor-days, sometimes even in cash, but so far no one in the Tivil *kolkhoz* had succeeded in gaining a place on one of the overcrowded courses. The fugitive had chosen the perfect golden key to open the door into the *kolkhoz*, because a tractor would halve the intensive work of the coming harvest.

"A tractor driver?" Fomenko repeated.

"Yes," she answered.

"You have the MTS certificate?"

"I have the certificate."

She was lying, Pyotr was certain she was lying. He could hear the little worms of deceit wriggling against each other as they burrowed into her words.

"This is excellent news," Stirkhov said. "*Otlichnaya novost.* The whole village will of course benefit, but . . ." He paused, his pale eyes suddenly flatter and harder. "But tonight I have come to inform you all of the quotas you are to fulfill with this year's harvest. The state demands that your quota of contributions be raised."

A ripple of shock ran through the hall, and one woman started to cry in harsh dry sobs. Moans made a rustling sound like rats in stubble. Then came the anger. Pyotr felt it like a wave of hot air, thick on the back of his neck, and he was sure the fugitive woman was in some strange way the cause of this dismay, that her presence was drawing disaster to his village.

"Silence!" Fomenko rapped on the table. "Listen to Comrade Stirkhov."

"We're listening," Igor Andreev, a brigade leader, said reasonably. His hunting dog whined at his knee. "But last December the Politburo ordered the seizing of most of our seed grain and our seed potatoes to feed the towns and the Red Army, so the harvest this season is smaller than a shrew's balls. We can't even fulfill the present quotas." He stared dully up at Fomenko. "Chairman, we'll be eating rats."

"If you work hard," Fomenko said quietly, "you eat. Stalin has announced the annihilation of begging and pauperism in the countryside. Work hard," he repeated, "and there will be enough for everyone to eat."

Stirkhov applauded vigorously. "Listen, comrades, only this week Stalin is opening the Belomorskiy Kanal. One hundred twenty million tons of frozen earth were removed by sheer hard work, and now the Baltic Sea is linked to the heartland of Russia. The trade increase in timber alone will bring a flood of prosperity and hard currency to our great Soviet State and its people. So do not talk of failure. See what can be achieved when we work together and follow the vision of our leader."

It was Leonid Logvinov who rose to his feet, the ginger-haired man they still called Priest, though his church was long gone. One hand clutched the ancient wooden crucifix at his neck.

"God forgive your murdering ways," he thundered, "and the blaspheming lies of your Antichrist."

"Too far, Priest, you've gone too far."

Stirkhov pounded his fist down on the metal table. But at the same moment the large oak door at the far end slammed open with a crash, rebounding on its hinges, and a wave of cold air swept into the hall. Mikhail Pashin strode into the central aisle, his brown hair windblown, his suit creased.

"Papa," Pyotr cried.

But Mikhail Pashin didn't hear. "Get out of here, all of you," he shouted. He pointed a finger at the men behind the table on the platform. "They've tricked you, those two. They've kept you in here while the forces of the Grain Procurement Agency are ransacking your houses. They're tearing your attics apart, hunting out hidden stores of grain, stripping your larders, and stealing your chickens to fulfill their quotas."

Alarm ripped through the benches. Panic forced everyone to their feet.

"Go home," Mikhail shouted above the noise. "Before you starve."

MIKHAIL Pashin could barely contain his anger. He expelled his breath violently and stepped aside to let the panicked villagers pass. They were pushing and pressing, struggling and shouting, a hundred of them fighting to get through the door as if the blue-capped wolves were actually nipping at their heels. It seemed to Mikhail that they were turning into sheep. Ever since the introduction of collectivization, starving peasants had thronged every railway station, clawing their way into the towns and cities, selling their souls for a few kopecks. Stalin was snipping off their tails, yet they didn't even bleat.

Urgently he scanned the bobbing heads. Where was Pyotr? He would be here somewhere. His son's infinite capacity for absorbing Communist propaganda made Mikhail clench his teeth, but right now all he wanted was to find him and get him safe. Tonight there would be violence. Even as the thought entered his head, the crack of a rifle shot ricocheted through the night air outside, bouncing off the *izba* walls, sending shivers through the valley. A woman screamed inside the hall, but the crowd was thinning. A stone abruptly exploded in through one of the side windows, scattering glass and drops of rain over the empty benches, as somebody expressed their rage. Mikhail took a deep breath.

"Pyotr!" he roared.

"Papa!"

With a huge sense of relief Mikhail caught sight of his son. Right at the front, struggling ineffectually in the massive grip of Pokrovsky. The blacksmith was holding him there, indifferent to the boy's kicks, quietly keeping him out of harm's way. Mikhail raised a hand to Pokrovsky.

"*Spasibo*," he mouthed. "Thank you."

Pokrovsky grinned in acknowledgment, but his eyes moved to the broken window and the lifeless leaves swirling in on the wind like omens. The big man ran the edge of his free hand across his own broad throat. *Smert*. Death. It was out there.

*Y*OU always seem to be the bringer of bad news."

Mikhail did not pause in his efforts to elbow a path down to the front of the hall but glanced fleetingly at the person who had spoken. To his surprise it was the girl he'd met in that candlelit moment before dawn this morning, the gypsy's niece, the one who seemed to have come from a different world. Her strange blue eyes looked at you as if seeing someone else, the someone you keep hidden from public gaze. She was standing in the aisle in front of him, still as stone, letting the flow of people break and re-form around her. Smiling at him. What the hell was there to smile at?

"These days most news is bad news," Mikhail muttered.

"Not always."

He wanted to push past to reach Pyotr, but something about her held him there for a second, and when an elderly *babushka* elbowed him against her, he found himself staring deep into her face, only inches from his own. Smelling the sweet scent of juniper on her breath.

She was painfully thin, bones almost jutting through her skin, and she had the bruised shadows of semistarvation in the hollows of her face. But her eyes were extraordinary. Wider and bluer than a summer sky, glittering in the light from the lamps, full of something wild. And they were laughing at him. For one strange and unnerving second he thought she was actually looking right into him and rummaging through his secrets. Abruptly he recalled the veiled threat she'd made the last time he spoke to her, and he forced himself to recoil.

"You should go home," he said, more abruptly than he intended.

"Home?" She cocked her head to one side and studied him. "Where is home?"

"You're living with the gypsies, aren't you?"

"Yes."

"Then show some sense. Go and stay there. This night has only just started."

"You and I," she said in a voice so low he barely heard it in the hubbub of voices around him, "have only just started."

He frowned and shook his head. Each time they met she seemed to have the knack of knocking him off balance. He broke free from her smile. "Pyotr!" he shouted again.

The boy was released and started to clamber over the benches toward him. But halfway down the hall Priest Logvinov was standing like a scarecrow, raised up on one of the bench seats, his red hair like flames around his head, the cross brandished like a weapon.

"Abomination!" he boomed out. *"Thou shalt have no other god before me, saith the Lord."* His finger pointed at Stirkhov's chest, as if it would drill through to the blasphemous heart within it.

"Don't, Priest," Mikhail shouted.

He saw Stirkhov, alone now on the platform, deliberately push over the metal table so that it fell with a screech on the floor below. With no sign of haste the *Raikom* deputy drew a Mauser pistol from inside his leather jacket and pointed it straight at the ranting figure less than ten meters in front of him.

"Priest! Get down," Mikhail bellowed and hurled himself toward the bench.

But it was the strange girl who saved him. "Aleksandr Stirkhov," she called, loud and clear above the noise in the hall, and then let rip with a shrill whistle that tore at Mikhail's eardrums and caught the deputy's attention. The muzzle of the gun wavered as he turned his head. All she did was smile at him, but instantly the soft pink tip of Stirkhov's tongue peeked out between his lips. Her smile widened, warm and distracting.

Time enough. For Mikhail to reach the exposed Priest, drag him down into the crowd, and push him along with the jostling flow to the door.

"Christe eleison," Priest uttered solemnly. "Christ have mercy on us in this unbelieving world."

Suddenly Pyotr's worried face popped up at Mikhail's elbow. He seized his son's arm in one hand and the girl's in the other and propelled them both through the door.

EIGHTEEN

Davinsky Camp
July 1933

ANNA stole half a potato from the camp kitchen. She was getting good at it. Or was it just that she was becoming invisible? That was more than possible.

When she looked at her own arms and legs, all she could see beneath the mosquito bites was a skeleton covered in an almost transparent gray film, so transparent that she could see the bones underneath. They peeked through with glimpses of white. She sometimes prodded them with her finger, to test how strong they were, she told herself, but really it was to make sure they were still there.

She didn't want to steal the potato, any more than she'd wanted to steal the bread last week or the greasy strip of pork fat the week before that. Each time she knew she'd be caught, and each time she was. A shriek of protest from a kitchen worker, a firm grip dragging her to the floor. But too late. She'd already crammed the food into her mouth before they could wrench it back from her. She'd taken the punishment beatings and prayed that none of the white sticks under her skin would snap. So far they hadn't. But they'd come close, and if she was caught stealing again they'd shoot her.

She felt the solid lump of boiled potato work its way, one millimeter at a time, down into her stomach, where it settled warm and comforting, like a friend. No, she patted the hollow cavity where she assumed her stomach still lay, no, not *like* a friend. *Because of* a friend. *Because of* Sofia.

Anna smiled and felt absurdly happy. She had achieved something positive, keeping herself alive for one more day, and it had been so simple this time, she couldn't believe it.

"You!" a guard, the one without eyebrows, had yelled at her when she was left behind in the yard after roll call. "Get over here. *Bistro!*"

She had to concentrate when she moved, slide one foot forward, then the other, then the first one again. Like pushing logs uphill. She was slow and he was impatient, so he clipped her elbow with his rifle butt.

"Unload those boxes into the kitchen. And be careful, *suka*, you stupid bitch. They're new."

It was that easy. Shift boxes. Unload pans. Keep eyes on floor. Place each iron pot on shelf. Slip potato in pocket. No beating. No punishment cell.

"For you, Sofia," she whispered, and again she rubbed the contented spot where the potato lay. She'd promised herself and she'd promised Sofia. But waiting was hard, and time and again she had to oust the thought that it would be much easier to lie down and die. With a raw gasp, she started to cough.

ISTEN!" Anna exclaimed, pausing from her task of stripping branches, ax in midair. "Listen to that." The other prisoners hesitated.

It was birdsong. A pure silken note that rose and fell and filled the air with the sweet sound of freedom. It set up an ache in Anna's heart.

"Get on with your work, if you've any sense," growled the short Muscovite who had toiled all day beside Anna with the silent precision of a machine and never missed her norm.

"It's beautiful," Anna insisted.

"What good is beauty to me? I can't eat it."

Anna returned to lopping limbs off the tree. The tall graceful pine lay stiff as a fallen soldier at her feet, oozing its sticky sap. She had long ago passed the point where she felt any sorrow for the forest and the systematic massacre of thousands of trees that was taking place in it, because in a labor camp there was no room for such feelings. Nothing existed except work, sleep, and eat. Work. Sleep. Eat. Above all, eat. It frightened her sometimes to feel her humanity slipping away from her; she feared she was becoming no more than a forest animal, chewing on twigs and scrabbling in the earth for roots.

And then a small drab-brown bird opened its beak and the sound that poured forth brought her winging back to the human race. To the memory of a Chopin waltz and a young man's arm sweeping her off her feet. The ache grew worse inside her.

"Yes," she said to the bent back of the woman from Moscow. "You can feed on beauty."

"Blyad!" the woman swore contemptuously. "You'll be dead before the year is out."

*A*NNA had no intention of dying. Not yet anyway.

Sofia, be quick.

She watched the forest each day for movement among the trees, for a shadow that shouldn't be there. A thousand times her heart leaped when she believed she'd seen Sofia's slight figure flit between the tall trunks or a sudden pale shape that looked like a face, but nothing materialized into reality.

She remembered well the first time she ever laid eyes on Sofia.

It was in the bitter winter of 1929 when Anna had not long been a prisoner in the camp and was as soft as the wood she was chopping into.

"Davay! Davay! Let's go, scum of the earth."

The guards had stamped their feet on the hard-packed snow, in a hurry to move the prisoner brigades on to the next timber haul a verst away.

"Bistro! Quickly!"

Anna had cursed her ax. It was too small and too blunt, the useless blade had stuck fast, trapped in the pale wood.

"Bistro!"

Anna had knelt on the branch, trying to widen the gap and release her ax. Everything hurt. The muscles in her back, the skin on her knees, the blisters on her feet, the tendons in her wrists, even the teeth in her head. And now lesions were appearing on her face, and they frightened her. She'd hacked again and again at the last two branches, but each time an iron-hard knot resisted her blows. She began to panic.

Frantically she tore at the branch with her hands, aware of the other brigades moving off, but her gloves had ripped and pain stabbed into her finger. A hand, strong and muscular, pulled at her shoulder and pushed her roughly to one side before she could object. An ax swung in a wide arc a hand's breadth from her cheek, a blue smear in the white air, its blade well oiled and finely honed. It had sliced neatly through the branch, which flew off with a crack into the trampled snow, followed almost instantly by the second one. The tree was stripped and ready to be hauled.

Anna had studied the owner of the ax. She was a tall young woman and wore the regulation rough camp dress swamped under a padded jacket with her prison number on front and back, and a wool cap with earflaps tied under her chin. Her legs were wrapped in layers of rags, and on her feet were shoes cobbled together out of birch bark and old rubber tires held together by string.

"*Spasibo,*" Anna had said gratefully.

Ax blows meant using energy, and energy was like gold dust around here, so you didn't waste it on others. Anna's rescuer possessed large blue eyes sunk deep in her head, and skin as gray as the sky. But no lesions.

"*Spasibo,*" Anna said again.

"Your chopping technique is all wrong," the other said. "Swing higher and the ax head gains momentum." She had shrugged and started to walk away.

"My name's Anna," Anna called to her retreating back.

The other prisoner turned and stared thoughtfully, eyes narrowed against the wind.

"I am Sofia," she said.

*T*HOSE were the early days in 1929, only four years ago, yet they felt like a lifetime away. Back in the time when four hundred grams a day of stinking black bread had seemed like starvation. When it lay heavy as damp clay in the stomach while she strove to work harder in the forest now that her technique with the ax had improved. The camp commandant made clear the simple rule: the more you worked, the more you ate. But only when she and her brigade reached the full norm would she receive the full *paiok* of seven hundred grams.

"For seven hundred grams of bread I would sell my soul."

She hadn't meant to say it out loud. But she'd noticed odd things happening to herself in those early days of shock at finding herself a prisoner. At night when her dreams grew too painful, she was digging her nails into her thigh so fiercely that they left scarlet welts in her flesh, and she'd started speaking aloud the thoughts that were meant to stay in her head. That worried her. She was losing control. She'd glanced around the barrack hut to see who might have heard.

Most of the women were huddled at each end, where the stoves gave out a trickle of heat, not enough to keep the ice off the inside of the grimy windowpanes but sufficient to give the illusion of warmth. Others lay silent on their beds. The hut contained ten three-story bunk beds, nudged tight against each other down both sides of the room, with every bed made of a hard board that was meant for two people but was packed with five each night, so that at times it was impossible to turn over in bed or do anything but lie rigidly on one's side. Hip bones soon developed sores, and there was a pecking order that settled the strongest and the fittest on the top boards. This evening by lamplight, some were playing cards they'd made out of scraps of paper and one group was bickering loudly on a top bunk as they bargained with each other for *makhorka* and salt.

"Your soul's not worth seven hundred grams of *chleb*."

Anna looked up, startled. It was Sofia, the girl who had helped her. Anna sat on the edge of her bedboard on the bottom bunk near the drafts of the door, attempting to mend a hole in her glove. The needle she'd created from a splinter of wood and the thread she'd unraveled from her blanket, and it was going surprisingly well despite the dismal light from the kerosene lamps.

"My soul," Anna said firmly, "is worth a good breakfast. And I don't mean the filthy *kasha* slop we're given every morning."

The blue eyes of the tall young woman scrutinized her carefully, as though she were a newly discovered specimen under a microscope lens. She was leaning against the upright of Anna's bed and looked tired, her shoulders wrapped in a dark brown blanket that made her silver-blond hair shine brighter by comparison. It was cropped short, as was all the women's hair, the authority's compulsory solution to the problem of head lice. Her skin possessed the gray ashy tinge of malnutrition, but she had no sores or lesions and her teeth were astonishingly white.

"I mean," Anna continued, "a breakfast of three fried eggs, yellow as suns on the plate, with whites as fluffy as summer clouds and a thick slice of pork, pink and succulent with a fine grain to it and a slender curve of yellow fat that melts on the tongue . . ."

"Go on, go on."

It was the Ukrainian *babushka* speaking and tapping a bony hand on Anna's back. She was lying on her tiny bed space behind Anna, who had thought her asleep because for once she wasn't coughing, but the mention of food had even penetrated her dreams.

"The bread," the old woman whispered, "tell me about the bread to go with the eggs and pork."

"The bread will be white, fresh from the oven, bread so light and moist that it soaks up the egg yolk like a sponge and tastes like heaven in the mouth."

"And the coffee? Will there be coffee as well?"

"Ah, yes." Anna closed her eyes and sighed with pleasure, unfurling it inside her like a delicate fan that she'd almost forgotten how to use. "The coffee will be so black and strong that just the aroma of it"—she and the old woman both inhaled deeply in an attempt to catch its fragrance—"will make your—"

"Stop it."

Anna opened her eyes.

"Stop it." It was Sofia. Her eyes were full of dark rage. "Why torture yourself?"

"One day I'll taste those eggs and that coffee again. I swear I will," Anna said fiercely.

"*Dura!* You're a fool," Sofia retorted, and she strode away to the far end of the hut.

Anna watched her climb up onto her top bunk and pull the brown blanket over her head, burrowing deep into it like an animal into its nest.

A bony finger dug into Anna. "And apples? Sliced up and sprinkled with cinnamon?"

"Yes," Anna answered. "And a pot of damson jam, deep purple and glistening with syrup."

"You know, *malishka*, I'd honestly sell my God-fearing soul for a breakfast like that before I die."

Anna swiveled around and smiled at the old woman, whose body was riddled with sores. She stroked the skin of the *babushka*'s hand, very gently because it was so paper-thin that the slightest touch left bruises like ink stains on it.

"So would I," she whispered.

The woman struggled to sit up, her birdlike chest straining against the first rumblings of a coughing fit, and closed her eyes.

"Hell couldn't be any worse than this place," Anna murmured. "Could it?"

THE next day one of the guards called out to her, "You. Come here."

The evening ordeal was finally over. The *poverka*, the roll call and counting of heads, was a process that dragged on and on sometimes for hours, even though the prisoners could barely stand after a hard day's labor in the forest, until the numbers that were lined up in rigid rows in the Zone tallied with the numbers on the lists in front of the commandant. The procedure was repeated rigorously every morning and every night, and every morning and every night someone died during it. The German shepherd dogs on chain leashes watched with gaping jaws for any movement in the rows.

"You. Number fourteen ninety-eight. Come here."

Anna's stomach dropped like a rock. When a guard chose to summon you out of the pack, it meant nothing but trouble. He was young. Barely shaving. She'd caught him watching her before, his gaze crawling greedily over her skin, worse than lice. He swaggered over to her across the icy ground, his rifle tucked snugly under his arm, its tip pointed straight at the spot between her legs to which his eyes kept sliding, even though it was bundled up under a skirt and a padded jacket.

"Number fourteen ninety-eight."

"Yes." She stared at the black patch of ground at his feet and linked her hands behind her back, as was required of prisoners when addressed by guards.

"I hear you are willing to sell your soul."

Her heart thudded.

"Is that so?" he asked, a sly smile tilting his mouth.

"It was a joke, nothing more. I was hungry."

Loathsome informers, the *stukachs*, like the yellow-toothed rats, they were everywhere. Swapping a scrap of information for a scrap of bread. No one could be trusted. Survival in the camp came at a high price.

He stroked the barrel of his rifle against her cheek, scraping one of the lesions and forcing her to turn her face aside while he poked the muzzle under the knot of her scarf at her throat. The metal was brutally cold on her skin. She could feel the pulse of her artery slowing at its touch.

"Are you hungry now?" he asked.

"No."

"I think you are lying, prisoner fourteen ninety-eight."

He smiled at her and licked his chapped lips. His back was to the nearest floodlight as it cut a yellow swathe through the darkness of the Zone, so that his eyes appeared as deep black holes in his head. Anna wanted to stick her fingers in them.

"No," she said.

"I don't want your soul."

"I didn't think you did."

"So will you sell your body instead in exchange for a good breakfast?"

From the depths of his greatcoat pocket he drew a package wrapped in brown greaseproof paper. Slinging his rifle over his shoulder, he unwrapped the packet and held it out to her. The wind tried to snatch it away, making the paper's folds crackle and snap. It contained two speckled eggs and a thin sliver of pork. Anna's eyes feasted lovingly on the sight of the eggs, on their plump brownness, on the delicacy of the speckles in grays and whites and liver browns, on the perfection of the curve of the shells. She didn't even dare look at the meat.

"So will you?"

He had moved. He was standing beside her now, his breath coming fast and forming small dense clouds of eagerness in the moonlight. Saliva rushed into Anna's mouth. There were women in the camp, she knew, who took favors from a guard, who sought one out for *protection*. Such women did not have lesions on their faces or death in their eyes, and they worked in the camp kitchen or in the camp laundry instead of in the killing fields of the forest. Was it so bad? To want to live.

Reluctantly she dragged her eyes from the beauty of the eggs and stared at the guard's expression. Now she could see clearly the look of loneliness in his young face, the need for something that felt like love even if it wasn't. He was trapped here the same as she was, about the same age as herself, cut off from all he knew and cared for. Russia had robbed them both, and he was desperate for something more. A little human contact. A stamping of self on a blank faceless world. It could help them both survive. Her famished body swayed imperceptibly toward his strong young frame.

"A good breakfast?" he whispered temptingly.

"Go fuck yourself," she said and swept away into the darkness.

NINETEEN

THAT night Tivil was stripped naked and raw. That was how it seemed to Pyotr.

"Stay indoors, Pyotr. And keep the house locked."

Those were Papa's words. With a frown he lit himself a cigarette, ruffled Pyotr's hair, and was about to disappear back out into the chaotic night when he stopped abruptly. He looked across at Sofia Morozova, assessing her. Mikhail Pashin had kept a firm grip on her arm, as well as on Pyotr's, when they left the church and he'd marched them both straight to the safety of his own home. Now he was leaving them.

"Will you do something for me?" he asked her. "Take care of my son tonight?"

"Of course. I'll guard him well."

Pyotr wanted to die of shame, but his father nodded, satisfied, and stepped out into the road. A cold drizzle was falling as he pulled the door closed behind him, and Pyotr could see the raindrops like diamonds in his father's dark hair. He tried not to be frightened for him. They were left standing in the tiny porch where boots were kept, the fugitive and himself, just the two of them alone in the house, eyeing each other warily. Pyotr picked up the oil lamp that Papa had lit on the shelf by the door and walked into the living room with it, hoping she wouldn't follow, but she did. Right on his heels.

Neither spoke. He placed the lamp on the table and headed straight for the kitchen. There he poured himself a cup of water, drank it down slowly, counted to fifty in his head, and went back into the living room. She was still there. She was leaning over the half-constructed model of a bridge on the table, one of the tiny slivers of wood between her fingers. Dozens of them were scattered over the surface, little lightweight girders.

"Don't touch," he said quickly.

"It must take a lot of patience to make."

"Papa is building it." He shuffled nearer. "I help."

She gazed at it, very serious. "It's beautiful."

He stared at one of the elegant wooden towers. Said nothing.

"What bridge is it?"

"The Forth Bridge in Scotland," he lied.

"I see," she nodded.

"Don't touch," he repeated.

She put down the piece of wood and looked around the room.

"You have a nice house," she said at last.

He wouldn't look at her. Of course it was a nice house, the nicest in the village. A huge *pechka* stove provided the heart of the *izba*, which had good-sized rooms, a large kitchen, and a handsome samovar decorated in Hochloma style. The house was light and airy, and the furniture was smart and factory bought, not hand hewn. He glanced around proudly. It was a house fit for a director of a factory, with the best wool runners on the brown-painted floor and curtains from the Levitsky factory's own machines. Only now did it occur to Pyotr that it might seem rather untidy to an outside eye.

"May I have a drink?" she asked.

He looked at her. Her cheeks were pink. Maybe she was hot. He didn't want to give her a drink, he wanted her to go, to leave him alone, but . . .

"A drink?" she repeated.

He scuttled back into the kitchen just as the cuckoo clock struck ten o'clock, and quickly he poured her a few drops of water in the bottom of the same cup he'd used. He didn't bother washing it. But when he hurried back into the living room she was crouched down in front of the three-cornered cupboard where Papa kept his private things. In one hand was an unopened bottle of vodka, a shot glass in the other.

"That's Papa's."

"I didn't think it was yours."

"Put it back."

She smiled at him, a very small movement of her lips. Pyotr watched her unscrew the cap and pour into the glass some of the liquid that looked like water but wasn't. He didn't know what to say. She carried the bottle and the untouched vodka over to the armchair and sat down in it. She raised her glass to him.

"*Za zdorovie!*" she said solemnly.

"That's Papa's chair."

"I know."

"How can you know?"

"There are lots of things I know about your father."

She tipped her head back and threw the shot of vodka down her throat. Her blue eyes widened and she murmured something.

"I'm going to tell," he said quickly.

"Tell what?"

"Tell Chairman Fomenko that you're a fugitive."

"I see."

She poured herself another shot of vodka and drank it straight off. She closed her eyes and licked her lips, breathing lightly. Her eyelashes lay like threads of moonlight on her cheeks.

"What makes you think I'm a fugitive?" she asked without opening her eyes. "I was just taking a break on my journey south, resting up in the forest." Quietly she added, "You have no proof."

He said nothing.

"I don't want trouble," she said.

"If you don't want trouble, why did you go to the meeting tonight?"

"To find you."

His stomach lurched.

"I had no idea when I met you in the forest that you are Mikhail Pashin's son."

Pyotr just stared at his shoes. He'd forgotten to clean them.

"Where is your mother?"

He shrugged. "She left. And never came back."

"I'm sorry, Pyotr. How long ago?"

"Six years."

"Six years is a long time."

He looked up at her. Her eyes were wide open now and filled with an emotion he couldn't make out. There was a sudden shout in the street and running footsteps. Pyotr felt a desire to be out there.

"Are you really a tractor driver?" he asked.

"Yes."

"Honestly?"

"Yes." She smiled at him, and he felt the sweet honey once again slide down his throat. She leaned forward, chin propped delicately on her hand. "Pyotr, please. We can be friends, you and I."

He could sense the strands of her web twisting through the air toward him, so fine he couldn't see them but he knew they were there. In her drab clothes she looked so harmless, but he recognized the determination in her, the same way he recognized the coming of thunder behind the gray skirts of a storm cloud. He turned and ran out of the house.

*E*LIZAVETA Lishnikova stood in the doorway of the schoolhouse and saw the boy race up the street as if his shirttails were on fire and disappear into the night. A light drizzle was falling but still she stood there, tense as she listened to the shouts and cries of panic that tore through the village. Black shapes moved stealthily through the darkness, and she caught sight of a fragile stick of a child creeping along the side of the fence that bordered the school. Her heart sank for the little one.

"Anastasia," she called out. "Come here."

The girl hesitated, eyes wide with fear. Under her arm she clutched a bundle of material.

"Come here, child." Elizaveta inserted a touch of her headmistress tone into the command.

The girl sidled through the front gate and scurried up the front path, her hurried footsteps like the pitter-patter of a mouse. She hunched in front of Elizaveta, her head hanging down, an expression of dismay on her narrow little face. The bundle in her arms was wrapped inside a piece of striped pillow ticking covered in damp patches from the rain.

Dear God, are we reduced to using our children to do our dirty work?

"What are you doing wandering around loose tonight, Anastasia?"

"The soldiers came to our house," the child whispered. Her nose was running and she wiped it on her sleeve.

"All the more reason to stay at home with your parents, I'd have thought."

"My father told me to . . . take something," she sniffed, ". . . and run."

She clutched the something closer to her bony chest, and the material moved in protest. The unmistakable squawk of an angry chicken issued from it.

"Why bring it here to the school, Anastasia?"

The top of the girl's mousy head nodded vigorously. "Pyotr told me to. He said . . ." Her small voice trailed away.

"What did Pyotr say?"

"He said the soldiers won't search the schoolhouse for food."

"Did he indeed?"

"He said it's the safest place to be tonight."

"I see."

The hopeful eyes looked up at her, straggly wet rat's-tails of hair stuck to her cheeks.

"Very well, Anastasia. This once you may go into the classroom. Sit there in the dark and make no sound. Keep your bundle quiet too. Wring its damn neck if you have to."

The pale face looked up at her with a gaze of adoration that Elizaveta knew she didn't want or deserve. All she could think of was that a chicken was not worth the risk she was taking. A man, yes. A chicken, no. For one brief second, her mind flitted back to a time thirty years ago when her father's glittering dining table would have boasted six roast chickens on it for one family supper alone, with the scraps thrown to the dogs at the end. Now she was risking her life for just one of the stupid creatures. The world had turned upside down.

In the street a pair of OGPU troops were forcing their way into the house opposite. Elizaveta stepped quickly back into the hallway, and Anastasia popped through the door and ducked into the schoolroom. Once inside, her small body became suddenly livelier and she held her head at a more confident angle on the stalk of her neck as she grinned up at Elizaveta.

"Pyotr was right," Anastasia chirruped. "He's always right."

Elizaveta sighed and turned her attention back to the street. Chairman Fomenko was just striding into the house opposite with a sharp word on his tongue, and Elizaveta felt an urge to go out there and rap her cane across his hands. What did the man think he was doing? You can't bleed a village dry and still expect its denizens to work for you. Yet sometimes the blasted man astonished her with his unexpected gestures of generosity, like when he personally drove one of the *kolkhoz* carts to take all the schoolchildren to the May Day celebrations in the next valley or when he dug up his own vegetable plot to provide a party for the whole village on Stalin's birthday, with soup and black bread and boiled chicken.

Off to one side she caught sight of a flash of blond hair in the torchlight. It was the stranger, the gypsy's so-called niece. Now why was she running about in the dark? And right near the church too. Elizaveta's heart thumped in her chest. Was the girl leading the troops to the church? Would they discover the chamber?

Pokrovsky, where are you?

Dear God, that was one of the reasons she'd not married. It was always the same. When you need a man, he's never there.

*R*AFIK fought them with his mind, one by one. He drew no blood, except in his own brain, but he raged.

The uniforms came. In ones and twos and threes. Their heads full of dry lifeless straw that he could ignite with a touch of his finger and a look from his eyes. He manipulated their feeble thoughts. House by house he turned them back, bought time for goods to vanish from larders into the forest's sanctuary. Sacks of grain, haunches of pork, slabs of cheese, they slipped away into the darkness. But the uniforms crawled everywhere, too many for him. The pain started when six faced him at once. Six was too many; they drained his strength, and when he saw the woman in the house weeping, entreating the stone faces to leave her family something to eat, he knew the cost he would pay if he didn't stop.

But he didn't stop and now he was paying it. A red hot pain erupted inside his brain. He staggered in the street, tasted blood.

"Zenia," he breathed.

Before the sound was out of his mouth, his daughter was there at his side in the shattered darkness, a tiny vessel of green fluid in her hand. Her gaze sought his and he saw the fear for him trapped in her eyes, but not once did she tell him to cease what he was doing.

"The potion won't stop the damage." She soothed his temples with a cloth that smelled of herbs. "But it will mask the pain, so you'll be able to continue. If you choose to."

Her black eyes begged him not to.

He touched his daughter's cheek and tipped the dark green liquid down his throat.

TWENTY

SOFIA was desperate. She couldn't find the boy. She slipped between the *izbas*, hugging the darkness, avoiding the torches and the swaying lamps and the voices giving orders. She searched everywhere, but he was gone.

In the chaos around her she seized the shoulder of a woman who was hurrying from her house, a scarf hiding her face from the troops that had fanned out through the village.

"Have you seen Pyotr Pashin?"

But the woman scuttled past her, bent double over a sack clutched in her arms, and melted away into the forest. In the center of the single street, blocking any movement, was a hefty truck, growling noisily and edging its way from house to house. At the back it was an uncovered flatbed already piled with more than a dozen sacks of various shapes and sizes, men in uniform hurling them up to a pair of young soldiers who were stacking them efficiently. Sofia tried to edge past it.

"*Dokumenti?* Identity papers?"

Sofia swung around. Behind her a man was holding

out his hand expectantly. He wore a long coat that flapped around his ankles and a rimless pair of spectacles that were spattered with rain.

"*Dokumenti?*" he said again.

"They're in my house, just over there." *Calm, keep calm.*

"Fetch them."

"Of course, comrade."

Walk. Don't run. Past the truck and down behind one of the houses. Everywhere voices were raised in anger and in entreaty. She reached the gypsy's house, breathless, but it was empty, though voices at the rear caught her attention and she crept over to find Zenia talking quietly with one of the procurement officers. He was pointing at the rows of vegetables. Silently Sofia slipped away and doubled back into the street. Where now? Where was the boy? Where?

She dodged down an alleyway between *izbas* and immediately spotted the tall figure of Mikhail Pashin. She opened her mouth to call out but swallowed the words just in time. He was carrying a torch in one hand and had the other arm around the shoulders of a young woman, so that their heads were close. Sofia recognized her at once. The mother of the blond child, Misha, the one to whom she told the story.

It was like drowning. She felt her lungs fill with something that wasn't air.

He was walking Lilya Dimentieva into her house as if he owned it, Mikhail Pashin slinking to his lover's bed. Sofia leaned against the wall behind her. A harsh moan escaped her. He had one son. Perhaps two. What chance did she and Anna have? She crouched down on the damp ground as the rain ceased and hid her face.

*S*OFIA."

It was Rafik.

"What are you doing out here?" His voice was faint.

"Searching for Pyotr Pashin. Have you seen the boy?"

He shook his head. It was that movement, slow and heavy, that made Sofia peer through the night's drizzle more closely, and what she saw shocked her. His black eyes were dull, the color of old coal dust. Sweat, not rain, glimmered on his forehead.

"Rafik, are you wounded?"

"No."

"Are you sick?"

"No." It was little more than a breath.

"Let me take you home." She lifted his hand in hers. It was ice cold. "You need—"

The crash of a rifle butt came from within the house beside them. He withdrew his hand.

"Thank you, Sofia, but I have work to do."

He headed off with an uneven gait toward a group of approaching uniforms, and her confidence in him was shaken. He was going to get himself killed if he interfered.

$\mathscr{P}$YOTR was running up to the stables when Sofia stepped out of the darkness and caught him. Her fingers fastened around his wrist, and he was astonished at the strength in them. One look at her face and it was clear she wasn't going to let him go this time.

"*Privet*," she said with no hint of annoyance that he'd run off before. "Hello again."

"I was just going to check on Zvezda," he said quickly. "Papa's horse. To make sure he wasn't taken by the troops."

She paused, considered the idea, and then nodded as if satisfied and led him up the rest of the narrow track to where the stable spread out around a courtyard. Once inside the stables she released his wrist and lit a kerosene lamp on the wall in a leisurely way, as if they'd just come up for a cozy chat instead of to escape from the soldiers. Pyotr wouldn't admit it, but he had been frightened by the savagery of what was tearing his village apart tonight. Her blue eyes followed his every move as he refilled Zvezda's water bucket, the horse's warm oaty breath on his neck, and for some reason her gaze made him feel clumsy.

"Zvezda is growing restless," she said, and she lifted a hand to scratch the animal's nose.

Pyotr wrapped an arm around the muscular neck and embedded his fingers in its thick black mane. The other horses were whinnying uneasily from their stalls, and it dawned on Pyotr that something wasn't right, but he couldn't work out what. It must be because of Sofia, he told himself. But when he slid his eyes toward her, she didn't look threatening at all, just soft and golden in the yellow lamplight. He was just beginning to wonder whether he'd gotten her all wrong when she put a finger to her lips, the way she did in the forest that time.

"Listen," she whispered.

Pyotr listened. At first he heard nothing but the restless noises of the horses and the wind chasing over the corrugated-iron roof. He listened harder, and underneath he caught another sound, a dull roar that set his teeth on edge.

"What's that?" he demanded.

"What do you think it is?"

"It sounds like . . ."

"Pyotr!" The tall priest burst into the stables and instantly checked the dozen stalls to ensure the horses were not panicked. "Pyotr," he groaned, "it's the barn, the one where the wagons are kept. It's on fire."

His windblown hair leaped and darted around him as if the fire were on his shoulders. His angular frame shuddered disjointedly while he moved from one horse to the other, patting their necks and soothing their twitching hides. He was wrapped in a horse blanket that was more holes than blanket.

"*I am a vengeful God, saith the Lord.*" His wild green eyes swung around to face Pyotr. "I tell you, this is the hand of God at work. His punishment for the evil here tonight."

His long finger started to uncurl in Pyotr's direction, and for one horrible moment Pyotr thought it was going to skewer right into the bones of his chest, but the slight figure of Sofia brushed it aside and hurried to the door of the stable. She looked out into the night and called, "Come here, Pyotr."

Pyotr rushed to her side and gasped. The whole of the night sky was on fire. Flames scorching the stars. It sent Pyotr's mind spinning. Once before, he'd seen an inferno like this and it had changed his life. He made a move to dash toward it, but Sofia's hand descended on his shoulder.

"You're needed here, Pyotr," she said in a steady voice. "To help calm the horses."

Pyotr saw the priest and the fugitive exchange a look.

"She's right," Priest Logvinov said. He flung out both arms in appeal. "I'll need as much help as I can get with the horses tonight. Right now they have the stink of smoke in their nostrils."

"But I want to find Papa."

"No, Pyotr, stay here," she ordered, but her eyes were on the flames and a worry crease was deepening on her forehead. "I'll make sure your papa is safe." Without another word she hurried away into the night.

TWENTY-ONE

GIGANTIC flames were ripping great holes in the belly of the night sky. Spitting and writhing, they leaped twenty meters into the air, so that even down at the river's edge Mikhail Pashin could feel the sting of sparks in his eyes, the smoke in his lungs. He was on his knees, his trousers wet and his knuckles skinned, crouched over the water pump on the riverbank, struggling in the darkness to bring it to life, but so far it had resisted all his coaxing and cursing. In frustration he clouted his heftiest wrench against the pump's metal casing, and instantly the engine spluttered, coughed, then racketed into action, sending gallons of river water racing up the rubber hose.

"The scientific approach, I see," a voice said out of the darkness.

In the gloom he made out nothing at first, just the slithering shadows etched against the red glow of the sky, but then he saw a pale oval. A face close by.

"It's Sofia," she said.

"I thought you were at my house, you and Pyotr."

"Don't worry. Your son is safe in the stables with Zvezda and the priest."

"Good. They'll be out of harm's way up there."

She moved closer, and as she did so one side of her face was painted golden by the flames, highlighting the fine bones of her cheek, the other side an impenetrable mask in the blackness. Mikhail liked the way she walked, silent as a cat. She stood over him, looking down, and for a brief second he was startled because he thought she was going to touch his hair, but instead she crouched down on her haunches on the opposite side of the pump. Their faces were on a level and he could see the firelight reflected off the glassy surface of the river and into her eyes. He was surprised by the humor in them on a night like this. She looked as if the fire were burning inside her.

"The whole village is helping," she said. Her words merged with the clanking of the engine.

"Yes, in an emergency the *kolkhoz* knows how to work together." He glanced over his shoulder to the spot where a long line of men and women, clutching buckets, snaked up from the river all the way to the burning barn. Each face was grim and determined.

"A human pipeline," Sofia muttered.

"Who the hell did this?" Mikhail felt a dull rage tighten his stomach. "Who would wish to burn down our barn?"

"Mikhail, look who's in the line."

"In the line? The villagers, you mean?"

"And?"

"The troops helping them."

"Exactly."

"What about them?"

He ran a hand over the engine to steady it, enjoying its heartbeat. The feel of machinery under his fingers always strengthened him in some strange indefinable way that he didn't understand. Sofia's hand reached out and lightly brushed his own.

"Look at them," she said urgently.

He frowned. What did she mean? He studied the troops striving hard in the line to prevent the fire from spreading to a second barn. Their caps were smut-stained, their skin streaked with sweat; some wore kerchiefs tied over the lower half of their faces to protect their lungs, some cursing and shouting for more speed, uniformed men all fighting side by side with the villagers.

"Look hard," she whispered.

He looked.

Nothing. He could see nothing. What on earth was she talking about? Just the blackness and the clawing flames. The effort of all those workers. Then suddenly it dawned. Damn it, she was right. His pulse raced as he realized that this was the moment when the troops' attention was totally diverted from the grain. Why the hell hadn't he seen it himself? He leaped to his feet, abandoning the water pump to its own steady rhythm, and raced up through the drooping willows toward the center of the village. Sofia matched him stride for stride.

*W*AIT here," Mikhail ordered. "And make no sound."

The small group of villagers nodded and huddled silent and invisible at the side of the blacksmith's forge, where the night wrapped them in heavy shadows. Four women, one of them sick, and two old men. Their backs didn't look strong enough to hoist the sacks, but they were all he could find inside the houses. Everyone else was up at the fire, so they'd have to do. Plus Sofia, of course. Just as he was about to edge away, she leaned close to him, her breath warm on his ear as she whispered, "Take care. I promised Pyotr I'd make sure you stayed safe."

He couldn't see her eyes, so he touched her hand in reassurance. It felt strong and swept away his doubts about the handling of the sacks.

"I'll be back," he promised and walked out into the main street.

It was dark and deserted now, except for the truck. Beside the truck stood a man with a long coat flapping at his ankles and a Mauser pistol in his fist. Mikhail glanced around but there were no other troops in sight. This one was leaning against the tailgate, cigarette in hand, waiting casually for his comrades to return and guarding the sacks on the flatbed, but there was nothing relaxed or casual about his face. His head turned constantly, eyes behind the thick spectacles scanning every point of access. He was no fool. He recognized the danger.

"*Oy moroz, moroz, nye moroz menya, Nye moroz menya, moevo kon,*" Mikhail began singing, loud and boisterous.

The words slipped and slid over each other in his mouth. He aimed himself in the general direction of the truck, but his feet wove from one side of the road to the other, stumbling and tripping, only just correcting themselves in time. He threw back his head and laughed.

"Hey, comrade, my friend, how about a drink?" His words came out slurred, and he brandished a bottle of vodka ahead of him while he looked around the dark street in a bewildered manner. "Where'sh everyone?"

The man pushed himself off the truck, threw the cigarette in the dirt, and ground his heel on it. He regarded Mikhail with caution.

"Who are you?"

"I'm your friend, your good friend." Mikhail grinned lopsidedly and thrust out the bottle. "Here, have a drink."

"No."

"Why not?" Mikhail upended the bottle and took a slug of the vodka himself. He felt it burn the knots in his stomach. "Is good stuff," he mumbled.

"You're drunk, you stupid oaf."

"Drunk but happy. You don't look happy, *tovarishch*."

"Neither would you if you had to deal with such—"

"Here." Mikhail thrust the bottle at the man again. "Some left for you. You could be out here all night."

The fire reflected in the man's spectacles. His hesitation betrayed him, so Mikhail seized the hand that had discarded the cigarette and wrapped it around the bottle. "Put fire in your belly." He rocked on his heels with laughter. "Fire in your belly instead of in our barn."

The man's mouth slackened. He almost smiled.

"Let's have it." He took a mouthful. Smacked his lips.

"Good?"

"It's cat's piss. It's no wonder you peasants are mindless. This homemade brew rots your brains."

"Come with me, Comrade Officer, and I will show you"— Mikhail lowered his voice in conspiratorial style—"the real stuff. The good stuff."

"Where?" Another swig.

"In my house. It's just over—"

"No. Piss off. I'm guarding this truck."

Mikhail yawned, stretched, scratched himself, and stumbled on his feet.

"Come, Comrade Officer, there's no one here. Your sacks are safe." He draped an arm across the man's shoulders, could smell cheap tobacco on his breath. "Come, friend, come and taste the good stuff."

*T*HE man was drunker than a mule. His eyes turned pink and his tongue seemed too large for his mouth, so that the words slid off it into his glass. But when Mikhail yanked him to his feet after an hour of pouring his best vodka down the bastard's throat, it came as a surprise at the door to find he still had a few wits clinging to him.

"You come too," the man said, his head lolling on his thick neck.

"No, my friend, I'm off to bed," Mikhail grinned.

He started to close the door but the man put his shoulder to it. "You come, my Tivil comrade. To the truck." With astonishing speed of hand for someone swilling with vodka, he produced the Mauser and pointed it at Mikhail. "You come. *Bistro.* Quickly."

So they stumbled up the road together, their path lit by the flames in the night sky. The truck loomed ahead. Even in the darkness it was obvious that the flatbed now held no more than a handful of sacks. The man stared at them and swallowed hard.

"Where's the grain?"

Shock was sobering him fast, and with a grunt of effort he swung the pistol at Mikhail's jaw, but Mikhail sidestepped it with ease. He was tempted to seize the gun and break the bastard's skull with it, but he knew any act of violence would lead to retribution for the whole village. Party officials were like cockroaches. You stamp on one, and ten more come out of the woodwork. He tried walking away, but the muzzle jammed against the back of his skull.

"Tell me where the fucking grain is, you thieving village bastard. Right now."

Mikhail didn't move. "Comrade," he said with a slur, "you've got me all wrong. I am just—"

"I'll count to three."

"No, comrade . . ."

"*Odeen.*" One.

"I know nothing about the grain."

"*Dva.*" Two.

Mikhail's body tensed, ready to lash out, but a quiet voice from the side of the truck distracted them both.

"Comrade Officer, I think you have made a mistake." It was Sofia. She and the gypsy approached out of the darkness together as if it were a cloak over their shoulders.

"Who are you?"

"I am Sofia Morozova. And this is my uncle, Rafik Ilyan, a member of the Red Arrow *kolkhoz.*"

"You know where my grain is?"

"Of course. It's here."

The gun released its pressure and Mikhail breathed. He swung around and saw Sofia waving what looked like a shawl in the officer's face, her lips bone white in the torchlight. Then suddenly Rafik was so close to the man that their shapes seemed to merge into one. The gypsy's black eyes were sunk like boreholes in his head and he was holding fiercely on to the man's arm, pressing his fingers into the flesh beneath the sleeve, and staring fixedly up into the narrow bloodshot eyes. The odd thing was that the comrade made no word of complaint. What the hell was going on? The officer was gazing back at the gypsy with a slightly baffled expression, as though he'd forgotten where he'd left his cigarettes rather than more than a dozen sacks of grain.

"You made a mistake," Rafik stated clearly, and as he said it his other hand whipped out and fixed on Mikhail's arm. The gypsy's voice was soft, but somehow it squirmed into Mikhail's head and crawled through the coils of his brain until he heard nothing else. "There were only ever four sacks in the truck, and you have them all there," Rafik said. "No grain is missing."

Mikhail and the officer stared at the sacks. Away in the forest an owl screeched, or was it a fox barking? The sounds were tumbling around indistinctly in Mikhail's head with the gypsy's words, and behind them was a dull roaring noise. He couldn't quite recall what that was.

Of course there had only ever been four sacks. What was he thinking of?

★ ★ ★

SOFIA watched in disbelief.

From nowhere the gypsy had appeared at her elbow when she was shifting another sack off the back of the truck, and he had helped her carry it to a small handcart. It was pushed away by an old woman with a crooked back and a mischievous grin that had more gaps than teeth to it. Hot cinders were floating down from the bloodred sky like fireflies that nipped at your skin, and Rafik draped a soft shawl over Sofia's bare arms.

"Come," he said and led her around to the front of the truck where they were hidden by the black shadow of the church. "You want to help Mikhail Pashin?"

"Yes."

"He has done well, but now the danger will be great for him when the officer returns."

Sofia could feel the skin of her face tighten and prickle. Like ants' feet walking over it. "What can I do?"

"I will deal with the man in my own way. But I need you to distract his attention so that I can get close to him."

It occurred to Sofia that the gypsy appeared so frail he didn't look as if he could deal with a pack of cards right now, never mind an armed OGPU officer.

"Rafik," she said with concern, "you're not well."

The sound of footsteps echoed up the shadowy street. Men's voices were coming closer and one was Mikhail's. She had no choice; she had to trust Rafik.

"Distract him, Sofia."

The sight of the gun jammed against Mikhail's skull nearly robbed her of control. But instead of hurling herself like a spitting wildcat onto the officer and probably triggering a shot from the gun, she managed to say calmly, "Comrade Officer, I think you have made a mistake." And a moment later she was flapping her shawl at him, the edge of it just clipping his jaw and making his eyes flare with annoyance. But what Rafik did then was beyond anything she'd ever seen. It left her speechless. In some strange and impossible way he seemed to take hold of the men's minds, first the OGPU officer's and then

Mikhail's, and manipulate their thoughts the way a child shifts and shuffles a set of toy bricks. She stared in disbelief at Mikhail, at the boneless way his arms hung at his side and the confused expression in his eyes, as the glare from the blaze turned them red.

"Sofia!" Rafik had to repeat it. "Sofia!"

She blinked and saw the gypsy stumble in the darkness. Her hand shot out to steady him, and she could feel the tremors shaking his body under the light cotton of his shirt.

"Go," he said and his voice was weak. "Run to the schoolhouse. Tell Elizaveta to bring the key to the chamber. Now. Run!"

*T*HE schoolhouse stood at the start of the village street, a modern box of a building with a neat low fence around it and a central doorway that threw out a yellow stain of light on the shadows of the path. A red glaze shimmered like oil across the windows as the billows of smoke and sparks in the night sky were reflected in the glass.

Sofia banged on the door.

It flew open immediately, and Sofia was convinced the teacher had been standing on the other side of it, listening for footsteps. Something about the tall gray-haired woman with the bright hawkish eyes steadied Sofia's racing heart.

She spoke quickly. "Rafik sent me."

"What does he want?"

"The key."

The teacher's mouth opened, then shut abruptly. "He told *you* about the key?"

"Yes, the key to the chamber, he said. He needs you to bring it to him."

There was a pause. Even in the darkness Sofia could feel the spikes of the woman's suspicion.

"Wait here."

But the moment Elizaveta Lishnikova disappeared back into the hallway of her schoolhouse, Sofia followed her and shut the door. Standing outside on the path, spotlit by the lamp in the hall, was an open invitation to any troops that might decide they'd had enough of firefighting, but the door on her right was ajar and the temptation to look too great.

What she saw astonished her. The room was like something out of a St. Petersburg salon. The deep maroon carpet covering the floor was of intricate Indian design, while the table and cabinets were clearly French from the last century, with ornate curlicues, gilt handles, and exquisite inlay of ivory, burrwood, and a vivid green malachite that brought the room to life. The curtains were wine-red swathes of heavy silk, and a magnificent ormolu clock ticked loudly in pride of place.

Sofia caught her breath, and Elizaveta raised her head from what was obviously a secret drawer in the side of a fine satinwood desk. Her long back straightened and she faced Sofia with a sudden pulse of color high on her cheeks.

"So I was right," Elizaveta said quietly. "You are a spy for Deputy Stirkhov, aren't you?"

"No."

The two women locked eyes, the older woman's face growing ever more angular, but Sofia said nothing more. If she did, she might say too much and not know when to stop. That frightened her more than saying too little.

"No," she repeated firmly.

The schoolteacher didn't dispute it further. Instead she said in an imperious tone, "I did not invite you inside this room. Please leave."

"I'll wait in the hallway. Be quick."

She left the beautiful room, and a moment later Elizaveta Lish-nikova joined her in the hallway with two keys in her hand. One she used to lock her private room, and then she slid it inside the thick coil of gray hair at the back of her head. Sofia was impressed. No one would search there.

"You have the key to the chamber—whatever that is?"

"Of course."

"Then let's take it to Rafik."

"Not you."

"What?"

"I want you to stay here. In the hallway. Don't leave it."

"Why?" Sofia was impatient to return to Mikhail.

"In case the troops come searching. They most likely won't but . . . they might." The older woman's careful brown eyes scanned

Sofia appraisingly. "You look the kind of person who could keep them out of my school. Guard it well. I'm trusting you."

With a whisk of her gray shawl over her head, the teacher was gone, the door slamming shut behind her. Sofia paced the scuffed boards in frustration. She wanted to be out there, ensuring that Mikhail and Rafik were not tossed into the truck in place of the sacks. She hated being left behind to watch over some irrelevant little schoolhouse.

What was there to guard anyway, other than some pieces of fine furniture? And what did Elizaveta Lishnikova mean when she said Sofia was the kind of person who could keep the troops out of the school? That she was in league with the OGPU forces? That she would argue well against them? Or that she had the youth and the feminine wiles to turn troops from their course?

Oh, to hell with the woman! Sofia banged her fist against the wall in frustration.

That was when she heard the noise. A tiny whimpery sound, like a mouse in pain. She wondered if it could be a creature that had fled from the barn fire. It stopped as suddenly as it started. Sofia resumed her pacing of the narrow hallway, her mind struggling to make sense of what she'd seen Rafik do to the officer and to Mikhail with what looked like no more than a touch of his hand. But before she'd conjured up the intense gaze that had burned in the gypsy's eyes, the noise started up again. Louder now. A recognizable wail this time.

It seemed to be coming from behind the other door in the hall, the one she assumed led into the schoolroom. Her breath grew shallow and she could feel the hairs rise on the back of her neck, but she wasn't going to stand here doing nothing. She lifted the oil lamp from its bracket and pushed open the door. The lamplight leaped in ahead of her, looping in great swaying arcs through the pitch darkness, jumping off the windows and lighting up a clutch of small pale circles. It took her a second to recognize them as faces. Children's faces, pale and wide-eyed with fear.

Children from less than five years old up to ten or eleven, each one silent at a desk. Eleven pale moons in the darkness and in front of each one on the desktop lay a bundle of some sort, some large and lumpy, others small and smelly. Nearly all the children had their thin arms wrapped protectively around the bundle of food they had saved from their homes, and one older boy had a zinc bucket at his feet piled high with what looked like grain of some sort.

The noise was coming from a tiny girl. She was sobbing, and an older girl had her hand clamped across the little one's mouth, but still the mouse-pain sound squeezed its way out. Quickly Sofia took the lamp back into the hall and replaced it in its bracket, so that no light showed in the schoolroom. She returned to the children and as she shut the door behind her, she heard their collective sigh. She groped her way to the teacher's chair at the front and sat down.

"Now," she whispered softly, "I'll tell you a story. But you must stay quiet as little mice."

TWENTY-TWO

*P*APA, wake up. Please, wake up. You're late."

Mikhail opened his eyes and a spike of morning sunlight lanced into them. He winced. He was on the floor of his own living room, curled up in his coat, a bottle nestled to his chest. An empty bottle. He swore softly under his breath, only to discover that his mouth tasted like cow dung.

"Papa, you got drunk!"

Mikhail sat up and scrubbed a hand through his hair. The ceiling swooped, then settled, and a heavy pulse started up behind his eyes and echoed dully in his ears. His mind struggled. It felt oddly empty, like the inside of a drum, just full of vibrating air. And a soft female voice whispering words he couldn't quite catch in his ear.

"I wasn't drunk, Pyotr."

"You were, you know you were." The boy's toffee-toned eyes glared, a long sulky beat. "And now you're late for work."

"What time is it?"

"Eight-thirty."

"Chyort!"

Mikhail felt an unfocused anger rise inside him, he wasn't sure at what or at whom, but he knew that somehow he had lost control and he hated his son seeing him like this. "Pyotr," he said sharply, "I'll drink if and when I have a mind to. I don't need your permission, boy."

"No, Papa."

Mikhail rose to his feet and groaned. Fuck it, this was a hangover like none he'd experienced before. His whole brain felt dislocated. He made his way out to the tub of water in the backyard, stuck his head in it, and kept it there until blood reached his brain. Today he'd have to ride Zvezda hard if he was to be at his desk before the blasted factory foreman started getting ideas above his station.

His shirt was wet around the collar and stank of alcohol, and of something else. He sniffed the sleeve cautiously. Was it her? The scent of her skin on his arm. The sudden memory of Sofia's face in the darkness, her mouth soft and full as she whispered words to him. What words? Damn it, what words? He couldn't remember. He shook his head viciously, and it splintered into jagged pieces but nothing became clearer. Had the vodka done this or . . . Dimly he recalled Rafik being there last night. What had the gypsy to do with it? Still feeling uncomfortable, he headed back into the house, where the boy was staring out of the window.

"Pyotr," he said gruffly, "you know I'm like a bear with a sore head if I sleep too long. You were right to wake me. *Spasibo.*"

His son continued to look out at the street, his back rigid, elbows stiff at his sides. Mikhail felt an urge to wrap his arms around his stubborn son's young frame, to hold on to it, to keep it safe and guard it from grain hunters and fire starters and slogan sellers. Instead he went into his own room, shaved, and changed his shirt, and when he came out again Pyotr was waiting for him.

"Papa, what happened last night?"

Last night. Mikhail shook his head again to try to clear the blurring that smudged his thoughts at the very mention of last night. What did happen? And why did he feel Sofia so close?

"What happened to the grain and the sacks, Papa? All the piles of them that the procurement officers stacked in the truck. People are saying it was stolen. That you were . . . involved."

The boy's face was tense, as if frightened to hear the answer. They both knew of the infamous case of the boy Pavlik, who only last spring had reported his own father to the authorities for anti-Soviet activities; the Politburo had used it as a major propaganda tool. One of Pyotr's feet kicked again and again at the floorboards.

"No grain was taken," Mikhail said firmly. "There were only four sacks."

"They say that's not true."

"Then they're lying."

Their gaze locked on each other.

"Pyotr."

The boy shuffled his feet.

"Pyotr, stay away from the barns today. That fire didn't light itself, and Fomenko will be looking for a culprit."

THE fresh air cleared Mikhail's head. Dusty white clouds trailed along the top of the ridge on each side of him as he cantered down the dirt road past the cedar tree that marked the village boundary and out into the valley, which lay before him sun-baked and vibrant with movement. The bushy green foliage of the potato crop rustled in the fields, and stooped figures wielded hoes and rakes along the long mounds of them. The whole *kolkhoz* workforce was already hard at it, striving to fulfill Aleksei Fomenko's labor quotas. One thing Mikhail couldn't deny was that Fomenko had pulled and prodded and bullied the Tivil collective farm into some semblance of productivity. He might be a bastard, but he was an efficient bastard.

Above, a solitary skylark soared up into the blinding blue sky, its wings fluttering like heartbeats, and Mikhail envied it its effortless flight. He used to work at the N22 aircraft factory in Moscow and he missed that wonderful sense of freedom that came with flight, but freedom was a word that had no meaning these days. With a shake of his head he wondered how Andrei Tupolev was getting on with the development of the ANT-4 airplane, and allowed himself a moment to indulge in the images of its corrugated duralumin skinning, like wave ripples in the sand. And the full-throated roar of its hefty twin engines that . . .

Abruptly he cut off the sounds in his head. Why torment himself?

Those days were gone. He heeled Zvezda into a longer stride, and the horse huffed through its broad nostrils, pricked its ears, and responded with ease. They were traveling fast, kicking up a trail of dust behind them, the valley widening out into the flat plain dotted with clumps of pine and alder along the silver twist of the river. It came as a surprise when he looked up and spotted a lone figure standing at the roadside some way ahead. His heart gave a kick of pleasure.

He recognized her at once, that distinctive way of cocking her head to one side, as if expecting something special from him. She was watching him, a hand shielding her eyes. The worn material of her skirt was almost transparent in the strong sunlight, and her fine fair hair ruffled around her face in the breeze. He reined Zvezda to a walk and approached with care, so as not to coat her in dust.

$\mathcal{G}$OOD morning, Sofia Morozova. *Dobroye utro.* You're a long way from home."

She looked up with a wide generous smile. "That depends where home is."

The smile was infectious. "Are you walking all the way to Dagorsk?"

She flicked at a fat blowfly that was irritating the horse's eye. "I was waiting for you."

"I'm glad, because I have something to ask you."

Mikhail slid off the saddle and landed lightly in front of her, the reins loose in one hand. The top of her head came up to the level of his lips, no higher, but a good height for a woman.

"Do you know what happened to the grain last night?" he asked, aware again of that odd disconcerting uncertainty in his mind at the mention of it.

Her eyes were an intense piercing blue. They caught his attention and held it with their directness, but now she was looking at him as though disturbed by the question.

"You were there," she said and shifted her gaze away from him and toward the village. "You saw them."

"That's what I don't understand." He ran a hand through his windblown hair and found himself studying the long white curve of her neck, exposed by the way she'd tucked her silver-blond hair behind her ear where it caught the sunlight. "I *was* there," he said. "But somehow it's all mixed up and I can't make sense of it. Pyotr claims I was drunk, and God knows I have a sledgehammer at work in my head this morning, but . . ."

She turned to look at him expectantly.

He shook his head. "I remember the fire, and you at the pump and a man with spectacles sweating over my best vodka, but then . . ." He stepped closer. "Just tell me, Sofia, how many sacks of grain were in the truck before everyone ran off to fight the fire?"

For a moment Mikhail thought she wasn't going to reply. Something in her eyes changed; a shutter slid down inside them, he could almost hear it rattle into place. Before she even spoke, he knew she was going to lie to him, and for some reason he couldn't quite understand, it made him feel sick.

"Mikhail, there were four sacks on the truck before the fire started and four sacks still there at the end of the night."

He said nothing.

"Rafik is sick," she said.

He tried to find a connection between Rafik and the truck and almost caught hold of it this time, but it slipped through his fingers and vanished.

"I'm sorry to hear that Rafik is unwell," he said.

"You don't look so good yourself."

"That's because I need to know what went on last night. Please, Sofia, tell me."

She looked away.

He seized her arm. The feel of it, the strength contained within its slender form, reminded him suddenly of having that same feeling at some point the previous evening, a point when he was standing close to her in the darkness, his skin touching her skin, her breath warm on his ear. But why? Where? That was when the blurring started again, like mist on the tips of a tree's branches, swaying and shifting so that there were no clear edges. His mind shied away from last night as Zvezda shied at a snake.

He shook her arm. "How many sacks, Sofia?"

"Four."

"The truth?"

"Four."

A stab of anger made him drop her arm, and in one easy stride he swung himself back up into the saddle, but whether the anger was at her for lying or at himself for not remembering, he chose not to ask. The old leather of the saddle creaked, and a small green lizard scuttled between Zvezda's hooves. The girl flicked her hair so that it sprang out from behind her ear, luminous in the clear air. All these things registered in Mikhail's head, each with the kind of indelible imprint that he knew meant he would not forget this moment.

He gathered the reins in one hand, on the verge of urging the horse into a gallop, but at the last second he looked down again at Sofia. And something in her held him, something in her intent gaze. Something he couldn't leave behind. He stretched out an arm. Instantly she seized it and he swept her up onto the horse behind him.

TWENTY-THREE

AT first neither spoke. Sofia leaned forward and felt the hard muscles on each side of Mikhail's ribs where she rested her hands lightly to hold on. The moment her feet lifted off the ground as she swung up on the horse, she felt the past drop from her arms like a heavy bundle of dead sticks she'd been dragging around with her, and she left them there, lying in a spiky jumble in the dirt.

She'd have to pick them up. Of course she would, she knew that. But later. Right now she felt alert, happy, and alive, and all that mattered was being here on his horse. With him so close she could smell the fresh clean male scent of him and study the strong curve of the back of his head and spot how his shirt collar was fraying where it chafed against his skin. She wanted to wrap her arms around his body and hold herself tight against him, feeling his sun-warmed back against her breasts, to burrow inside his jacket and shirt, her cheek next to his naked skin, and listen to his heart beating. But she didn't.

Instead she held on lightly and let her own body move with the rhythm of the horse beneath her. It was traveling at a good pace. Fields of potatoes flitted past in long straight ridges as far as the eye could see, occasionally edged with a haze of clover flowers that drew the greedy bees to them. Was she a greedy bee? Drawn to her own personal flower?

But he wasn't hers. She was stealing him. An ache started up in her chest and her fingers fluttered involuntarily against his ribs, making him half-turn his head to her.

"Are you all right back there?" he asked.

She could see a shadow on his jaw where he hadn't shaved well this morning and the dark length of his eyelashes.

"I'm fine. Your horse must possess a strong back to carry the two of us so effortlessly."

Mikhail laid an affectionate hand along the horse's neck, fingers kneading the heavy muscles. "You and I are no more than a gnat's wing to Zvezda. He's used to hauling massive carts all day around Dagorsk."

"For your factory?"

"No, for a Soviet haulage business. You didn't think he rested in a stall with a hay net and a young filly to amuse him till sundown, did you?" he laughed. "Like I'm sure Comrade Deputy Stirkhov does all day."

She could feel the laughter under the tips of her fingers, vibrating his rib bones, and it sent a joyous echo through her own veins.

"Mikhail, you are too free with your insults." She pointed up to a wood pigeon whose heavy wings clattered noisily as it swooped low over their heads. "I expect that bird is in the pay of Deputy Stirkhov, carrying our every word back to its master."

He laughed again and raised two fingers in an imitation gun, aiming at the pigeon.

"I mean it," she said softly. "You should take more care."

He shrugged his big flat shoulder blades as if she'd laid an unwelcome weight on them. "Of course you're right. You'd think I'd have learned by now. That's why I've washed up here in this backwater instead of . . ." His words trailed into a sigh.

"Instead of where?"

"Moscow."

"Did you like Moscow so much?"

"I liked the Tupolev aircraft factory."

"Is that why Rafik calls you Pilot?"

"Yes. But I was never a pilot. I'm an engineer. I worked on the engine designs and stress testing of the ANT planes."

"That must have been exciting."

A pause. Two dragonflies chased alongside for an iridescent second before darting back to the river.

"Yes." That was all he said.

"Very different from a clothing factory out here in the middle of nowhere, that's certain," she said lightly. "Sewing machines aren't much good at flying."

He laughed once more, but this time the sound of it was empty. "Oh yes, I'm well and truly earthbound these days."

It wasn't hard to picture him soaring through the blue sky, eyes bright with joy, mouth shouting insults at the silent clouds to his heart's content. But she didn't ask the obvious question, made no attempt to search out the why or the how. Instead she laid her cheek against his shoulder. They rode like that in silence and she could feel the thread between them spinning tighter, drawing them together till she wasn't sure where she ended and he began.

After several minutes, as though he could hear her thoughts, he said flatly, "I was dismissed. I wrote a letter. To a friend in Leningrad. In it I complained that some of the equipment was agonizingly slow in arriving at the N22 factory because of incompetence, despite the fact that Stalin himself claimed to be committed to expanding the air-craft industry as a major priority."

"Foolish," she murmured and tapped his head. His hair felt soft.

"Foolish is right." He leaned back a fraction in the saddle, so that his shoulder pressed harder against her cheek. "I should have realized all employees in such a sensitive project would have their letters mon-itored. Bloody idiot. It was only because Andrei Tupolev himself intervened for me that I wasn't sent to one of the Siberian labor camps. Instead I was exiled out here in, as you so aptly put it, the middle of nowhere. But I'm an engineer, for Christ's sake, Sofia, not a clothes merchant."

"You were lucky." Sofia sat up straight once more, lest he hear her heart cracking with fear for him. "You must be careful, Mikhail."

"I admit I've had a few run-ins with Stirkhov and his *Raion* Committee already. I'm an engineer, and since all the big public show trials of the engineers he doesn't trust me and is always wanting to interfere."

"What show trials?"

It slipped out. She wanted to cram the words back inside her mouth.

"Sofia, you must have heard of them, everyone has. The trials of the industrial engineers. The first one was the Shakhty trial in nineteen twenty-eight. Remember it? Fifty technicians from the coal industry. The poor bastards were accused by Prosecutor Krylenko of cutting production and of being in the pay of foreign powers. Of taking food out of the mouths of the hungry masses and of treachery to the Motherland."

She could feel his back growing rigid with rage.

"Everyone clamored for their deaths while they were forced into confessing incredible and absurd crimes, slavish and servile in court. They betrayed the whole engineering industry, humiliated us. Endangered us." He paused suddenly, and she wondered where his mind had veered, but she soon found out.

It was in a totally different voice that he said, "You'd have to be blind and deaf and dumb not to know of the trials. They were a huge spectacle. Used by Stalin as propaganda in every newspaper and radio broadcast, in newsreels and on billboards. We were completely bombarded for months." Abruptly he stopped speaking.

"I was ill," she lied.

"Blind and deaf," he murmured, " . . . or not in a position to read a newspaper."

"I was ill," she repeated.

"You can read, can't you?"

"Yes. But I had . . . typhoid fever . . . I was sick for months and read no newspapers."

"I see."

He said it so coldly she shivered. They rode the rest of the way into town in silence.

★ ★ ★

*T*HE town of Dagorsk seemed to press in on Sofia as she walked its pavements alongside Mikhail. The buildings were tombstone-gray and huddled on top of each other, either old and scruffy or new and scruffy. There was beauty there in some fine old houses but it was hidden under layers of dirt and neglect. Doors and windows remained unpainted because paint was scarcer than white crows these days, and the pavements were broken and treacherous. It used to be a quiet market town tucked away on the eastern slopes of the Ural Mountains, but since Stalin had vowed in 1929 to civilize the backward peasants of Russia and to liquidate as a class the *kulaks*, the wealthy farmers, Dagorsk had been jolted sullenly into the twentieth century. The austerities of Communism seemed to cast a shadow over the town, with shop windows like empty black holes and goods impossible to obtain.

Factories had sprung up on the edge of the town, circling it like barbed wire, and turning the air gray with the soot from their chimneys. The people had changed too. Gone was the easygoing familiarity of faces as the new forbidding apartment blocks and tenements filled up with strangers looking for work or, even worse, strangers who had been exiled to this remote region because of crimes committed against the state. Dagorsk was busy with people avoiding each other's eyes and with cars and carts avoiding each other's axles, as the web of suspicion and paranoia spread through the streets. Sofia felt uneasy.

"It's always frantic here," Mikhail said as they walked quickly past a squat onion-domed church that lay in ruins. "It's why I choose to live out in the peace and quiet of Tivil, though I'm not so sure my son agrees with me. He's still young. I think he'd prefer the energy of Dagorsk."

"No, I get the feeling he likes the countryside. Especially the forest."

"Maybe. He certainly enjoys working in Pokrovsky's smithy in his free time." He sounded pleased. "And you?"

"I'm not good with crowds."

"So I noticed."

He smiled at her, and she realized that since leaving the horse in the haulage yard and setting off on foot through the maze of streets, through the press of other people's bodies, she had gravitated nearer and nearer to Mikhail. He had slowed his stride to her pace and brushed against her, aware of her unease. She could feel the weight of his arm beside her, the nearness of his shoulder. Did the smile mean he had forgiven her the lie?

"My spinster aunt didn't like crowds either; she preferred pigs," Sofia said because she wanted another of his smiles.

"Pigs?"

"Yes. One gigantic sow in particular, called Koroleva. She used to walk the pig up the mountain twice a year, regular as clockwork. It was to meet up with a farmer and his boar from the next valley who walked up from the other side of the mountain, rain, wind, or shine. They'd spend a few days up there away from all crowds while the pigs enjoyed more than just the pine nuts and then came down again until the next time."

"I bet they produced strong litters after all that walking."

"Yes, good sturdy ones. But as a child it took me years to realize that Koroleva wasn't the only one getting serviced on the mountain. Regular as clockwork."

He threw back his head and laughed. "You're making it up."

"No, I'm not," she lied, flushing slightly.

They stood still for a moment, smiling into each other's eyes. She loved him for his laugh in a world where people had forgotten how to make that sound. He threaded her arm through his and guided her along the twists and turns up to the central square, steering her past the clutching hands of the beggars who pulled at her clothes like thorns. They came to an abrupt halt at a broad crossroads where the radio loudspeakers were blaring out into the street. It was one of Stalin's speeches read by Yuri Levitan, hour after hour of it. Oblivious to the long line of silent women outside the bakery, Mikhail turned Sofia to face him, holding her shoulders. His gray eyes were bright with curiosity, and his mouth curved in an echo of the laughter.

"Sofia, what exactly are you doing here?"

"I've come to visit the *apteka*, the apothecary on Kirov Street. For Rafik."

She knew it wasn't what he meant. He meant what was she doing in Tivil, but she wasn't ready for that. Not yet. It was too soon to tell him about Anna, too soon to be certain he wouldn't report her as a fugitive from one of the forced-labor camps. If he did, all hope of saving Anna would be lost. He kept his gaze on her face, watching her intently, and then his fingers took hold of her hand, turned it over, and placed a fifty-rouble note from his pocket on its palm. One by one he wrapped her fingers over the note.

"I must leave you now, Sofia. Go buy yourself some food." Gently he touched a fingertip to her cheek. "Put some flesh on your bones."

His hand was so male. She noticed that about it. She'd been cut off from maleness for so long. His palm was broad, with short hard nails on his fingertips. She took a deep breath. Now was the time to ask.

"Mikhail, will you give me a job?"

"Oh Sofia, I—"

"I'll do anything," she rushed on. "Sweep floors, oil machines, type invoices . . . and I can sew too if—"

A passing motorcycle roared up the street, smothering the life out of her words, but not before she had seen despair leap into Mikhail's face.

"I'm sorry, Sofia. There are lines of people at my factory gate every day, nothing but pathetic bundles of rags and rib bones, people who are desperate."

"I'm desperate, Mikhail."

He frowned. His gaze moved over her body in a way that made her blush. "You're not starving," he said quietly.

"No. That's true. Thanks to Rafik I'm not starving. But—"

"And you'll have work on the farm." He smiled again. "I hear you're the famous tractor driver who will lighten the load of the harvesters this autumn."

"Work on the *kolkhoz* is no use to me," she said impatiently. "I'll do all I can for them and it'll put a roof over my head and food in my stomach, but it won't provide me with what I need, which is . . ." She stopped.

"Money?"

"Yes."

"I'm sorry, Sofia. I can't."

"Just one or two days a week?"

"You don't seem to understand," he said bleakly. "I can't give work to everyone. I have to choose. Choose between who earns enough money to eat that day and who doesn't." His eyes grew as dark and dull as the pavement under their feet. "I'm forced to decide who lives and who dies. It's"—he looked away at the road ahead—"my penance."

"Please," she whispered. Ashamed to beg. Their eyes held. "It is life or death, Mikhail. If it weren't, I wouldn't ask. I need money."

He stared at her a moment longer, and she could see herself through his eyes. She was filled with disgust at what must look like her greed. She stepped away from him.

"Think about it, anyway," she said, with a try at lightness and a smile that cost her dearly. "Thanks for the lift on your horse. And for this." She held up the note and ducked out into the road, dodging a handcart piled high with old newspapers tied with wire. Her disappointment was so solid it almost choked her. She'd spoiled everything.

When she reached the other side, she turned to wave and saw that Mikhail was still standing exactly where she'd left him on the pavement, staring after her, but he was no longer alone. Beside him stood a slight female figure in a light summer dress. It had a patch near the hem but otherwise looked fresh and clean, unlike Sofia's own shabby skirt. With a shock she recognized Lilya Dimentieva, the same woman she'd seen so intimately entwined with Mikhail last night, the one who'd come to the house to whisper with Zenia. The one with the child, Misha. That one.

She was smiling up into his face with tempting brown eyes and as Sofia watched, Lilya slipped her arm through Mikhail's, rubbing her shoulder against him like a cat. Together they set off down the street.

*S*OFIA was furious. She wanted to snap something brittle between her fingers. Something like Lilya Dimentieva's thin neck. She was furious with Mikhail and knew she had no right to be. He wasn't hers.

She hurried down Ulitsa Gorkova with long unforgiving strides, indifferent now to the crowds milling around her, as though she could outpace the rage at that possessive little movement of Lilya's. But she couldn't. It burned as fiercely as hellfire, melting her from the inside.

* * *

*A*s Sofia emerged from the gloomy *apteka* into the bright sunlight on Kirov Street, she clutched Rafik's paper package in her hand and headed down toward the factories hunched together on the riverbank. Here the River Tiva had widened out to a busy thoroughfare where long black barges nudged up alongside the warehouses and men shouted and hurled ropes. Sofia looked at its oily restless surface and wondered how far a small rowboat might travel on it. It was something to consider. Traveling back up north for thousands of kilometers on foot would take too long, and she was acutely aware that each day was a fight for survival for Anna. She had to find a way to speed up the journey, yet without money she stood no chance.

She had no trouble finding the Levitsky factory. It was an ugly red brick building that rose three stories up from the muddy bank, with derricks jutting out over the river at the rear, and at the front a set of studded pine doors large enough to swallow carts whole. Attached to it at one side was a modern concrete extension with rows of wide windows that must flood the place with sunshine.

Is she in there? she wondered. *With you, Mikhail?*

Are you at this very moment holding out a glass of chai *to her? Or lighting her cigarette, your fingers brushing hers, so that you can lean close and smell her perfume? Even catch a glimpse down the front of her pretty summer frock?* Sofia's cheeks slowly colored. She stood outside the factory for more than an hour, and at the end of that time she shook herself and walked away, pushing past the *bezprizorniki*, the hollow-cheeked street urchins who scavenged on the edge of survival by thrusting whatever they had to sell under your nose. Today it was Sport cigarettes for ten kopecks each. They smelled foul. She retraced her steps to Lenin Square, dominated by an imposing bronze statue of Vladimir Ilyich Lenin himself with arm upraised in exhortation and by the colorful propaganda *plakati* that declared SMERT KAPITALIZMU! (*DEATH TO CAPITALISM!*) and WORKERS OF THE WORLD, UNITE!

The first person Sofia saw was Zenia. The gypsy girl was standing in the shade under the spreading branches of a lime tree near the newspaper boards with her bare arms draped around the neck of a young man and his hand curled snugly at her waist. He was wearing a uniform with pale blue cap-crown and epaulettes, the uniform of OGPU, the secret police. Quickly Sofia whirled away in the opposite direction, nipped past the open archway of a large market hall, and ducked around a corner.

"Ah, what have we here? The beautiful tractor driver from Tivil, I do believe."

It was Comrade Deputy Stirkhov from *Raikom*. And he was blocking her path.

TWENTY-FOUR

Davinsky Camp
July 1933

SOFIA is dead."

"No. You're lying."

"Anna, you've got to stop this. This stupid waiting." Tasha glanced up from the cards in her hand. "You've got to accept the fact that she's not coming back. Not ever. For fuck's sake, who in their right mind would turn up in this shit-hole unless . . . ?"

"Shut up, Tasha," Anna said, but without rancor. "Sofia will come."

They were sitting on Anna's bedboard playing poker with shabby homemade cards, and as usual Nina was winning. The stakes were threads of cotton yanked from their skirts.

"Nina, you'll be opening a clothing factory soon," Anna laughed, throwing down her hand of cards in disgust. "Who dealt me this rubbish?"

"I did." It was the new girl, Lara. She was nineteen and tall, with pale skin and pale hair. None of them mentioned it, but she reminded them of Sofia and somehow filled a gap for them all. "Anna," she asked with a quick flick of an ace, "what makes you believe she'll come back? The temptations out there must be so strong."

Tasha and Nina exchanged glances, but Anna ignored them. "You don't know her," she said firmly.

"But Tasha is right, she can't be in her right mind to risk coming back here."

"She promised me."

"But a promise in here," Lara explained gently, "is not the same as a promise out there." She nodded toward the world beyond the barbed wire fences. "In the real world people don't gamble for pieces of thread to mend their clothes. And they don't keep promises that are insane."

"The trouble with you, Lara, is that you haven't been in here long enough yet."

"What do you mean?"

"It drives us all a bit insane."

SOFIA is dead.

Tasha's words stuck in Anna's head like needles, and she couldn't pull them out. Yet still she refused to believe them, and as the night hours crawled past she set about breathing life into her memories of Sofia. She was convinced that if she let her friend walk and talk and laugh and cry in her head, it would help keep her walking and talking and laughing and crying out there in what Lara called the real world.

But at the same time she knew Tasha was right. Only someone insane would return to Davinsky camp out of choice, and for the very first time doubt crept down her spine with cold fingers.

"Sofia," she murmured, "what is out there? What is holding you?"

She'll come. I know she'll come. She is tenacious.

Even as a girl she had been tenacious. Anna recalled a story about Sofia's childhood that she had told her one day on the endless trek to the Work Zone.

The sound of a whip is like a branch snapping, over and over. That was what Sofia had said. When she was eleven years old, her father was tied to a tree in the center of the village and whipped to death in front of her. He was a priest. But in January 1917 he was known to be working with the Bolsheviks, and that was as good as a death warrant.

The troops of Tsar Nicholas II, Emperor of All the Russias, had ridden the eight versts from Petrograd, their bridles jangling in the cold still air as they entered the village, and they had unleashed their knotted knout on him. He didn't scream or curse, just prayed silently into the bark of the tree.

Sofia waited till after the funeral, and then in the early morning mist she plaited her long blond hair into a thick braid down her back, pulled on her *lapti* boots, and took herself into her father's store shed in the backyard. There she filled a sack with a mixture of their winter-storage vegetables that she'd grown herself—potatoes, rutabagas, and a few handfuls of turnips—and set off on the long road to Petrograd.

The heavy sack hung down her back like a dead animal. Ice lay on the sides of the road like broken glass, and the clouds above were a dirty white with the smears of sooty fingerprints pressed into them. She walked fast, as though she could outpace the grief that snapped at her heels, taking big bites out of her. Everything had shifted. She could hear it clicking into a new position both inside and outside her head, so that at times when she looked at the familiar landmarks along the way—the old water tower, the sawmill, the lopsided weathervane on top of the barn—she barely recognized them.

Her mind felt as brittle as the ice at her feet. She had a great desire to yell at the top of her voice, but instead she thought about her father's limp body stretched out on the kitchen table. She had hugged it close and refused to let go. She cried into his fingers and kissed the cuts on his neck, but when they took his body away from her to put it in a box, she knew she was going to have to build a new life for herself. Her uncle had offered her his own house as a roof over her head, but he'd told her it was up to her now to put aside her books—the ones she and her father had loved to read together—and start earning a living. She tightened her grip on the sack.

*T*HE city of Petrograd smelled of danger. There was a nervousness in the air that Sofia breathed in the moment she stepped onto its pavements, and it made her blood pump faster in ways she didn't quite understand. She had always loved Petrograd—not that she'd been in its busy streets more than a dozen times in her life—with its tall pastel-painted houses and its elegant shops and glittering people drifting in and out of them on the wide boulevard of Nevsky Prospekt. The place pulsed with the constant noise of traffic, an animated jangling of carriages and cars and trams.

Ice edged the gutters and hung like frozen tears from the balconies as she pushed onward to the street market in Liteiny, but business was bad there today. No one had roubles to spend. So after three hours she scooped up what was left of her sack and headed back to the bustling center, always taking her bearings from the golden Admiralty spire just as her father had instructed her.

The sky was white and glossy, as if storing more snow up there behind glass, but in her quilted coat and her bright yellow hat and mittens that she'd knitted herself, Sofia wasn't cold now that she was moving once more. But that sense of nervousness was strong again, the feeling of a city holding its breath, and she studied the people around her carefully to discover where this strange feeling was coming from. The ones in fur coats and silk scarves hurried along the streets noisily, talking in loud voices, but she noticed that the ones in the shabby jackets and the cloth caps huddled in tight groups on street corners among the dirty ridges of old snow, heads close together.

She edged toward one ragged group and watched them with interest. Yes, this was where the tension lay. She could see it billowing off the men along with the smoke from the hand-rolled cigarettes that they clutched between their fingers so ardently, like a badge of membership. She swallowed hard, then shifted the sack into a more comfortable position on her shoulder and headed for the huddle of three men. They were tucked in the mouth of an alleyway next to a laundry that spelled out its name in colored glass, and she couldn't help noticing that the shoes of all three men had holes in the toes. She moved closer, swinging her sack.

"Go away, little girl."

The words were muttered by the youngest of the three when he spotted Sofia near enough to overhear their conversation. He had round brown eyes with eyelashes longer than a girl's and thin bony wrists.

"Go away and play."

It was the way he said *play* that annoyed her. "At least I'm busy working," she retorted, giving him a cool look that was meant to irritate.

It succeeded.

"So are we, you *durochka*."

The second man bared small white teeth at Sofia and asked, "What's in the sack, little girl?"

"Something to interest you."

"What's that? Kerensky's head?"

The three men laughed and tugged at their caps. Sofia knew the name. Aleksandr Kerensky was head of the Provisional Government.

"No," she said. "Vegetables. Good ones, not half rotten." Their mouths opened wider at the mention of food. "I thought you looked hungry," Sofia added, keeping it polite this time.

"Of course we're hungry," the third man said in a mild voice. He was older than the other two, with deep creases scored on his cheeks, and a sadness sat around his mouth. "The whole of Petrograd is hungry, the bread rations are miserable . . ." As he spoke, a carriage swept past with four matched horses, and a liveried coachman, driving with easy arrogance through the slush, sent up a spray of ice onto the pavement. A slow ironic smile crept across the third man's face, and he shook his head. "Well, maybe not every bastard in this city has an empty belly."

Something struck Sofia as odd then. These men were not quite what she expected. Oh yes, their faces were sharp-edged and their clothes thin and patched, clearly part of Petrograd's underclass, yet they didn't stand around with a posture of defeat. Their heads were up like prize cockerels hungry for the fight. Their eyes burned with expectation of . . . she struggled to work out what it was and then it came to her . . . expectation of triumph.

Triumph over what?

She swung her sack again, trying to waft the smell of turnips under their noses to regain their attention. "Interested?" she prodded.

The eyes of the men followed the sack.

"We have no money."

"I didn't think you did."

"So what do you want in exchange?"

"Cigarettes."

"For yourself?"

"That's my business."

"How old are you, child?"

"Eleven."

"Okay, let's have a look at what you've got in there." It was the one with the girl's eyelashes. He reached forward to take the sack from her, but she stepped back nimbly.

"No, I'll show it to you."

Sofia started to open up the sack, but again the bony wrist shot out and fingers with big knuckles began to close on it. Something inside her knew instantly that if this man snatched her sack from her, she would never see it again—nor any cigarettes in exchange. Her heart thudded.

"No!"

She threw the word at him with all the strength of her mind and saw the man's eyes widen with alarm. As he started to recoil, she followed it quickly with a thump of her fist right in the middle of his skinny chest. He stumbled backward, limbs clutching at air.

"Little devil," he cursed.

"Serves you right," the older man chuckled.

"Here, girl," said the one with the teeth. "If you're so tough and want cigarettes, smoke this one." He thrust the smoldering butt at her. It looked disgusting. There were no more than a few puffs left in it, and one end was damp with spittle.

She knew it was a test of some kind. With a casual shrug of her thin shoulders, she took the cigarette, put it to her lips, and inhaled. The three men grinned as she swallowed smoke, choked back a cough, and blinked furiously as her eyes filled with water. It was like swallowing scalding lava and made her stomach heave. She pushed her mouth into a smile.

"So, what's your name?" the older man asked.

Gently he removed the cigarette from her fingers, took a long drag on it himself, and tossed the remains into the gutter, where it hissed.

"Sofia Morozova."

The men immediately exchanged a glance.

"Any relation to the priest, Morozov?"

The question caught her by surprise. Her throat tightened at the mention of her father. She nodded.

"He was well known here," the bony-wrist man said, and his whole manner had changed. It was as soft as his eyelashes.

"My father." She managed to squeeze the words from her throat.

"Well, Sofia . . ." The older man bent toward her and lowered his voice to a whisper. "There's going to be real action today, so a basinful of vegetable soup in the belly will give us all the stomach for it. My name is Igor." She could see his sad mouth curve into a smile. "I think we can do business."

SOFIA took up a position outside the Alexandriinsky Theater, where there was a constant bustle of cars and carriages and patrons in their finery. She sneaked in close whenever she could, touting her cardboard tray of cigarettes, but more often than not she was shooed away by the uniformed attendant. It made her feel like a stray dog.

The cigarettes had been a good idea, easy to sell. Out of the forty-eight she had started with, she was down to seven. Not bad. She was looking around for her next customer when she spotted a man in a top hat and a dark cape with bright silk lining heading straight toward her on the icy pavement. He planted himself firmly in front of her and looked down at the tray through tiny half-moon spectacles. She inspected him back. He was glossy, as a fur coat was glossy. Even his hair shone like boot polish in the lights from the theater entrance.

"Hello, little cigarette girl."

He picked up one of the grayish cigarettes and held it stiffly between finger and thumb as though it might bite. Then he shifted his gaze to Sofia's face, and suddenly she felt she was the one about to get bitten.

"It's good tobacco," she lied.

"Oh yes? So where did these come from? Stolen from your father's pocket?"

She wasn't going to admit they were soup cigarettes. Igor had jumped at her idea. He and his fellow strikers had stood around a big iron brazier on a patch of wasteland on the snowy banks of the Fontanka, a whole group of gaunt-cheeked faces, and heated her vegetables in a massive pan over the flames, turning them into a soup that drew men from the street corners across the city. Each paid one cigarette. Soup cigarettes.

"Yes," Sofia said, and she looked the man straight in his soft-lidded eyes. "They're from my father's pocket." She paused and let her shoulders droop. "He's dead."

It made him blink. He pulled a five-rouble note from his wallet and dropped it on her tray.

"You're very pretty, my dear. Maybe you need someone to take care of you now." He slid a good imitation of a fatherly sort of smile onto his face. "You don't want to be standing out in the cold on a night like this; it could be dangerous."

She twitched her plait, making it swing in an irritated arc onto her shoulder. He watched it, fascinated.

"You've bought my cigarettes," she said flatly, "not me."

With a precision she was proud of, she spat on the ground next to his shoe, a habit she had acquired from her afternoon companions. If her father had been here, he'd have cuffed her, but he wasn't here anymore. She snatched up the money, thrust the tray and its contents into the glossy man's hands, and then slipped away into the dark streets.

She should go home now. Curfew was at eight o'clock. It would be foolish to linger. But already she could hear the marchers and their shouts ringing out as they advanced on Palace Square. She'd just take a quick look. That was all.

*I*T was like being part of a wall. That was what it felt like to Sofia, a good strong wall. She saw herself as a brick, a small and flimsy one admittedly, but still a brick. Her arms were linked with Igor on one side and a vociferous woman on the other, and their arms were linked with other arms, and more arms, right across the width of the road, hundreds of them blocking all traffic and causing chaos in the city. Behind them were row after row of other linked arms, and in other streets and other squares the demands were shouted out in voices that grew bolder with each brick added to the wall.

"We want bread!"

"We want work!"

"Down with the tsar!"

Before the crowd could finish the words, the sound of horses' hooves was heard advancing at speed and a troop of cavalry burst into the street, charging straight at the head of the marchers with the intention of crushing the leaders. The sight made Sofia's legs tremble, but she was certain the wall would hold fast. It wouldn't break, it was strong and invincible. Her knees felt weak and something was stopping her from breathing properly, but surely the wall wouldn't break.

"Igor," she cried out.

"Death to the Duma!" he bellowed at the oncoming horses. "Death to the Duma!"

She could see the animals' breath now, rising like incense in the street as they came out of the darkness, and then she saw the determined faces of the soldiers, eaten into strange shapes by rage. Her heart turned into a wild thing behind her ribs and she clutched tight to the arms.

Then the sabers flashed.

A woman screamed in pain and the wall broke. Arms were snatched away and bodies were pressed against shop fronts, anything to avoid the scything of the blades as the horses charged. Sofia could hear their big hearts beating as their hooves pounded on whatever and whoever fell under them. The bricks crumbled into dust. Screams and panic flared through the crowd; people fled, stumbled, ducked into alleyways as the night air was torn apart as easily as the wall.

Sofia ran. Igor had been ripped from her in the stampede, but the woman on her left had yanked her into a side street and together they hurtled away from the metal sound of the hooves, the echo of each other's footsteps giving them hope. They twisted and turned and dodged around corners, ducked between fences, gasping for breath, dragging icy air into their lungs. Sofia neither knew nor cared where she was. Strange streets crowded in on her and she could hear the breath of the woman at her side growing harsher, felt her stumble.

"This way." Sofia steered them into a quiet avenue where large houses were set back behind tall forbidding gates. Here at last they'd be safe. She knew she should be thanking God for their escape, but she could find no words for him. Instead she felt only a dull anger hot in her stomach. To be hunted through the streets like an animal filled her with sick humiliation.

"They treat us like vermin," the woman whispered and slowed to a walk.

"I'm not a rat."

"You can certainly run fast as one, girl."

"Are you a Bolshevik or a Menshevik?" Sofia had heard both words thrown around this afternoon.

In the dark she could barely make out the woman's face, but she saw the headscarf lift and heard the grunt that the woman gave. It could have meant *Da*. Yes. Or it could have meant *Shut your mouth, suka*.

At that moment a lone cavalry officer appeared at the end of the street, and in a flash he had heeled his horse into a gallop, the tip of his blade carving a path through the damp night air straight to the woman's throat.

The woman broke into a run.

"No," Sofia shouted. "He'll ride us down."

"Stupid girl, we are going to die whatever we do."

To Sofia's surprise the woman dropped to her knees in the middle of the road, head bowed, hands clasped together, and started to pray.

The horseman was closing, saber ready to strike.

When Sofia looked back on this moment, it was as if time stopped in this quiet avenue in Petrograd. Stillness filled her young mind. The panic and fear that had been banging holes in her ribs seemed to drain out of her, leaving her mind clear and white. She waited until the horseman had raised himself to a standing stance in the stirrups and the blade was cutting through the thread of the woman's prayers like a knife through smoke as it swept toward the pale curve of her defenseless neck. Then Sofia leaped forward.

She came at the horse from the side and slammed her fist down onto the animal's rump with all her strength. Startled, the creature whinnied and jinked sideways away from her, but she followed and slapped it again and again. It reared up on its hind legs, twisting around to face its attacker. The officer shouted a command and sawed at the reins, but it was too late. Unbalanced by his attempt at a saber strike on the woman, he was thrown backward and crashed down onto the road.

He lay immobile. Sofia darted forward and snatched up the horse's reins. The animal was panicked, but she knew horses and was not going to let this one escape. She murmured to it and rested a hand on its sweating hide as she slowly drew the reins toward her. The horse rolled its eyes and bared its teeth at her, prancing on its toes, but it submitted to her calming touch.

The woman clambered to her feet. "God preserve you, my little rat," she shouted with a great laugh of relief, and she strode over to the form of the officer unconscious on the freezing ground. She thudded her boot twice into the side of his head. "God answered my prayers, soldier."

"Listen!" Sofia hissed.

A new sound broke the silence. Running feet, a troop of them, pounding the night air. Sofia stared down the black tunnel of the road and made out a tall youth racing up toward her; behind him a black stain spread out, flowing in all directions like spilled ink. More troops, but this time on foot.

"Quick!" she shouted to the woman, pulling the horse around.

By the time the youth reached them, they were both on the horse, one in front and one behind the saddle, so all he had to do was make for the stirrups. As he did so, he released a battle cry that ripped from his lungs and echoed from the walls around them. It both startled and delighted Sofia. Then he kicked the skittering horse into an easy gallop away from his pursuers, handling it with skill, and within seconds the troops were a receding stain once more. In Sofia's hand was the saber.

*T*HEY rode hard and in silence, avoiding the main thoroughfares, keeping to any street that was dark and dismal. He seemed to know the layout of Petrograd intimately, as though accustomed to chasing through its alleys, and several times he swerved under a bridge or down unexpected passageways to avoid a sudden surge of uniforms. They were everywhere, but always he kept the horse one step ahead of them.

Seated behind him, Sofia wrapped her arms around his back, feeling the strength of his spine and the rise and fall of his ribs as he breathed hard, sometimes even a sudden thud of his heart through the thin material of his jacket. At times his thick red scarf flapped in her face and he made little yips of encouragement to the horse. As they wound their way through the streets, she began to recognize landmarks—a shop here, a factory there—and knew they were approaching the spot where she had entered the city this morning. She tapped his broad shoulder blade and called out.

"This is my road."

Immediately he reined the horse to a walk and she slid easily off the back, landing on her feet in the snow.

"*Do svidania*, young anarchist," he called. "*Spasibo.* Thank you, my friend." He waved a hand as he swung the horse's head.

Sofia didn't wave back. She'd not even seen more than a shadow of his face, but she watched him ride away like a gray ghost into the night, the woman hunched awkwardly in front of him. She waited until he had disappeared from view completely before she turned and set off on the long walk home in the dark. Only then did she let loose the wide smile that was caught on her lips and the shiver of excitement that had been trapped in her bones. Tonight she had learned a lot. With a whoop that echoed through the still air, she lifted the saber she'd stolen from the officer and whirled it above her head in a circle, cutting slices out of the night.

But already she missed the energetic young rider, missed the warmth of his body against her chest. It was with a strange reluctance that she kept her feet walking away from the city, and one of her father's favorite words—*tenacity*—floated down into her young mind, as soft flakes of snow began to fall.

THE scarf, the red scarf.

That was the detail that always caught in Anna's mind and snagged, the way a sleeve snags on a briar. She couldn't unhook it however hard she tried. Of course, with so many young men fighting for the Bolsheviks, probably half of them were wearing red scarves.

But she couldn't shake her stubborn brain free from the knowledge that she had given a red scarf to Vasily that Christmas. She had knitted it herself specially for him, and he'd kissed her with a great whoop of delight and sworn to wear it always.

Could he have been this impetuous horseman of Sofia's childhood? Anna always wondered about it and plagued herself with the wondering. Vasily had repeatedly refused to take Anna on any of his wild escapades, declaring that it was too dangerous, yet—if it was

Vasily that night—he was willing to ride through the gates of hell with Sofia clinging to his back.

A tiny worm of jealousy squirmed into being, and she stamped on it again and again until it was nothing but a green lifeless smear. Sofia would never betray her.

TWENTY-FIVE

DEPUTY Stirkhov's office was not at all what Sofia expected. It was stylish. A spacious chrome-legged desk with shiny black top, a gleaming chrome clock and desk lighter, and curved tubular chrome chairs with pale leather seats. Of course it boasted the usual bust of Lenin on a prominent shelf and a two-meter picture of Stalin on the wall, but Lenin with his pointed beard was carved out of white marble rather than plaster, and the portrait of Stalin was an accomplished original oil painting. On another wall hung framed lithographs of Rykov and Kalinin. This was a man who knew how to get hold of what he wanted.

Sofia sat in one of the chairs and crossed her legs, swinging one foot casually though the pulse in her scarred fingertips was pounding like a fresh wound, a sure sign of nerves. She accepted a glass of vodka, even though it was still only midmorning. She felt it heat the chill that had seeped so suddenly into her bones.

"Thank you, Comrade Deputy. I didn't expect to find such a modern office in a town like Dagorsk."

"Modern in mind, modern in body," he said self-importantly, settling himself behind the expansive desk.

He flicked open a Bakelite box and offered her an elegant tan-colored cigarette that didn't look Russian to her. Imported goods were not often to be seen these days, not openly anyway, though everyone knew they were available in the special shops that only the Party elite could enter. She shook her head and he lit one for himself, drew on it deeply, and scrutinized her with an appraising look. She still hadn't worked out exactly what this pale-eyed man wanted from her when he'd suggested "a talk in my office."

"You are new to this area. And to Tivil?"

"Yes."

"I am very interested in Tivil."

She didn't like the way he said it. "It's a hardworking village," she pointed out, "much like any other. Of no particular interest, it seems to me."

"That's where you're wrong, Comrade Morozova."

He threw back his shot of vodka and poured himself another. Sofia waited, aware of the value of silence with a man like this, who would always be tempted to fill it. He seemed to puff himself up with each drink, his round face growing rounder. His skin was shiny on his cheeks, as if he polished them each morning like apples. His suit was crisp, though slightly worn at the elbows, and he had the look of a sleek tomcat. She had no doubts about the sharpness of his claws.

"Tivil," he said flatly, "is not like any of the other villages in my *raion*. It keeps tripping up my officers and making fools of them. They go out there to ensure that quotas are filled, that sufficient live-stock and crops are handed over, that taxes are paid and the required number of labor-days worked for the *raion* digging ditches and mending roads. But what do they come back with?"

He leaned forward in his chair and stared at her expectantly. She stared back, and it was as if something flowed into the silence between them, something menacing.

"They come back with lists," he snapped. "Lists all neatly ticked, goods checked off, each page endorsed with an official stamp." His fist came down on the desk, making the clock quiver. "It's nonsense. At the end of each week there is a discrepancy between what is and what should be. That's why I went out there the other evening to settle matters myself."

Sofia sipped her drink and showed little interest in his tale of woe.

"But it happened again," he growled. "Everything went wrong. And I know who to blame."

"Who?"

Stirkhov hunched his head between his shoulders. "That's not your business."

"So why," she asked with just the right touch of impatience, "have you asked me here?"

"Because you are an outsider. You are not yet a part of that close-knit community. Instead of shitting all over each other to gain extra privileges for themselves like other villages do, the Tivil bastards keep their mouths shut and stare at you with stone-hard eyes as if you'd crawled out from under a dog turd. Yet I can't . . ." Frustration made him fumble for words. ". . . I can't find the crack in their shell that will . . ." He shook his head from side to side and lifted his glass to his lips.

"A man like you would keep a Party spy in their midst," Sofia said amiably, "I'm certain."

"Of course." He waved a dismissive hand. "But the *bedniak* is worse than useless except for petty tittle-tattle. Spends too much time inside a bloody vodka bottle." He seemed oblivious to the irony as he knocked back his third vodka of the morning.

"So why have you asked me here?"

"To warn you."

"To warn me? Of what?"

He smiled smoothly. "Of danger."

"What kind of danger?"

"Word is going around that it was you who started the fire."

Her breathing grew tight as her lungs turned to lead. She gave a light laugh, but Stirkhov wasn't smiling now.

"That's absurd," she said. "I had nothing to do with it. Why on earth would I set fire to the barn?"

"A grudge?"

"No, Comrade Deputy Stirkhov, I assure you I bear no grudge against the village. My uncle has kindly taken me in, and I am grateful to him and to Tivil. Who is spreading such malicious rumors? Tell me. Is it your spy? Because if so, you should get rid of the fool. Believe me, I wouldn't ever commit such a criminal act against Soviet property or . . ." She stopped and released her tight grip on the edge of the desk. Her knuckles were white. "Thank you for the warning, Comrade Deputy. I will take care. It's obvious that whoever torched the barn is trying to shift the blame onto me."

He was observing her with shrewd eyes. "Interesting," he murmured softly. "Not much like a gypsy, are you?"

"My father's sister, who brought me up, was married to Rafik's brother."

Stirkhov picked up his gold-tipped fountain pen and scribbled a note on the pad in front of him, considered it for a moment, then placed his elbows on the desk.

"Let me see your *dokumenti*, comrade."

It was an offense not to carry identity papers at all times, papers that stated her place of residence, her date and place of birth, and her father's name. And to leave the *kolkhoz* without official permission to do so was a second offense. She recrossed her legs, slowly, and watched his eyes follow the movement.

"Deputy Stirkhov, I have a suggestion to put to you first."

He stood up, walked around to her side of his desk, perched his plump bottom on its edge, and rested a hand on her knee. She refrained from slapping his wrist away.

"What kind of suggestion?" he asked.

"It seems to me that you need someone new in Tivil. Someone . . . with fresh eyes."

"Someone like you."

"Exactly like me."

His smile returned, a smile meant to charm, and the tip of his pink tongue popped out for a brief second. "You will report to me only."

"Of course."

"And in exchange?"

"You pay me. Each week. One hundred roubles. Fifty now to seal the agreement."

"Hah! You must think me stupid." He leaned over her, and she could smell French tobacco on his breath. "Don't underestimate me,

Comrade Morozova." His hand tightened on her knee. "You bring me information and then we'll talk money."

She laughed and stood up, tipping his hand off her leg. "An empty stomach dims one's eyes and ears, Deputy Stirkhov. I do not hear well when my stomach growls."

She held out a hand, palm upward.

He looked at it, then at her. And licked his lips.

"Very well. Ten roubles now."

"Fifty."

He narrowed his eyes.

"Fifty," she repeated. "It will be worth it to you."

"It had better be."

"It will, I promise."

He reached into his inside pocket and produced a fifty-rouble note, which he placed in her hand. As her fingers curled around it, he stepped forward to kiss her, but she swung her head so that his lips barely brushed her ear. She hid a shiver, lowered her eyes demurely, and escaped to the door.

"Comrade Morozova," Stirkhov said sharply. "I expect much of you."

She gave him a dazzling smile. "So do I."

I saw you watching me." Zenia stepped out into Sofia's path as she left the *Raikom* offices. "I'm supposed to be at work in the factory already, but . . ." Her cheeks flushed and she lowered her eyes shyly.

The young gypsy girl's wild hair was tamed under a bright yellow kerchief tied at the nape of her neck, and her scoop-necked blouse, though old, was clean and showed more of her smooth olive skin than perhaps Rafik would approve. A green cotton skirt swung from her hips. Sofia could understand why any soldier would come calling.

"Zenia," she said, "you look lovely. Who was your friend?"

Zenia blushed deeper. "His name is Vanya."

"He works for OGPU, I see, the secret police."

Zenia's black eyes darted defensively to Sofia's face. "I haven't told him anything. About you, I mean."

Sofia stepped nearer and could smell the musky scent of sex on her. "Zenia," she whispered, "the secret police are clever. You will tell him things without even knowing you're doing it."

Zenia tossed her head scornfully. "I'm not a fool. I don't say . . ." but she paused as though remembering something, and her eyes clouded. "I don't say anything I shouldn't," she finished defiantly.

"I'm glad. Guard your tongue, for Rafik's sake."

Zenia looked away.

"It's all right, Zenia, I won't say anything."

The dark eyes narrowed suspiciously.

"I won't say anything about Vanya. To Rafik, I mean," Sofia added.

Zenia smiled, a sweet grateful smile that made Sofia lean forward and brush her cheek against the girl's. "But be careful. They will be stalking Tivil village after what happened with the procurement officer, and you may be their way in."

"He loves me," Zenia said simply as she flounced away, young hips swaying and head held high, attracting glances from passing men.

"He loves me," Sofia echoed, as if trying the words for size in her own mouth. Then she turned and retraced her steps through the shabby streets back toward the river.

TWENTY-SIX

IKHAIL'S office was dark. Its small window let in a square patch of sunlight that was sliding across the floorboards toward the door as if trying to escape. He was often tempted to relocate to an office in the bright new extension he'd had built alongside the old factory, but he always changed his mind at the last moment because he knew he needed to be here, overlooking the factory floor, visible to his workers each time they raised their heads from their machines. It discouraged malingering.

His office was up a flight of stairs that led off the vast expanse of the factory floor, so that the incessant rattle and clatter of the bobbing needles were as much a part of his work life as breathing. Nothing more than a wall of glass divided him from his workforce, which meant he could look down on the rows of hundreds of sewing machines and check the smooth running of his production line at a glance. He'd installed modern cutting machines in the extension, but in here the machines were so old and temperamental that they needed constant attention, damn them. He had to watch them like a hawk because spare parts were like gold dust and the girls at the machines weren't always as careful as they should be.

He stood looking out at them now, hands in his pockets, feeling restless and unable to concentrate. On his desk a stack of forms, permissions, orders, and import licenses awaited his signature, but this morning he could summon up no interest in them. He loosened his tie and rolled up the white sleeves of his shirt. She'd unsettled him with her lies. With the challenge in her eyes, as though daring him to do something but refusing to say what it was.

He laughed out loud. At himself and at her. Whatever it was that Sofia Morozova was up to, he was glad she'd arrived in Tivil like a creature from the forest, wild and unpredictable. She made his blood flow faster and in some indefinable way altered the balance in his mind, so that he was left with the feeling that he was flying high in the air once more. He gave another laugh but then frowned and lit himself a cigarette, trying to breathe her in with the smoke. All kinds of memories were stirring, ones he'd thought were dead and buried, but now they were coming to life. They picked and prodded and chipped away at him so that he ached all over. What was it about Sofia that had set this off? Just because she was fair-haired and blue-eyed and had a fiery spirit like . . . ?

No, he slammed the door shut on it all. What good did looking back do? None at all. He drew hard on his cigarette and exhaled over the glass, fogging it with smoke so that the women and their machines became an indistinct blur. He tried to imagine Sofia down there, working all day at one of the benches and couldn't. It twisted his brain into shapes it wouldn't take. Sofia was a skylark, like himself. Too much of an individual in a country where individuality and initiative were stamped on by the heavy relentless boot of the state. Conform or die. Simple.

A knock on the door distracted him.

"Come in," he said, but he didn't turn. It would be his assistant, Sukov, with yet another pile of the endless paperwork for his attention.

"Comrade *Direktor*, you have a visitor."

Mikhail sighed. The last thing he wanted right now was an ignorant official from *Raikom* breathing down his neck or a union inspector looking for trouble.

"Tell the bastard I'm out."

An awkward pause.

"Tell the Comrade *Direktor* this bastard can see he's in."

It was Sofia. Slowly, savoring the moment, he turned to face her. She was standing just behind his assistant, eyes amused, breathing fast as though she'd been running, and even in her drab clothes she made the office instantly brighter.

"Comrade Morozova, my apologies," he said courteously. "Please take a seat. Sukov, bring some tea for my visitor."

Sukov rolled his eyes suggestively, the impertinent wretch, but remembered to close the door after him. Instead of sitting, Sofia walked over to stand beside Mikhail at the glass wall and stared with interest at the machinists at work. Her shoulder was only a finger's width away from his arm. A faint layer of brick dust lay on the angular bone of her elbow, where she'd nudged against something, and down the side of her skirt. It made her look vulnerable, and he had to stop himself from brushing it off.

"A pleasure to see you again so soon and so unexpectedly." He smiled and gave her a formal little nod. "To what do I owe this treat?"

She gave him a sideways glance, raising an eyebrow at his ironic tone, but instead of answering she tapped the glass with one finger.

"The worker ants," she murmured.

"They work hard, if that's what you mean." He paused, studying the way her skin whitened under the curve of her jaw. "Would you really want to be one of them?"

She nodded. "It's money," she said, and she abruptly swung around to face him. "It's very noisy in here."

"Is it?"

"You mean you don't notice?"

He shook his head. "I'm used to it. It's quieter here than down there in the sewing room. I issue earplugs, but half the women don't bother to wear them."

She looked out at the hundreds of heads bent over the machines. "What nimble fingers they have."

"They have to work fast to meet their quotas."

"Of course, the quotas."

"The curse of Russia," he said, and he touched her shoulder, just on the spot where a tear in her blouse was mended with tiny neat stitches.

She didn't draw away. "It looks to me," she said thoughtfully, "as though the machines are working the women rather than the other way around."

"That is Stalin's intention. No people, just machines that do what they're told."

"Mikhail!" Sofia hissed sharply, glancing toward the door. In a low whisper she warned, "Don't talk so." Her eyes met his. "Please."

The door opened and they stepped apart. Sukov entered with a tray that he set down on the desk with a show of attention that made Mikhail want to laugh. He was a pale-skinned young man with tight blond curls who usually made a point of resenting any menial task now that Mikhail had elevated him from the tedium of quality control to *Direktor*'s Assistant. But he was well in with the union leaders and knew how to keep them off Mikhail's back, so Mikhail tolerated his idiosyncrasies. He was astonished to see two *pechenki* on a china plate. Where on earth had Sukov found cookies? A bribe from somewhere, no doubt. Mikhail would remember that.

"*Spasibo,*" Mikhail said pointedly.

Sukov rolled his eyes once more and tiptoed out of the room.

"I apologize," Mikhail laughed as they settled down opposite each other at the desk, "for my assistant's excess of discretion."

"Well, he must think it's your lucky day. First one female visitor and now another."

She said it with eyes sparkling, deliberately provoking him, but he wasn't blind.

"If you mean Lilya, she walked with me to the factory gates, that's all." He picked up one of the glasses of tea in its *podstakanik*, a metal holder, noticed it had a picture of the Kremlin on it, swapped it for the other one with a picture of Lake Baikal, and presented it to her. "She's in need of a job."

"Like me."

He offered her the plate with the two cookies. She took one. "No," he said, "she's not like you. Not at all like you."

She bit into her cookie, a crisp sharp snap.

"Shall I tell you a joke?" she asked.

Her words made him almost choke on his tea in surprise. "Go ahead."

She leaned forward, eyes bright. "Two men meet in the street and one says to the other, 'How are you?' 'Oh, like Lenin in his mausoleum,' comes the reply. The first man cannot work it out. 'What do you mean, why like Lenin?' The second one shrugs, 'Because they neither feed us nor bury us.'"

Mikhail tipped his head back and roared with laughter. "That is very black. I like it."

She was grinning at him. "I knew you would. But don't tell it to anyone else because they may not see it quite the way we do. Promise me."

"Is that what we Russians are reduced to? Neither dead nor alive?"

"I'm alive," she said. "Look." She put down her tea on the desk, raised her arms above her head, and performed a strange kind of snake dance with them in the air. "See, I move, I drink." She sipped her tea. "I eat." She popped the rest of the cookie into her mouth. "I'm alive." But her blue eyes slowly darkened as she looked at him across the desk and said softly, "I'm not dead."

It was as if an electric shock hit him. Abruptly he stood up. "Sofia, let's get out of here."

*H*IS hands almost fitted around her waist as he swung her up onto the rusty iron perch of the freight wagon. She was so light he thought she might take flight in the clear bright air.

"It's a good view from here," she said, shielding her eyes from the sun as she gazed out across the drab muddy waters of the River Tiva.

"And from here." Mikhail was still standing among the weeds and dirt of the disused railway siding, looking up at her face.

She smiled. Was she blushing? Or was it just the breeze from the river tickling her skin? It wasn't much of a place to bring her, but there was nowhere else—nowhere private, anyway. He'd walked her past a string of warehouses and down to the railway line that tracked along the river to the point where the rails forked into this forgotten siding. Screened by scrub and trees, it was used as a graveyard for abandoned freight wagons. He chose one without sides, tossed a stone at a sharp-faced rat that was sunning itself on what remained of the wooden planking, and lifted her onto it.

He leaped up easily and sat beside her, legs draped over the edge. He noticed her shoes were new and finely stitched, and when she bent to brush dust off them he saw again the white scars on two of her fingers and wondered how they came to be there. He felt an absurd desire to touch their shiny surface. Somewhere out of sight the sound of a train wheezing its way into the station reminded him that a large consignment of army uniforms had to be freighted out today, and he should be there to ensure no slip-ups.

"To hell with it," he said.

"To hell with what?"

"This crucible."

Her gaze left the river and studied his face. Her eyelashes were long, catching the sunlight and even paler than her hair. "Tell me what you mean."

"I mean Russia. This Motherland of ours has become a crucible, and we're all caught in it. Men and morals of every kind are being melted down and reshaped. No one can stay the way they were." He looked at her fragile bone structure and wondered what kind of steel held it together. "We all have to re-form ourselves."

"Have you?"

"I've tried." He tossed a stone in a high arc toward the river in front of them, which was dragging itself northward, brown and lifeless, its surface filmy with white-flecked pollution pumped from the waste pipes of Dagorsk's factories straight into its waters. "But right now, I'm not interested in changing anything. Least of all you."

A smile flickered to her lips, but she looked away as if to keep it secret.

"Sofia, look at me."

She turned back to him, shyly.

"Why did you come to my office today?" he asked.

"Because there's something I want to ask you."

"Ask away." He said it easily, but he felt a part of himself tighten.

"Are you proud of your father? Of what he did?"

Mikhail had a sense of scaffolding falling away, leaving him balanced on a precarious ledge.

"Isn't every son proud of his father deep in his heart?" he responded in the same light tone but it sounded unconvincing even to himself.

"No."

"Why do you ask such a question?"

She looked at him with that odd directness of hers, head tilted to one side, pinning him down, and then suddenly she smiled her widest smile and let him go.

"I wondered what kind of relationship you had with your father," she said softly, "because you obviously love Pyotr very much. He's a fine boy."

"Pyotr and I are too alike. I see so much of myself at that age in the boy. That unshakable belief that you can mend the world. It's enviable in some ways because it gives your life a rigid structure. Like the model bridge that I'm building, each girder firm and inflexible, except the girders come from blueprints laid down by someone else, by Lenin or Stalin or God or Muhammad. It doesn't come from within."

"So you no longer think you can mend the world?"

"No, I leave the world to take care of itself. I have no more interest in saving it."

She sighed and let her gaze drift with the river. "All right, so you cannot save the world. But would you save a person? One individual?"

This was the question. He could feel it, as though a wheel had started to turn. Although she asked it casually, this was the question that had brought her to his office, he was certain. Would he save an individual?

"Save them from what?"

"From death."

"That's a big question."

"I know."

On her lap her fingers twisted around each other, and Mikhail couldn't take his eyes off the imperfection in the perfect flesh. Her hands looked accustomed to hard labor. Farm work? Or was it something worse? Why had she never heard of the Shakhty trial? Was it because she'd been dragging trucks down deep mines or carting rocks out of the earth like a pack animal?

She was waiting for his answer, not looking at him.

"Would I save an individual? That would depend," he said very deliberately, "on the person. But yes, if it was the right person I would try."

She lifted her hands to her mouth, but not before he'd seen her lips tremble. The sight of that weakness, that momentary dropping of her guard, touched him deeply.

"That's a big answer," she whispered.

"I know."

Mikhail reached out for her scarred hand, wrapping his own large hands around it to keep it safe.

"Why?" she murmured.

"It's just the way I see things," he said, stroking one of her damaged fingers with the tip of his thumb. He could feel the ridges on it. "Someone has to fight back."

"But you said you have no interest anymore in changing the world."

He laughed, and her fingers twitched inside his. "Not the world, but maybe my small corner of it. I'm no good at following another man's orders, especially when that man is Josef Stalin."

Sofia gasped and glanced quickly around their sleepy sunlit corner. "Don't, Mikhail."

He looked at her gravely. "I'm not easy to control, Sofia. Ask Tupolev at the aircraft factory, ask Deputy Chairman Stirkhov here in Dagorsk; they'll all tell you how difficult I am."

He lifted her hand and brushed his lips along the back of it, feeling the veins and the pulse of her blood. She watched him intently as he spoke.

"When you let yourself become an impersonal cog in the vast machine that is the state, it's all too easy to forget that you are a person, and you do things you later regret. But I'm Mikhail Pashin. Nothing can alter that."

"Mikhail Pashin," she echoed. "Does the name Dyuzheyev mean anything to you?"

"No."

The word came out too fast. Her shoulder, slender in the colorless little blouse, leaned against his, and he could feel the heat of her seeping into his flesh.

"I've seen people, Mikhail, who have been robbed of who they were. By Stalin and his believers." Her voice was no more than a murmur. "Don't underestimate what they can do to you."

He touched one of the scars on her fingers. "Is this what they did to you?"

"Yes."

Their eyes held, and it was as though she threw wide the doors inside herself and let him in. She opened her mouth to speak again, but a noise caught his ear, the scrape of something hard on metal.

SHH," Mikhail murmured and placed a finger over her lips.

Her eyes widened, then grew wary, but she made no sound as he slipped off the flatbed and lifted her down. They stood still, both listening. After a moment he pointed silently to a covered freight wagon a few meters behind them. Its rusty rear wheels were dislodged off the rails, enmeshed in weeds and blackened chunks of planking that had rotted off the wagon and fallen to earth.

Sofia nodded. She took a breath and stretched up on tiptoe so that her mouth was close to his ear. "It's not safe to—"

Noise exploded around them as the chilling crunch of a squad of army boots quick-marched into the quiet of their haven. A magpie lifted into the air with a raucous cry of alarm that sent a pair of pigeons clattering up out of their dust bath into the trees. Twelve soldiers poured into the siding, driving out all sense of privacy, and swarmed over the four box wagons that drowsed lethargically in the sunshine. After a brief glance the officer ignored Mikhail and Sofia, but from one wagon there rose a shout and a cry of terror.

A man came hurtling out of it. Mikhail felt Sofia's body tense. The man had a dense gray beard and was dressed in black, but something flashed on his chest as he tore past the flatbed, something golden that caught the sun and betrayed him. It was a cross. In his hand was a studded Bible, clutched fiercely as he ran.

"Mikhail," Sofia cried, and she started to head into the path of the pursuing uniforms.

Instantly Mikhail seized her, dragged her back into his arms, and kissed her hard. She struggled and swore and lashed out but he didn't release her, his arms holding her rigidly against him. He felt the thin material of her blouse tear a fraction at the back as he fought to keep her still, his lips crushing hers, bending her head back till he feared her neck would snap.

The soldiers shouted to one another as they raced past the embracing couple, but they did not break their stride. A moment later came the crack of a rifle shot and a scream of pain. A black crow cawed above them like an echo, and Sofia froze in Mikhail's arms. Still his mouth was on hers, his teeth touching hers, silencing her, but her blue eyes were huge with anger. He could feel the sparks from them on the skin of his face.

He wanted to shake her, to rattle those eyes of hers in her head until they could see straight. Instead he eased the pressure of his grip on the flesh of her shoulder so that she wouldn't bruise, and was acutely aware of her hip bone cutting into his stomach, her breasts tight against his chest. Another rifle shot. A shout of triumph. Then the splash of water as a body hit the river's slick surface and was swallowed into the filth beneath.

Sofia shut her eyes, and her body went limp. Mikhail held her on her feet, his arms still around her but gently now. His lips released hers, and she buried her face in his shoulder.

"You did nothing," she moaned.

"I kept you from getting us both killed," he said sharply into her hair. "An informer had already signed that man's death warrant."

The soldiers marched back out the way they'd come, indifferent to the lovers, and immediately the pigeons settled down in the dust again, strutting with curiosity around the fluttering wafer-thin pages of the Bible where it lay in the dirt.

"You didn't even attempt to save that man from death," Sofia accused him.

"I told you. Only for the right person."

He could hear her breathing, fast and furious. His own heart was hammering, but he didn't know whether it was because of the soldiers or because of Sofia, soft and pliant in his arms. They stood like that for a long while in silence, letting the tremors pass, feeling the heat of their bodies together drive out the chill of death that had invaded the air they breathed and the ground they stood on. Her hair felt soft as down on his cheek and smelled of sunlight, while somewhere unseen another train growled its way toward Dagorsk station.

Gently, as if he might break her, Mikhail lifted her head off his shoulder, drawing back so that he could look into her face, but he didn't release his hold on her. Her limbs felt fragile, thin as kindling sticks, yet her eyes burned. He took her face in his hands, slowly studied the fine lines of her full lips, the tilt of her eyebrows, and the delicate flare of her nostrils, and felt something come alive deep within himself that he'd thought was dead forever. He recognized it instantly. It was trust. Long ago he'd learned to exist without it, each day, each month, each year, dimly aware of the dull ache of loss, but suddenly here in this unlikely place it had leaped back into life. Bright and gleaming, polished to perfection like a newly minted rouble. He wanted to shout with joy to the skies. Because without trust you can't love.

Softly, frightened that this magical creature in his arms might vanish before his eyes, he kissed her mouth. It tasted of sugar from the cookie earlier and of something else that he couldn't place. Her lips parted and a faint moan escaped her as her body melted against his. His hands caressed the long line of her spine, fingers exploring each bone of it, gentling the muscles of her back, sliding hungrily down to her narrow waist. Her arms twined around his neck with an urgency that set his blood racing, her mouth opened to his probing tongue and the sweet taste of her flooded his senses. He neither saw nor felt anything but Sofia in his arms.

"Stand apart!"

A young soldier was facing them across the dusty platform of the flatbed wagon. Patches of sweat darkened the khaki material under his arms; a rifle bristled in his hand.

"Stand apart," he repeated, taking aim at Mikhail's head.

"Do nothing foolish," Mikhail murmured to Sofia as he stepped back from her, one step, no more. "We're doing no harm here," he said reasonably to the soldier.

"You were loitering near an enemy of the people, that superstitious propagandist of bourgeois ideas we hunted out of the wagon."

The soldier's face was thin, his brown eyes single-minded, one of Stalin's believers. "I requested permission to come back to make sure you are not subversive members of his religious cell." He swung the rifle barrel from one to the other and back again.

"Comrade," Mikhail said, easing himself forward so that he stood partly in front of Sofia, "we know nothing about the man in hiding here. We'd never seen him before and had no idea he was in the wagon."

"Show me your papers, the pair of you."

Mikhail felt rather than saw Sofia flinch. Instantly his heart sank. Her eyes sought his and told him all he needed to know. He smiled at the young soldier. "Certainly, comrade," he said easily, and he started to walk around the flatbed, his shadow staying behind with Sofia as though reluctant to leave. "I am *direktor* of the Levinsky factory and here are my *dokumenti*."

He was within touching distance of the soldier now, could see the beads of sweat on his upper lip. The rifle was still pointing at him.

"Here," he said, and from his trouser pocket he withdrew a packet of cigarettes along with a lighter and his identity papers, at the same time nodding casually toward Sofia as if she were nothing. "The girl's husband works for me, so I'd appreciate it very much if you'd just leave her out of this." He gave a shrug. "You're a man of the world, comrade; you understand how these things work. She amuses me today, but her husband is a valued engineer and I couldn't afford to lose him just because he got wind of my . . . well, let's call it a dalliance with his wife." He laughed and offered a cigarette.

The soldier took one and accepted a light. "I see," he said and removed another cigarette that he slipped behind his ear. He twisted his mouth into a leer at Sofia and shook his head dismissively. "Not to my taste," he said with a sneer, exhaling smoke. "Not enough flesh on her and breasts like peas. I like something I can grab by the handful."

You can grab my fist by the handful, in your bloody mouth, you bastard.

But Mikhail kept his fist at his side and handed over his papers instead. He drew on his cigarette and glanced across at Sofia, who looked poised to run. He gave a small shake of his head. He saw the soldier's eyes glint greedily as he opened the documents and found a hundred-rouble note inside.

"I think we understand each other," Mikhail said.

"Of course we do, Comrade *Direktor*. Girl, piss off and sell your skinny cunt elsewhere today."

Sofia hesitated, eyes focused on the soldier's weapon as though she had other ideas.

"Go," Mikhail said.

She gave him a long look, then turned and raced away with loose-limbed strides. Mikhail remained with the soldier leaning against the wagon, keeping him talking and smoking until he was sure Sofia was safe, then he walked briskly back to the factory. In his office the glass she'd drunk from was still on his desk and he lifted it up, touching his lips to the spot where hers had touched.

TWENTY-SEVEN

Davinsky Camp
July 1933

Hundreds of skeletal figures in ragged clothes stood in rows in front of the shabby wooden huts, waiting. The women's patience stretched beyond endurance. It had been a hard day out in the Work Zone and an exhausting march back to camp, but now they were being made to stand in the compound. They stared at the ground, slapping at the marsh flies and mosquitoes.

Two hours they'd waited for the roll call to begin under gray evening skies, no talking and hands behind backs. Around them the barbed-wire fences and well-guarded watchtowers breathed out a menace that the prisoners had learned to deflect with their own private rituals, maybe a memory here, a snatch of a song there. Or even a shifting of weight from one foot to the other in a secret internal rhythm inside their *lapti*, their birch-bark shoes.

The door to the building finally opened. The commandant emerged and all eyes turned to admire his smooth plump cheeks, the way one admires a pig's fat flank before slitting its throat. He strutted, swished a long lead-tipped cane, and ordered the start of evening roll call, but his speech was slurred, his tongue slow and labored. He strode through the rows while the numbers were called out, disgusted by the fleshless bodies and the bloodless lips, but his cane enjoyed its daily dance on fragile bones and tender tissues.

"You." He rapped a shoulder. "Name?"

"Prisoner fourteen ninety-eight." Eyes on his leather-clad feet. "Fedorina, Anna."

"Crime?"

"Convicted under Article fifty-eight, section—"

The lead tip of the cane slipped under her chin and raised her head, silencing her. She looked straight at the commandant, at his soft loose lips and his greedy unfocused eyes, and coughed. A slender trickle of blood and sputum flew from her lips to his. He lashed out with his cane on her cheek and scrubbed his mouth with his sleeve, but turned and lurched drunkenly away from her.

She managed not to smile. But the faintest of chuckles issued from Nina at her side, and Anna was aware that the whole row of women experienced a surge of fresh energy.

NINA, there's a civilian worker in the office, isn't there? The tall dark-haired one."

They were on the return trek from the Work Zone.

Her big-boned companion nodded her head, like a horse chasing flies. "Yes. She walks in from the civilian camp each day and deals with the paperwork."

"You talk with her sometimes, I've seen you."

Nina laughed softly. "I think she fancies me."

"Would she know about any escapees and what happened to them? Surely there must be a record in the office."

It wasn't much to go on. Just a flicker of Nina's eyes to one side before she shrugged her broad shoulders and said, "Knowing how drunk our beloved commandant is most of the time, I don't think there's much chance of an efficient filing system in his office, do you?"

But the flicker of the eyes was enough for Anna.

"Nina, you're lying to me."

"No, I—"

"Please, Nina." Anna brushed her arm against the other woman's sleeve. "Tell me."

They shuffled along in silence for a few steps, the sky almost drained of color as the sun slid away from them. Around them nothing but the vast pine forest listened to the sighs of the hundreds of women.

"What have you heard?" Anna pressed.

Nina's mouth tipped downward and she spoke quickly. "An unnamed female escapee from this camp was reported found at the railway station in Kazan." She hesitated, then added. "Found dead, shot in the head."

Anna's feet stumbled, blind and boneless. White noise, which she knew was the sound of pain, filled her head. Nina was still speaking, but Anna couldn't hear her words.

"No," she shouted, "it's not her."

Her lungs started to close. She stumbled, bent double, fighting to drag in air, and the crocodile behind her shuffled to a halt.

"Move yourself, *suka*, you bitch!" The nearest guard raised his rifle butt and brought it down with impatience on the small of her back.

She crunched to her knees on the dusty pine needles, but the shock of it jerked her lungs back into action. Nina yanked her onto her feet and into some kind of forward motion before the guard could strike again.

"That bastard needs his rifle butt shoved up his ass," Tasha muttered from behind.

"It won't be her," Anna whispered. "It won't be Sofia."

Beside her Nina nodded but said nothing more.

AFTER that, Anna had no ability to control what went on in her head. It took all her strength just to keep the feet and the lungs working long enough to prevent a repetition of the rifle whipping. Sweat gathered in sticky pools in the hollow of her throat, and her thoughts seemed to slide into them and drown.

Despite all her efforts, her mind returned again and again to the day in 1917 that she still thought of as the Cranberry Juice Day. She shivered despite the heat of the evening.

The day had started well, in the Dyuzheyevs' drawing room.

When Anna moved her bishop, Grigori Dyuzheyev had frowned and tapped his long gray teeth.

"Anna, my girl, you are becoming lethal. I've taught you too well."

Anna laughed and looked out the window at the snow drifting down from a leaden sky, to hide the ripple of pleasure she felt. Papa wasn't interested in chess; he was over by the fire buried in yet another of his dreary newspapers. But when she was young she had badgered Grigori to teach her, and she'd learned fast. It seemed she had a natural flair for strategy, and now, four years later, she was threatening to steal his king from under his nose. He never gave her any quarter and made her battle for every piece.

But at the very last moment she saw his heavy eyebrows swoop together in a spasm of what looked like pain at the prospect of losing to a twelve-year-old slip of a girl. Suddenly she'd had enough. She didn't want to humiliate this generous man, so she left the back door open for his king and let him win.

"Well done, my girl," Grigori snorted his dragon sound. "That was close, by God. Next time maybe you'll do better—if you're lucky!"

Papa glanced up from his paper and chortled. "Got you on the run, has she, my friend?" But he leaned his head back against his armchair and stroked his whiskers the way he did when he was unhappy about something.

"What is it, Papa?"

He tossed the copy of *Pravda* aside.

"It's this damn war against Germany. It's going so badly for us because of sheer incompetence, and two more factories are on strike here in Petrograd. It's no wonder young men like Vasily are up in arms and on the march these days."

"They should be horsewhipped," Grigori growled. He blew out smoke from his cigar in a blue spiral of annoyance.

"Grigori, you can't hide yourself away among your Italian paintings and your Arab stallions and refuse to see that Russia is in crisis."

"I can, Nikolai. And I will."

"Damn it, man, these young people have ideals that—"

"Don't give me that tosh. *Ideology* is a word used to hide evil actions behind a cloak of justice. These bloody Mensheviks and Bolsheviks will bring about the disintegration of our country, and then we can never go back."

"Grigori, I love you like a brother, but you are blind. The Romanovs' Russia is not an ordered utopia and never has been. It's a doomed system."

Grigori rose to his feet and strode over to stand with his back to the log fire, the color deepening in his whiskered cheeks. "Do these fools really think their Party membership card will be the answer to all their problems? I tell you, Nikolai, they have a lot to learn."

"Maybe it's we who have a lot to learn," Papa said hotly.

"Don't be absurd."

"Listen to me, Grigori. Do you know that Petrograd, this glorious capital city of ours, has the highest industrial accident rate in Russia? At the Putilov works alone, there are fifteen accidents a month and no one is doing a damn thing about it. No wonder the unions are angry."

"Papa," Anna interrupted, quoting something she had read herself in the newspaper the day before, "this is the twentieth century, yet nearly half the homes in this city are without a water or sewage system."

"Exactly my point. But does Tsar Nicholas care? No, no more than he does about the bread shortages."

"That doesn't mean we have to face the downfall of the tsars," snapped Grigori.

"I rather fear it does," Papa retorted.

"Enough, gentlemen!" From her place on the sofa beside the fire, Svetlana Dyuzheyeva scolded her husband and his friend and shook an elegant finger at them both. "Stop your politicking at once and pour us all a drink, Grigori. Anna and I are bored to tears with it all, aren't we, *malishka*?"

But Anna wasn't actually bored. Recently she'd taken to dipping into Papa's newspaper when he'd finished with it and was alarmed by the reports of saber charges by the cavalry in the street. Blood had been spilled on both sides.

"Isn't Vasily supposed to be here by now?" she asked, careful to keep her concern out of her voice.

"The infernal boy is late again," Grigori grumbled as he went over to the drinks table and picked up the vodka bottle.

The furnishings in the drawing room were as ornate and elaborate as the house itself, all elegant tables and highly polished cabinets on delicately carved legs. Two sweeping electric chandeliers glittered down on beautiful objects of fine porcelain, each as thin as paper.

"Give him time," Svetlana smiled, as indulgent as ever.

Anna abandoned the chess table with its inlaid squares of ivory and ebony and took up a new position on the padded window seat.

Don't die without me.

She whispered the words to the windowpane and watched it cloud over with the warmth of her breath, blocking off the white frosted world outside.

Don't die without me, Vasily.

All kinds of deaths jostled each other inside her head as the reason why Vasily hadn't yet appeared, each one more gory than the last, and sent shivers down her spine.

"Are you cold?" asked Maria, Anna's governess, who was quietly bent over a piece of needlework on her lap.

"No, I'm not cold."

"Anna, why don't you come and sit over here by the fire?" Svetlana Dyuzheyeva asked with an encouraging smile. "It's warmer than by the window."

Anna looked around at her. Her own mother had died when she was born, so her ideas of what a mother should be were all pinned on Svetlana. She was beautiful, with alabaster skin and soft brown eyes, and she was kind. Vasily complained that she was too strict, but when Anna whispered it to Papa, he said it was for the boy's own good and in fact a sound thrashing occasionally would keep him more in line, instead of roaming the streets with the trade unionist demonstrators and getting himself into trouble.

"No, thank you," Anna replied politely to Svetlana. "I prefer to sit here."

"Don't worry, he won't be much longer, I'm certain," Svetlana smiled gently. "Not when he knows you're here."

Anna nodded to please Svetlana, though she didn't believe a word of it. She knew too well how strongly the activity in the streets drew him into its coils. On the other side of the window the lawns were covered in a crisp coating of fresh snow that glittered sharp and silent in the intermittent sunshine, as they tumbled away from the house like flouncy white skirts all the way down to the lake. She made a tiny round space exactly like a bullet hole in the mist on the glass and put her eye to it. The drive was still empty.

She couldn't ever remember a time in her life without Vasily's laughter and his teasing gray eyes, or his soft brown hair to cling to when he galloped her around the lawns on his back. But recently he had become more elusive, and he was changing in ways that unnerved her. Even when he did sit quietly at home she could see his mind rushing out into the streets. *Turbulent*, he called them, and that just frightened her more. That was when she suggested she should go with him.

"Don't be silly, Anna," he'd laughed, and his laughter hurt. "You'd be trampled to death. I don't want you to be harmed."

"That's not fair, Vasily. I don't want you to get hurt or be trampled to death either."

He laughed and shook his head, drawing himself up taller. She'd noticed he was growing so fast these days, he was leaving her far behind.

"Life's not fair," he said.

"It should be."

"That's the whole point." He waved his arms around in exasperation. "Can't you see, that's why we're all out demonstrating on the streets for a fairer society, risking—" He stopped the words before they came out. "The government will be forced to listen to us." The gray of his eyes swirled with as many shades as the sea up at Peterhof, and Anna wanted to dip a finger in it.

"Vasily," she said impatiently, "take me with you next time. Please, Vasily, I mean it."

"You don't know what it's like out there, Annochka. However bad you're imagining it, it's far worse." Slowly his eyes darkened, like the tide coming in. "The government leaves us no choice but violence." He took her hand between his own and chafed it hard. "I don't want you hurt, Anna."

And now he was late as she was stuck here gazing out of the window. *Don't die without me, Vasily.*

*T*HERE was the swish of a troika, the jingle of its bells.

Before she'd even jumped off the window seat, the door swung open and in strode a tall youth with gray eyes that sparkled brighter than the chandeliers. A dusting of snow still lay on his brown hair as though reluctant to leave him, and his cheeks glowed red from the wind. He brought a great swirl of vitality into the room, but instead of his usual immaculate jacket and trousers he was wearing what looked to Anna like horrible workman's clothes, brown and baggy and shapeless. A flat cap was twirling in his hand.

There was a bustle of kissing cheeks and shaking hands, and then Vasily bowed very stylishly to Anna.

"Don't look so fierce, Anna," he chided her. "I know I promised to be here earlier but I was . . . distracted." He laughed and tugged at a lock of her hair, but she was not ready to forgive him yet.

"I thought you'd had your head cut off," she said accusingly, turning her back on him just in time to catch Papa giving Grigori an amused wink.

She flounced over to the chaise longue where Svetlana was sitting, elegant in a dove-gray costume, the sleeves trimmed with smoky fur at the cuffs like mouse bracelets. Anna inhaled the wonderful scent of her and glared at the three men.

Vasily came over and knelt before her on the Persian rug. "Annochka"—his voice was low and it made her scalp tingle— "please forgive me for being late."

"Vasily, I was so . . ." But before the words *scared for you* rushed out of her mouth, something in her sensed he would not welcome her fears, so she changed it just in time. ". . . So tired of waiting. To dance." She kissed his cheek. It smelled of tobacco. "I want you to dance with me."

With another elegant bow that made her heart thump, Vasily swept her up into his arms and twirled her around and around, so that the dress billowed out like a balloon.

"Mama," he called, "let's have some music for our ballerina."

"Let me," Grigori offered, moving over to the grand piano at the other end of the room. "Here, how's this?" With a flourish he struck up a lilting piece.

"Ah, a Chopin waltz," Svetlana sighed with pleasure and rose to her feet, as graceful as the swans on the lake. "*Doktor* Nikolai, will you do me the honor?"

"Enchanted," Papa responded courteously, and he took her in his arms.

They danced around the room. Outside, the world was cold and growing colder each moment, but inside this room the air was warm and echoed with laughter. Smiling down at her, Vasily held Anna tightly by the waist so that as she twirled in circles her cheek rubbed against the rough serge of his jacket. Every bone in her body was transfixed with joy. She blocked out all thoughts of workers and demonstrators and sabers. Vasily was wrong, she was certain. This world would last forever.

A knock. The drawing-room door burst open and Maria, her governess, entered, followed by a maid in black uniform and white lace cap who bobbed a curtsy. Maria's voice was tight and awkward.

"Excuse me, madam, but there's been an accident."

All dancing ceased. The music stopped midphrase. Anna felt a shiver of shock in the air.

"What kind of accident?" Grigori Dyuzheyev asked at once.

"There's been trouble, sir," Maria said. "Down by the orchard. The head gardener is hurt. A bayonet wound, they say, a bad one." She was punctuating each sentence with little gasps. "By a troop of Bolsheviks. I thought *Doktor* Fedorin might be able to help."

Instantly Papa was all business.

"I'm coming right away. I'll just fetch my medical bag from the car." He was rushing to the door. "Tell someone to bring clean water, Svetlana," he called over his shoulder, and then he was gone.

Svetlana hurried from the room. Grigori and Maria followed. Vasily was still holding Anna in his arms, and she could feel the rapid pumping of his heart.

"Well, my little friend, it looks like it's just you and me. Let's have one last dance," he said, his eyes serious. "There won't be any more dancing after today, Anna."

He started to twirl her around the room again, even though the music had stopped and voices were shouting outside. He kissed her on the forehead, and she inhaled quickly to capture the scent of him. A single shot rang out. A scream outside. Instantly Vasily was pushing her to the floor and bundling her underneath the chaise longue. She could smell old horsehair and the acid tang of her own fear.

"No, Vasily," she whispered.

"Yes, Anna. Lie still. You must stay here. Do you hear me?" He was on his knees, tipped sideways to peer into the low gap between the floor and the seat. The lines of his face had changed, sharper now and suddenly older than his fourteen years. "Whatever happens, Anna, don't come out. Stay here." He took her hand, kissed a fingertip, and was gone.

But she had no intention of being packed away like a china doll and immediately started to back out from under the chaise longue. She scurried across the floor on her hands and knees, feet catching in her hem, to the window, where she placed her hands flat on the icy pane, cheek pressed beside them. Why was there a pool of cranberry juice in the snow? As though someone's cold fingers had dropped a jar of it. But next to the pool lay Grigori Dyuzheyev. He looked asleep.

TWENTY-EIGHT

*R*AFIK."

Sofia leaned closer. The gypsy's answering murmur was faint. His slight figure lay unmoving under the bedcover, a fragile disturbance of the gaily colored patchwork. At times his eyes seemed to glaze over as they stared up at the ceiling with its moons and planets and its all-seeing eye. The black of his pupils had changed to dull ash gray.

"Rafik."

Gently she took his hand in hers. She couldn't understand exactly what had happened to make him so ill, and Zenia was no help. When Sofia asked what the problem was, the gypsy girl averted her eyes, looking suddenly younger, and said, "You must ask Rafik." But he was in no state to ask anything. Though his hand was small and narrow-boned in hers, it felt unexpectedly heavy and possessed a heat that seemed to come from deeper than just skin and muscle. She ran a finger over its knotted veins, willing them to keep flowing.

"Rafik, my friend, you don't look so good. Can I

give you more . . . ?" She waved a hand at the murky bottle beside the bed, hesitating to call it medicine.

Zenia had left the strange-smelling liquid for him before going to work for the day, with strict instructions for a mouthful to be taken every few hours, more if his head pain worsened. But Rafik had sent Sofia to the Dagorsk *apteka* specifically to fetch something stronger. The pain must be bad. Sofia feared for him as she spooned the white powder onto his tongue, but when he closed his eyes, his lips continued to move silently, as though his dreams were too powerful to ignore.

She leaned so close her hair brushed his. "Stay," she whispered. "Stay with me."

A heavy knock on the front door made her jump, and when she opened it she was surprised to find the broad figure of the blacksmith on the threshold.

"May I come in, Comrade Morozova?" he said without preamble. "I want to speak with you."

She suddenly remembered the ax, the one she'd stolen. Was that what this was about? She watched his eyes. That was where she knew to spot danger. But no, the blacksmith's eyes were solemn, no threatening ripple disturbing their dark surface. She stepped back and allowed the big man to enter.

His collarless shirt was undone at the neck, revealing thick corded muscles, and he was still clad in his leather apron that smelled of grease, but his manner was polite and his voice soft. It was as if he knew his shaven head and massive size were intimidating enough without needing to add to it. The carefully trimmed spade of a beard revealed a touch of vanity that sat oddly on him. She wondered if there was some woman in his life he was aiming to please.

"So, Comrade Pokrovsky," Sofia said, "what can I do for you?"

His brown eyes narrowed as they studied her. "I've come with an offer for you."

"An offer? What kind of offer?"

"A job."

"You're offering me a job?"

"Yes. Zenia told me you were looking for one. Is that right?"

"Yes."

"Then I'm here to offer you one."

"I'm not at my best with a hammer and bellows," she said with a smile.

He frowned, then opened his mouth wide and roared with laughter. The sound almost took her head off. "Not in the forge. In the school."

Sofia folded her arms and said nothing. This didn't feel right.

"Well?" the blacksmith urged.

"Why you?"

"What do you mean?"

"Why have *you* come to me with the offer? Instead of the schoolteacher herself?"

"Oh, she's busy with the children—she lost her other assistant. Anyway, she . . ." He paused, his heavy beetle brows pulled together, and Sofia wasn't certain whether the look he gave her was one of annoyance or embarrassment. Either way, she wasn't about to take a chance.

"Go on," she said softly.

He drew a deep breath, filling his barrel chest until it stretched the seams of his shirt. "Anyway," he continued, "she wants my opinion."

Sofia blinked. "Of me, you mean?"

He nodded, studying her closely.

"But I spoke to her only last night at the school," she said.

"I know."

A small silence grew between them. Sofia was the one to break it.

"Elizaveta Lishnikova must have considerable respect for your judgment."

He shrugged. "She has made mistakes in the past. She's not good with . . . us peasants." He showed his big teeth in a smile. "Like the last teacher she employed. He's gone now."

"So what will you report back to her?"

He chewed ponderously on his beard, the way a bull chews on the cud. "That you have a smile that would keep the boys in order. A soft voice that would comfort the little ones. That your eyes are sharp and trust no one, but you're the kind of person to have at one's back in time of trouble. Unless," his eyes narrowed to slits, "unless you're coming with a knife, that is."

Another silence landed between them.

"Comrade Pokrovsky," Sofia said after a moment, unfolding her arms, "would you care to join me for a cup of tea?"

$\mathcal{T}$HEY didn't talk much. Just sat at the table holding their cups and eyeing each other with interest. Sofia could feel the suspicion in the room as solid as a third person, but neither seemed to mind it much. They were used to living with it, breathing its fumes, and both were careful not to mention what had gone on in the village the previous night. She looked at his hands, scarred and lined, the forge imprinted in the shape of every massive nail and knuckle.

"Have you always been the blacksmith in Tivil?"

"All my life. And my father before me."

"The village must have changed a lot."

"It has."

He clamped his lips shut and said no more, but his dark eyes were not so cautious and a deep anger sparked in them. She looked away to give him a moment to hide it.

"So you've known Rafik for many years?" she said.

"I have. He's the best man you could wish for when handling a horse."

"And when handling a mind?"

He leaned forward, fists on the table, making it creak. "Seen him do it, have you?"

"Yes."

"It's frightening, isn't it?"

"What is it he does?"

The smith's hand stroked the smooth skin of his head, unconsciously protecting the contents of his skull.

"It's gypsy enchantment," he growled.

"What kind of gypsy enchantment?"

"*Chyort!* How would I know, girl? An ancient power of some kind, I suppose." Sofia watched him spread his arms out wide, taking in the whole baffling breadth of the universe. "It might be," he added in a lower voice, "drawn from the black arts, for all I know."

She laughed softly. "I don't think so."

He reached across the table as if to seize her by the throat, but instead he plucked out a thread of her hair and wound it around his thick finger. "Rafik can twist your mind as easily as I twist your hair. If you're his niece, as he claims you are, you must know all about gypsy skills, anyway."

Sofia's heart thumped. She wasn't usually so clumsy, damn it. This blacksmith may have lived in a Ural village all his life but he was no fool, and he kept laying snares for her to run into, just as he would for the animals on the forest trails.

"My aunt married Rafik's brother, but I possess no gypsy blood." That was the story she and Rafik had concocted and she was determined to stick with it. "So I was taught nothing of their traditions or ways."

He unwound the blond strand on his finger and dropped it into the palm of her hand. "That explains it then." And he laughed, a boisterous sound, though she couldn't for the life of her see the joke.

"Stop teasing the girl, Pokrovsky."

"Rafik!" Sofia leaped to her feet.

The gypsy was standing in the doorway. His slight frame looked unsteady, leaning heavily on the doorpost of his room. How long he'd been there, she wasn't sure, but she sensed it was no more than a second or two. His shirt, which should have been a pale gray, was dark with sweat and hung loose over his trousers.

"Rafik, you should be in bed."

"No." He accepted the arm she offered him and let her lead him to the maroon armchair. "We are under a cloud, black as"—Rafik tipped the corner of his mouth in a slender smile—"as Pokrovsky's fingernails over there. It hangs above us and—" He stopped. Listened to something. Sofia didn't know if it was to something inside or outside his head.

"What do you mean?" she asked quietly.

"Not the village in danger again?" Pokrovsky moaned.

"No." Rafik turned his black eyes on Sofia. "No, it's you, Sofia." He pulled himself to his feet and skirted a hand over her head without actually touching her. "It's cold," he murmured. With jerky movements he wiped a large red handkerchief across his face. "Now," he said calmly, "we will take you to the *kolkhoz* office to—"

A rap at the door interrupted him. He nodded, as though it was what he'd been expecting. Sofia saw a flicker of something—was it pain or was it knowledge of what was to come?—tighten his lips before he walked to the door and opened it. A rush of bright sunlight tumbled in.

"Good day to you, Comrade Fomenko."

The *kolkhoz* chairman stood more than a head taller than the gypsy, and for one fleeting moment Sofia thought he was going to brush Rafik aside, there was such a determination in the way he stared straight at her, ignoring the two men. It made her uneasy.

"Comrade Morozova," he said brusquely, "you haven't registered yet as a resident of Tivil, I am told."

"I was just about to take her down to the office to do so," Rafik responded quickly.

"Good. We need her in the fields. You'll be assigned to a brigade, Comrade Morozova."

Sofia's tongue dried in her mouth. Just the mention of the word *brigade* brought back images of the labor camp and sent a cold shiver through her. She made no comment, just returned his stare. Did this man think of nothing but his fields and his quotas? But his observant gray eyes were giving nothing away. They turned and studied Rafik for a long moment, and then with a brisk nod he was gone. Sofia experienced a distinct reduction of the energy inside the *izba*, as though something had been sucked out of the room.

"Pokrovsky," she said thoughtfully, "tell your teacher that if she wants an answer, she must come and ask me herself."

I lied to Mikhail."

"It was for his own good," Rafik pointed out.

"He knows I lied to him."

"It was to protect him. The less he remembers about the sacks, the safer he is."

"I know. But—"

"Leave it, Sofia." There was an edge to his voice.

"Sometimes, Rafik, you scare me."

"Good. Because you scare me, my dear. Like you scared Fomenko."

"Did I?"

"That's why he came himself to check up on you. It's clear he's not sure about you. Our chairman likes to be in control, so yes, you worry him."

Sofia laughed softly and felt his answering smile strengthen the bond that had forged between them.

"Are you sure this is such a good idea?" she asked.

They were making their way down the dusty street to the *kolkhoz* office. It was by far the most conspicuous *izba* in the village, draped with placards and colorful posters listing the latest production figures and urging greater commitment from *kolkhozniki*. To emphasize the point, painted in large letters above the door was the statement FIRST FIVE YEAR PLAN IN FOUR. No one was going to accuse Stalin of not driving his people hard. Gray clouds were creeping up on the horizon, hovering above the ridge as if waiting for a chance to slip down into the valley, and there was no breath of wind to scour Tivil clean. The smell of burned wood and ash still hung between the houses like a physical presence.

Rafik had changed into his bright yellow shirt and was walking carefully, one hand lightly on Sofia's arm for support. She knew the effort was too much too soon, but she hadn't argued against it. Never again would she put Mikhail's life in danger the way she had today in Dagorsk because of her lack of *dokumenti*. Just the thought of how close it came, of the bullet pointed at his head, sent acid surging into her mouth.

As they passed the blacksmith's forge, Pokrovsky raised an oily hand, but Sofia only had eyes for Mikhail's son, Pyotr, who was standing there with him. He was a small figure beside the great bulk of the blacksmith, a pair of tongs in his young fist. The boy wiped a hand on his heavy burlap apron and then across his mouth, leaving a smear of grease. Sofia smiled at him but he didn't respond.

Rafik stumbled.

"You shouldn't be doing this," Sofia told him. "You should be resting."

"Don't fuss. If you don't register as a member of this *kolkhoz* today, people will start asking questions." His black eyes sparked at her. "You don't want that, do you?"

"No, I don't want that. But neither do I want to see you ill."

A drawn-out growl rattled inside his chest. "And I don't want to see you dead."

THE man behind the desk stood no chance. He was in his forties and was proud of his position of authority in the *kolkhoz*, his mouth faintly smug. His steel-rimmed spectacles reflected the bright lamp that shone on his desk despite the sunshine outdoors, and his hand kept fiddling with the cord of the telephone, the only one in the village. A telephone was a status symbol that he did not care to be parted from, even for a moment.

"Identity papers, *pozhalusta*, please, Comrade Morozova," he asked politely. He stroked his mustache, held out his hand, and waited expectantly.

Sofia hated the office from the second she stepped inside it. Small, crowded, crammed with forms. Walls covered in lists. Just the stench of officialdom turned her stomach. She'd seen how it could warp a man's mind till people became numbers, and sheets of paper became gods that demanded blood sacrifice.

"*Dokumenti?*" the *kolkhoz* secretary asked again, more forcibly this time.

Sofia did exactly as Rafik had instructed her. She took a folded blank sheet of paper from her skirt pocket and placed it on the desk. The man frowned, clearly confused. He picked it up, unfolded it, and spread its blank face in front of him.

"What is this, comrade? A joke?"

Rafik rapped his knuckles sharply on the metal desk, making both Sofia and the man jump.

"No joke," Rafik said.

Words in a language Sofia did not recognize started to flow from the gypsy's mouth, an unbroken stream of them that seemed to wash through the room in waves, soft, rounded sounds that made the air hum and vibrate in her ears. A resonance echoed in her mind. She fought against it, but at the same time her eyes registered that the man at the desk bore a blank expression, as though the waves had swept his mind as empty as a beach at low tide. Sofia swore she could even taste the salt of sea spray in her mouth, and she wondered if her own face looked as blank.

"No joke," Rafik reiterated clearly.

He walked around the desk, his bright yellow shirt as hypnotic as the sun, till he was standing beside the man, and he placed one hand heavily on his shoulder. The other slapped down with a loud crack on the sheet of paper.

"Identity papers," he purred into the man's ear.

Sofia saw the moment when understanding flooded the man's eyes. It was as sudden and savage as a punch in the stomach. He blinked, ground his teeth audibly, and gave a brisk nod of his head.

"Of course," he muttered in a voice that had grown thick and unwieldy.

While Rafik returned to stand beside Sofia, the man rifled through drawers, yanked out forms, flourished the Red Arrow *kolkhoz* official stamp. But she barely noticed. All she was aware of was the tang of salt on her tongue and Rafik's arm in the yellow sleeve firm against her own. How long it was before they stepped out into the street again, Sofia wasn't certain, but by the time they did so, the clouds had slunk into the valley and Tivil had lost its summer sheen. In her pocket was an official residence permit.

"Rafik," she said quietly, "what is it you do?"

"I wrap skeins of silk around people's thoughts."

"Is it a kind of hypnotism?"

He smiled at her. "Call it what you will. It kills me slowly, a piece at a time."

He could barely breathe.

"Oh, Rafik."

With an arm around his waist and taking most of his weight on herself, she walked him around to the patch of scrubland at the back of the office away from watchful eyes. With great care she eased him to the ground. He sat there trembling, knees drawn up to his chest and his eyes focused on the ridge of trees beyond the river. Without warning he was violently sick. Sofia wiped his blue lips with her skirt.

"Better," he gasped. "In a moment I'll be . . . better."

"Shh, just rest."

Sofia wrapped her arms around him, drawing him onto her shoulder and accepting the guilt into her heart.

"Thank you, Rafik," she murmured.

"Now," he said in a voice held together by willpower, "tell me why you are here."

He didn't touch her. The sinewy hands, which in some inexplicable way possessed the key to people's minds, lay lifelessly on his lap. He did not even look at her. The piercing eyes were closed, no waves sent to wash through her brain. He was leaving it up to her, to tell him.

Or not to tell him.

TWENTY-NINE

SOFIA hurried to the stables. She wanted to reach them before Fomenko spotted her running loose instead of heading to one of his blasted brigades. The track was rough under her feet, rutted and patterned with hoof-prints. She had come in search of Priest Logvinov, and she was nervous. He was the kind of person around whom someone always got hurt, and she couldn't afford to get hurt. Not now, not when she was so close.

The experience with Rafik in the office had made her doubt the reality of her own thoughts, and it had taken an effort of mind to drag them away from Mikhail. But her body was less controllable. It kept reliving flashes of memory, the feel of Mikhail's mouth on hers, so hard it hurt at first and then so soft and enticing that her lips craved more. She walked harder, faster, driving her body to concentrate on other things.

She reached the dingy wooden buildings that rose haphazardly around three sides of a dusty courtyard. They were set far back enough from the village to take advantage of the gentle slope that climbed up toward the ridge, and on this higher ground Sofia caught the breeze full in her face. It carried with it the scent of dense vegetation where creatures scuttled at will, and the temptation to vanish back into their world was strong.

"Is Priest Logvinov around?" she asked a dark-skinned youth sweeping the yard with slow lazy strokes. He had scabs on his head and his bare arms.

"In with Glinka," he muttered, tipping his head toward one of the open stable doors without breaking the rhythm of the hazel broom or his soft tuneless humming.

"*Spasibo*," Sofia said.

The gloom inside the stable came as a relief after the harsh glare in the courtyard, and it took a moment for her eyes to adjust. She inhaled the smell of horse and hay, and at first could see no one, just a row of empty stalls, fresh straw on the floor and buckets filled with clean water. The horses were out working in the fields or hauling timber out of the woods, but the stamp of a hoof and a soft murmur drew her to the far end.

The priest did not turn at her approach, though Sofia was sure he knew she was there. His tall scarecrow figure in a sleeveless deerskin jerkin was draped over the low door that fenced in one of the stalls, and his knuckles were rhythmically kneading the forehead of a small bay mare whose eyes were half-closed with pleasure. Close to her side stood a black colt on spindly legs much too long for him. He must be the one born the other night. He stamped the ground in a show of bravado as she approached and rolled his long-lashed eyes at her.

"That's a fine colt," she said.

"He has the devil in him."

The colt thudded a hoof against the back board as if to prove the point.

"Priest, were you here in Tivil before the church was closed down?"

He twisted his head around to look at her. His long thin neck pulsed with a web of blue veins and his red hair hung lank and dull, but his green eyes still burned.

"Yes, I was the shepherd of a God-fearing flock. In those days we were free to worship our Lord and chant the golden tones of evensong as our consciences dictated."

The sadness in his voice touched her. He was a strange man.

"So you were familiar with the church building inside? Before it was stripped of decoration and painted white, I mean."

"Yes. I knew every inch of that house of God, the way I know the words of the Holy Bible. I knew its moods and its shadows, just as I knew the moods and shadows of my flock as they clung to their faith. Lucifer himself stalks the marble corridors of the Kremlin, and he drags his cloven foot over the hearts and minds of God's children." His gaunt face crumbled. "An eternity of hellfire awaits those who forsake God's laws because they are stricken with fear." His voice grew hoarse with sorrow. "Fear is like a terrible black stain spreading over this country of ours."

"It is unwise to say such things aloud," she warned. "Take care."

The tall man spread his scarecrow arms wide, making the colt snort with alarm. *"Yea, though I walk through the valley of death, I will fear no evil, for thou art with me."*

"Priest," she said softly, "you don't yet know what evil mankind is capable of, but if you carry on like this, believe me, you soon will. It eats into your humanity until you don't even know who you are any more . . ." She stopped.

His green eyes were staring at her with fierce sorrow. She lowered her gaze, turned away from him, and asked the question she'd come to ask.

"Was there a statue of St. Peter in the church before it was closed down?"

"Yes."

"Where did it stand?"

"Why the interest?"

"Does it matter to you? I need to know where it used to stand."

The noise of the colt suckling and the scratch of the hazel broom over the yard were the only sounds. At last Priest Logvinov scraped a hand across his fiery beard.

"They came one Sunday morning, a group of *Komsomoltsy*," he said bitterly. "They tore down everything, destroyed it with hammers. Burned it all in a bonfire in the middle of the street, tossed in all the ancient carvings and icons of the Virgin Mary and our beloved saints. And what wouldn't burn they took away in their truck to melt down, including the great bronze bell and the altar with its gold cross. It was two centuries old." She expected him to shout and rage, but instead his voice grew softer with each word.

"The statue of St. Peter?"

"Smashed." His fleshless frame shuddered. "It used to stand in the niche beside the south window. Now there's a bust of Stalin in its place."

"I'm sorry, Priest."

"So am I. And God knows, so is my flock."

"Stay alive. For them at least."

"I know thy works and where thou dwellest, even where Satan's seat is."

Again she had a sense of the man teetering on the edge of willful self-destruction, and it filled her with a deep feeling of gloom and waste, so strong that she actually shivered. Quickly she thanked him and left the stables, but as she retraced her steps down the rutted track back to the street she was uncertain exactly what had upset her.

What was wrong?

Was it fear for Rafik? Or was it because of Mikhail? And the way Lilya had rubbed her shoulder against him as though she owned that piece of his flesh. Were her own carefully constructed defenses crumbling so easily? The wind seemed to ripple through her mind, stirring up her thoughts, and it carried to her again Priest Logvinov's words. *Fear is like a terrible black stain spreading over this country.* And then she understood, because she'd heard almost the same words months ago in the mouth of Anna.

Anna. Whose fragile heartbeats would run out if she didn't reach them soon.

*T*HE church—or assembly hall, as it was now called—was the only brick-constructed building in Tivil. Gray slabs of corrugated metal tipped with soft yellow lichen covered the roof, and the walls were divided by rows of narrow pointed windows with plain glass, though one was boarded up. A reminder of the violence on the night of the meeting. A stubby open-sided tower sat above the door. Presumably where the bell had once hung. The tower was empty now, full of nothing but warm air and pigeons.

Sofia tried the large iron handle, but the door didn't budge. She cursed and pushed harder. *Chyort!* But she was beginning to realize that Chairman Fomenko was not the kind of person to leave anything to chance, certainly not the safety of his assembly hall. She took a good look up and down the street. At this hour there wasn't much activity, just a child and a goat ambling out to the fields, but closer in the shade sat two old women. They wore headscarves and long black dresses despite the heat and seemed to be almost part of the landscape. As Sofia approached them she realized one was reading aloud from a book on her lap.

"Dobroye utro, babushki," Sofia said with a shy smile. "Good morning."

The old woman with the book reacted with surprise. Her ears were not good enough to have heard Sofia's soft footfalls. The book slid instantly under a handwoven scarf, but not before Sofia saw it was the Bible. It was not against the law to read the Bible, but it labeled you if you did. It marked you out as someone whose mind was not in line with Soviet doctrine, someone to be watched. Sofia pretended she hadn't seen it.

"Could you tell me who has a key to the assembly hall, please?"

The one who had not been reading lifted her chin off her chest, and Sofia saw the milky veil of blindness over her eyes, but her hands were busy in an effortless clicking rhythm with knitting needles and a ball of green wool.

"The chairman keeps it," she said. She tilted her head. "Is that the tractor girl?"

"*Da*, yes, it's her," responded the other. She puffed out her lined cheeks into a warm smile. "Welcome to Tivil."

"*Spasibo*. Where will I find Chairman Fomenko?"

"Anywhere where work is being done," said the blind *babushka*. "Poleena and I expect him to arrive here any moment now to count the number of stitches I've knitted so far this morning."

Both old women gave good-natured chuckles that mingled with the sun on their laps.

"But his house isn't far, just the other side of the chu—of the assembly hall. His is the *izba* with the black door. You could try there."

"Thank you. I will."

★ ★ ★

$\mathscr{B}$UT the black door didn't respond to her knocks. So she retraced her steps to the church and started to circle its walls, just as she'd done before, but then it had been furtive and in the dark with her ears alert for any stray sound. This time she inspected the building openly, seeking a way in.

She edged along the narrow side path through weeds to the gloomy rear of the church and came to the small door, so old it looked like part of the stones. It was barely the height of her head, half hidden behind a prickly bush, and bore the raw marks of her knife blade around its lock.

"Trying to find something, are you?"

Sofia snatched back her fingers and swung around. Behind her stood a narrow-shouldered man in a rough smock. He was smoking the stub of a hand-rolled cigarette and had a face that made Sofia think of a rodent—small featured, sharp toothed.

"I'm looking for a way in."

"You could always use a key, but that's just an old unused storeroom in there." He was watching her with an expression that made Sofia's skin crawl.

"I'm told that Chairman Fomenko has the key to the hall, but he's not at home."

"Of course not. He's out working in the fields."

Sofia tried to step around him, but he blocked her path and gave her a slow smile that she didn't like.

"Your name, I recall from the meeting the other night, is Sofia Morozova. Mine is Comrade Zakarov."

Instantly Sofia's chest tightened. She recalled Zenia's words: *Boris Zakarov. He's the Party spy around these parts.* So he wasn't creeping up behind her by chance.

"Why so eager to get inside our hall, Comrade Morozova?"

"I think that's my business, don't you?"

"If you made it mine, I might be able to help you."

"Do you have a key?"

He took a long pull on his cigarette. "I might."

She stared at him coldly. "I dropped a key of my own at the meeting. It got lost in the stampede and I need to look for it, that's all."

"What value do you put on this key of yours?" he asked and smiled his toothy smile. "Worth a kiss?"

His words echoed in a cold cave inside her mind. *Here's a crust of moldy bread.* Worth a kiss? *Here's a scrap of felt for gloves.* Worth a kiss? *Here's a pat of butter.* Worth more than a kiss? How much more?

She brushed past Boris Zakarov without a word and ran directly into Aleksei Fomenko himself. He was striding up from the low field by the river, a net of cabbages over his shoulder and a long-legged wolfhound at his side. He didn't look pleased to see her idling on *kolkhoz* time.

*F*IRST, *know your enemy.*

She'd learned that lesson well. *Know him. And seek out his weak spot.* More than anybody in the village Aleksei Fomenko was the greatest threat to her, but his weak spot was well hidden. His back was turned toward her as he opened the door to his house, a proud muscular back that he had no fear of turning on anybody, and Sofia envied him that. From behind she studied the neatness of his ears, emphasized by the short cropping of his brown hair, and she was certain his mind was equally neat. A line of sweat ran down the spine of his workingman's cotton shirt. Why on earth did this chairman of a large collective farm concentrate so hard on being a common peasant? What was driving him?

"Have you registered?"

His manner was curt, but the look he gave her was again one of sharp interest. It occurred to her that he was more curious about others than he was willing to admit. Zenia had told her he wasn't married, so Sofia wondered what his home was like. It was clear that he expected her to wait outside, but she didn't. After the dog entered, its claws clicking on the wooden flooring, she followed him in.

"Yes, I have registered."

Her eyes darted quickly around the room she'd entered. *Know your enemy.* What did this lair tell her about the man? It was startlingly barren. Nothing on the walls, strictly no bourgeois frills or pretensions. A chair, a table, a stove, some shelves, and that was it. Chairman

Fomenko obviously didn't believe in pampering himself. Instead of a property of distinction worthy of a *kolkhoz* chairman, the house was indistinguishable from any of the other village *izbas*, and he kept the floor well swept and the roof beams free of cobwebs. It was the house of a tidy mind. Or a secretive one.

No clues, except the dog. Sofia extended her hand. The animal touched her fingers with its damp black nose, and when it was satisfied, it allowed her to run a hand down its gray wire-brush coat. It was an elegant Russian wolfhound, a bitch with a narrow muzzle and soft brown eyes, and it gazed up at her with an expression of such gentleness that Sofia felt herself fall a little in love with the creature. But it was no more than a minute before the hound returned to its position next to Fomenko's thigh and stayed there.

"She's beautiful," Sofia said. "What's her name?"

"Nadyezhda."

"Hope. An unusual name for a dog."

He rested a hand on the hound's head, his fingers instinctively fondling one of its ears, and he looked at Sofia as though about to explain the name, but after a second's thought he made an abrupt turn and picked up a large iron key from a shelf of books at the rear of the room, too far away for Sofia to read any titles. He moved briskly now as though pressed for time, but when it came to handing over the key, he paused.

"You lost something in the hall, you say?"

"Yes. A key."

"I can't spare time to help with a search myself, comrade, but if I give you the key to use, you must return it to the office as soon as you've finished with it."

"Of course."

"Then report to one of the potato brigades."

"I'll work hard."

Still he weighed the key in his hand, and she had a feeling that despite being short of time, he still had something to say to her. That made her nervous. He subjected her to a careful scrutiny, his gray eyes so intent on her that she had a sudden sense of the loneliness inside this man and of the effort he put into hiding it.

"A tractor driver will be of great use to our *kolkhoz* next month when we start harvesting," he said thoughtfully.

"I'm glad." She had no intention of still being in Tivil next month.

"But everyone knows that a tractor driver can also inflict great damage to the crops if he or—more to the point—*she* chooses."

"Comrade Chairman, I am offering myself as a helper, not a wrecker."

"But it is significant that the moment you appear in Tivil, a barn burns down and sacks of grain go missing."

Sofia's pulse thudded in her throat. "It is a coincidence that someone else here is manipulating."

"Who?"

"How do I know?" she shrugged. "I'm new here."

"That is my point." The key tapped the firm lines of his jaw. "Come to the office at noon tomorrow. I'd like to ask you some questions."

"Chairman, I take exception to such a demand. I am here to give assistance to the *kolkhoz* of my uncle."

His gray eyes caught her out. "In which case you won't mind answering my questions, will you?"

"Questions about what?"

"About where you've come from. Who your parents were. About your family." He paused again and observed her minutely as he added, "About your uncle."

"Uncle Rafik is not well."

"It's interesting how often the gypsy is sick after the procurement officers have come calling in Tivil." He gave an ironic half-smile. "So often, in fact, that I'm beginning to wonder if there is a connection."

"I believe he grows sick at heart when he sees the village suffer."

Fomenko didn't like that; his mouth tightened. "He should be sick at heart at the thought of the men and women and children going hungry throughout our towns and cities. It is my job to make sure they don't, by making this *kolkhoz* productive. We must help fulfill our Great Leader's Plan."

The pause he left demanded a patriotic response from her, but the words wouldn't come to her tongue. Instead she held out her hand for the key.

★ ★ ★

THE church was cool, hushed, as Sofia locked the door behind her. The sunlight slid through the windows in bright golden beams that captured the dust and emphasized the shadows. She breathed deeply, shocked to find she was shaking.

How could Fomenko have that effect on her, just by breathing the same air? She stared down at her palm and almost expected to see the imprint of his fingers there. That was a foolish notion, so she pushed it aside and looked around her. Gone were the icons, gone the mosaic images and the gold latticework that once lined the central nave, no candles, no collects to honor the Mother of God. The soul of the building had been painted over with stark white.

For a moment she was rooted there, wondering what her father would have made of it, then she took a deep breath. *That's the way it is now. Accept it. Don't waste time grieving for what can never be brought back. You're here for Anna, only Anna. Now search this barren place, just as she told you to.*

Quickly she sought out the bust of Josef Stalin's head. It was easy to find, displayed prominently in a niche on the side wall, as Priest Logvinov had said. She stared with dislike at its lifeless eyes and arrogant chin, and wanted to climb up there to give it the same treatment the *Komsomol* thugs had given St. Peter.

No risks. Not now. Get on with the search.

First she examined the bricks beneath the niche. Her fingers traced the outline of each one, seeking a loose corner or some disturbed mortar that would indicate a hiding place. But no, the bricks were smooth. She traced them all the way to the floor with no success and then knelt on the boards and set to work, running a hand along each one, tapping it, picking at its edges, testing whether it would lift or rock unevenly. Nothing. Nothing at all. Except the cold lead of disappointment in her stomach. Frustrated, she crouched on the floor, elbows on her knees, and stared at the white wall. Where? Where was the hiding place? Anna's governess, Maria, had whispered that a secret box was concealed here, but where, damn it, where? Where would someone hide something they didn't want found?

The oak door rattled. She leaped to her feet. Someone was trying to enter.

"Comrade Morozova, are you in there?" It was the Party man, the weasel man, the informer, Comrade Zakarov.

In a final rush she scanned the wall beneath the head of Stalin once more. *A box buried at St. Peter's feet.* That was what she'd been told, but it was so little. Abruptly she dropped to her knees.

"St. Peter," she whispered, "grant me inspiration. Please, I'm begging. Isn't that what you want, you and your God? Humility and supplication."

Nothing came. No shaft of sunlight to point the way. Sofia nodded, as though she'd expected no less, and just then the door shook again, louder this time. "Comrade Morozova, I know you're in there."

What now? With a sudden droop of her shoulders she buried her face in her hands and felt a wave of loneliness chill her bones. She had to leave. She stood, made her way up the central aisle, and inserted the key in the lock, and as she did so a longing for Mikhail came with such force it took her breath from her.

"Mikhail," she whispered, just to feel his name on her tongue.

He could help her. But would he? If she told him all she knew about Anna and his past and about what was hidden in the church, would he turn her away like a thief? He'd said he would help the right person, but was she that right person? Was Anna? He was in a position of authority now and worked for the Soviet State system; he had a son whom he loved. Would he risk it all if she asked? Would he?

He'd be insane to do so.

She straightened her shoulders and turned the key. If she asked for his help, she risked failure, and failure meant death. Not just her own.

THIRTY

Davinsky Camp
July 1933

THE cat crept into the camp out of nowhere. Its arrival occurred at the end of one of the fierce summer storms; the small creature picked its way daintily around the puddles in the yard as if walking on eggshells. It was young and painfully thin, its bedraggled fur a sort of noncolor, neither gray nor brown but somewhere in between. But there was a jauntiness to its movements that attracted attention in a world where limbs were heavy and movements slow.

The women couldn't help smiling, and a group of them tried to herd it into a corner, but it looked at them with scornful green eyes and slipped effortlessly through their legs. It scampered straight into one of the huts, gazed with interest at the array of bunks, and leaped up onto Anna's. It nudged its bony little head against her arm and plunged its needle claws into her blanket, kneading with a steady rhythm that tore holes in the threadbare material. Anna touched its head, a light tentative brush of her fingertips over the damp fur, and immediately the young cat started to purr.

The loud rackety sound did something to Anna. Happiness sprang into her chest like something solid. She could feel it warm and contented in there, soothing the inflamed pathways in her lungs. Like the cat, it seemed to have come from nowhere. She scratched a finger under the furry chin until it stretched out its neck with pleasure and watched her through half-closed eyes that desired nothing more.

Other prisoners were gathering around the bunk board.

"It's so pretty," one crooned.

"It needs meat."

"Don't we all!"

"It'll be riddled with fucking fleas," Tasha warned.

Anna laughed. "We've already got bedbugs, mosquitoes, and marsh flies; what difference will a few fleas make?"

The young animal suddenly hiccupped, and everyone chuckled. Tasha put out a hand to stroke its soft fur, but at that moment one of the guard dogs outside barked and the cat hissed and flattened its ears, its sharp claws raking Tasha's skin.

"Fuck the little bastard!"

The cat shot off the bed, its hollow belly low to the floor, and disappeared out of the door in a flash of noncolor. Several of the women chased after it.

"I hope they eat the miserable piece of gristle," Tasha said, sucking at her hand.

Anna stared at the spot where the cat had torn a hole in her blanket and felt an even bigger hole torn in her chest. "Oh Tasha, that's what this place does to us. I'm sure they will, eat it, I mean. I just hope the poor little creature has enough sense to head straight for the barbed wire."

"Wouldn't we all like to do that?"

"Give me your hand. Here, this will help." She took Tasha's hand between hers and pressed hard to stem the blood. The tiny needles had done no more than scrape the surface, and the trickle soon stopped.

"Thanks," Tasha said, and she went over to the grimy window to watch the chase.

But Anna didn't hear because she was staring blindly at the wall opposite. The brief sensation of a hand pressed hard against her own had whisked her without warning back to that day at the Dyuzheyev villa when the dancing had been stopped forever by a light knock on the door.

"No." Maria had hissed the word. "No, Anna."

The twelve-year-old Anna had come hurtling out of the house, but her governess seized her with a grip that hurt and yanked her back onto the front steps, tight against her skirt. Maria placed one hand on Anna's shoulder and the other gripped her hand, and she was not going to let go.

"Say nothing," she breathed, not taking her gaze from the group spread out on the drive in front of her.

Gray uniforms were everywhere, red flashes on their shoulders, snow trampled and dirty under their boots. A circle of rifles, glinting in the sun, was aimed at the three figures in the center of it: Vasily, Svetlana, and Grigori. Grigori was splayed awkwardly on the snow in a sleep that Anna knew wasn't sleep and in a pool of red juice that she knew wasn't juice. She choked and gasped in the cold air. Svetlana was kneeling beside her husband, a terrible, low, bone-scraping moan escaping from her lips, her head bowed to touch Grigori's chest. There was more of the cranberry juice on the front of her beautiful gray dress and on her sleeve. On the fur and on her chin.

Vasily looked strange. He was standing stiff, his limbs rigid as he spoke to the soldier with the peaked cap, the one with a revolver still pointed at Grigori's motionless body, and the words that rushed out of Vasily were hot and angry.

"You'll get the same, whelp, if you don't stop yapping." The soldier's eyes were hard and full of hate. "You and your family are filthy class enemies of the people. Your father, Grigori Dyuzheyev, was a parasite, he exploited the workers of our Fatherland, he had no right to any of this—"

"No." Vasily was struggling for control. "My father . . . treated his servants and tenants well, ask any of them what kind of—"

The soldier spat on the snow, a jet of yellow hate. "No one should own a house like this." His mustache twitched with anger. "You should all be exterminated like rats."

Anna mewed.

The soldier swung his gun so that it was pointing directly at her. "You. Come here."

Anna took one step forward, but that was as far as she could go because Maria still held her tight.

"Leave her alone," Vasily said quickly. "She is only a servant's brat."

"In that dress? What kind of fool do you think I am? No, she's one of your kind. One of the rats."

"Leave her," Vasily said again. "She's too young to make choices."

"Rats breed," the soldier snarled, and without shifting the aim of the gun he turned his head to address a boy of about sixteen standing alertly at his shoulder, his cap low over his forehead. He was wearing ragged boots and his chest was heaving, and Anna noticed that despite the chill winter air his young skin was damp with sweat. His uniform was someone else's castoff, with sleeves and trousers flapping loose and a telltale hole just over his heart.

"Son, fetch the rat."

The boy looked directly at Anna. His pupils were so huge she feared they would swallow her up, black and bottomless. She glared back at the boy as he started toward her.

"No, comrade." It was Maria. Her voice was as cool and crisp as the snow. "The girl is mine. My daughter. I am a servant, a worker, and she's a worker's child, one of the Soviet proletariat."

"No worker wears a dress like that."

"They gave it to her." Maria gestured to the body of Grigori and to Svetlana bent over him. "They like to dress her up in fine clothes."

The soldier rubbed an old scar on the side of his head, and Anna saw he had no ear there. He turned to Svetlana. "Is it true? Did you give the brat the dress?"

Svetlana ignored the soldiers but smiled lovingly at Anna.

"Yes," she said quietly, "I gave dear Annochka the dress. But you are the rats and the scum. My husband spent his life at the Foreign Office helping his country. What have you ever done for Russia? You are the rats that will gnaw the heart out of Mother Russia until there is nothing left but blood and tears."

The shot, when it rang out in the stillness of the January day, made Anna jump, and her feet would have skidded off the step if Maria had not held her. She bit her tongue, tasted blood. She saw Svetlana hurled backward off her knees, her head flying so fast that her neck was stretched out, revealing blue veins and translucent white skin above the gray collar. A red hole flowered in the exact center of her forehead and leaked dark tendrils.

Vasily roared and ran to her.

Anna stared at the soldier boy in the too-big uniform and cap, rifle steady in his hand, and realized he was the one who had fired the bullet. The older soldier placed a proud hand on his shoulder and said, "Well done, my son."

The other soldiers murmured an echoing contented sound that was passed from one to the other, so that rifles relaxed and attention lapsed.

Vasily came fast. It took no more than a second for the knife that suddenly materialized in his hand to sink into the soft throat of the older soldier in command, the one without the ear, and for Vasily to leap up the steps and vanish back into the house. Anna smelled the sweet familiar smell of him as he raced past her, and the old red scarf hanging from his pocket flapped against her cheek. A hideous sickening certainty hit her that the red scarf would be the last thing she would ever see of Vasily. The soldiers fired after him and a bullet grazed Maria's temple, but they were too slow. Their shouts and stomping feet echoed in the marble hall and up the stairs as they searched, and there was the sound of shattering glass inside.

Anna didn't move her lips, but she turned her eyes to Maria and whispered, "Do you think he's safe now? Vasily has escaped, hasn't he?"

Her governess's face was gray as stone except for the small trickle of blood, and she was staring at the body of Svetlana. It was only then that Anna realized tears were pouring down her own cheeks. She dashed them away, scraping her cold fingers over her face, and that was when she saw Papa. He was running, except to Anna it looked like flying. His long dark cloak was billowing out around him like great black wings as he ran up the slope of the snow-covered lawn to the drive, his face twisted in anguish at the sight of his two dearest friends sprawled on the trampled snow.

"Stop there," one of the soldiers shouted.

He was older than the rest, with heavyset shoulders and a troubled brown gaze that kept glancing back to the body of his superior on his back in the snow, with eyes staring up at the sky as though daydreaming.

"What happened?" Papa demanded. "Why have you shot these people?" Anna could see the tic in his cheek muscle. "I shall report you."

"Who are you?" The older soldier raised his voice.

"I am *Doktor* Fedorin. I was tending to someone wounded by your men here on the estate."

He stepped back and dropped on one knee next to Grigori, but his eyes glanced over at Anna. Imperceptibly he shook his head. He touched first Grigori's wrist, then Svetlana's, his head bowed. Anna saw his lips move soundlessly, and a deep shudder gripped him. She felt it ripple in an echo through herself.

"The boy killed my comrade here," the soldier growled.

Papa looked up. Slowly rose to his feet. "What boy?"

"The Dyuzheyev son."

Papa stood very still. "Where is he?"

"My men are searching for him now."

Papa looked at Anna but said nothing.

"I am taking over this house," the soldier suddenly declared. "I requisition it in the name of the Soviet people and—" He stopped abruptly and pointed at the black Oakland car parked farther along the drive, its headlamps sparkling in the thin sunshine. "Whose is that vehicle?"

"It's mine," Papa said. "I'm a doctor. I need a car to visit the sick."

"The rich sick," the boy soldier spat. "The sick who possess big houses and big bank balances." He pointed his rifle at the Oakland and fired. The windshield exploded, and glass flew like ice.

The older soldier scowled. "Why ruin a perfectly good car? We could use it for—"

"It is American. It stinks of injustice just like this doctor does."

"Tell me, *Doktor*," the older man in command demanded sharply, "do you also live in a big house? Do you also keep servants? Do you own horses and carriages and more silver samovars and fur coats than you can ever use?" The man took a step closer. "Do you?"

Anna saw Papa's eyes go to the silent bodies of Svetlana and Grigori. Suddenly he yanked the handsome silver watch from his waistcoat pocket. "Here," he shouted, "take this. And these." He hurled his cigar case and his beaver hat onto the trampled snow at their feet.

"And take my house too, why don't you?" His heavy bunch of keys hit the boy's toecap. Papa's rage frightened Anna. "Take everything. Leave me nothing, not even my friends. Will I then be fit to doctor your glorious proletariat? And are *you* fit to decide who is fit to be cared for and who isn't?"

The boy's eyes filled with loathing.

Anna watched Papa take four long strides toward her. *Odeen. Dva. Tre. Chetiri.* One. Two. Three. Four. Her heart leaped at the sight of his familiar reassuring smile, at his eager blue eyes, his hair ruffled by the wind. The cloak that so many times had wrapped her close against his warm cigar-smelling body swirled in welcome, as though seeking her out. His hand reached for her, and she felt Maria's fingers uncurl.

There was a loud crack. Anna knew now that it was the sound a rifle makes when it's fired. The boy, she thought, shooting at the car again. She expected Papa to be angry with him, but instead his mouth jerked open into a silent *oh*, and his eyes rolled up in his head, so that only their whites showed. His knees went soft. And then he was falling, face first as he used to do in the enticing waters of the Black Sea to amuse her when they spent the summer at their dacha. Face first into the snow. The back of his head was blown open. The boy soldier was gripping his rifle proudly.

Anna ripped herself free of her governess and started to scream.

THIRTY-ONE

ZENIA dealt the tarot cards, the *gadalniye karti*. Her hands were quick and skillful, each card laid neatly on the table, flicking a second and a third to overlap it. The images of noose and naked bodies and long curved sickle tumbled on top of each other. The room in the *izba* was gloomy, shutters closed, the air scented with a cloying ball of goose fat that hissed and spat in a dish of beaten copper. In the center of the table sat a basket of woven birch bark, a lid of coarse netting stretched over it, a knife positioned in a vertical line across its surface. The blade pointed due east. Inside the basket something moved.

The shadows shifted and Rafik's voice was deep with tension as he placed a hand on the knife and said, "Again, Zenia."

The gypsy girl gathered the cards. Shuffled and dealt again. The same. Noose and sickle and pink-skinned naked bodies entwined in long curling loops of silvery hair.

"The lovers," Zenia announced. "They bring death to Tivil."

An intake of breath while a shutter vibrated, though there was no wind. Rafik picked up a teacup that stood on the table, the one Sofia had drunk from earlier in the day with Pokrovsky. Inside it tea leaves were bunched at the bottom and spread into intricate shapes that Zenia had studied.

"Are you sure?" he asked, though in his heart he didn't doubt his daughter's reading.

"Yes, I'm sure."

"A journey for her. One that brings sorrow to Tivil."

"Yes."

They both gazed at the brown envelope that lay next to the basket. On it was written one word: *Sofia*. Rafik felt the weight of each of the bold black letters.

"Tonight," he said, "I will walk the circle."

THE field was emptying. Sofia stood, straightening her cramped muscles, and watched the women head back toward the village in twos and threes, their chatter adding to the tinkling bell of the cows as they ambled in for the night.

"That's it for today," the woman tending the next potato row called across to her. "Come on, you can finish now. Enough for today."

Sofia shouldered her hoe. "So Chairman Fomenko does allow us to stop work eventually, then?"

The woman chuckled, and together they trudged up the valley, talking quietly about the condition of the crop this year, while the evening sun sent their long shadows skimming ahead of them. As they approached the cedar tree, Sofia spotted the huddle of three children crouched in the dust at the base of its wide trunk, playing a game of some kind with small stones and a rubber ball. A pair of bright brown eyes met hers and looked away quickly. It was Pyotr. So he was nervous of her. Sofia felt an unexpected tug at her heart.

She waved to him and smiled to coax him into friendship, but part of her felt like going over there and giving the boy a good shake. She didn't, of course. She was just as nervous of him, that was what was so stupid. They were uncomfortable together, too well aware of each other's weakness. He knew she was a fugitive, and she knew he hadn't reported her, not yet, anyway.

"Hello."

Sofia blinked. A skinny little form had detached itself from the group and skipped over to her. Sofia halted, and her companion from the field nodded pleasantly and walked on. She had her husband's meal to cook. It took Sofia a moment to recognize the narrow face and the uncombed hair at her side. It belonged to one of the girls from inside the schoolroom last night, one of the silent little mice.

"It's me, Anastasia."

"Hello, Anastasia."

"My mother said to thank you."

"For what?"

Anastasia glanced furtively around with exaggerated care, though no one except the two boys was within earshot. "For the story."

"It was my pleasure."

The girl grinned up at her, little mouse teeth showing. "We asked our teacher if you can come in again. Will you?"

Well, that explained the Pokrovsky visit. And why a number of the women in the potato field this afternoon had gone out of their way to include her in their banter.

"*Da*." Sofia smiled. "Yes, I'll come in again. If I'm officially invited."

"Did you hear that, Pyotr? Comrade Morozova might be coming into our school."

Pyotr looked up from his position in the dirt. His gaze darted to Sofia's face.

"But you're a tractor driver."

"Yes." She could see the uncertainty disturbing his young eyes and knew he was trying to deal with questions he couldn't answer. Would it be so bad to have a fugitive in his school? Should he report it? What would happen if he did? Or if he didn't? "Pyotr, I am many things." She laughed, to show him she understood. "Don't—"

The other boy jumped to his feet, his knees dusty, his eyes sharp. With a sinking heart she remembered him from the meeting, the youth who looked as if he'd stepped out of a propaganda poster.

"Has Chairman Fomenko been informed of this?" he asked.

"Don't be silly, Yuri." Anastasia waved a dismissive little hand at him. The gesture made Sofia smile, it was so obviously copied from her teacher. "The school is run by Comrade Lishnikova, not Chairman Fomenko." She turned to Pyotr with a bright expression that grew brighter as she faced him, even though he was crouched once more over his pile of stones and didn't look up. "Isn't it, Pyotr?"

The boy shrugged and tossed a stone high into the cedar branches.

"Don't take any notice of Pyotr," Anastasia sighed apologetically. "He's sulking because his father is leaving Tivil."

Leaving. Sofia's heart knocked against her ribs.

"Leaving?"

Pyotr traced the outline of an airplane in the dust, his shaggy hair falling over his face and hiding any expression from her.

"Pyotr, is your father leaving Tivil?" she asked softly.

Reluctantly he nodded. "He's going to Leningrad."

"When?"

"Tomorrow."

One word. That was all it took, and the evening sky grew dark.

*W*HY didn't you tell me?"

"This morning, Sofia, with you eating my cookies, I had no interest in tomorrow. I was enjoying today too much to think about leaving."

"You could have told me."

"Would it have changed anything?"

"No. Except—"

"Except what?"

"Except make me . . . more aware of what I had, and . . . of what I was losing."

The look Mikhail gave her in response made her pulse quicken and made the long wait alone in the dark worth every minute. The sun had set several hours ago, but she had sat patiently on the edge of the stone water trough in the stableyard, listening to the contented sighs and snores of the horses, while a bat flitted erratically above her head snatching mosquitoes out of the air. She was growing used to waiting for him.

By the time she caught the sound of the steady tread of a horse's hooves on the slope up to the stables, the moon had risen and stars glimmered like diamond splinters in the great arc of black night that hung over the mountains of Tivil. The air was moist. Her skin grew chill in the breeze, her breathing fast. When Mikhail walked into the yard leading the big horse Zvezda on a loose rein, both man and animal moved with a tired step, limbs heavy and heads low. It had been a long day. He carried his jacket slung over his shoulder, and a leather saddlebag was hooked on the pommel. In the colorless shaft of moonlight they seemed to drift like ghosts, silver and luminous, and for one second Sofia believed they were figments torn from her dreams. Only the metallic ring of the hooves convinced her otherwise.

"Mikhail."

His head lifted, eyes astonished. And the smile he gave her roused such a need to touch him that she forced herself to remain seated. If she stood, she might steal the rein from his grasp and slip her own hand into its place.

"Sofia," he said, "is something wrong?" His easy smile slipped into a frown of concern.

"Yes."

Instantly he strode forward. His face was divided by shadows, so that she was uncertain of his thoughts, but the way he leaned over her made her sway toward him, the tip of her hair brushing his sleeve.

"What is it?" he asked urgently.

"You're leaving Tivil."

He drew himself upright again with a light laugh. "Oh, is that all? I thought it was something serious."

She swayed away from him, silenced by his indifference. He stepped aside and started to unbuckle the horse's girth. The animal blew out its stomach with a snort of pleasure, and Mikhail ran a hand over Zvezda's thick neck so that it gleamed in the sheen of moonlight.

"*Spasibo*, my friend," he said softly, and Sofia was jealous of the deep affection in his voice. Without looking around, he asked as though it were unimportant, "Did you get my letter?"

"What letter?"

"I gave a letter to Zenia to deliver to you. I knew I wouldn't be back until late tonight because I had to finish writing a report. Didn't you receive it, the letter?" He swung around and gazed intently at her face.

"No. I came here straight from working in the fields."

"Oh, Sofia!"

She didn't know what he meant by that. A bat dipped close to their heads as though listening in on their conversation before it swooped up over the gray outline of the stable roof and disappeared into the darkness. The freedom of its movement suddenly galled Sofia, and she felt a spike of anger at Mikhail, who seemed to possess that same freedom, able to travel anywhere, but considered it too inconsequential to mention.

That was when she said, "Why didn't you tell me?"

Now he was looking at her as if expecting a response, but a response to what? She had the feeling she was missing something here, something big. Mikhail opened his mouth to speak, but just then the horse stamped its foot impatiently and instead he gathered the reins in his hand.

"Come on, my midnight wanderer."

Sofia didn't know if he was talking to her or the horse, but was content when together they left the yard and walked into the sweet-scented stable. There she lit an oil lamp while Mikhail unsaddled Zvezda and started brushing him down with long soothing strokes. Sofia filled the water bucket and hay net. They worked in companionable silence except for Mikhail's low murmurs to the horse, and Sofia enjoyed the ordinariness of working alongside him; it gave her a sense of satisfaction she hadn't expected. When eventually he blew out the lamp, they retraced their steps out into the yard, and she was taken by surprise when he stopped by the trough where she had been sitting earlier.

"You must be cold after waiting so long."

He took up his jacket and draped it over her thin blouse, his hands lingering on her shoulders. She could smell the scent of him wrapped around her body, and it released some of the tension from her skin.

"Tell me what was in the letter, Mikhail."

"I'm not sure that you'll want to hear this."

"Try me."

"It's about tomorrow."

Her stomach tightened. "You're going to Leningrad." Her voice sounded flat.

"Yes, I am."

"Weren't you going to say good-bye? Or is that what the letter is for?"

"If you haven't yet read my letter, how did you know I was leaving?"

"Pyotr told me."

"Ah yes, Pyotr. The boy is unhappy at being left behind in Tivil."

She stared at him aghast. His face lay in deep shadow.

"You're abandoning your son?"

There was an odd little pause, a kind of blink in time, and then Mikhail placed a hand on her arm and shook it hard. The movement shocked her, as did his rough laugh.

"So you think me a deserter," he said.

She had offended him.

"Yes."

"The boy will survive."

"I'm sure he will."

But will I?

"The delegations meet for only a few days."

"Delegations?"

"Yes. It's the summons to report to the Committee of Soviet Production and Distribution. An annual chore that . . ." He stopped, removed his hand from her arm, and stepped back. One half of his face slid into the moonlight, and she could see that his cheek muscle was taut. "You thought I was going away forever," he said quietly. "Didn't you?"

She nodded.

"You thought I was going off permanently to the bright city to enjoy myself without my son and without saying good-bye . . . to you."

Sofia ducked her chin to her chest miserably and nodded again. Then the fact that Mikhail was coming back to Tivil in just a few days sank in and got the better of her. She looked up at him with a wide grin.

"It wasn't your going away that I minded. It was that I wouldn't get a ride on Zvezda anymore. I'd have to walk all the way to Dagorsk."

He threw back his head and laughed, and the unfettered joy of it made her blood pulse. A sudden gust of wind twitched his hair as if it would laugh with him, and Sofia wanted to touch the long line of his throat with her fingers to feel the vibration inside it.

"Come," he said.

He drew her arm through his as he headed smartly out of the courtyard and down the slope toward the silent village. Walking with him at night felt good—secretive and involving, as though the darkness belonged just to them. She breathed deeply, the rich damp odor of the black earth bringing a sense of belonging into the empty corners of her mind. Her fingers rested on the warm muscles of his forearm.

"Shall I tell you a story?" he asked.

"If it's a funny one. I'm in the mood to laugh."

"I think this one will amuse you."

She lengthened her stride to his, her feet finding their way easily along the silvered path. On either side, cabbages looked like shaggy gray chickens roosting for the night.

"Tell me," she said.

"Well, you recall the steep flight of stairs up to my office at the factory?"

"Yes."

He chuckled and she found herself smiling in anticipation.

"My assistant, Sukov—remember the smarmy bastard who brought us our tea this morning—he fell down them today. All the way from top to bottom and broke his leg in two places."

Sofia halted and stared at his delighted smile. "What is remotely funny about that?"

Mikhail's smile widened, but his gray eyes grew dark and serious. "He was coming to Leningrad with me in the morning. Now it means there's a train seat and a travel ticket going spare."

THE river gleamed like polished steel in the moonlight. Sofia waded into it, naked, but even the touch of the chill water on her skin couldn't cool the heat in her blood.

One week with Mikhail. She was to have one whole week. Just the two of them. It was more than she had ever dared hope for, much more. Just the thought of it set her heart drumming in her chest, and she gazed up at the dazzling array of stars above as if they'd been put there tonight just for her. She laughed out loud. The happiness wouldn't stay inside, it just bubbled out into the silent night. She splashed a spray of water up toward the stars and laughed again when she heard a plop in the water where some night creature took fright at her antics.

Sleep had been impossible. She could no more close her eyes than she could close her heart, so she had come down to the river, alone and unseen, and washed away the dust of the fields from her limbs.

Anna, are you looking at this same moon? These same stars? Waiting for me? Oh Anna, I'm coming, I promise. Hold on. I'll know. By the end of this week together I'll know if I can ask him to help. Your Vasily. She hesitated, then spoke the words aloud this time so that her ears would have to hear them.

"*Your* Vasily. Don't hate me, Anna. It's for you. I swear it's for you."

She plunged under the surface of the water, a cold black world where you couldn't tell which way was up and which way was down.

A shadow, among many shadows. The night was full of them: the swaying of branches in the breeze, white drifts of mist rising to swallow the paths, a fox or a vole scampering on its nocturnal run, but still she saw the shadow.

She was dressed and standing on the riverbank when the narrow track across the river changed fleetingly from silver to black, and then again farther along. Instantly she was alert and retreated into the overhanging curtain of a willow tree. From there she watched the shadow and quickly made out that it was a man, and he was walking away from her. The moonlight painted the back of his head and sketched his long limbs, and for one breathless moment Sofia thought it was Mikhail come to seek her out. But then a wisp of light caught the long back of the ghost dog at the shadow's side, and she realized it was Aleksei Fomenko with his hound.

Fomenko? What was the chairman doing prowling the night? From behind the feathery veil of willow leaves, she observed them, the way they strode along the wooded track without hesitation. Both man and animal knew the way.

The way to where?

★   ★   ★

*T*HERE was just enough breeze to rustle the night. It shuffled the leaves and sighed among the branches, just enough to hide the brush of her skirt on a thorn or the crack of a twig underfoot as she followed them.

The dog worried her. The animal's ears were sharp, but it seemed intent only on what lay ahead. Sofia stayed a good distance behind them, concentrating hard on the small sounds of their movement to guide her through the forest. They were tracking up over the ridge, and her mind raced for an answer to explain Fomenko's surprising nighttime wanderings.

A lover? In the next valley?

It was possible. She'd heard no mention of any woman in his life. The idea of this self-controlled man losing himself to such an extent appealed to her, his desires getting the better of his quotas. That thought made her smile and quicken her pace. Around her the forest grew darker, the trees denser, denying the moon anything more than a trickle through the thick canopy of foliage. The path beneath her feet became rougher and steeper as they passed from valley to valley and then higher into the mountains, and still the man and dog pushed on. Sofia's pulse began to quicken. Thoughts flickered in her head. Moths fluttered in her face.

The dog whined as its claws scrabbled up a gully, and the sound of it was so familiar it made the hairs on the back of her neck rise. She became convinced she knew where they were heading.

The hut.

*I*T was strange to be in the clearing again. So much had changed for her in the last few days, yet here everything seemed the same. The hut still leaned like an old man and the boughs of the fallen tree still lay white as dead bones in the moonlight, but Sofia didn't venture among them. Instead she sheltered in the undergrowth, tight against a tree trunk, and watched a flame flare into life in the small window of the hut after Fomenko entered with the dog.

Was he meeting someone?

That time when she had hidden down by the stream and come

back to find the two men in the hut and the horse outside, she was sure now that it was Fomenko and that the dog was Hope. But this time he was on his own, alone and secretive. Secrets always meant weakness. *Know your enemy. Know his weakness.* She listened to the sounds of the night, eyes fixed on the yellow rectangle of the window, but a sudden snort right behind her made her leap from her position. Her blood raced. She swung around but could make out nothing among the black shapes of the forest.

A person? A moose? Even a bear?

Damn it, she wasn't waiting to be clawed to death. Ducking low, she crept out into the clearing, only too aware that she was now visible to watchful eyes. She moved silently to the window and with caution peered in at one corner, but she needn't have worried. Aleksei Fomenko was kneeling on the dusty floor, totally engrossed. His long back in the familiar work shirt was angled toward her, but she could just see that he was bent over a hole in the flooring. A hole? She hadn't noticed one when she had slept here, but it was explained by the sight of two wooden planks lying to one side, the floorboards, and next to them a candle, its flame casting uncertain light around the room. Sofia eased farther along the window frame, and over his shoulder she caught a glimpse of what was holding his attention so seriously. A square olive-green object. It took her a moment to recognize it for what it was

A two-way radio, all dials and pointers and knobs. A sudden burst of static took her by surprise, and she ducked down below the sill, her breath raw in her throat. A secret radio. Why did the chairman need a secret radio?

As she crouched low to the earth, her mind struggled to find an explanation. Was it to connect him directly to OGPU, to give him a direct line to the secret police where he could betray the secrets of his *kolkhozniki* in private? But what was wrong with the office telephone? Maybe this radio bypassed the normal channels and took him straight to the man at the top? She shook her head. *No,* she told herself, *don't get carried away,* most likely nothing as dramatic. Probably just a secret lover crooning sweet talk in her ear. She decided to risk another glimpse and slid up slowly till her eyes were again on a level with the cobwebbed glass. This time she took in more of what was in front of her: the stillness of Fomenko's powerful shoulders, the earphones on his head, the mouthpiece he was murmuring into, the notebook open at his side and covered with lines of dense writing.

Why on earth would he need notes for a lover?

With a small sense of shock she became aware of the dog. It was stretched out on the floor, licking dirt from from one paw with long sweeps of its tongue, but abruptly it stopped. Its head lifted, eyes and ears alert. It gazed at the closed door and, making no sound, it raised its lips to show its long teeth in a silent snarl. Sofia didn't know what its quick ears had picked up, but she wasn't going to hang around to find out. She pushed herself away from the hut and raced back down the track to Tivil.

THIRTY-TWO

Davinsky Camp
July 1933

AFTER the business with the cat, Anna lay awake, propped upright against the damp wood of the hut wall to ease her breathing. Beside her on the bedboard lay a squat nervy woman who spent every waking hour angry and resentful, to the point that she could barely sleep at night. She lay on her side staring wide-eyed at the degraded world inside the hut, hating it with a passion that was killing her.

Anna didn't want to be like that; she didn't want to hate until it was all that was left inside her. She'd seen it again and again, the way prisoners died from hate, and she tried to spit out its insidious bitter taste in the mouth, but sometimes it was hard. Especially without Sofia to make her laugh. She missed Sofia.

Ever since the cat she had missed Sofia even more. Sofia would have known how to rid her head of the images that swarmed inside it, images that buzzed and stung like bees. It was that stupid cat's fault, scratching Tasha's hand like that. Because now that Anna had let that terrible Cranberry Juice Day back into her head, it settled there like a carnivore, gnawing at her and refusing to go away. Even as she hacked away at the branches all day in the forest and tried to block her mind with thoughts of the futile arrogance of the guards or the fragrance of the pine sap, the memory sank its powerful teeth into her and kept dragging her back to Petrograd and that cold winter of 1917.

She had became a shadow after her father died in the snow. No longer a person, just a twelve-year-old shadow inside a cramped and stuffy apartment that belonged to Maria's brother, Sergei, and his wife, Irina. Her skin turned gray; she rarely spoke and only picked at the barest crumbs of food. But she learned to call Maria "Mama," and she wore a plain brown peasant dress without complaint and ate black bread instead of white. At night she shared Maria's narrow cot and spent the hours of darkness lying obediently on the sour-smelling mattress, but never seemed to close her eyes. They had changed from their bright cornflower blue to a dull muddy color that matched the winter gloom of the River Neva. Yet still she wouldn't cry.

"It's not natural," Irina said in a low voice. "Her father has just died. Why doesn't she cry?"

"Give her time," Maria murmured to her sister-in-law as she ran a hand over the silky blond head. "She's still too shocked."

"A shock is what that girl needs," Irina said, miming a quick little slap with her hand. "It's like having a corpse in the house." She shivered dramatically. "The child gives Sergei and me the creeps, she does. How you can sleep with her in your bed, I don't know."

"Irina, please. She's silent but she's not deaf."

"No, you're not deaf, are you, Anna? Just willful. Well, child, it's time to snap out of it and give your poor Maria a chance to get on with her own life. She's starting a new job tomorrow and can't spend time fretting about you."

Anna's muddy eyes turned to Maria, panic fierce in them. "Can't I come with you?" Her voice was barely a voice. "I can work too."

"No, my love." Maria kissed her forehead in the dark. "I'm working in a factory, putting washers on taps. It'll be noisy and dirty and unimaginably boring. You'll enjoy it much more here with little Sasha and Aunt Irina."

"You might die tomorrow. Among the taps."

Maria put an arm around Anna and rocked her gently. "Neither of us will die, I swear to you. You must wait patiently for me to return."

A soft moan escaped from the back of Anna's throat.

ANNA spent the day at the window. She kissed Maria good-bye at the door of the second-floor apartment and then ran to the window to wave to her all the way down the street, but the moment Maria was out of sight, a suffocating blackness swarmed into her mind. It stopped her breathing. Air wouldn't go into her lungs and sometimes she had to beat her ribs with her fists, pushing her chest in and out to make air suck in and blow out. Irina clipped her on the ear for doing it, saying she was being silly and mustn't scare Sasha, who was watching Anna from his colorful rag rug with a big grin on his face. His ears, which stuck out like wings, listened to every sound she made.

Anna counted. She counted her fingers, she counted the number of blue flowers on the wallpaper, the spots on Sasha's chin, the chimneys on the roofs, the tiles on the house opposite, the people in the street, the pigeons in the gutter. She even tried to count the snowflakes when they fell from a colorless sky, but that was too hard. Only when the sky grew dark and Maria came home, only then did Anna believe Maria was still alive.

THEY came for Maria in the middle of the night. They barely gave her time to pull a dress on over her nightgown, but she was quick to push Anna firmly against the wall.

"Stay there," she said fiercely.

So Anna stayed there. But when the big man in the arrogant boots and the long overcoat patted her on the shoulder and told her not to fret, she wanted to bite him. To sink her teeth into his wrist where the ugly blue veins bulged above his black leather gloves and make his blood flow onto the floorboards. Maria said little, but when she bent to pull her felt *valenki* on her feet, Anna could see the white skin on the back of her neck twitching as if spiders were crawling over it.

It was Sergei who put up the fight.

"What do you want with my sister?" he demanded. "She's a good worker. She's done nothing. We are a loyal Bolshevik family. I marched on the Winter Palace with the best of them. Look"—he yanked open the front of his nightwear to reveal a livid shiny scar across his chest—"I am proud to bear the mark of a saber."

"I salute you, comrade," said the man in the overcoat. His face was shrewd. "But it's not you we want to question, it's her."

"But she's my sister and would never—"

"Enough, comrade." He held up his hand for silence, a man accustomed to being obeyed. "Take her outside," he ordered two of his soldiers.

"Maria." It was Irina who darted forward. "Take this." She thrust her own warmest fur hat onto her sister-in-law's head and a piece of cheese into her hand, and gave her a quick peck on the cheek. "Just in case," she whispered.

Maria blinked but couldn't speak. Her face looked frozen.

Just in case? Of what? Anna wanted to scream. What would they do to her, these huge soldiers whose shoulders packed the small room with their hard muscles and their long rifles and the stink of their damp uniforms?

"And this pretty little kitten with the eyes that would kill me." The officer's laugh held no humor. "Who is she?"

"She's my niece," Sergei said. He placed a protective arm around Anna's shoulders. "She's not important. She helps with our baby, so that my wife can spend more time knitting scarves and gloves for our brave soldiers."

The man walked over, placed his hands on his knees, and lowered his face until it was at the same level as Anna's. He inspected her closely.

"So. Shall I take you down for interrogation as well?"

Anna gave a faint nod.

He smiled a snake's smile, and she spat at him. Her spittle hit his cheek and slithered down. Without a thought, his gloved hand slapped her face, bouncing her head off the wall. She didn't cry, but Maria did.

"The child didn't mean it," Maria called out. "She's upset and frightened. Apologize immediately, Anna."

Anna glared at the man. She wanted him to take her wherever Maria was going, so she started gathering more spittle in her mouth.

"Anna!" Maria begged.

"I'm sorry," Anna whispered.

Abruptly he lost interest. "Come," he said. Suddenly they were gone, and only the smell of them remained.

*F*IVE days. Anna counted the breaths.

Twenty-five breaths in a minute. Fifteen hundred breaths an hour. Thirty-six thousand breaths in a day and night.

She wasn't so sure about the nights. When you sleep you breathe more slowly. But alone in the bed she didn't sleep, and when she did close her eyes on the sofa during the day, she woke up with nightmares. Irina scolded her for disturbing Sasha with her screams.

Five days. One hundred forty-four thousand breaths.

*O*N the sixth day Maria came home.

She said little and didn't go to work. She lay on her side on the bed hour after hour, eyes wide open. Anna sat on the floor beside the cot and twisted her fingers into the quilt because it was the nearest she could get to Maria without touching her. And she knew that if she touched the fragile figure, Maria would break.

So she sat still, made no noise, just fed tiny cubes of pickled beetroot into Maria's mouth. They turned Anna's fingers and Maria's lips the color of cranberry juice.

*W*HEN eventually Maria did emerge, her hair was styled differently but it didn't quite hide the ugly marks on the side of her neck.

"What are they?" Anna whispered.

"Cigarette burns."

"Was it an accident?"

"Yes," Maria said quietly. "An accident of beliefs."

Anna didn't understand, but she knew she wasn't meant to understand.

"You have to go."

Anna couldn't believe the words.

"You have to go, Annochka. Today."

"No."

"Don't argue. You have to go."

Maria was holding a small burlap bag in her hand, and Anna knew it contained her own few belongings.

"No, Maria, please no. I love you."

That was when tears started to slide down Maria's face and the bag shook in her hand. "It's time for you to go, my love," Maria insisted. "Please don't look so terrified. Sergei is going to take you to the station, and then a good kind woman will travel with you all the way to Kazan."

Anna wrapped boneless arms around Maria's neck. "Come with me," she whispered.

Maria rocked her. "I can't, little one. I've told you, the men who came here to the apartment want to ask me more questions."

"Why?"

"Because they want to know where Vasily is. He killed one of their own when they shot his parents and they don't forgive that. They questioned me about where he could be hiding and I told them I know nothing, but they . . . didn't believe me. So they want to ask me more. It's all right, don't tremble so, I'll be fine."

"No accidents?"

"No, no more accidents." But Maria couldn't stop a shiver. "Even though your papa is dead, they have declared him an enemy of the people, and that means that you are in danger. You must leave. I'll come for you as soon as I can."

"You promise?"

"Yes."

"I'll write to you, so—"

"No, Anna, it's too dangerous. In six months, when all this blood-letting is over, we'll be together again. You'll be staying with a distant cousin of mine, but eventually I'll come and care for you, as I promised your dear papa. I love you, my sweet one, and now we both have to be strong." Gently but firmly she detached Anna from her neck. "Now give me a smile."

Anna smiled and felt her face crack into a thousand splinters.

THIRTY-THREE

THE train jolted to a halt. Mikhail reached across and pulled the leather strap, so that the window slid all the way down. Sluggish air drifted into the carriage from outside, hot and heavy and laden with smuts from the engine. On the platform, vendors fought to peddle baskets of food.

"This compartment is like a bloody oven," complained the man in the seat on Mikhail's right. It was his chief foreman from the factory, Lev Boriskin, a stocky man but powerfully built, with thick gray hair and a habit of fingering his lower lip.

"I'll see if there are any rain clouds ahead," Mikhail said.

He leaned again toward the window because it meant he would brush against Sofia. She was seated in the corner next to the window, her blond head turned away from him, looking out at the crush of bodies on the platform. All day she had spoken very little, but could he blame her? From the start things had gone wrong. They had traveled into Dagorsk in a cart with four others, including a married couple who quarreled at full volume all the way to the station. Then on the platform he had introduced her to Boriskin and to Alanya Sirova, Boriskin's secretary, a woman of about thirty with ambitious eyes behind thick tortoiseshell spectacles. It was only when he saw Sofia's face grow rigid with dismay and her gaze turn to him questioningly that he realized that in his delight at inviting her to Leningrad last night, he'd forgotten to mention their traveling companions. He'd ushered her into the seat by the window, dismissing Boriskin's pointed remark.

"I thought," the foreman said with a sideways shift of his eyes to Sofia, "that as *direktor fabriki*, you should have the best seat instead of—"

"Comrade Morozova has been commissioned to write a report," Mikhail cut in sharply, "on this delegation. She will cover our contribution to the committee as well as our travel arrangements. So I think she is entitled to the window seat, don't you?"

Boriskin paled, pulled at his lip, and shook open a copy of *Pravda* with a show of indifference. Mikhail sat himself next to Sofia, a barrier between her and his foreman. She looked at him with stern blue eyes, but in their depths he could see a ripple of laughter.

THE crowded carriage made it easier. For much of the time there was movement and chatter as passengers retrieved or replaced packages from the rack above their heads. The man over by the door was constantly fiddling with his pipe and muttering to himself, while Alanya Sirova, on the far side of Boriskin, shuffled documents in and out of her briefcase with a zeal that Mikhail felt certain was aimed at the mythical report. The noise and bustle meant he could talk to Sofia in a low voice without anyone noticing.

"I'm sorry," he murmured.

"No need," she smiled.

"It's a long journey. There'll be moments."

"As long as there's no quota to them." She raised a teasing eyebrow at him.

They couldn't say more, not with Boriskin at Mikhail's elbow, but it was enough. He felt the warmth of her arm along the length of his own, and occasionally their feet touched as though by accident. Mikhail was unable to relax, but through half-closed eyes he watched the railway lines snake past the window like silver veins and once spotted a hawk rising in a spiral, as if weightless on the bleached air, its great wings outstretched, but its shadow fell like a dead body on the field beneath.

"Look," he pointed out to Sofia. And in a lower tone he added, "The spirit of Russia."

"Don't," she breathed.

*T*oo many hours were spent reading the documents that were passed down the line from Alanya Sirova to Boriskin to himself, pages of facts and figures that danced in front of his eyes. He had no interest in the damn things. He became increasingly restless and everyone in the carriage irritated him, especially the pipe smoker and the military man who snored. They all prevented him from being alone with Sofia. Even the well-meaning woman opposite who picked at food constantly like a plump pigeon, drawing from the depths of a large red carpetbag *blinis* and *kolbasa* sausage, which she broke into tiny pieces and popped into her mouth. Kindly she offered some to Sofia, but Sofia shook her head.

Vast regions slid past. Forests that stretched forever, pine trees burnished gold by the sun, and silver birches that shook their delicate threads as the train roared by. Sometimes a river or a ragged village appeared to break the monotony, but not often. Or once in a long while a crooked water tower and a bustling station where everyone was shouting and great clouds of white breath shuddered from the engine, while hawkers thrust out filthy hands offering *pelmeni* or hard-boiled eggs and pickled cucumber in paper cones.

"Come, Comrade Morozova," Mikhail said, rising to his feet, at one such station. "Time to stretch the legs."

"Comrade *Direktor*," Alanya Sirova intervened quickly, "first I'd like your comments on this report from—"

"Later," Mikhail said curtly.

He yanked open the door, took hold of Sofia's hand, and escorted her out into the fresh evening air.

"Do they believe you?" Sofia asked in an amused voice once they were on the platform. "That I'm here as an observer of the delegation?"

Mikhail laughed easily. "Who cares? You're here, that's all that matters. And they're so used to the system being riddled with informers that there's no reason for them to doubt your role. It's simple really. Alanya Sirova informs on Boriskin, Boriskin informs on me, but who is there to inform on Alanya?" He grinned at her. "You, of course. It makes sense."

She grinned. "Ingenious."

He carved a path through the jostling crowd to where passengers were replenishing their teakettles with *kipyatok*, boiling water from the station samovar. He filled a tea flask and poured a drink for them into a *kruzhka*, the enameled metal mug that all travelers carried. They took it over to a quieter spot near the station railing. As far as the eye could see, a wide flat plain spread in every direction, dotted with the hunched figures of *kolkhoz* workers and a few straggling cattle seeking shade in the long evening shadows. The land shimmered in a lazy golden haze as if it had all the time in the world.

"Have I told you that you look lovely today?" Mikhail let his eyes feast on Sofia openly at last, as he watched her sip the tea.

"You did mention something similar earlier this morning," she laughed. "Thank you for the dress."

"If I tell you I chose it because it matches your eyes, will you scoff at me?"

"Definitely."

"Okay, the truth is that I grabbed the first garment off the top of the pile in the factory storeroom."

She looked at him, her blue eyes the exact shade of the cornflowers on the dress, and he could see she didn't believe a word of it.

"That's more like it," she smiled, and something about the mischievous sideways glance she gave him made the hour he'd spent yesterday, searching out a style and size of dress and jacket that would be perfect for her, worth every second. When he'd handed over the leather satchel to her last night, she had grown soft in the moonlight, seeming to melt inside. It was obvious she was unaccustomed to receiving gifts.

"Tell me about this conference I'm supposed to be reporting on," she said.

"No, that's far too dreary. Let's talk instead about escaping from our chaperons in Leningrad and taking a stroll along the banks of the Neva and through the Field of Mars with you looking like a breath of summer, and we'll stop for a beer and—"

"Mikhail!" She was frowning at him. "Tell me about the conference. I need to be prepared. It's"—she glanced back at the train, at the dirty windows and the pair of spectacles staring out from behind them—"it's how I stay safe."

Mikhail felt a sharp surge of anger scald his throat. He was able to laugh off any threats to his own safety, but not to hers. The fact that Sofia felt in danger from these people he employed made him want to sack them on the spot.

"Very well," he said seriously. "There are some points you will be expected to remember. First of all, you must express admiration for the much vaunted 'liquidation of unemployment.' The expansion of industry has provided jobs for all. This achievement will be mentioned over and over again."

"But Mikhail"—her eyes abruptly lost their summer blue—"I've seen the unemployed people begging in the streets and lining up hopelessly at the factory gates."

He gave her a sardonic smile. "Now that, my dear Sofia, is the kind of comment that will get you tossed into prison for anti-Soviet incitement before you can blink an eye."

She stared at him, and nodded. "Tell me more."

"No mention of hoarding of coins because the paper rouble is worth nothing. Or of the rampant inflation. Or the wholesale shortage of food and goods because the Kremlin in its wisdom is disposing of Russia's wheat, fish, eggs, butter, petroleum, wood pulp—shall I go on?—to foreign markets at absurdly low prices to gain hard currency or—"

She reached up, pretending to brush a smut of engine soot from his cheek, and let her finger soothe the heat from his skin.

"Enough," she murmured.

He silenced his tongue.

"Your speech to the committee," she said softly, "avoids these issues, I assume."

"Oh yes," he growled, "I can lie with the best of them."

"Good. I was just checking."

"Remember, Sofia, they look for scapegoats when things go wrong. They attacked Bukharin and even Rykov, though he was chairman of the Council of People's Commissars. Just sit there with your pen and pad, take notes, look serious, and say nothing."

She nodded, her blond hair bobbing skittishly in the last of the sunlight. "Now tell me," she said, totally flooring him with that sideways smile of hers, "what are the arrangements for sleeping tonight?"

He pulled a face and gave a savage snort. "Not good, I'm afraid."

MIKHAIL stubbed out a cigarette and lit another. It burned a hole in the darkness of the flat wilderness around him. He was leaning against the wall of the hotel where they were spending the night, though *hotel* was really too grand a word for it—a wooden building packed with rooms the way a matchbox is packed with matches, all crushed against each other, all occupants carefully supervised and accounted for to OGPU.

He'd been a fool to bring her on this trip, to risk her safety, but to leave her behind in Tivil would have been like leaving part of himself behind. And she'd wanted to come, she'd made that clear with a kiss. He inhaled deeply, recalling the sweet softness of her lips on his. The night was dark now; clouds had edged their way down from the north, and he wondered if Sofia was asleep in her bed. Or wide awake, listening to the snores of Alanya Sirova in the bed beside her, and thinking of . . . what? *What do you think of, Sofia?*

Mikhail couldn't sleep, so he'd come outdoors in the hope that the night wind would flush the unwanted memories from his mind. It was always the same when he traveled to Leningrad. It was like traveling back in time, back to his boyhood in St. Petersburg. The train that carried him westward and then north toward the Gulf of Finland seemed to unravel his life with each turn of its wheels, as though pulling at the delicate thread he'd used to stitch the years together. The experience was so vivid that it startled him. The *whoosh* of steam from the engine and the echoing sob of its whistle through ancient forests stirred up images from the past and set them tumbling through his mind.

He didn't want to eat. And he couldn't sleep. The important conference lay ahead of him, but his thoughts were elsewhere, just when he needed to be sharp. Two more days of this journey to Leningrad, pistons thundering beneath him as loud as in his head, and pointless delays when the train would be shunted into sidings for idle hours at a time. Two more days to drag his senses back to the present.

Which meant only two more days of a soft arm at his side and blue cornflowers spilling onto his knee. But what then?

THIRTY-FOUR

*H*OW do they do it?

Sofia gazed around at the sea of faces, at the concentration on them. Did they really care so much, or was it all an act?

The great dome above the hall was supported by massive pale marble pillars, and beneath it rows and rows of packed seats curved in a wide sweeping arc. Sofia tried to concentrate on the speeches. But it was impossible. However eagerly she made herself start to listen to each new delegate up on the rostrum, boredom invariably seeped in as lists of production figures and target levels were recited for each *raion*. The only rousing moments came when Party slogans were hammered out with fists on the lectern and a thousand voices roared back from the floor as one.

The pillars. Her eyes were drawn to them instead of to the pad on her lap. Bone-white pillars. Tall and graceful, like pine trees stripped of bark. She couldn't keep her eyes off them, and each one made her think of Anna, still out there in the forest, her blade slicing through the flesh of a tree. *Don't stop, dear Anna. Breathe, my friend, breathe.* She swallowed the rage that rose in her throat at the injustice of it, but she must have made some noise because in the seat next to her Alanya Sirova turned and studied her.

"Are you all right?" Alanya asked.

"I'm fine."

Still Alanya stared at her. "You haven't written down anything for the last half hour." She nodded at Sofia's blank page.

Slowly Sofia turned her head to look into the suspicious brown eyes. The two women's communication with each other had so far been stilted, despite sharing a bedroom at night and being seated next to each other for the last six hours in the conference hall. Sofia could feel Alanya's curiosity like something palpable crouched between them and was amused by her sudden show of concern.

"Comrade Sirova," she said in a muted tone, giving it just the right touch of condescension, "I am listening. This delegate on the platform"—she gestured to the bearded man in the shabby brown suit speaking so passionately in favor of engineering expansion—"is telling us something that is crucial to our understanding of how the Levitsky factory can be moved forward, step by step, until it is able to surpass even our Great Leader's targets of technological development and progression. It is essential to think things through first and write afterward." She narrowed her gaze. "Do you understand me?"

"Yes, comrade, yes, I do." The sleek brown head nodded eagerly.

"And," Sofia continued, "I advise you to bear that in mind—if you want to progress further than a lowly secretary. I'm sure you have the ability to do so."

The ambitious eyes gleamed behind the thick lenses, and her sallow cheeks took on a pinkish tinge. "*Spasibo*, comrade. I promise I will in future."

Sofia allowed herself a faint smile. That was Comrade Sirova dealt with. She turned back to the pillars, to the pine trees.

IT was out among the pine trees one hot mosquito-ridden afternoon that Sofia had learned from Anna about her visit to Maria, the woman who had been her governess as a child. Maria who, during all those years that Anna was living with the distant cousin in a village hundreds of miles away near Kazan, had never come for her. Never once wrote. Never got in touch. Nothing. As though Anna had ceased to exist. Anna had waited and waited, and pinched her own skin to make sure she was still real, always believing that one day Maria would come. Her lonely young heart clung to Maria's words, "I promise I'll come for you."

But she didn't come.

Now in the damp forests of a Siberian Work Zone, Anna shook her head. "I was foolish. I wouldn't let it go. So when the woman who had taken me in suddenly died—she was trampled by a bull when I was twenty-one—I spent a time grieving for the stern old vixen, and then I took the small amount of money she left me in her will, bought myself a train ticket and travel permit, and went in search of Maria. It took me months to get a seat on a train, but finally I traveled back to Leningrad."

Sofia was honing Anna's ax, squatting down among the wood chippings with a flat stone in front of her, keeping down below the eyeline of the guards. Anna was leaning back against a tree trunk, each breath wheezing as she spoke.

"Don't talk, Anna. Rest your poor lungs."

"No, you must know this. For when you go."

She didn't say where, just *go*. It wasn't something they talked about, but both knew it would be soon.

"Very well, tell me," Sofia said, one eye on the nearest guard. His back was turned to them at the moment.

Anna sighed with satisfaction. "I found the house."

She stopped as if that were enough, and when Sofia looked up she saw that Anna's eyes had closed, her thin chest struggling. Her lips were turning blue. Quickly Sofia drew from her pocket her last small scrap of black bread crushed with the pulp of pine seeds from the forest floor.

"Here, chew on it." She pushed it between her friend's lips.

Anna took it and chewed, until eventually she dragged a shallow breath into her lungs and then another. Slowly the rhythm returned.

"I found the house in Liteiny district," Anna whispered, "the one where Maria's brother, Sergei Myskov, and his wife, Irina, lived. It was just around the corner from the tap factory." She paused, resting a moment, her sunken blue eyes on Sofia's face. "I remembered the iron staircase and the *kolodets*, a courtyard with a well at its center. And there was a lion's head carved above the archway. It frightened me when I was young."

"Hey, you two." The guard had caught sight of them. "Get back to work."

"*Da*," Sofia called out. "Right away." She shifted her position, as if to do as ordered, and the guard turned away.

"Anna, there's no time now and you're not—"

But Anna put out her hand and seized Sofia's wrist. Her grip was still strong. "Listen to me. It's important. You must remember this, Sofia. It will help you."

Sofia lifted her hand to wipe the sweat from her friend's gaunt face, but Anna swept it aside impatiently, and the flash in her blue eyes reminded Sofia of the old Anna.

"I'm fine," Anna hissed. "Just listen."

Sofia laid aside the ax and crouched beside her, attentive.

By the time I found the apartment building it was raining and I was wet through but I barely noticed, I was so excited at the prospect of seeing Maria again after nine years. When I knocked, the door to the apartment on the second floor was opened by a youth with wavy brown hair and ears that stuck out like a baby elephant's. I recognized him at once.

"Sasha?" I gasped. It was Sasha, Irina's son. He was about eleven then. "I'm a friend of your Aunt Maria."

"Tiotya Maria doesn't have friends."

What did he mean? Why didn't Maria have friends?

"Where does she live now, Sasha?"

"Here."

"Here?" This was too easy. "May I come in and see her?"

He stepped back and called over his shoulder, "Tiotya Maria, a visitor for you."

"Who is it, Sasha?"

It was Maria's voice. I rushed into the room and a pale-faced woman with white hair was sitting in a chair by the window. It was a much older Maria, but still my dearest governess.

"Maria," I breathed, "it's me."

A tremor ran through the silent figure, and then tears started to slide down her cheeks.

"*My Anna,*" she sobbed, and the fingers of one hand clawed at the air to draw me to her chair.

I clasped my arms around her neck while she touched my wet hair and murmured soft words against my cold skin.

"*Why didn't you come?*" I whispered the words. "*I waited for you.*"

Maria placed a shaky hand over her eyes. "*I couldn't.*"

"*Why didn't you write?*"

"*Aunt Maria had a stroke.*" It was Sasha's voice. I had forgotten he was even still in the room. "*It happened when she was tortured.*"

My thoughts beat panicked wings in my head. White hair? Maria could not be more than forty. Why white hair? Her eyes were still beautiful, still luminous brown, but over them hung a veil, gossamer fine, and behind it lay a world of bafflement and confusion. And there was the omission of rising to her feet to greet me. It all made agonizing sense.

"*Oh Maria, my poor dearest Maria. Why didn't you ask your brother Sergei to write to me? I'd have come . . .*"

Maria frowned a lopsided frown and murmured, "*Hush.*" She glanced quickly in Sasha's direction and back again to my face. "*It's not important.*"

"*Of course it's important. I would have taken care of—*"

"*No, no, not you, Anna Fedorina,*" Sasha interrupted roughly. "*My parents would never have written to you or wanted you in this house.*" He stood with his hands on his hips and his chin jutting forward. "*Aunt Maria suffered the stroke when she was tortured on account of her connection with your family, with you and your father and your father's friends. I grew up on the story of how her hair turned white overnight in the prison cells.*"

His words caught like fishhooks in my throat.

"*Your father was declared a class enemy and—*"

"*Shut up,*" I shouted.

"*Leave us, Sasha,*" Maria moaned. "*Please.*"

He glared at me for a long moment, then marched out of the room, slamming the door behind him. Quiet settled on the room after that. Maria dismissed my apologies for what she'd suffered, so instead I kissed her, told her I loved her and would take care of her now that I had found her again. I made us tea from the samovar in the corner of the cramped room, and then I pulled up a stool and told tales of my long years in Kazan. As the daylight started to fade from the room, I risked the question that burned inside me.

"*Did you ever hear what happened to Vasily?*"

Maria laughed, soft and low like in the old days. "How you worshipped that boy! You used to trail around after him like a little shadow. Do you recall how you used to make him dance with you? Or maybe you've forgotten that."

"No, I haven't forgotten."

"And he adored you." She chuckled again. "He came looking for you, you know."

My heartbeat stopped. "When? When did he come?"

"I'm not sure. I can't . . . Think, stupid brain, think." Maria rapped her knuckles against her own forehead, denting the pallid flesh. "I forget every-thing now."

I stroked the spot soothingly. "It's all right, there's no rush. Take your time. Can you remember what he looked like?"

The crooked mouth smiled its crooked smile. "Oh yes, he was tall. Grown into a man."

"And still as handsome?"

"Yes, still as handsome. He came twice and told me he'd changed his name for safety."

"To what?"

Again the look of bewilderment.

"Did you tell him where I was, Maria?"

"No, my love, I'm sorry, I couldn't remember where you were."

"Was he . . . disappointed?"

"Oh, yes. That's why he came twice. To see if I had remembered." Tears filled her eyes. "But I couldn't."

I hugged her close and whispered without hope, "Where is he living now?"

To my surprise Maria nodded. "He wrote it down."

From a large battered canvas bag that lay at her feet she withdrew a Bible, its cover well worn to a faded black. Tucked inside its pages was a scrap of gray envelope and on it printed in black letters: Mikhail Pashin, Levitsky Factory, Dagorsk. Home: Tivil Village, near Dagorsk. But just as I was holding the piece of paper in my hand, the door to the room crashed open and uniforms marched into the small space, their leather boots and broad shoulders using up all the air in the room. Five stern faces turned on me. Behind them, with the sternest face of all, stood eleven-year-old Sasha.

"Anna Fedorina?" The officer wore a black Cossack mustache that seemed to bristle and threaten, but his eyes were calm. "You are Anna Fedorina,

daughter of Doktor Nikolai Fedorin, who has been declared an enemy of the people."

"But that was years ago."

The officer gave me a smile that was not a smile. "We don't forget. Or forgive."

Strong hands seized my arms and dragged me off my feet.

"Anna!" Maria screamed with all the power of her frail lungs, her one good hand clawing the air again. "Let me kiss her, let me kiss my Anna goodbye."

The soldiers hesitated, then thrust me at Maria's chair. Maria clamped her arm fiercely around my neck and buried her face in my hair, kissing my cheek, my jaw, my ear, all the time whispering, whispering, whispering. So that when the rough hands stole me from Maria's grasp, I was aware of nothing but the words that seemed to be stuck like burrs in my brain.

"His mother's jewels. In a box. He's buried them in the church under St. Peter's feet. He told me. In the village where he lives."

THIRTY-FIVE

Leningrad
July 1933

"WHERE are you going, Comrade Morozova?"

Sofia had risen to her feet in the conference hall because she couldn't bear it inside this hothouse of lies and paranoia a moment longer. All the promises of quotas that were impossible to achieve, and the incessant ranting against wreckers and saboteurs, set off a griping pain in her stomach, as though rats were chewing in there.

Alanya Sirova's expression was poised halfway between curiosity and suspicion. "Are you leaving?"

"*Da*. Yes, I have work to do."

"But I thought . . ."

"While Comrade *Direktor* Pashin and Comrade Boriskin are away reporting to the committee"—Sofia tossed her pad and pen on the lap of Alanya's navy-blue suit—"I want you to take notes of everything that goes on here."

The secretary's cheeks glowed pink with pleasure. "*Spasibo*, comrade. I won't let you down, I promise."

It made Sofia want to cry.

★ ★ ★

*T*HE streets of Leningrad had changed. As Sofia walked their pavements she began to wish she hadn't come back. The tall pastel-painted houses with ornate window frames and wrought-iron balconies, which she had once thought so smart and elegant, had been transformed into sooty drab buildings crammed full of sooty drab people who scurried to the bread lines and the candle lines and the kerosene lines, where they waited for hours like sheep in a slaughter-house. Their clothes were shabby and their chins tucked tight to their chests. Against the cool breeze that skidded off the canals? Or against the expression in other people's eyes? Suspicion was so strong in the air, she could smell it.

As she hurried down Nevsky, the trams rattled past her, packed with gray empty faces. The new factories pumped a thick filth into the air that settled like black widow's weeds over the buildings, and when Sofia leaned eagerly over the bridge as she had as a child to catch sight of the Fontanka, the stench that drifted up from it caught at her throat and made her eyes water. What were they dumping in there?

She was here to search out the apartment where Anna had lived briefly with Maria and Irina, but she had no exact address to go on. She walked fast along the bank of the Neva, over the little humpback Gorbatiy Mostik and then turned left across Liteiny Bridge. Once in the Liteiny district she set about combing the spider's web of streets with their dismal tenements, but it took her an hour to find it: the tap factory. It was still there.

What else had Anna told her?

An iron staircase. A *kolodets*, a courtyard with a well, and a lion's head carved above an arch. But the dark rows of crumbling tenements all seemed to have iron staircases to the upper stories and courtyards where ragged children crawled among the woodpiles. It was only when she spotted the lion's head above one of the arches that Anna's voice pulsed in her ears. *You must remember this, Sofia. It will help you.* She walked the street twice just to make sure no other lions lurked nearby and then approached the entrance. It was like all the others, no paint, with cracked and swollen woodwork. She lifted the big knocker and rapped on the door. Her hand was shaking.

★ ★ ★

A woman's wrinkled face peered around the door.

"Yes?"

"I'm looking for Maria Myskova. I believe she may live here."

"Who wants to know?"

The woman was wrapped in a thick woolen headscarf despite the heat of the day and wore a dark brown blanket draped around her shoulders, so that in the gloomy hallway her head appeared disembodied. Her eyebrows were drawn together above what was clearly a glass eye, but her other brown eye was bright and intensely curious.

"Who are you, girl?" she demanded, holding out a hand in a fingerless glove for identification papers.

Sofia stood her ground without giving her name. "Maria used to live here with Comrade Sergei Myskov and his wife and child. On the second floor. Do you know where they are now?"

"At work."

"You mean they still live here? When will they be home?"

"Who wants to know?" The woman's eye gleamed.

"Are you the *dezhurnaya*?"

"*Da*. Yes, I am." She unwrapped the blanket enough to reveal an official red armband.

Everyone knew that caretakers were paid informers of the secret police, keeping a watchful eye on the comings and goings of the inhabitants of their building for OGPU, and the last thing Sofia wanted was to rouse those wasps from their nest.

"I'll come back later if you'll tell me when they—"

The crash of a piece of crockery and a man's voice raised in a curse erupted from somewhere at the back of the hallway. The woman swiveled around with a squeal and scurried back into the shadows toward a door that was half open. Sofia didn't hesitate. She stepped inside and leaped up the stairs two at a time, trying not to inhale the smell of boiled cabbage and unwashed bodies that clung to the walls. It brought the stink of the barrack hut at Davinsky camp crashing into her head.

When she reached the second-floor landing, she turned to her left, where a boarded window let in a few dim streaks of light. To her surprise, packed tight against the wall of the dingy corridor were three beds, low and narrow. One was tidily made with a folded quilt, the second was a jumble of stained sheets, and the third was occupied by a bald man stinking of vomit, whose skin was yellow as butter. This was Sofia's first experience of the *communalka*, the shared apartments where several families were crammed into the space that had once belonged to only one.

She squeezed past the first two and spoke in a whisper to the man in the third.

"Do you need anything . . . ?"

It was a stupid question. Of course the poor wretch needed something, something like a decent bed in a decent hospital with decent food and medicines and clean decent air to breathe, but he didn't reply. His eyes were closed. Maybe he was dead. She felt she should tell somebody. But who? On tiptoes, so as not to wake him, she crept to the door at the end of the landing and knocked quickly. The door opened at once. A dark-haired woman stood in front of her, shorter than herself but broad across the bust. Sofia smiled at her.

"*Dobriy vecher,*" she said. "Good evening. I am Anna Fedorina."

*S*HE'S dead. Maria died two years ago. Another stroke."

The words were stark, but Irina Myskova spoke them gently.

"I'm sorry, Anna, I know how much she cared for you. It's so sad that she didn't live to see you released."

"Tell Sasha that."

The woman's face stiffened at the mention of her son. His part in Anna's arrest clearly sat uneasily on Irina's heart, and she ran a hand across her large bosom, stilling whatever turmoil erupted in there. Her clothes were neat but old, the material of her skirt darned in several places. The apartment was the same, clean and tidy with striped homemade *poloviki* rugs on the floor, but everything looked old and well-used. Only the white plaster bust of Lenin gleamed new and the bright red posters declaring FORWARD TOWARD THE VICTORY OF COMMUNISM and WE SWEAR, COMRADE LENIN, TO HONOR YOUR COMMAND. Sofia ignored them and looked across at the chair by the window. It was Maria's chair, and now it stood empty and solitary, clearly not used by the family anymore.

"Sasha was only doing his duty," Irina insisted loyally.

Sofia hadn't come here to argue. "Those times were hard and—"

"But you're looking well, Anna," Irina interrupted. She eyed Sofia's new dress and her shining blond hair thoughtfully. "You were pretty as a child, but now you've grown quite beautiful."

"*Spasibo.* Comrade Myskova, is there something of Maria's I could have? To remind me of her."

Irina's face relaxed. "Of course. Most of her possessions have gone . . . sold," she added self-consciously, "but Sergei insisted on keeping a few things back." She walked over to a cupboard and drew from it a book. "It's Maria's Bible." She offered it to Sofia. "Maria would have wanted you to have it, Anna."

"Thank you."

Sofia was touched by the gift. The feel of the book under her fingers, its pages so soft and well thumbed, raised a sudden sense of her own childhood and her own father's devotion to Bible study. She handled it with care.

"Thank you," she murmured again, and she moved toward the door.

"Wait, Anna." Irina came over and stood close. Her mouth twitched.

"What is it?" Sofia felt an odd rush of sympathy for this woman caught between her love for her son and her love for her husband's dead sister. Gently she said, "What's done is done, Irina. We can change the future but we can't change the past."

"*Nyet.* And I wouldn't wish to. But . . . if I can help you . . . I know from Maria that you were always fond of the Dyuzheyevs' boy."

"Vasily?"

"Did Maria tell you he came here once? He's going under a different name now."

"Yes. Mikhail Pashin. She said he came twice."

"I wasn't here, but I believe it was only once. Maria got confused sometimes. The other time it was a different man altogether who came to see her."

"Do you know who?"

"Anna, I think you should know that the man had come trying to find you."

"Me?"

"*Da*. It seems he was the young Bolshevik soldier, the one who shot your father and Vasily's mother. He was searching for you."

Sofia's heart seemed to hang loose in her chest. "Who was he?"

"That's the odd thing. He said he'd been sent to work in a village in the Urals."

"His name?"

"Maria wasn't any good at remembering, but she told Sasha the name and he remembered it."

"What was it?" She held her breath, and a sense of foreboding made her grow cold despite the heat in the apartment.

"Fomenko. Aleksei Fomenko."

MIKHAIL didn't sleep. The journey home was hard with no overnight stops. They slept sitting upright in their seats as the train plowed its way through the darkness, its lonely whistle startling the wolves as they prowled the forests. Rain fell spasmodically, pattering against the black windows like unseen fingers asking to be let in.

Mikhail quietly smoked one cigarette after another and tried not to move too much in his seat. Sofia's pale head lay on his shoulder, Alanya's dark one on the other. He didn't much care to be used as a pillow by the secretary and knew she would be embarrassed if she knew. Why Boriskin and Alanya had swapped seats, he wasn't sure, but he suspected it had something to do with the dressing-down he'd given his foreman for declaring too accurate a picture of the labor problems at the factory.

His foreman had let him down badly. What was the point of bemoaning the lack of a skilled workforce in a peasant community when even a cabbagehead like Boriskin knew that such complaints would lose them important orders? And, more crucially, lose them the vital supply of raw materials? God knew there was enough friction at the conference without adding to it needlessly. That was the trouble with some of these blasted jumped-up union men; they had no idea how to . . .

He stopped himself. No point going over it all again. He'd have to deal with Boriskin's idiocy—or was it willful incompetence intended to make Mikhail himself look bad?—back in the office. Not tonight.

Tonight he'd had enough. Instead he brushed his cheek across the soft silk of Sofia's hair and marveled that even with the stink of his own cigarettes and a fat cigar in the seat opposite, her hair still smelled fresh and sweet. Its fragrance reminded him of bubbling river water, though he wasn't sure why. He listened for her breathing but could hear nothing above the thunder of the wheels beneath him.

His own part in the conference had gone smoothly. The report he'd delivered to the committee had been well received—it could hardly be otherwise, considering the production figures he was presenting to the hatchet-faced bastards—and his speech to the delegates in the hall had been suitably dull and steeped in boring numbers. No one had listened, but everyone had applauded and congratulated him at the end. That was the way it worked. *You protect my back, I'll protect yours.* Mikhail took a long frustrated drag on his cigarette. No, he couldn't complain about the conference. It was the rest of it that disturbed him on a much deeper level. The way Alanya attached herself to Sofia and stuck tight as a tick to her side so that it was impossible for him to make time alone with Sofia. And then there was the small matter of her disappearance.

Damn it. Where did she go?

It was late in the evening before she returned, and to explain her absence he'd made up some claptrap about her attending a dinner with the members of the Party elite. But that had backfired because when she reappeared, Alanya and bloody Boriskin had both fussed over her like mother hens and asked who had been at the dinner and what they'd had to eat. He chuckled to himself at the memory. Sofia had handled it brilliantly. She'd given Mikhail that slow mischievous smile of hers, then put a finger to her lips as she shook her head at Alanya.

"No details, Comrade Sirova. Wait till you are invited to such an event, and then you will learn for yourself."

"Of course, comrade. You're right."

Boriskin nodded pompously, and Mikhail had to fight to keep a straight face, but nothing was the same after that. In some indefinable way, she withdrew into herself. Oh yes, she still slid him secret smiles and brushed her shoulder against his jacket or let her fingers entwine with his when no one was looking. But it wasn't the same. And on several occasions he caught her gazing at him, when she thought he wouldn't notice, with an expression in her eyes that frightened him. It was as if a light had been turned off.

What had happened to her during those missing hours?

He eased Alanya off his shoulder and back onto her own headrest, then turned and gently kissed the top of Sofia's head.

"Stay, my love, stay with me," he whispered.

He stroked her hand, running his thumb over the tight white scars, and lifted them to his lips. They felt smooth and slippery against his tongue. As he kissed them, her fingers came to life and curled around his jaw, their tips stroking his skin with a slow sensuous touch that sent a fierce heat rippling through him.

"Mikhail," she whispered, "kiss me."

While the rest of the carriage slept, he took her beautiful face in his hands and kissed each delicate part of it, her eyes, her nose, her cool forehead, the sweep of her chin, even the sweet tips of her pearly ears. She uttered a soft little whimper. Finally he kissed her lips and tasted her. And knew it was a taste he could never give up.

THIRTY-SIX

*P*YOTR put on a clean white shirt, dusted off his shoes, and combed his hair. He thought about what he was about to do. It frightened him a little. He licked his teeth to moisten them. In the kitchen he cut himself a slice of black bread, but his stomach was too churned up to eat, so instead he drank a glass of water and left the house.

Each person must be reborn. Each person must be taught to rethink.

That was what it said in the Communist pamphlet he kept under his pillow. That was what Yuri had explained to him in detail today at Young Pioneers.

Everyone will have a new heart.

Yes, Pyotr understood that. Unless you erased the old and the bad, how could there be room for the new and the good? Which was why he was going to speak to Chairman Aleksei Fomenko. She'd be grateful in the end, the fugitive woman, he was sure she would. When she had her new heart.

★ ★ ★

*P*YOTR knocked on the black door that belonged to Chairman Fomenko, making a spider scuttle sideways across the wooden panel. When he received no answer he knocked again, but still no response. He stood on the doorstep so long his shirt grew sticky and he watched the sun slide behind the mountain ridge and the shadows creep up the street toward him, as the workers started leaving the fields.

"Hey, Pyotr, what you doing?"

It was Yuri, his face flushed from running.

"I'm waiting for the chairman."

"What for?"

"I've something to tell him."

Yuri kicked a stone with his toe. "Must be important."

"It is."

Yuri's eyes brightened with interest. "What's it about?"

Pyotr almost told him. It was on the tip of his tongue, the words to betray Sofia. He wanted so much to spit them out of his mouth— *She's dangerous*—but a strange quivering feeling in the depth of his stomach held him back. He knew that everything Yuri had said this morning about needing people to *rethink* was right, it made sense. Of course it did. He wanted to do what was right, but now that it came to doing it, he wasn't so sure. Once out there, the words would gain a kind of life of their own and he could never take them back. If he told Yuri, Yuri would tell the chairman, the chairman would tell the OGPU, and they would march in and arrest her and then . . . His mind couldn't go further.

"Well?" Yuri urged. "What's it . . . ?"

At that moment Anastasia came hurtling down the dusty street and skidded to a halt in front of them. Trickles of sweat were carving tracks through the dirt on her thin face. She often helped her father with hoe or sickle in the fields, and it was obvious that she'd just come from there. Her fingernails were filthy.

"What are you doing here, Pyotr?" She grinned at him. "Not in trouble, are you?"

"Of course not," Pyotr objected.

"He's got secret information to tell the chairman," Yuri said grandly.

"Really?" The girl's eyes widened. "What is it?"

Pyotr felt himself cornered. "It's about a girl in this village," he said in a rush. "About her anti-Soviet activity."

To his astonishment, tears leaped into Anastasia's eyes and she started to edge fearfully away from him.

"I must go home now," she blurted out, and she ran off down the road, her rat's-tail hair flying out behind her, dust kicking up behind her heels. Quite clearly Pyotr could see the bulges under her faded yellow blouse at the back where it was tucked into her shorts. The four bulges jiggled as she ran.

"Yuri," he said to distract his friend's attention from noticing them, "I'm not waiting any longer."

Anastasia had stolen potatoes. Only two weeks ago a woman in a village the other side of Dagorsk had been sentenced to five years in one of the labor camps for stealing half a *pud* of grain from her *kolkhoz*. Pyotr suddenly felt cold, and dismay spilled into his mind. If he told Chairman Fomenko about Sofia, wasn't it his duty to tell about Anastasia too? He looked up and saw his father striding up the street toward him.

"What are you up to, boys?"

"Nothing much."

"You're standing on the chairman's doorstep for nothing much?"

But instead of being annoyed, Papa was laughing and his face was free from the usual shadows it wore after a day's work. Ever since he'd come back from the conference yesterday, he'd been in a good mood. It must have gone really well in Leningrad.

"Good evening, Comrade Pashin. *Dobriy vecher*," Yuri said politely. "Have you heard if there's any news yet about the sacks of grain that went missing?"

That was typical, always digging around for information. But Papa wasn't pleased, and his face lost its smile.

"I know nothing at all about that. Come, Pyotr," Papa said firmly, taking hold of his son's arm. "We're going to Rafik's house."

They walked up the road in an awkward silence.

"Why do you dislike him, Papa?"

"Dislike who?"

"Yuri."

"Because I don't want the young fool turning you into him."

"No, Papa. I think for myself."

His father halted in the middle of the street and turned to him. "I know you do, Pyotr. I've seen the way you make your choices after working out what's right and what's not." He smiled. "I admire that."

Pyotr felt a kick of pride. And it must have shown on his face because his father seized him in his arms and held him tight against his chest as though his heart could pump his own blood into his son's veins.

*I*T was the first time Pyotr had ever been inside the gypsy's *izba*. It smelled funny, and half the forest appeared to be dangling from the roof beams. He hung back near the door, unwilling to go too deep.

"*Dobriy vecher,*" Papa said to Rafik. "Good evening."

"*Dobriy vecher,* Pilot. And good evening to you too, Pyotr."

The gypsy was swallowed up by a huge maroon armchair and was grinning at Pyotr, so that his eyes were crinkled at the edges. "How's the colt up at the stable?"

"He bit Priest Logvinov today."

Rafik laughed. "He has spirit, that one. Like you."

Pyotr gave a quick nod. The fugitive woman was seated opposite Zenia at the table, and the gypsy girl had laid out a row of playing cards, the rest of the pack still in her hand, but her black eyes smiled a welcome. Pyotr studied the cards with interest. They were like no others he'd ever seen. Instead of the usual numbers on them they had pictures, and not just boring old kings and queens. There was a hangman and an angel with widespread wings. Pyotr slid a step closer.

"I'm pleased to see you're feeling better, Rafik," Papa said.

"Much better."

"Good."

Then his father turned courteously to the two women at the table and gave them a small old-fashioned bow, which surprised Pyotr. Papa's eyes were gleaming with excitement. What was going on?

"Good evening, Sofia."

She swiveled in her chair, stretching out one of the long golden legs that Pyotr remembered from the forest. He had avoided looking at her face so far, but now he risked it, and immediately he wished he hadn't, because he couldn't look away. Her eyes were shining, deep blue and swirling with light the way he imagined the sea to be. Her lips opened a fraction when she looked up at Papa, just as Anastasia's did at school when she looked at Yuri's slice of bread and honey. As if she wanted to eat him. And Papa was doing the same. Pyotr felt an uncertain flutter of panic in his stomach. *Look away, look away.*

"I have a surprise for you all." His father turned to him. "For you too, Pyotr."

"What is it, Papa?"

"The *Krokodil* is coming to Dagorsk next week."

All sense of danger and fugitives vanished right out of Pyotr's head and he gave a whoop of delight that filled the room. "Can we go and see it, Papa? Which day? How long will it be here? Can we take Yuri too and . . . ?"

His father chuckled, "Slow down, boy. Yes, of course we'll go and see it." He turned back to the others in the room and said with that formal little bow again, "You're all invited."

"I'll come," Zenia said at once and dealt another card. A golden chalice.

Rafik shook his head and ran a hand roughly through his thick black hair. "I don't ever leave Tivil, but the rest of you go and enjoy yourselves."

"What is the *Krokodil*?" Sofia asked.

"It's an airplane," Pyotr explained excitedly. "One that's painted to look like a crocodile."

Mikhail nodded and sketched its outline in the air. "It's one of the squadron of Tupolev PS-9s. They're part of Stalin's propaganda drive, and it flies around the country to demonstrate Soviet progress to the people. The idea is to give film shows and hand out leaflets and things like that. One of the Politburo's better ideas, we think, don't we, Pyotr?"

"Yes," Pyotr grinned.

"Pilot." It was the gypsy.

Something in the way he said it made everyone turn to look at Rafik. He'd left the chair and was standing rigidly in the center of the room. His hands were pressed to his temples as though holding in something that was trying to get out, and his black eyes looked sick.

"Pilot." This time it was a shout. "Get out of here, now, quickly. Run."

Instantly Zenia was at his side.

"Tell us, Rafik."

"They're coming for him, to seize him. Run, Mikhail."

The air in the room changed. Pyotr almost could see it turn into a gray mist. Sofia leaped to her feet.

"Papa?" Pyotr cried out.

"Go, Mikhail," Sofia urged. "Go."

But his father didn't move. "What the hell do you mean, Rafik? Who on earth is coming for me?"

The door burst open with a crash. Uniforms streamed into the room.

THIRTY-SEVEN

THE cell door slammed shut behind Mikhail. The stench hit him like a blow to the face. How many men in here? Ten? Twenty? Thirty? In the semidarkness he couldn't tell, but there was no air to breathe, no place to sit, so he stood.

It was night, but a grubby blue lightbulb glimmered faintly behind a metal grille on the ceiling like a malevolent watchful eye over the prisoners. This was a different world he'd entered. His first instinct had been to lash out at his captors, and now he bore the rewards of that. A split lip, a rib that grated at each breath, a kneecap booted out of place.

Fool, he'd been a bloody fool not to control his temper. But the soldiers took no notice when he pointed out that they were making a terrible mistake and that he'd done nothing to warrant arrest. Then the sight of Pyotr being slapped like a puppy for clinging to his father had brought his walls of control tumbling down. He fought to remember now, snatching at images that kept fading from his grasp.

Most clearly he could summon up Pyotr's frightened young face and Sofia's urgent mouth arguing with the officer, her eyes blazing. Hazier was Rafik, silent and remote, and Zenia at the table with her head in her hands, hiding behind her mane of black hair. And then there was the memory of Sofia begging. It drifted in and out. But oddly it wasn't the soldiers she was pleading with, it was Rafik, imploring him for something, down on her knees and begging. Then Pyotr's panicked shout . . .

Pyotr. *Dear God, who will take care of my son?*

As he stood upright by the door, his back away from its foul surface, he shut his eyes. In the silence he heard a *drip-drip-drip*, the cell walls running with damp, and a sudden movement. A huddled figure trampled over sleeping forms and there were cries of "bastard" and "shithead," but most didn't move, locked in their own despair and nightmares. The figure reached the overflowing slop bucket only just in time. The stench worsened.

Earlier the prison guards had taken pleasure in their work, as they'd ripped out his bootlaces and tossed aside his belt. Stripped him naked. He knew its purpose was to humiliate and belittle, to humble his arrogant subversive soul so that the interrogator's job would be that much easier when it came to the time for questions. In return he had given nothing but stone-hard hatred. They'd thrown his clothes back at him and marched him with hands clasped behind his back down long gray corridors to this underground overcrowded cell. Into this different world.

This was the new reality and he'd better get used to it. A cold-eyed unblinking reality. Stuck in this wretched hole. He would still be here tomorrow, and the next tomorrow, and the tomorrow after that. He spat on the floor, spitting out his fear, and he struggled for something clean and cool and strong to hold on to, and he found a pair of eyes. Eyes that looked at you straight, blue as a summer sky and bright with laughter. He drew them to him and filled every part of his mind with them, even the dark rotten places where he didn't like to look. And he felt the claws that were raking his insides grow blunt and lifeless.

"Sofia," he whispered. "Sofia."

SOFIA stood on line. Hour after hour. Till her feet went numb and her heart ached and her hand itched to bang on the hatch to demand attention. The long L-shaped office was painted green and smelled of disinfectant, but someone had placed a vase of vivid red flowers on the windowsill. Most of the people in the line were women: wives, mothers, sisters, daughters, all in search of their loved ones. Some with desperate eyes and panicked faces, others with the patience of the dead, shuffling forward with no hope.

So why come, Sofia wondered?

But in her heart she knew. You hold on with every sinew left in you because if you don't, what is there? Nothing. You lie down and die, that's what. And if you die, they win. *No. Nyet.* She said it aloud in the room. *No. Nyet.* Others stole a surprised glance at her, but she ignored them and turned to Mikhail's son at her side, a slight silent figure who had barely spoken a word all day.

"Pyotr."

He lifted his head. His brown eyes were gaping holes of misery.

"Pyotr, are you hungry? Would you like some bread?"

She spoke quietly to avoid the envious ears around her and held out a small slice of black bread wrapped in greasepaper that Zenia had pushed into her hand before Sofia left the house early this morning. He shook his head. His fists were sunk deep in his pockets and his shoulders were hunched over, so that he looked like a wounded animal. She touched his arm but he flinched away.

"Not long now," she said.

"That's what you said two hours ago."

"Well, this time it must be true."

He looked at the twenty or more people ahead of them and at those behind them in a line that snaked out the door, then shrugged his young shoulders. She wanted to rub his bony back, to brush his hair off his face, to raise his head and coax some energy back into him. From the moment the troops drove off with Mikhail in the black prison van, the boy had lost his hold on who he was. He had turned gray, empty, colorless. Sophia had seen too many like that in the camps, seen the gray slowly darken and turn black and the black turn to death. Or worse than death, to nothingness.

She seized his shoulder and shook him till she saw a flash of annoyance in response.

"Better," she snapped. "Your father is in prison. He's not dead and he's not in a labor camp. Not yet. So don't you dare give up on him, do you hear me?"

"Yes."

"Say it."

"Yes, I hear you."

"Better. Very soon now we'll find out exactly what he's accused of." She glanced over at the hatch with impatience. "If ever that snail-faced bastard decides to speed things up."

An old woman was standing in front of the uniformed official, tears running down her cheeks, trying to thrust a brown paper package through the hatch. "Give him this," she was sobbing, "give my boy—"

"No parcels," the bored official rapped out and slammed down the shutter.

Pyotr looked frightened. Sofia touched his arm, and this time he didn't pull away.

"Your father is a valuable worker for the state, Pyotr. They won't waste his knowledge and expertise by—"

"He's not my father," Pyotr shouted at her, his cheeks suddenly bright red with shame. "He's a thief. He deserves to be locked up."

"NAME?"

"I'm inquiring about Mikhail Antonovich Pashin. He was taken from Tivil last night, but—"

"Who are you?"

"I'm here with his son, Pyotr Pashin."

"Papers?"

"These are Pyotr's."

"And yours?"

"I'm just a friend. I'm helping Pyotr find out what—"

"Your name?"

"Sofia Morozova."

"Papers?"

"Here. It's my resident's permit at the Red Arrow *kolkhoz* in Tivil, though I don't see why I—"

"Wait."

The shutter slammed shut.

SOFIA."

"No need to whisper, Pyotr. It's all right, we're outdoors now. No one can overhear."

"I know what happens when a person is arrested."

"Do you?"

"Yes. It happened to Yuri's uncle. The person is interrogated, sometimes for months, and if he's innocent he's freed, so . . . Why are you laughing?"

"No reason. Go on."

"So do you think Papa will be freed?"

"The bastards wouldn't tell us anything today, where he is or what he's charged with. But I insisted he's innocent."

"So he'll be freed?"

Sofia's heart went out to the boy. She swung him to face her, her hands pinning the slender bones of his shoulders.

"He'll be set free," she told him fiercely. "Your father is a good man. Don't ever believe he's not, and don't ever disown him again in my hearing."

His cheeks colored scarlet, but his brown eyes didn't drop away. "He's not my father."

"Pyotr, don't you dare say such a thing."

Still the brown eyes stared miserably into hers, but his voice lowered to a whisper. "He's not. Ask Rafik. My father was the miller in Tivil. Six years ago my mother ran off with a soldier to Moscow and my father burned down the mill with himself inside it."

"Oh Pyotr."

"I had no one, no family. My father was labeled a *kulak* even though he was dead, so no villager would help me. The authorities were going to send me to an institution." He stopped and dragged a hand across his eyes. "But Mikhail Pashin adopted me. He was new to the village and he didn't even know me, but he took me in."

Sofia drew Pyotr to her and gently stroked his hair.

"He'll be set free," she whispered. "I promise."

★　★　★

*N*AME?"

"I am Mikhail Antonovich Pashin."

"Occupation?"

"*Inzhenir.* Engineer First Class. And *direktor fabriki.* Factory manager."

"Which factory?"

"The Levitsky factory in Dagorsk. We make clothes and military uniforms. It is a loyal factory with dedicated workers. This month we exceeded our quota of—"

"Silence."

The peremptory order made the small interrogation room shrink further. There were no windows, just a bright naked lightbulb dangling from the ceiling. A metal table stood in the center, gray and scarred, two chairs behind it, another one alone and bolted to the floor in front of it. He stood very erect, focused on what he intended to say, and forced himself to swallow his anger. He felt it burn his throat as it sank to his stomach.

"Sit."

He sat.

"Place of birth?"

"Leningrad."

"Father's name?"

"Anton Ivanovich Pashin."

"Father's occupation?"

"Wheelwright. He was a man loyal to the Revolution and he died for it when—"

"Why did you leave the Tupolev aircraft factory?"

"I'm damned sure you know why I had to leave. It'll be written down in that fat file in front of you. So why bother to ask me?"

For the first time the man behind the desk showed a flicker of interest. He was tall and elegant, in a uniform that was well-cut and bore a row of medals.

"Answer my question." His eyes were slightly slanting, and he had small neat features that wouldn't have looked out of place on a woman.

"I left because I was forced to."

"And why was that?"

Keep it calm. Wrap the anger in a tight shell of control. Play it their way.

"Because I made an error. I criticized the system of delivery. I was so eager to build the ANT-4 airplane for our Great Leader that I allowed my disappointment at the delay in the arrival of some essential items of equipment to cloud my judgment."

"You admit you were wrong."

"I admit it freely. I didn't consider the magnitude of what our leader had undertaken. I know now that the railways had to be expanded first before they could deal with the loads they had to carry." He lowered his voice. "I was young and foolish."

The slanting eyes watched him for a long while, then with a sudden push of his chair, its legs squealing over the tiled floor, the interrogator rose and started to pace back and forth across the narrow space behind his desk.

"Don't lie to me, you filthy wrecker."

"I am no wrecker."

"Don't lie to me. You tried to wreck the Tupolev factory and now you are wrecking the Levitsky factory. Working against the forces of progress outlined for us all in the First *Piatiletka*. It is people like you who cause the shortage of goods."

"No, I told you we exceeded our targets."

"Who is paying you?"

That came as a shock. "Nobody."

"You were seen with a German diplomat in Moscow."

"That's a lie."

"I am the one who decides what is a lie and what is not," the examiner shouted across the desk. Spittle gathered in the corner of his mouth.

"This is a mistake."

"Are you saying that the Soviet Intelligence System is wrong?"

"Only that this is—"

"You were seen to wreck the Tivil Red Arrow *kolkhoz* grain procurement system."

"No."

"Yes. There are witnesses."

"Who?"

"Silence, scum. Who is paying you? Foreign powers are frightened of our great success. It is well known that they employ subversives to destroy our industry, subversives like you who commit treason and deserve to be shot."

Mikhail's blood was pounding. This was worse than he expected.

"Confess the truth, you piece of dog shit."

"I am innocent of these charges, I swear it. I am a Communist, loyal to Russia."

The interrogator stopped pacing as abruptly as he'd started. With exaggerated steps he returned to the desk and lowered himself onto the seat once more. His enraged expression melted away, and he looked at Mikhail with disappointment in the line of the mouth, disapproval in the narrowing of the eyes.

"Examiner, you are wrong. I swear to you I had nothing to do with the grain in Tivil."

The interrogator sighed and shook his head with studied regret. "Let's start again."

"I've told you everything."

"Name?"

"You know my name."

"Name?" A hand slammed on the desk. "Name?"

THIRTY-EIGHT

Davinsky Camp
July 1933

*I*T'S a railway."

"What?"

"They're saying we have to build the railway."

"Oh fuck."

Anna looked around the group of women lined up with her outside the medical hut. They'd already been waiting in the yard for an hour, stripped to their ragged underwear, an emaciated bunch with ribs popping out like elbows and knees wider than their thighs. Most had sores of some kind or other. A railway? How could this army of skeletons construct a railway?

"Why on earth would they want a railway up here anyway?" she asked. "There's nothing but trees."

"Trees and mosquitoes," one woman groaned, swatting an insect on her arm.

Each year as soon as the surface snow melted in the forest, the area became a quagmire of marshy ground, covered by a constant layer of stagnant water where the huge mosquitoes loved to breed in their millions. They were the curse of the summer. Infected bites caused more deaths than anything else at this time of year.

"Gold," Nina said, and she went back to picking a thorn out of her thumb.

"What do you mean?"

"There's gold up here."

"Christ," a freckled girl from Leningrad exclaimed, "just tell me where."

"I heard they're opening another mine and transporting more male prisoners up here to work it."

The men's labor camp was only four versts away and was twice the size of the women's. They were the ones who felled the pines in the first place and hauled them down to the river when the women had finished trimming them. Throughout the summer great rafts of trunks floated downstream to the timber yards, and one of the most feared jobs was riding on them.

"Railwork is savage," Nina groaned.

"That's why they're putting us through this charade of a medical."

"What do they do?" the freckled girl asked.

"They just stand around gawping," Tasha sneered, "while a man in a white coat tells you to strip naked so he can pinch your buttocks to test your muscle tone and then listen to your lungs."

"And the swines prod you," Nina added, "in places they don't need to prod you."

Anna frowned at her. "Don't scare her, Nina."

The older woman shrugged. "That's nothing. Something to be scared of is what I heard the bastard shitheads did to one of the men who broke an ankle out in the forest the other day when a tree crashed on it."

"What?"

"The guards knew he was no use to them anymore, so they tied him naked to a tree and took bets on how long it would take him to die from mosquito bites." She leaned forward and lowered her voice to a whisper. "Apparently they settled in black swarms on his balls and—"

"Shut up, Nina," Anna snapped.

"Oh come on, I want to hear—"

"Scum!" A guard in the hut doorway waved a rifle in their direction. "Get in here. *Bistro!*"

At once they trooped silently into the hut, where a row of tables was set up. Behind each sat one of the favored prisoners who worked for the administration and achieved a status within the camp that brought them the first rung of power. They ate more and labored less. Anna was pushed toward a table where the favored prisoner had a bored expression on her face, but beside her sat a cheerful-looking man wearing metal-rimmed spectacles and a white coat. A stethoscope hung from his neck.

Behind them both stood a guard. Anna knew him at once and gave him a long sullen look. For a moment he rested his tongue between his teeth, then treated her to a slow interested smile.

"Strip," he ordered.

ANNA hated that guard more than any other. Each time their paths crossed, just the sight of his smug face and his thick greedy fingers made her feel as though she were part of some lesser species that he could stamp on whenever the mood took him. It made no difference whether she was clothed or not. His gaze on her flesh was sticky as slug slime slithering down her skin, and at times she had even scooped up handfuls of dirt from the ground and rubbed it over her arms and legs, rubbed it hard to rid herself of the slime. When she came out of the medical hut she did it again, grabbed the dirt and scrubbed. It gave her a strange level of relief, but it also made her smile because she knew, if Sofia were here, that she would have raised a skeptical eyebrow and given that low laugh of hers.

"It's what's inside that counts," she'd have said, flicking the grit from Anna's skin. "The outside—well, that's just onion peel."

It was with Sofia in the early spring before her escape that this particular guard hammered into Anna's mind the level of degradation they had reached. It was a time when the long winter nights were growing shorter and the dull skies, which for many bleak months had sagged so low they touched the tips of the pine trees, abruptly lifted. The sun was climbing higher each day and the air had begun to sparkle with a clarity that dazzled the eyes. Lungs stopped hurting, skin started to heal. Muscles became warmer, worked faster.

"Smoke break! *Perekur!*"

"Ax sharpening," Sofia shouted across the rows of felled trunks to the nearest guard. "For two."

"Bistro!" he grumbled. "Quickly!"

Sofia beckoned to Anna and led the way to the ditch dug out on the edge of the forest as a latrine for the hundreds of workers. Behind it lay a boulder that was still half buried in snow, and she slid easily down the other side of it into a steep-sided hollow at the bottom of which flowed a steady stream of meltwater. Immediately Sofia crouched at the water's edge, honing her ax blade with smooth strokes on one of the wet stones. She turned her head, not breaking the action, and smiled at Anna. It always astonished Anna, that smile, because it still contained so much hope. How had she kept it all in there hidden behind her cool blue eyes? Was there a secret store of it inside her thin chest?

"A guard is coming," Anna warned.

Sofia shrugged, her hands still scything the blade expertly across the stone.

"He likes to kill, this one," Anna said.

Only yesterday this same guard had clubbed to death a woman from the Tver region for no more than stumbling and sending the top branch from the pile in her arms crashing down on his foot. Sofia looked up toward the forest and made a strange little grimace as she saw that the guard had arrived on the boulder above them.

"What the fuck do you scum think you're doing?" His rifle was pointed at Anna's head. "I didn't give you bitches permission to stop to sharpen axes."

"It's our smoke break," Anna pointed out. "We're not wasting work time, and anyway we did ask permission."

"We want to work more efficiently for our Great Leader and Wise Teacher," Sofia said coldly. "We don't intend to hold back our brigade from meeting their norm."

The guard's eyes narrowed, and he pushed back his *shapka* hat with the tip of his rifle. Neither prisoner moved a muscle, and finally he nodded.

"Go ahead. *Bistro!*"

Anna knelt down beside Sofia and started to hone her blade, but she was nowhere near as good at it as Sofia. The ax was a sad and pathetic object with its dull chipped blade and its head bound in place by string and a scrap of wire, but the haft was strong and well shaped to the curve of a hand. Sofia took it from Anna with the flicker of a smile and again resumed the steady rhythmic sharpening of the steel on the flat wet rock, first one side, then the other. She made it look easy.

"Your fingers have the skills of a swordsmith," Anna murmured. They were long and muscular except for the two that were scarred.

"After my father was whipped to death," Sofia whispered under her breath, "I worked on my uncle's farm for years. But anyway I was the last of a line of seven daughters, so my father taught me the skills of the son he never had."

"No talking," the guard yelled, and he suddenly leaped down onto the stretch of shingle below, so that he was only half a dozen strides from them.

Anna saw him glance furtively back over his shoulder to ensure no one had followed, and immediately she knew he intended trouble. She stood quickly and faced him. He hadn't shaved this morning and his heavy jaw was dark and threatening, his eyes hungry. His nose was crooked, as though it had been broken at some time, and Anna experienced a strong urge to break it again—with her ax. Lazily he swung the point of the rifle till it was aimed at Sofia's unprotected back. Sofia must have sensed the threat, but she didn't move. Just her hands, *snick-snick-snick* as they sharpened. The guard licked his soft lips.

"I don't like you," he snarled at Sofia.

"I don't like you either," she answered softly without turning around. She might have been talking to the ax blade.

"Give me one good reason why I shouldn't put a bullet between your ribs."

Anna stepped quickly between them, blocking his view of the figure still at the water's edge.

"Ah, pretty one, so you want to play, do you? I tell you what." His mouth spread into a wide wolfish grin that revealed teeth as crooked as his nose. "I won't put a bullet through your disrespectful friend if you give me a kiss from those luscious red lips of yours."

Anna felt a hot rush of fury, less for the guard's abuse of her than for the fact that he made her want to kill him in cold blood, and that raging desire frightened her. She started to move toward him.

"*Nyet!* No, *nyet!*" It was Sofia. She was rising from the ground, uncurling like a snake, the ax already swinging in her hand.

But Anna threw herself forward before Sofia could reach him, clasped her arms around the guard's hard-muscled neck, and pressed her lips on his mouth. It tasted foul, of tobacco smoke and onions and acid lust. She wanted to spit, to bite, to rip his face off with her teeth. But his lips were opening under hers, yawning into a pair of cavernous jaws that started to devour her. She fought to pull away, but his arms were strong around her, jerking her body into hard contact with his. Their coats were bulky between them, but his hand pushed in, squeezing, pinching, prodding at her breast. His tongue rammed into her mouth, repulsive as a rat, huge and choking. She couldn't breathe.

"Enough!" Sofia's voice, ice cold.

Abruptly he was gone from Anna. His smell still clung to her body, but he had backed off and was staring at Sofia. She was standing with his own rifle in her hands, which she had snatched from his grip while his mind and his hands were in his trousers.

"Shoot him," Anna hissed.

"Hush," Sofia murmured soothingly. Her face was bone white, and a muscle was trying to tear itself loose under one eye. "Here," she said to the guard, throwing him the rifle.

Anna was sure he would shoot them both, but some deep part of him had lost its nerve and he didn't. He stared grimly into Sofia's cold eyes, spat an oath at them both, and then leaped onto the boulder and disappeared back to the Work Zone.

Anna bent over and vomited the taste of him from her mouth.

A soft hand touched the back of her head. "Anna."

Anna straightened, wiping her mouth on her sleeve. "How many more years of this can we take? We should have let the bastard shoot us."

"No, Anna," Sofia said fiercely. "Don't ever think that."

"Why didn't you kill him while you had the chance?"

"Because they'd all have been down on us like a pack of hounds, tearing us to shreds and relishing every second of it. Men such as these enjoy their work. When I was very young and my father was out performing his priestly duties in Petrograd with me on his back, men just like this one—except they wore the tsar's colors instead of Stalin's—came to our house and killed my mother and six sisters." Her eyes had darkened to the color of an evening sky, but the shadows beneath them had sunk into deep dark hollows.

"Sofia," Anna said quietly, "not all men are like that."

Sofia laughed, a harsh, scathing sound as chill as the meltwater. "So how in God's name do you know which ones you can trust?"

THIRTY-NINE

IKHAIL wasn't frightened of the pain. Of course it would be bad, he was under no illusion about that, but they hadn't brought him here to kill him. Not yet anyway. So they'd make sure he survived the beatings. No, what frightened him was the degradation. The humiliation. Their obscene seizing of his sense of self and wiping the floor with it, ripping him apart mentally.

They would be expert at it, he was in no doubt of that, with their sharpened verbal scalpels. And he knew he was a proud man, too proud maybe. Would he, Mikhail Pashin, the person he knew so intimately and had learned to both love and hate with a passion over thirty years of life, would he survive? Not his body. Him. His self.

That was what frightened him.

HE cement floor was wet, freshly hosed down. Barefooted, Mikhail was marched into the empty cell by two warders, hands cuffed behind his back. The door swung shut with a heavy metal clang. The warder with the lean face and impatient eyes locked it with an iron key that was attached to his belt by a chain, then turned a smile on Mikhail. Except it wasn't a smile, it was a baring of the teeth. The second warder sniggered in anticipation. He was a solid big-muscled ox of a man with almost no forehead and broad beefy fists, which he flexed and unflexed while the pupils of his vodka-shot eyes grew huge with desire. An objective part of his mind registered that these two men were well chosen for the work. But the subjective part of Mikhail's mind, the part that knew how to hate, hated them as bastard brutes who needed to be put down the way you put down a mad dog. He could smell the rabies in them.

Fight or yield? It would make no difference. Two heavy rubber nightsticks and a metal bar would be the victors. Fists that were chained behind your back were no fists at all. He had no weapons, except his hatred. His heart was pounding, but he kept his breath steady and his body braced for the first blow. Casually he spat on their freshly hosed floor.

The metal bar swung. He ducked and it whistled past his ear, but from the other side a fist sledgehammered into the exact center of his chest. He made no sound. A brick-hard rubber stick slammed onto his mouth, blood exploded on his teeth, and he spat out a sliver of something white.

"Is that all you've got?" he taunted.

The next blow crashed down on the spot between his neck and his arm, sending pain searing through his skull. Neither his shoulder nor arm would move. With a bellow of rage he rammed his head into the lean one's jaw and had the satisfaction of hearing a sharp click as something snapped and a high scream, like a pig's squeal, issued from the warder. Immediately a crunch from the metal bar to the back of Mikhail's legs brought him buckling to his knees. Then it came, the real pain. Again and again, blows like rain. To his back. His ribs. Knees. Kidneys. The nape of his neck. The soles of his naked feet. Worse. To his testicles. That pain was special. White hot. A steel furnace, flames leaping and scorching his every nerve end, a throbbing sickening agony.

"Confess," one of the warders roared in his ear.

He was disintegrating. He could feel the parts inside him coming loose.

"Devil curse you, you bastards," he spat through blood.

An explosion of pain registered in his brain, but he could no longer tell where it came from in his body. At long last, he let go. He stopped holding the parts together and tasted a sticky tar clogging the channels of his mouth and nose. He couldn't breathe.

SOFIA hitched a lift back to Tivil. Pyotr swung himself up on the back of the cart beside her, relieved to catch his breath. She'd set a punishing pace on the road that he couldn't match; the visit to the prison had knocked all the air out of him. Old Vlasov had come clattering up behind them with his horse and two-wheeled cart, empty now that he'd delivered his load of logs to the bakery in town. They jumped on, and Pyotr threw himself on his back in the sawdust where he wrapped an arm tight across his eyes, hiding from the world outside. Hiding from himself and from his betrayal. It gnawed at his heart.

He didn't look at Sofia, but he could feel her seated next to him, upright and alert, hugging her knees. The road was rough, the sky gray-bellied. When Pyotr eventually rolled onto his side he saw a flight of swallows dipping over the river, but today he had no interest in them and he studied Sofia instead. Deep in thought, she had the knack of being very still, so still she became almost invisible, like an animal in the forest. He wondered what made her like that.

"Sofia."

She turned to him, her gaze coming from somewhere far away.

"I didn't mean it."

"I know you didn't." Her voice was gentle.

"He is my father."

"Of course he is. He loves you, Pyotr, and you love him."

"You won't . . ." He hesitated.

"No, I won't tell him."

Pyotr grunted a kind of thanks. "He's been . . . better."

"Better than your real father, you mean?"

"Yes. He never beats me and more than anything he wants me to have schooling. He says it's the way forward for Russia. And he doesn't get drunk." He laughed. "Not all the time, anyway."

He hadn't meant to say it to her. Any of it.

She studied him, solemnly. "Your father is a loyal citizen of Russia."

"Yes, he is."

"Don't doubt him."

"He's read all Lenin's and Stalin's writings, like *The State and Revolution*, and I'm always pushing the latest pamphlets under his bedroom door for him to read at night when he gets home."

She smiled. "I bet he appreciates that."

"He does."

"Who are you trying to convince, Pyotr? Me? Yourself? Or the men in the interrogation room?"

"Papa will be released if he is innocent," he insisted.

"And is he innocent? Or did he take the grain off the truck? What do you believe?"

The question knocked a hole in Pyotr's chest, letting in the confusion once more. He threw himself back on the floor of the cart and this time wrapped both arms across his face.

"I don't know," he muttered.

Instantly she was on him. Snatched his arms away, so that he was looking up into her fierce blue eyes as she leaned over him.

"It doesn't matter," she snapped, "whether he's innocent or guilty. Can't you see that? What matters is that he's your father. He loves you. You owe him, this man who took you in as his own son when you were tainted by the *kulak* label of your miller father." She dug her fingers into his arms. "You owe him everything. That's what matters—love and loyalty."

Abruptly she released him. Pyotr felt as if he'd been run over.

"Not," she added softly, "a power-frenzied devil with a mustache and a withered arm who gets his thrills by signing death warrants in the Kremlin."

Pyotr sobbed. The thoughts in his head were crashing into each other, and then suddenly she was close again, her breath brushing his cheek.

"Help me, Pyotr. Help me get Mikhail out of that stinking prison."

THE village was coming into sight when she spoke again.

"Pyotr, tell me about Lilya Dimentieva."

"What about her?"

"She and your father are . . . friends."

"Yes."

"Good friends?"

"Yes."

"What is she like?"

"She's all right."

"And the child, Misha?"

"What about him?"

"Is he . . . your father's?"

"No, of course not, don't be stupid. Misha's father was killed in an accident when he was clearing trees off the high field last summer."

"Oh."

"Papa helps Lilya out when she needs it, like when Misha broke her window. And she cooks us meals sometimes."

"I see."

"She's easy to like."

He watched the color rise into her cheeks, slowly at first and then faster, darker. She looked away, and Pyotr was sorry. He hadn't meant to hurt her.

FORTY

SOFIA left Pyotr outside the *kolkhoz* office. She hurried past the pond, where two boys were making a lot of noise trying to capture a duck, and up to Rafik's *izba*. She burst into the cottage calling his name.

"Rafik?"

No answer; the place was empty. Where was he? She had questions to ask, and time was trickling through her fingers too fast.

"Comrade Morozova."

Sofia spun around. Outside on the step stood Eliza-veta Lishnikova, the schoolteacher, and in her hand she carried a book. Her gray hair was pinned up tidily in a pleat at the back of her head and her gray narrow-waisted dress was as immaculate as ever, but something about her made Sofia's heart miss a beat. It was in the crispness of her manner, in the shine of her eyes, a bright expectation. She knew something that Sofia did not.

"Comrade Lishnikova, I intended to come and speak to you today."

"Well, I've saved you the trouble." The woman held out the book. "Here, I've brought you a gift."

Sofia accepted it, surprised. It was a good-quality copy of Dostoyevsky's *The Idiot.*

"Thank you, comrade."

"I expect you've read it."

"Yes, I have, but I will enjoy reading it again." She thumbed through the soft pages thoughtfully. "*Spasibo.* But why should you bring me a gift?"

The long face with its fine bones seemed to shift slightly. "I thought you might need it. Something to calm you before tonight."

"Tonight? What's happening tonight?"

"Ah," Elizaveta hesitated, then smiled politely. "I see, you don't know yet. Excuse my mistake." She turned to leave.

"Comrade," Sofia said sharply. "I was coming to thank you for the offer of a job at the school."

The teacher raised her elegant eyebrows expectantly.

"I would like to accept," Sofia continued.

"Indeed? That would be a help to me, but Rafik tells me you will soon be gone."

"Gone?"

"From Tivil."

"Why do you say that?"

"Ah, comrade, you must ask Rafik himself. But let me tell you this, that man knows more than you or I put together." She laughed, a clear low-pitched sound that belonged to a younger woman. She started to move away.

"Tell me," Sofia called out after her, "what happened to your previous assistant teacher?"

Elizaveta Lishnikova froze for no more than a second, but Sofia spotted it.

"He left," the older woman said.

"Suddenly?"

"Yes." Sofia thought she was going to finish it there, but she continued stiffly, "He spoke out of turn one day and a pupil reported him." She shrugged. "It happens."

"Was it Yuri? The pupil who reported him." Mikhail had told her on the train about Pyotr's friend.

Elizaveta said nothing, but she sighed, and a layer of her brightness faded. Without another word, she walked away.

*S*OFIA tried to make sense of it. The schoolteacher's message had unnerved her. Tonight? What did she mean? Why did her mind need to be calmed? What was going to happen tonight?

Suddenly she was frightened. She felt the fear cold and hard in a tight ball just under her heart and she rubbed a hand there to release it.

Anna, oh Anna. I'm not strong enough. I can't do this.

She sat down in Rafik's maroon chair, dropped her head in her hands, and let the moment crash down on her; all the misery and suffering of the last four months when she'd battled halfway across Russia, footstep by footstep, crushed her so that she could barely breathe. She remained like that for a long time, till her fingers grew stiff in her hair, and the whole time she thought hard. About Mikhail. About Anna. About what she was about to lose. And at last when the level of pain became manageable once more, she rose and walked over to Rafik's carved wooden chest against the wall, the one he had drawn her shoes from, the one she'd never opened. The lid was carved with serpents. She lifted it. She didn't know what she'd expected, but it certainly wasn't what stared up at her.

Two bright black eyes and fur whiter than snow, sparkling like ice. She touched it. It was the complete pelt of an Arctic fox, beautifully tanned to such perfect suppleness it was hard to believe the animal wasn't still alive. She stroked the soft fur and gently lifted it out, but underneath lay a folded pile of white sheets, and beside all this whiteness a bundle in the corner sang out. It was a bright red piece of material.

She snatched it up, almost expecting to find blood on her hands from the scarlet fibers, and could feel something weighty inside. Cautiously she unwrapped it. A single pebble tumbled onto her lap, and she felt oddly disappointed. She'd expected something . . . something more revealing, but she picked it up and examined it anyway. The pebble was bone white with silvery veins running through it but otherwise quite ordinary. What on earth did Rafik use it for? It was absurd but the more she stared at the stone, the less she wanted to relinquish it back to the chest. It felt oddly comforting in the palm of her hand, so that she lifted it to her cheek, running its milky surface along her skin.

Her mind grew calm and she breathed more easily. Whatever was going on here, the fear and weakness of a few moments ago had drained away. It was strange. Maybe Rafik had handled this stone so often that he'd left a small piece of himself in its silvery veins. Was it Rafik's strong spirit that was steadying her, or was it something rising to the surface from within herself? She was uncertain.

With an impatient shake of her head, she bundled the pebble inside the red cloth again and returned it to its position in the chest. She needed to find Rafik, but as she stepped out of the house, she heard the sound of hooves and glanced up to see Chairman Fomenko astride a long-boned black horse heading down toward the *kolkhoz* office. He reined the animal to a halt in front of her.

"Good day, Comrade Morozova."

Sofia gave him a cold hard stare. This man was the young boy soldier who killed Anna's father in cold blood sixteen years ago and also shot Svetlana, Mikhail's mother. She wondered for the thousandth time whether Mikhail was aware of the truth and whether she should tell him. Just because Fomenko had turned up at Maria's apartment searching for Anna, it didn't excuse anything.

"You haven't yet attended my office, as I requested."

"I was in Dagorsk today."

"Did you find out what has become of Comrade Pashin?" His broad shoulders seemed to block out the morose charcoal sky.

"*Nyet.*"

He studied her for a moment in silence, and the skin around his gray eyes creased with a concern that surprised her. "Tomorrow morning then. Eight o'clock at my office."

She nodded.

"Comrade Morozova," he said in a gentler tone, "may I suggest that you eat something."

"What do you have in mind?" she asked. "Grain?"

Instead of cursing her as she expected, he laughed, and the sound of it made her want to claw his tongue out.

★ ★ ★

*S*OME instinct for danger made her skirt around the back of the village. The stables seemed the most likely place for the gypsy to be, but instead of taking the direct track up between the cabbage fields, she kept to the forest edge and climbed the slope of the ridge, breathing in the sweet fresh scent of pine. It meant she came at the stables from the back and from above. She looked down at the long wooden buildings but could spot nothing that shouldn't be there. The courtyard was empty except for a tangle of farm ironwork in a huddle in one corner and the trough in the center.

So what the hell was making the hairs on her neck stand up?

The solitary village street lay below, sleepy except for a hound belling somewhere and the urchins shrieking with delight in the murky pond. In the distance figures littered the fields like scarecrows with hoes in hand while others hunched on their knees, laboriously weeding the potato ridges. A flat sky lay like a lid on the valley. Nothing strange, nothing out of place.

So why the taste of fear in her mouth?

And then she heard it, faint but unmistakable, the rhythmic cadence of a religious chant. It drifted from the wall of the stable building like incense, charging the air. It was a rich golden sound that brought back her father and her childhood in a rush, but the priest and his secret flock were deluding themselves if they thought their God could combat the might of Communism. She looked around quickly. A sentry, surely the priest must have set a sentry. She couldn't see one at first, but by moving off to her left so that she could see the approach through the cabbage fields, she spotted him. There at the head of the track stood the figure of the young boy with the scabs and the broom, but he wasn't sweeping this time. He was arguing, arms flailing in all directions. Uniforms swarmed over him like wasps on a honey jar, poking him in the ribs, cuffing his ears.

Sofia ran. She hurtled back down the slope to the rear of the stables and hammered her fists on the dusty planks. Instantly the chanting ceased. She raced to a high narrow vent in the wooden wall and leaped up to it, scrabbling through the tiny gap, nimble as a squirrel. She dropped inside, blinked in the gloom and found herself in some kind of harness room, surrounded by leather and brass. She heard movement and rushed out into the long section where the stalls were situated, but there was no sign of anyone. Just a horse's heavy nose turned in her direction, bristling with curiosity and soft sighs. The smell of incense was strong.

"Priest," she called softly.

From her right came a sound she recognized, the faint tinkle of a brass censer. The priest was standing alone in front of what looked like a solid wall of old timbers, but his appearance bore no resemblance to the way she'd seen him last. He was clothed in full Russian Orthodox priest's regalia, a long black cassock that enveloped him with a stillness that filled the small space. Around his neck lay an embroidered stole, and a tall black hat on his head transformed his shaggy red hair into a golden halo, but it was his eyes that had changed most. The wildness had vanished and in its place was a cool green sea of peace. They studied Sofia with calm authority.

"God be with you, child." He made the sign of the cross.

"Quick," she urged. "*Bistro*. The soldiers are here at the front."

He knew she could be laying a trap for him. His green eyes probed hers, but something in them must have satisfied him because he pushed against one of the planks of timber. Silently, on well-oiled hinges, it swung open all the way to the roof beams, leaving a tall slender gap. Sofia put her head around it. A room lay behind it, long and thin, crammed with people, scented with candles and incense and the spice of prayer. More than twenty faces were turned to her, old men with gray beards and tired eyes, old women wearing black head-scarves and crosses at their necks. A large black Bible lay open on a lectern, gilt letters glittering promises in the candlelight.

"*Bistro*. Quickly, out," Sofia whispered. "Soldiers."

A gasp of panic and then they poured out through the gap, squeezing their fleshless bodies through little more than a hand's breadth.

"Which way?"

"They'll kill us."

"God be merciful."

"Beloved Mother of Christ, blessed Virgin, hear our prayers."

"This way," Priest Logvinov said.

He led his flock into one of the stalls, his threadbare cassock trailing over the straw and picking up stalks while one woman sobbed quietly into her handkerchief. He bent down and flipped a wooden latch that instantly released the end plank, so that it sprang open. Outside lay the rocky slope up to the forest. Sofia had to admit he was better prepared than she expected.

"Go, my children."

Each villager stopped to kiss the ring on the priest's hand, "Thank you, Father," but every second of delay caused Sofia agony.

"Faster," she urged. "*Bistreye!*"

A clatter of boots sounded in the courtyard at the front, and the boy lookout squealed as though struck. Sofia fought the overwhelming desire to flee up that inviting slope to the cool refuge of the trees.

"Priest," she said, "I'll try to delay them. Get out of those clothes and if you ever want to say another prayer again, hide that Bible." She snatched the ceremonial hat from his head and thrust it into his hand. "Be quick."

"God will protect us, my child," Priest murmured.

"My tongue will do a better job of it," Sofia snapped back. She turned and raced through the stables to face the uniforms in the yard.

*W*HY was she doing this? Why risk so much?

The question sprang into her mind unbidden the moment she saw the soldiers strutting across the courtyard. Just the sight of the boots and the peaked caps turned her stomach, and memories of the labor camp guards stabbed like spikes in her brain.

"*Tovarishchi,*" she called out. "Comrades."

They were young, or they would not have halted so readily for a female voice.

"*Tovarishchi,*" she said again, this time with a welcoming smile. Each second's delay meant another fleeing figure reaching the safety of the trees. "I'm glad you've arrived. We've been waiting for you, but you've come to the wrong barn. It's the one on the other side of the river."

The ragged group of soldiers swung their gaze in her direction, except for one, tall and lanky with an Asiatic face and straight black hair. He was heading directly for the tumbledown door that led into the section of stable where the secret room was hidden, as though an informer had earned his thirty pieces of silver.

"Comrade Chairman Fomenko will want to speak to you all first," she added quickly, "before you start work."

The lanky soldier halted and watched her through narrowed eyes.

"What are you talking about?" asked a lean-faced young man who seemed in command. He frowned. "We are not here to do work for your chairman."

"Oh," Sofia tossed her hair at him. "I thought you were the ones coming to help put up a new barn for us."

"We are OGPU soldiers," he said, proudly pushing out his narrow chest, "not peasant laborers." But his eyes lingered on her. All their eyes lingered on her.

"My mistake." She smiled and swayed her hips. "So why are you here?"

"To search these premises." He shifted his rifle in his hand to emphasize the point.

"For what?" Seconds were ticking past.

"For illegal gatherings of religious enemies of the state."

Sweat lay on his downy upper lip. The air was hot and close under the heavy gray sky, and as the officer glanced around uneasily, Sofia had the feeling that this was the young officer's first command. He was as anxious as she was.

"In here." The Asiatic soldier gestured impatiently with his rifle at the dim interior of the stable. "Bring the girl." He stared at Sofia with suspicion.

The officer nodded, relieved to have the decision made for him, and Sofia braced herself.

"Water?" It was Rafik. In his bright yellow shirt and a white bandanna around his head. "Water is what you young men need after your march up here, I'm certain."

He was standing casually in the doorway in front of the suspicious soldier, blocking the entry. In one hand he held a large enamel jug, chipped at the rim, and in the other two tin mugs. "Fresh cool water from the well. Come and drink."

FORTY-ONE

THE words drew blood. In the small windowless room lit only by a single naked bulb, the interrogator was facing Mikhail across the table again. The man's lips were pale and his skin sallow, as though he'd spent his whole life burrowing like a mole through the dirt of prison. Mikhail stood, hands behind his back as instructed, and fought to keep his mind concentrating.

"Mikhail Pashin, you employed a woman at the Levitsky factory who once worked as a servant girl for the tsarina. Her father fought for the Whites."

"That was a long time ago. She is a good Communist now."

"You have arranged for her to sabotage Red Army uniforms as they are sewn."

"That is untrue. I make sure every uniform is checked."

"Why do you check them? That proves she is not trustworthy."

It was his dead friend's sister. She had come to him begging for work, her big-knuckled fingers entwining in his shirt front. She was tainted, a pariah; no one would employ her because she had once worked in a palace.

"No, that's not the case. Every garment is routinely checked before it leaves the factory because any of the girls can make a mistake with her stitches."

"Saboteurs hide behind such platitudes."

"She is not a saboteur."

"But you are."

Mikhail caught his breath. The room seemed to be closing in on him, and his testicles throbbed in a steady sickening pulse from the beating in the cell, but he spoke his next words clearly. "No, I am no saboteur."

"Don't lie to me, you piece of dog shit. Can you deny that you spoiled three sewing machines last week, delaying production, on orders from your masters in Berlin?"

"Yes, I do deny it."

"But the machines broke."

"Yes."

"You broke them. You are a filthy spoiler."

"No. They broke because they're old."

"Just like you broke a turbine when you worked at the Tupolev aircraft factory."

That caught him off guard. It was always the same, the questions twisted and turned, the accusations sliding under his carefully constructed defenses.

"No, the turbine broke because a part needed replacing, but—"

"Were you well paid for that?"

"I've already told you my salary at Tupolev's."

"Well paid by your foreign paymasters for that treachery?"

"That is insane. There were no foreign paymasters. I produced—"

"Is that why you let the German firms palm off defective machinery on you?" The mole eyes narrowed to slits.

"The machines are—"

"To sabotage quotas."

"We exceeded quotas last—"

"Wrecker."

"No."

"Spoiler."

"No."

"Traitor."

"No." He shouted it. To make it enter this man's thick skull.

"You try to deprive the army of uniforms."

"I told you, I exceeded the set quotas."

"You lie."

"Look at the production figures of the Levitsky factory."

"You falsify the figures, you muddle up the numbers, you are a saboteur, a spoiler, a traitor." The man's voice rose abruptly to a shrill command. "Confess."

The room swayed. Or was it him? A fog seemed to thicken the air, and a buzzing sound scraped his nerve ends as the electric lightbulb spluttered and flickered briefly. His mind was trying to shut down. He closed his eyes. Somewhere inside the fog he heard a soft voice that whispered in his ear. *You should take more care.* It was Sofia, warm against his back on the horse, the feel of her breasts so close and her fingers tickling his ribs.

"You bastards," he growled.

But again her solemn voice in his ear, *You are too free with your insults.*

Her words were real. This room could be nothing but a nightmare, a dismal wretched one. He opened his eyes, but the nightmare was still there in front of him, the interrogator leaning forward, his thumbs pressed together, his gaze full of distaste.

"Confess."

"I am a loyal Communist."

"Spit that word out of your mouth, you filthy bourgeois capitalist. You are not fit even to speak of Communism. You don't know the meaning of the word; you lie and you cheat and you take a traitor's gold."

"No."

"You expanded the Levitsky factory, tying up a portion of the state's investment finances that could have been used elsewhere. You were trying to undermine the Russian economy."

This twist of logic finally dislodged Mikhail's precarious temper. "You stupid bastard," he snapped, raising his hands as though he would seize the man's throat, "I expanded the factory in order to boost production and *help* the Russian economy. If you throw everyone who comes up with new and productive ideas into prison, this country will fall to its knees and weep."

A silence settled and the room seemed to vibrate with it. Mikhail could hear his own labored breathing. The interrogator opened the file in front of him, but his pale lips were working in anger and his eyes barely scanned the page.

"You took in a *kulak's* son," he stated. "The child of a class enemy. You don't deny it because you can't. The *kulak* was a class enemy who sabotaged the village mill. You all work together, you wreckers, in a conspiracy. Admit it. Confess. Sign this statement."

"No. I refute the charge."

"You are a class enemy. You steal from the state."

"No."

"You stole sacks of grain."

"No."

"I have a witness."

"They're lying. It's not true. Who is this false accuser?"

"Your son."

FORTY-TWO

SHE wasn't coming.

Pyotr leaned his forehead against the bleached wood of the meeting-hall door, as if its warmth could still the chills inside him. He was alone, and his heart ached for his father. He kept his back turned to the road because he refused to watch yet another villager pass by and turn their face away from him, as though he were invisible. Sofia wasn't coming. He was an outcast even to her, a leper and untouchable for the second time in his life, but what had he done? Nothing. He kicked angrily at the door, rattling it on its ancient hinges.

"Pyotr."

She was here. He turned, relief filling his throat with that strange sort of honey taste that always came when he was near her.

"Did you get it?" she asked.

He nodded and held out his hand. Across his palm lay the heavy iron key to the meeting hall. It had grown warm from contact with his flesh.

"*Molodiets.* Good boy." She snatched it from him.

"Did they believe you? That you wanted to contribute to the *kolkhoz* by cleaning up the hall for them?"

He nodded again, but with the handle of the hazel-twig broom in his hand he pointed at one of the sheets of paper pinned on the door, the lists of that week's individual achievements for each worker. His own name was on it. Time spent at the forge. Already someone had drawn a heavy black line through Pyotr's name to show that he no longer existed. He heard Sofia draw in breath sharply.

"Shall I tear it down?" she asked, as casually as if she were asking him if she should sew on a button.

"No," he said, shocked.

"Why not?"

"No, don't."

Her hand lightly touched the hair on the back of his head. "Why not, Pyotr?"

"It's not . . . not . . ." He struggled for the right word. "Not wise."

"Why? Because Chairman Aleksei Fomenko put it up?"

"There are soldiers," he told her in a whisper, "here in Tivil. I saw them."

"So did I."

"It'll just make . . . more trouble," he muttered.

She took her hand away from his hair. No one had touched him like that since the night his mother went off with her soldier. Not even Papa.

"Pyotr," she said, and her voice was so quiet he had to listen hard, "if everyone is frightened of making trouble, how will we ever make the world better? Even Lenin was a great one for making trouble."

He hunched his shoulders.

"The people of Russia will rot in their misery," she breathed, "like your father will in his cell. Like I did. Like Priest Logvinov will if he's not more careful than he was today, like all the other stinking prisoners will if we don't make trouble, you and I."

His heart jumped in his rib cage, but he didn't know if it was excitement or fear. Her eyes were fixed on his.

"You were a prisoner?" he whispered.

"Yes. I escaped."

It was like a gift. She was trusting him. He wasn't invisible.

"Open the door," he said. "I'll help you."

* ★ ★

*T*HEY searched the hall together and took half each. Pyotr was quick as a ferret, darting from one likely spot to another, exploring it, moving on, eager to be the one to find the hiding place. She was slower, more methodical. His fingers wormed their way into cracks and scrabbled under benches seeking hidden compartments, but nothing yielded to his touch. Only the gray metal table with the two pencils and the two chairs he left alone because it was Chairman Fomenko's territory. Pyotr felt like an intruder there. His cheeks were flushed, but he didn't want to stop, not now.

"Do you know," Sofia's voice came to him from across the body of the building, "that in the Russian Orthodox church, worshippers always stood? No benches to sit on, and services could go on for hours."

Pyotr wasn't interested. Most of the church buildings had been blown up anyway. He pulled at a strip of plasterwork in the shape of an angel's wing and it came away in his hand, but nothing lay behind it.

"It was to prove their devotion, you see," she explained.

Why was she telling him this? She had her cheek against the opposite wall, eyeing the line of it, her fingers feeling for false fronts to the bricks.

"Do you know why they had to do that?" she asked.

"No."

"It's not that they had to prove it to God. They had to prove it to each other."

Pyotr thought for a long moment and scratched at his head. "Like when we have meetings here and workers denounce each other for slacking in the fields that day. Is that what you mean?"

"Exactly. It's to prove to others what a true believer you are. To avoid damnation, in hell or in a forced labor camp. Both the same."

He squatted down on his haunches and trailed a finger along the edge of a floorboard. He knew she was wrong, of course. Stalin warned against saboteurs of ideas as well as of factories, but he didn't want to tell her that, not right now anyway.

His finger snagged.

"Sofia."

"What is it?"

"I've found something."

She hurried across the hall. "What?"

"This. Look."

He lifted a filthy piece of string, no more than the length of a man's hand. It was attached to one of the planks.

Sofia crouched at his side. "Pull."

He yanked and a meter-long section of floorboard flipped up. Pyotr let out a shout and fell back on his bottom but scrambled to his knees to peer into the gap. He'd found the hiding place. Now he would have the means to free Papa; that was what she'd promised him. He didn't know quite what it was they were searching for, except that it was in a box and was definitely going to be something good. Sofia was tugging at the next section of flooring to widen the gap but it wouldn't move, and for the first time he noticed the scars on her fingers. They pressed their faces eagerly to the edge of a hole, black and deep. Too black and too deep to see what lay at the bottom.

Sofia frowned. "Not what I expected."

"I'll squeeze in," Pyotr said quickly. He didn't want her to doubt his find. "I'll drop down."

"No." Her hand gripped his shoulder.

"Why not?"

"We don't know how deep it is or what's down there."

"Fetch something to drop down into it then, that's how they test wells."

Instantly she hurried off toward the pencils lying on the table at the front of the hall, but Pyotr didn't wait. He swung his legs through the narrow gap, lifted his bottom, raised his arms above his head, and slipped through as smooth as an eel. He plunged into the darkness and hit a hard floor with a crunch, knocking the breath from his body. He looked up to where several meters above his head a small rectangle of light broke up the solid blackness and gave him his bearings.

"Pyotr."

He could hear the shock in her voice.

"I'm still alive."

Her pale oval face popped into the gap above, blocking the light.

"Are you hurt?"

"No." He rubbed his knee and his palm came away damp, but he just wiped it on his shorts. "It's very dark."

She laughed. "What did you expect, you idiot?"

But she didn't tell him off. He liked her for that.

"Now you're down there, feel around but be careful. See if you can find a box or a bag of some kind. Maybe even some candles."

Pyotr scrabbled to his feet and stood still for a moment, staring into the darkness, waiting for his eyes to adjust. Faint shapes began to emerge, gray on black. He took a deep breath, and the air smelled dry and faintly sweet. He stretched out a hand in front of him and took two cautious steps. That was when the plank was slammed into place above him and total darkness swallowed him whole.

FORTY-THREE

Davinsky Camp
July 1933

ANNA was too sick to work. She knew the day was close when she wouldn't be able to get enough air into her lungs to allow her to walk, never mind work, but she hadn't expected it so soon. She lay on her bedboard in a half-sitting posture and fought against the coughs that were tearing holes in her half-starved body.

The strange thing was that she became convinced that each spasm in her chest was the growling of a sharp-toothed monster inside her, with eyes like glowing coals and slick green scales for skin. It was a fantasy, she knew that, but she couldn't shake free of it however hard she tried.

"It's lack of oxygen," she gasped aloud. "It's turning my brain to pulp."

But she could smell its foul breath coming out of her own mouth and hear its scales rustling and crackling inside her lungs as it shifted position.

HERE, eat this."

Nina was pushing a small piece of black bread

between Anna's lips, and her broad face was creased with concern. Anna let the heavy morsel of food settle on her tongue, and she sucked it slowly to make it last.

"And this."

Tasha did the same with another nibble of bread, and her fingers caressed Anna's damp brow. "Stupid bitch, you are," she said gruffly.

Anna sucked the bread and smiled. She couldn't speak, but it wasn't just the coughing that stopped the words. It was the fact that these two women, who each day were fed nowhere near enough to fuel the hard manual labor they were forced to perform, were sacrificing some of their *paiok*, their ration, to her. You didn't ask that of anyone, not even friends. It was like asking for their life.

With a great effort she swallowed hard and said, "I'll be better tomorrow. I'll work again then."

"Sure you will."

"After a day of lazing around doing nothing, you'll be strong as an ox."

"You're just jealous," Anna murmured.

They laughed. "You bet we are."

Anna put out a hand and lightly touched Nina's muscular arm. "*Spasibo*," she whispered.

Nina shrugged. "Don't be stupid. It's only because I want you back in the line to tell us stories once more. We're dying of boredom on the march without you, aren't we, Tasha?"

"Hell, yes. Nina tried to amuse me today with a tale about her experience of birthing a breech calf. I tell you, it fucking made me vomit." Her prim little mouth pulled tight. "Get some sleep now, you idle layabout, and you'll feel better tomorrow."

"*Spasibo*."

Anna closed her eyes, grateful for the blackness because her eyes were becoming increasingly sensitive to light, which caused little pinpricks of pain in her eyeballs. She recalled Sofia having the same problem that time she was ill with her hand and was eating nothing.

"I can't see," Sofia had said one evening in the hut, and Anna had heard the suppressed panic in her voice despite her determination to hide it.

Anna had waved a hand in front of her friend's eyes. "It's pellagra."

"I know."

Pellagra, like scurvy, was caused by vitamin deficiency and was the curse of the prisoners, and one of its effects was an inability to see in the dark. Anna took Sofia's undamaged hand and quietly steered her through the rows of bunks to her bedboard. She was shocked by the fire raging in her friend's veins, and that was the moment she decided to go to find Crazy Sara.

SARA."

"Get away, you whore."

Anna tried again. "Sara, I've brought you some bread."

The wild green eyes rolled in their sockets. "Putrid bread from a whore."

But the wizened claw shot out, snatched the gray knob of clay-bread from Anna's hand, and rammed it into her toothless mouth before the gift was retracted. Anna waited patiently for the woman to cease snuffling a stream of obscenities and scratching herself.

"Sara, I'm told you have knowledge. Of what lies out there in the forest that can heal ailments."

The woman cackled and pointed a crooked finger at Anna. "More than you'll ever know."

They were standing beside the vast rubbish dump at the far end of the camp. It was raining, a gloomy chill downpour that had gone on all day, making the rocks slippery to handle on the road, but in the distance the sun hovered on the horizon where it would sit until morning, reluctant at this time of year to leave. The stench of the dump was foul, as of dead bodies buried in the filth, but Anna gave no sign of repulsion.

Sara was one of the *brodyagas*, the garbage eaters, the band of pathetic wretches who lived off what they could scavenge from the dump. They scurried over it like crabs, seeking out things to thrust past their white gums, and welcomed the advances of any guard desperate enough to handle their diseased bodies. Most were insane, their minds rotting as fast as their limbs, but this one, this Sara, was Anna's only hope. She clung to it.

"They say you are a witch." Anna spoke slowly and clearly to ensure that the woman heard above the rain, but she didn't risk coming too close. "That you can—"

Sara shrieked, and it took Anna a moment to recognize the noise as laughter. The woman's lungs were wheezing with delight. She had lost all her hair long ago, including her beetle-black eyebrows, and her pink scabby scalp glistened in the rain.

"What will you pay?" Her hands were grasping like claws.

"What do you ask?"

"Butter, bread, and beetroot. And"—she swung her head from side to side, searching in her bewilderment for some other demand— "and your coat. Yes," she screeched the word, "*da*, your coat. I want it now . . . now . . . now . . . now. I want . . ."

Anna recoiled. Demanding a coat? It was summer now, but come the winter . . .

"I need a cure for an infected hand. If it heals, you shall have my coat. But not before."

The woman's hand slithered forward between the raindrops like a snake's head and fastened on the wet collar of Anna's coat, fingering the padded material. Her sunken mouth started to drool.

"Bring me butter," she crooned. "Then I will see."

Anna nodded and, holding her breath against the stink of decay, hurried away from the dump and the scuttling crabs. The woman's cackle was not drowned out by the rain.

*I*T didn't take her long to get it. She brought butter and bread for Sara, and in exchange received herbs in a poultice for the splitting flesh of Sofia's hand. Some of the women in the hut stopped speaking to Anna when they saw her draw a brown greaseproof packet of meat and fat and even a sweet biscuit from her pocket each day.

Everyone knew, but Anna didn't give a damn about them as she watched Sofia heal. She could feel their scathing disgust like sandpaper on her skin. People whispered behind their hands, and even out in the Work Zone fingers pointed when guards sidled up to smile at her. Whatever filth the women thought of her, it wasn't even close to what she thought of herself. But that didn't stop her, and each evening she walked out from behind the tool-hut with food in her pocket and fire in her belly.

One night as she was gently feeding tiny strips of yellow pork fat into Sofia's cracked lips, she saw the feverish eyes fix on her face as though trying to work out what was reality and what was a trick of her confused mind.

"Anna." A raw whisper.

"I'm here."

"Tell me . . . something . . . happy."

Anna was engulfed by a huge wave of tenderness. She was standing right next to Sofia's top bunk, and she leaned her head against the sick girl's arm. How could something look so dead and yet burn so hot?

"Tell me, Anna." So soft it was no more than a shimmer of air. "Tell me more about Vasily."

Anna pushed a dried currant into Sofia's mouth. She never touched a scrap of the food herself. Just the thought of where it came from made her retch. "Chew," she ordered and started to talk.

Pirate Island, we called it. It sat, small and stubby, in the middle of the lake on the Dyuzheyevs' grand estate. No one ever went there except the swans. There were two of them—Napoleon and Josephine we named them because they were so horrible, always hissing and flapping their great white wings like angry angels that had fallen to earth. One lazy summer day Vasily decided we would attack the island, so we set off in the row boat pretending to be Tsar Nicholas's best troops driving the hated Finnish pirates off Russian soil, and Vasily had made us wooden swords.

"Come on, Captain Konstantin, row harder," Vasily bellowed as if we were in the middle of a vast sea with a howling gale.

The sun glittered on the water and the air was humming with the beats of insects' wings. A brilliant blue butterfly landed on Vasily's cap, and I clapped with such delight that I nearly lost my oar. To be honest, I was quite nervous of invading that tiny island.

"Vasily," I warned, "I don't think that the swans—I mean the pirates— will be very friendly."

"Of course the bastards won't, Captain, they're filthy pirates, aren't they? They guard their treasure well, but together we'll defeat them and lop off their heads."

"But you're the general. I'm only a captain, so you'll lead the charge, won't you?"

I didn't want to land. I thought it would be just perfect to float in the boat with Vasily forever, but we bumped up against the island. Vasily put his finger to his lips. In silence we crept up the rocky bank into the undergrowth, where Vasily suddenly gave a shout of pain, clutched his chest, sank to his knees in the mud, and collapsed on his side.

"Vasily!" I screamed.

"I'm shot, Captain Konstantin," he gasped.

"What?"

"The pirates have done for me." He writhed on the ground as though in agony. "It all rests on you now, my brave captain. You must attack their camp alone."

"Vasily," I said crossly, plucking like a little bird at his soft brown hair. "Don't be silly."

"Captain, are you a yellow-bellied coward?"

"No!"

"I knew I could trust you, soldier. Here, take my sword as well and don't forget to make the charge with a bloodcurdling scream to frighten the cursed pirates off the island."

I gazed at him in horror. His eyes were firmly shut, his strong young limbs crumpled and lifeless. Why couldn't I lie down beside him and be shot by pirates too? In a panic I glanced quickly around, imagining black-tipped beaks with razor teeth lurking behind every bush, yellow eyes gleaming with menace. I picked up Vasily's long sword, but my hand was shaking.

"Vasily," I whispered, "a swan is bigger than me."

He didn't move.

I took a tentative step toward the heart of the island. "I'm going after the pirates now."

No answer.

I listened hard for any sound of the swans, but I could only hear my own heart beating in my ears. I was so terrified I forgot to breathe. I could see the leaves shivering in the wind, and I knew even they were frightened for me. I was going to die.

I ran. With a bloodcurdling screech and both swords whirling in crazy circles, I charged into the undergrowth, branches taking swipes at my head. Straight away Josephine heard me and came flying out with head high and wings wide, uttering a deafening war cry. I launched my attack, swords scything through the air. For one second the bird was so surprised she backed off, and I was fooled. This is easy. I'm a great warrior and I can . . .

She ran at me, eyes spitting fire. I went down, head over heels in a flurry of arms and legs as she bowled me over and swung her long sinuous neck back ready to strike, huge yellow beak gaping wide. She was about to swallow me whole. I screamed and stuck out my sword. But before she or I could move, I was scooped off the ground and tucked under a strong arm, and with a battle cry fit to crack open the world my rescuer raced in a slither of stones and nettles back to the shoreline. Josephine chased us like a fiend from hell, but we tumbled into the boat and pushed out into the lake. My general had saved me, but I was so angry I refused to sit on the row bench with him. I wouldn't even speak.

"Oh, come on, Princess, don't sulk. That was a great adventure." He splashed me with an oar.

"Why, Vasily? Why did you do it?"

"Come here, Annochka." He pulled me onto the bench beside him and kissed the top of my trembling head. "Don't be cross. I did it to show you that you can do anything, anything in the world if you set your mind to it. You have the heart of a lion."

I snuggled close against him, his white linen shirt turning green wherever I touched him.

"But I was frightened," I moaned.

"We're all frightened sometimes, my angel. The trick is to roll up your fear into a ball, put it in your pocket, and just carry on. Like you did today."

"Next time," I said loftily, "you can be the pirate and I will run you through with my sword."

He grinned, and then abruptly his dove-gray eyes grew dark as slate and he hugged me close. "Annochka, terrible times are coming soon to Russia. Only blood will quench the anger of our people and it will be hard on the likes of your family and mine. You will need every scrap of your courage. All this was to show you that you can do far more than you think you can. I want you to be ready."

"I'm ready," I whispered.

FORTY-FOUR

SOFIA was trapped. Not in the dark like Pyotr or in some stinking hellhole like Mikhail, but trapped just the same. Chairman Fomenko ushered her into his office, and the moment he shut the door she felt the tension tighten like an iron band inside her head.

"Please, sit down."

"I'll stand."

Just the sight of this man sent loathing snaking through her veins She stood with folded arms, and to her annoyance he gave her a slight smile, amused by her stance. He sat down at his desk, arranging his limbs with neat precision.

"Cigarette?" he offered.

"No."

From a drawer he pulled out a slender tin of hand-rolled *makhorka* cigarettes, thin and misshapen, and lit one carefully with a match. Why did he smoke the cheapest foul-smelling tobacco? Surely he didn't need to. He probably did so to prove his identification with the ordinary workers in the fields. And that just annoyed her further. Nor did she like the intelligent way he looked at her through the haze of smoke or the feel of his eyes summing up her clothes, her shoes, and the strong curves of the muscles in her legs.

"I think we'll have our meeting today, instead of tomorrow, now that you're here, Comrade Morozova."

Sofia said nothing.

"Do you like it here in Tivil?" he asked.

"Yes."

"And you enjoy living with the gypsies?"

"Yes."

"Do they strike you as strange at all?"

"No."

"I hear tales about them, about their . . . antics."

"I don't know what you mean."

He flexed his broad shoulders under his brown checked shirt, faded by the sun, and Sofia recognized it as a gesture of frustration, a warning that she should be civil.

"You don't look much like a gypsy yourself," he pointed out.

"I am by marriage, not by blood."

"Please explain."

"My aunt who brought me up was married to Rafik's brother. She wasn't a gypsy, but her husband was."

"What about your own parents?"

"They died."

"I'm sorry. What happened?"

"They were both railway workers. There was a train crash." That was the story she was sticking to. It invited fewer questions.

He nodded in silence. "These things happen."

"When someone is incompetent."

"Incompetence is often a disguise for sabotage."

Why did he say that? Was he testing her? To see if she would bleat agreement like one of his docile flock? Or perhaps to trap her into insisting that incompetence was the result of tiredness and hunger and fear of taking decisions that might expose you to accusations of *wrecking*. Was that it?

She said nothing; instead she glanced around the office. So far she'd taken no notice of it, concentrating only on Fomenko himself and trying to decipher every lift of his eyebrow, but now she took her time staring at the red banners and portraits on the whitewashed timber walls. They were the usual clutch of beauties: Lenin and Kirov, and in pride of place, of course, Josef Stalin in military tunic and cap. She'd heard he was living a plain, almost austere life in his Kremlin stronghold, but what good is austerity when you have an insatiable thirst for the blood of your people?

She looked away, unfolded her arms, and took a step nearer the desk. Its metal top was painted black, chipped from long use, and its surface was smothered in piles of papers, all in separate orderly stacks. At one end sat a wooden tray with something lumpy on it, but she couldn't see exactly what because a red cloth was draped over it.

"If you've asked all your questions, may I leave now? I would like to finish sweeping out the hall, but I need the key." She held out her hand.

Fomenko had come marching into the hall when she was peering down at Pyotr in the hole, and he'd demanded to know what she was doing there. With a flick of her wrist she had pushed the plank back into place before he noticed it and then explained that she was sweeping out the hall, instead of Pyotr. She held up the broom to prove the point. He had remained suspicious and she knew she hadn't fooled him, but his manner was scrupulously polite as he removed the key from her and escorted her to his office.

Aleksei Fomenko leaned back in his chair now and made no attempt to take the key from his pocket for her. His eyes narrowed speculatively and his lips parted a fraction to exhale tobacco smoke. Something about his stillness made her uneasy.

"Sit down," he said, pointedly adding, "Please, comrade."

She thought about it, then did so.

"I wish to see your *dokumenti*."

She removed her residence permit from her skirt pocket and dropped it on the desk.

"Your travel permit?"

"Your secretary in the outer office inspected all my documentation when he issued this permit of residency." She waved at the door. "Ask him."

"I'm asking you."

She forced her mouth into the shape of a smile. "What more do you need to know?"

The stiff lines of his face softened into an answering smile, and then he ran a patient hand over his short hair and took a form from one of the piles. It irritated her that his hands were so broad and capable, as if they were accustomed to achieving what they set themselves to do. They stubbed out the cigarette in a small metal dish that served as an ashtray and picked up a fountain pen. It was the first thing she'd seen in connection with the chairman that had even a hint of status about it. It was a beautiful black-cased pen with a fine gold nib. A silence hung in the room for a second, and into it the wind outside blew small shards of sound: the jingle of a horse harness, the rumble of a cartwheel, the throaty shriek of a goose.

"Your father's name and place of origin?"

"Fyodor Morozov from Leningrad."

"Your aunt's name and place of origin?"

"Katerina Zhdanova from the Lesosibirsk region."

"How long did it take you to travel to Tivil?"

"Four months."

"How did you travel?"

"Walking mostly, sometimes a lift in a cart."

"No money for a train ticket?"

"No."

He put down his pen. "A long journey like that could be dangerous, especially for a young woman alone."

She thought of the farmer with foul breath and greasy hands who had found her asleep in his barn. By the time she left him unconscious in the straw, his mouth had lost its gold tooth and she had the price of a week's food.

"I worked some of the time," she said, "dug ditches or chopped wood, sorted rotten potatoes and turnips into sacks. People were kind. They gave me food."

Get out of here, you scrawny bitch. We don't want strangers. Stones had rained into the mud at her feet as a warning. Stiff-legged dogs had snarled a threat.

"Good, I'm glad," Fomenko said, but the edges of his gray eyes had darkened and she wondered what was passing behind them. "Russian people," he continued, "have kind hearts."

"You have a higher opinion of them than I do."

He placed his elbows on the desk, watching her closely. "They are kind to each other now because since the Revolution there is greater justice, so they have no reason not to be."

She thought of Mikhail in his cell and shivered visibly. The movement alerted Fomenko, and his face formed into lines she couldn't read, his eyebrows drawn together in concentration but his mouth unexpectedly gentle. He leaned to one side and flicked the red cloth off the tray on the end of the desk with a quick gesture that enforced his efficiency in her mind.

"Are you feeling weak? Is that it? Have you not eaten today?"

Laid out on the pinewood tray was a square of black bread, a slab of creamy cheese, a glass tumbler, and a bone-handled knife. Beside them stood a stubby blue pitcher.

"Here, have some food."

He tore off a chunk of the bread, smeared the moist cheese on it, and offered it to her, but she would rather choke than touch his food.

"I won't rob you of your meal," she said firmly.

He hesitated, his jaw flexing so that she could see the muscle twitch beneath the skin. With no comment he replaced the bread on the tray.

"*Kvass?*" he offered.

Kvass was a traditional brew, fermented from bread, yeast, and sugar, that Sofia had no taste for, but she nodded politely. He poured the brown liquid into the glass and handed it to her across the desk.

"*Spasibo,*" she said. She sat holding it in her hand but didn't raise it to her lips.

As though he suddenly felt the need to put some distance between them, he rose from his chair and walked over to the window. He stood there with his broad back to her, saying nothing, just gazing at the fields outside, at the *kolkhoz* he was so committed to driving toward greater productivity. She could see the strength of his determination in the line of his shoulders and the stiffness of his neck. She placed the glass silently on the desk and at the same time whisked his box of matches into her pocket.

"Is that all?" she asked.

He coughed, an odd kind of sound that was more of a growl than a cough, and when he turned, his face was in shadow, his expression hidden from her.

"May I have the key to the hall to finish the sweeping?" she asked.

His whole body grew unnaturally still. "Why the hall? What is this preoccupation of yours with our hall?"

She stood. "I am offering to help because Pyotr is upset by the arrest of his father, that's all. No preoccupation with anything."

"Let me give you some advice, comrade. Stay clear of the boy. He will have to denounce Mikhail Pashin at our next *kolkhoz* meeting."

"No, Chairman, that is asking too—"

"Asking only what is right. Our Young Pioneers know their duty. In the meantime stay away from him or you could be in trouble yourself."

"It's not an infectious disease he has. His father is being interrogated."

"Comrade Morozova"—the chairman's voice was insistent—"we in the Red Arrow *kolkhoz* will not tolerate a saboteur in whom the motives of greed and self-seeking are rampant. The Revolution has shown us a better way."

"He's just a boy of eleven years old, that's all. What kind of threat to the state, or to me for that matter, can he possibly be when—"

"I wasn't referring to Pyotr Pashin when I mentioned saboteurs."

"Then who?"

"You."

A silence descended that seemed to last forever. Sweat prickled on Sofia's back and she inhaled deeply.

"Comrade Chairman, you are a powerful man here in Tivil." She saw his surprise at the abrupt change of subject. "And maybe in Dagorsk too."

He was studying her carefully.

"Mikhail Pashin has been arrested—"

"I am aware of that," he interrupted.

"—arrested wrongfully," she continued. "He had nothing to do with the sacks of grain that went missing."

"That is for the interrogators to establish."

"But if a person in authority, a powerful man like yourself, reported to these interrogators that their prisoner was a loyal Communist who at the time of the theft was drinking inside his home with an OGPU officer and was clearly innocent of any . . . sabotage, then they would release him. They would believe your word."

His face changed. It lost the tautness that usually held it together and curved into a wide genuine smile. "Comrade," he said with a soft laugh, "I am concerned. I think hunger has addled your brain."

"No, Chairman, I think not. No more than listening to a radio in the forest has addled yours."

It was as though she'd slapped him. He rocked slightly on his heels. A dull flush rose to his cheeks while one fist clenched and unclenched at his side, so that for a brief second she thought he was about to seize hold of her, but he didn't. Instead, with stiff courtesy, he walked over to the door and opened it.

"Don't let me keep you from sweeping the hall," he said in a soft voice and held out the key.

Sofia's fingers closed over it, and as they did so she could feel the heat in his flesh. She walked out without a word.

*P*YOTR," Sofia called urgently.

She crouched down by the broom that lay where she'd dropped it in the assembly hall and put her mouth close to the floorboards.

"Pyotr," she called again.

She heard a scrabbling noise beneath her feet.

"Sofia?"

"Are you all right?"

"I'm fine."

But the boy's voice was so thin it made her heart lurch. She yanked at the string and the short piece of flooring shot up so she could peer in, but at first she could make out nothing in the gloom.

"It's all right, Pyotr, I'll get you out." She lay down flat on her stomach, slid her head and shoulders through the hole and felt around blindly with her hands. "Whoever makes use of this place can't bring a rope in with them every time. It would be too conspicuous. There must be—"

"I can see it, I can see it. There beside you, there, on the right . . .

no . . . farther over." His young voice was rising. "That's it, just there by—"

"Got it."

Her fingertips had touched the bristled twists of a rope hanging down under the floorboards. She tugged at it and instantly it uncoiled, snaking one end into the black cavern beneath.

"A ladder," Pyotr cried out, "it's a rope ladder."

Sofia shinned down the swaying rungs and jumped the last section onto an earthen floor. She was struck by the change in temperature. It was a cold underground room.

"Pyotr."

His pale face was close, and she wrapped her arms around him, hugging him tight to her. "I'm sorry," she breathed into his hair. "Fomenko came."

She could feel the boy's bony body rigid at first, but slowly it grew soft in her embrace and that was when it started to tremble. Only faintly, but enough to tell her what he'd been through, shut away in the dark on his own. His shirt was damp with sweat despite the cool air. She held him until the trembling ceased, then stepped back and tapped his chin teasingly.

"Look what the chairman kindly gave me for you."

From her pocket she drew out the box of matches she'd stolen from his desk, and in the dim light she placed them in Pyotr's hand. His fingers were quick to strike a match, and holding it in front of him he crossed to a narrow shelf, picked up the stub of a candle that lay there next to a Bible, and lit it. The flame flickered and hissed, but by its light she saw Pyotr's face clearly for the first time. One of his lips was bleeding where he'd been biting at it.

"Come on, let's get you out of here," she said cheerfully, and she held out one end of the rope ladder to him. "You first."

"No." He shook his tousled brown hair. "Look at this."

Holding the candle high, he led the way to the rear of the room. She swerved to avoid a wooden chair piled with half a dozen bulging sacks in the middle of the floor, all propped carefully on top of each other, and her heart tightened when she realized Pyotr must have heaped them like that, struggling in the darkness to reach the ceiling, but there weren't enough of them. Did he shout? Did he scream and cry for help? Or wait quietly, believing in her?

"Look," he said again.

Had he found the jewels? Her pulse leaped at the thought. The walls were lined with wooden planking coated in pitch that had been repaired in places, and on one side was an ancient door with heavy iron hinges.

"It's locked," Pyotr said when he saw her glance at it.

He stretched out the candle, and its uncertain light revealed that the rear wall was covered with a heavy brocade curtain instead of planking. It was hard to tell its color in the gloom, but Sofia had the impression of a deep purple glimmering among the darting shadows.

"Is it . . . ?"

"Wait," Pyotr whispered. Then with all the panache of a magician he swept the curtain aside.

The wall was full of eyes. Sofia felt her stomach sink as she realized it wasn't the box of jewelry she was seeking.

"So, Pyotr," she murmured, "it looks like God hasn't been driven out of Tivil after all."

The alcove behind the curtain was a meter deep by about three meters wide, and every scrap of birch-lined wall was covered in religious icons and statues and crucifixes. Sad-eyed saints carried the burdens of the world's sins on their gilded shoulders, and hundreds of Virgin Marys gazed with adoration at the soft-faced Child Jesus. Lovingly arranged in groups on the floor were statues of them painted in vivid reds and blues and golds.

Pyotr was staring open-mouthed.

"So," Sofia said, "this is where the village hid their beliefs." She spoke quietly, as in a place of worship, and after a moment she reached up and pulled the curtain back across the alcove. Pyotr flinched, and the look in his eyes was far away.

"So shocked?" Sofia asked.

He rubbed his free hand across his face in a rough gesture and nodded. "They're so . . ." His voice trailed away.

"So powerful?" she finished for him.

"*Da*. I didn't realize."

"You've never been inside a proper Orthodox church with frescoes and carvings and gold crosses and air so laden with prayers and incense that you can barely breathe it in."

He shook his head. "But it's just superstition." It was meant as a statement, but somehow it came out more as a question. "Once they realize that, won't they let it go?"

"No, Pyotr, they won't." She stopped herself. Now was not the time for saying more. "Come on, let's see what's in those sacks you piled in a heap."

"Just grain and potatoes and rutabagas." He kicked one of the sacks with his foot, spraying dust through the air. "Hoarders' food." He said it with disgust.

"Let me put the candle back on the shelf." She pushed him toward the rope ladder. "Time to leave."

He twisted his head to look her full in the face. "Sofia, I thought you'd cheated me. When you said there was something here to help my father, I thought you must mean that you'd shut me down here because all I had to do was pray to the Virgin Mary and Papa would be freed."

"Oh Pyotr." Sofia leaned forward and kissed his cheek. "I'll never cheat you. What I'm searching for is worth thousands of roubles, and in this country roubles will buy you anything if you have enough of them, even freedom. We'll get him out, one way or another." She stroked his damp hair. "I promise."

His brown eyes glistened, and the lonely feel of his hand as it slid into hers tore at her heart.

A light rain was spitting in the wind. Sofia locked the church door and glanced cautiously up and down the street for any sign of Chairman Fomenko, but there was none. Two young girls came skipping up the muddy street and waved to Pyotr, but he ignored them.

"Pyotr, one more thing I need from you."

"To help Papa?"

"Yes. And to help me."

He looked at her expectantly. The wariness seemed to have disappeared from his eyes. "Yes?"

"I want you to take the key to the smithy where I saw you working and—"

"Make a copy."

He was quick. "Is that possible?" Or was she asking too much of Mikhail's son?

He puffed out his skinny chest. "Of course. And Pokrovsky the blacksmith will give me help if I need any."

"Will he keep it secret?"

"For Papa he will."

She grinned at him. "Thank you, Pyotr. When it's done, take the original back to the *kolkhoz* office. Understand me?"

"Yes." He tossed his head and strutted off in the direction of the smithy.

"Mikhail," she breathed, "you can be proud of your stiff-necked son."

Then she faced up toward the far end of the village. It was time to speak to Rafik.

I'VE been waiting for you."

Rafik was seated at the rough table when Sofia entered, still wearing his yellow sunshine shirt. His black eyes were half-hooded, his olive skin seemed darker, and his black hair was hidden from sight under the pelt of the white fox. His shoulders were hunched over like an old man's. This was not a Rafik she recognized, and her mouth grew dry. The room was dim despite the daylight outside, the air scented and heavy, and the moment Sofia breathed it in she could sense a strangeness in it.

What had he done? Warily she sat down opposite him.

"So the soldiers at the stable let you go," she said.

"Did you think they wouldn't?"

She shook her head. "I was searching for you up there. I didn't expect to see the troops. I was worried for you."

"It was priests they were seeking today, not gypsies. Next time I may not be so fortunate."

"Did the worshippers escape?"

"Every last soul of them."

"And Priest?"

"He is safe . . . but not safe."

"It's a miracle that he hasn't been arrested and put to death before now."

"I look after him."

She understood now exactly what he meant by that: he used this strange hypnotic power of his. "So why wouldn't you look after Mikhail when he needed it and I begged you?"

"Oh Sofia, don't look so angry. You have to understand that there were too many troops swarming around him and it was impossible. The time was all wrong, but now . . . the time has changed. Tonight is the moment when your eyes will open."

She didn't know what he meant, but there was a strange, unfamiliar formality in the way he spoke, his tongue clicking against his teeth. His gaze was distant, and she was not sure he was even seeing her at all.

"Rafik," she whispered. "Who are you?"

He didn't answer, but the whistle of his breath grew louder in the room, and a movement of his hands made her look down at the table where they'd been clenched together. Now they lay apart, placed on the worn wooden surface with fingers splayed like stars, and between them lay the white pebble. It seemed to draw all light from the room deep into itself, and Sofia felt her skin grow cold.

The stone was the one she'd found earlier in the chest. Then it had seemed harmless, but now for some unknown reason it made her nervous, yet her eyes refused to turn away from it. Her breath quickened.

"Sofia." Rafik's voice was deep. He reached out and rested a heavy hand on her head.

Instantly her eyelids drifted shut, and for the first time in the darkness of her own skull she became aware of a powerful humming sound, a vibration that rattled her teeth. To her dislocated mind it seemed to be coming from the stone.

FORTY-FIVE

ARE you ready?"

"Do I look ready?"

Pokrovsky had just stepped out of his *banya*, the bath hut behind the forge, with nothing but a towel draped around his barrel waist and a grin on his face. Elizaveta Lishnikova wasn't sure whether she found the grin or the massive naked chest more disconcerting. The sun was about to dip down behind the ridge, but not before it had set fire to the clouds in the west, a flaming red that draped a glowing sheen over the blacksmith's oiled skin.

"You're beautiful," she murmured. "Like Odysseus."

"Like who?"

"Odysseus. A Greek warrior from"—she was going to say Homer's *Odyssey* but changed it to "from long ago."

Pokrovsky laughed unself-consciously and flexed both his arms to emphasize his huge biceps for her entertainment.

"Like rocks," he said.

"Granite boulders, more like."

He laughed again and put his muscles away, leaving her wondering what they would be like to touch. Until she came to teach in Tivil sixteen years ago, her experience of men had been limited to waltzing with cavalry officers or walking through the gilded gardens of Peterhof on the arm of an elegant naval captain. Even then she had enjoyed the feel of their hard masculine flesh under their uniforms, but they were as remote from Pokrovsky as the bright orange lizards that darted under his *banya* were from the gray monster crocodiles of the Nile.

Elizaveta was fifty-three now. Wasn't it time she stopped this girlish rubbish? It wasn't as though she'd never been asked, despite being tall. Three offers of marriage she'd turned down, much to her parents' anguish. She had even allowed one of the suitors to kiss her on the terrace, a recollection of a bristling mustache and the taste of good brandy on his lips, but she hadn't loved any of them and preferred her own company to that of fools.

"Pokrovsky," she said in her teacher's voice, "how old are you?"

"That's personal."

"How old, man?"

"Forty-four."

"Why aren't you married?"

"That's none of your damn business."

"I expect you frighten the females with those great granite boulders of yours. You'd crush any girl to death with them."

"Hah!" But the blacksmith was grinning again. "The trouble with you, Elizaveta, is that you think you know everything. If you're so damn clever, tell me, how old are you and why aren't you married?"

"Don't be so bloody impertinent, Pokrovsky. Go and get yourself decent at once. You'll be late for tonight if you don't hurry. Don't you know that you shouldn't even be talking to a lady in that rude state of undress?"

He roared with laughter and rubbed a great hand across his neat little beard, then ambled off to his *izba*. Elizaveta took her time heading into the forge; she didn't want him to think she was anything other than calm and indifferent to his gibes. But once inside, she poured herself a stiff glass of vodka and knocked it back in one. Only then did she permit herself a smile and imagine the heroic Odysseus with a chest like that.

★ ★ ★

*T*HE noise of a bell came first, sweet and silvery. Five pure notes in the darkness that wasn't darkness. It was more an absence of being, and Sofia even wondered if she was dead. Was this her own death knell she was hearing? But the ringing of the bell changed. It expanded and grew and surged and swelled until it was a rich rounded sound that reverberated all around her, making the air quiver and dance.

Yet the tolling of the bell seemed to arise from inside Sofia's head, not from outside. She could not only hear it, but feel it—the great brass clapper rapping against the delicate inside of her skull, clanging out each bass note in a crescendo of sound that she feared would crack her bones, the way glass will shatter when the right note is hit. And through it all came a voice in her ear, soft as love itself, yet so clear she could hear every word.

"Fly, my angel, fly."

She looked down for the first time and discovered that she was high up in the air at the topmost pinnacle of a tall spire that was attached to no building, just a towering needle of gold that pierced the sky. Like the Admiralty spire in St. Petersburg that used to glint like a blade of fire in the sunlight when she was a child.

"Fly, my angel, fly."

In one smooth movement she spread out her arms and found they were wings. She stared with astonishment at the fluttering of the feathers, long pearl-white gossamer feathers that smelled as salty as the sea and rustled as she breathed. She moved her wings gently up and down, flexing them, testing them, but they weighed nothing at all. Far below her stretched a wide flat plain full of silver-haired women, their faces turned up to her, thousands of pale ovals, each one with arms raised above her head. All whispered, "Fly, my angel, fly."

Sofia felt the breath of it under her wings and launched herself.

*S*HE opened her eyes. She had no idea where she was or how she'd arrived there, just that she was standing upright in the dark, arms outstretched to each side. White figures circled her, four of them. Flickering lights in their hands, candle flames, and the scent of cedarwood.

Rising from the floor a mist wove around her. She inhaled, a short sharp breath, and tasted the tang of burning pine needles, which made her look down.

At her feet on the blood-red cloth from Rafik's wooden chest stood a small iron brazier, and in it were things she could only guess at but which were alight; all crackled and spat and writhed. Her feet were bare. Outside the circle of light all was darkness, but she could sense instantly that she was indoors, somewhere cool, somewhere damp, somewhere deep inside the black womb of Mother Russia. The four figures stood silent and unmoving around her, one at each point of the compass, loose white gowns covering their bodies.

"Rafik," she murmured to the one directly in front of her.

As she did so she became aware that her own body was draped in a white gown. It rustled when she lowered her arms.

"Sofia."

Rafik's single word was like a cool touch on her forehead.

"Don't be afraid, Sofia, you are one of us."

"I'm not afraid, Rafik."

"Do you know why we have brought you here tonight?"

"Yes."

She didn't know how she knew, but she did. Her mind struggled to clear itself, but it was as though her thoughts were no longer her own.

"Speak it," Rafik said. "Why are you here tonight?"

"For Mikhail."

"Yes."

There was a prolonged silence while words pushed against her tongue, words that didn't seem to rise from her own mind.

"And for the village, Rafik," she said clearly. "It is for the village of Tivil that I am here, to make it live a life instead of die a death. I am here because I need to be and I am here because I am meant to be."

She barely recognized her own voice. It was low and resonant, and each word vibrated in the cool air. She shivered beneath her gown, but not with fear. She gazed around at the four figures, their eyes steady on hers, their lips murmuring silent words that drifted into the mist, thickening it, stirring it, causing it to linger as it brushed Sofia's cheek.

"Pokrovsky," she said, turning her eyes on the broad bear of a man whose wide shoulders stretched the white robe to the edge of its seams. "Blacksmith of Tivil, tell me who you are."

"I am the hands of this village. I labor for the workingman."

"*Spasibo*, Hands of Tivil."

She lowered her eyes from the blacksmith to the slight figure with the full lips and bold gaze. "Zenia, who are you?"

"I am a child of this village." Her voice rang clear and strong out past the flames and into the darkness beyond. "The children are the future and I am one of their number."

"*Spasibo*, Child of Tivil." Sofia swung around farther to face the figure in place to the east of her. "Elizaveta Lishnikova, schoolteacher of Tivil, tell me who you are."

The tall gray woman, with the nose like a bird's beak, stood very straight. "I am the mind of this village. I teach the children who are its future and bring knowledge and understanding to them the way the dawn in the east brings each new day to our village."

"*Spasibo*, Mind of Tivil."

Finally Sofia stepped around to look once more deep into the intense black eyes that burned with their ancient knowledge.

"Rafik," she asked, softly this time, "who are you?"

Ten heartbeats passed before he spoke. His voice was a deep echoing sound that made the flames shimmer and sway to a different pulse. "I am the soul of this village, Sofia. I guard and guide and protect this small patch of earth. All over Russia villages are destroyed and trampled by the brutish boot of a blood-addicted dictator who has murdered five million of his own people, yet still claims he is building a Workers' Paradise. Sofia," he spread his arms wide to include all the white robes, "the four of us have combined our strengths to safeguard Tivil, but you have seen the soldiers come. Seen the food stolen from our tables and the prayers clubbed to death before they are born."

"I have seen this."

"Now you have come to Tivil and the Pentangle is complete."

Sofia observed no signal, but the four white-clad figures stepped forward out of the shadows as one, until they were so close around her that when they each raised their left arm it rested easily on the shoulder of the person to the left. Sofia's heart was racing as she felt herself enclosed inside the circle. Rafik scattered something into the brazier at her feet so that it flared into life and the mist thickened into a dense fog. She could feel it crawling far down into her lungs every time she breathed. She swayed, her head growing too unwieldy for her neck, and a pulse at her temple throbbed in time with her heartbeat.

"Sofia." It was Rafik. "Open your eyes."

She hadn't realized they had closed. Their lids were heavy and slow to respond to her commands. What was happening to her?

"Sofia, take the stone into your hand."

He was holding out the white pebble to her, and without hesitation she took it. She expected something from it, some spark or sign or even a pain shooting up her arm, but there was nothing. Just an ordinary warm round pebble lying in the palm of her hand.

At a murmur from Rafik the circle sealed itself tighter with hands touching shoulders, and a slow rhythmic chanting began. Soft at first, like a mother crooning to her infant, a sound that loosened Sofia's limbs and stole her sense of self. But the chanting rose, the language unknown to her, until it was a rushing wind that tore at her mind, ripped out her conscious thoughts, and swept them away until only a great echoing chamber remained inside her head and only one word leaped out of it.

"Mikhail!" she cried out. "Mikhail!"

Hands touched her head, and she started to see things and hear things that she knew were not there.

A small room. A small desk. A small man with a small mind. Long rabbity teeth and pale cheeks that looked as though they'd never seen the sun. His elbows on the desk, his thoughts on the prisoner in front of him.

The prisoner angered him, though he kept all sign of it from his face. He shifted the lamp on his desk to angle the beam more into the prisoner's eyes and had the satisfaction of seeing him wince. One of the prisoner's eyes was swollen and half-shut, his jaw bruised, his lip as split and purple as an overripe plum, yet still the prisoner clung to the wrong attitude. Hadn't he learned that it didn't matter whether he was guilty or not guilty of the crimes he was charged with?

Wrong attitude.

That was his real crime, that he still believed he could pick and choose which bits of the Communist creed he would adopt and which ones he would reject.

Wrong fucking attitude.

The prisoner's mind was a danger to the state. Time to change what was in it or discover that the state could break the strongest of wills and the strongest of minds. The state was expert at it and he, the interrogator, was an instrument of the Soviet State.

There would be only one fucking winner.

"Mikhail," she breathed.

"Mikhail," the circle echoed.

The white stone in Sofia's hand seemed to grow chill. Or was that just her own skin? She wrapped her fingers tighter around it, digging her nails into its cold hard surface as though they could gouge out the eyes of the man with rabbit's teeth.

"A curse on you, Interrogator," she hissed.

The flames in the brazier surged as if they fed on her hatred.

"Mikhail," she intoned into the shadows. "Come to me."

HY me?" Sofia asked.

The clouds were low and there was no moon, so the night felt heavy and cloying despite the breeze that rustled up from the river, fretting under the eaves of the *izbas* and stealing Sofia's words from her lips.

"Why me?" she repeated.

"Don't you know?" Rafik asked in a low voice. He was pacing with a smooth unbroken stride over the uneven tangles of roots and soil, skirting around the fringes of Tivil. "Don't you know now who you are?"

"Tell me, Rafik, who I am."

"Feel for it, Sofia, stretch your mind back to the beginning and to before the beginning. Reach deep into yourself."

A bat flitted out of the night sky, circling jerkily above their heads, followed quickly by another, and the shadow of their wings seemed to press on Sofia's mind. Something stirred inside her, something unfamiliar. She experienced again that sense of being high up on a golden pinnacle with the silver-haired figures below her, sending their breath to lift her wings. She shook her head, but still the image wouldn't go away. It lodged there.

Rafik did not push her, but he gave her time. Together they were pacing out the circle that the gypsy trod nightly around Tivil. Through the fields, past the pond and around the back of each *izba*, weaving what he called a protective thread. When he led her out of the ritual chamber, she was not surprised to discover that the mysterious ceremony had taken place inside the church, not in the main hall but in the old storeroom at the back of the church where the lock still bore the marks of her knife.

"Now," Rafik had said with his hands on hers, a prickling sensation growing between their palms as if they were being stitched together, "now you shall tread the circle with me." His eyes probed hers, and she was certain he could see clearly even in the moonless night air. "Are you ready, Sofia?"

"Yes, I'm ready."

Her blood was pounding in her ears. Ready for what? She didn't know, but without anything being said, she understood that this was the bargain she had struck with Rafik. His help with the safety of Mikhail in exchange for her help with the safety of the village. But it was all so strange, and she had a feeling that the cost of this bargain to both could be high.

"I'm ready," she said again.

Suddenly he smiled a gentle smile and softly kissed her cheek. "Don't fear," he whispered in her ear. "You are strong and you have the power of generations within you."

MORE bats came. In ones and twos at first, and then a steady trickle of beating wings pursued them, until finally a swirling black cloud of the creatures swung down from the mountain ridge, rising out of the depths of the forest and hurtling in a screaming, screeching, scratching wall of eyes and teeth and sharp scything claws toward the point where Sofia was pacing the circle. Rafik walked an arm's length ahead of her.

She lashed out at them, but there were too many. The dense black shadow fell on her like a net, and instantly they were in her hair, nipping and tearing. Tiny leathery wings squeezed under the collar of her blouse, furry bodies burned hot against her skin, their razor sharp teeth cutting strips from her throat and her shoulder blades, slicing into her cheeks, hooking their dagger claws into her eyelids.

She fought them in the seething dark. She swept them from her body, scraped them from her face, dragged them out of the air, and ripped off their wings. She stamped on their evil little distorted faces, attacking them with her hands, her elbows, her feet, and even her teeth. Fending them off her eyes . . .

As suddenly as they came, they were gone. A great susurration of wings and then nothing. There was total silence, not even the wind in the trees, and that was the moment she realized that the plague of bats had left Rafik untouched. They had descended on her, but not him. Why? And why had Rafik offered no help? She was shaking violently and raised a hand to her face but found no blood, no scratches, no pain. Had it all been in her mind?

Rafik nodded and raised his eyes to where the moon was hidden behind the ancient boughs of the cedar tree at the entrance to Tivil. "I told you," he said.

"Told me what?"

"That you are strong."

I poured you a drink."

It was far into the night when Sofia slid gratefully into the big armchair that was Mikhail's and wondered how long the drink had been waiting for her on the table.

"Thank you, Pyotr. I certainly need it." She tried to smile. "I'm sorry I'm so late."

The boy, clothed in a pair of cut-down pajamas, picked up the glass of vodka and handed it to her. His brown eyes were so pleased to see her that she risked a light reassuring brush of her hand against his. His skin felt wonderfully warm and alive, as skin should feel. Not like her own. Her own was drained of moisture, dry as paper to the touch, as though everything of worth had been sucked out of it tonight, sucked out of her. A pulse throbbed behind her eye.

"I couldn't find you anywhere tonight, Sofia. I thought you'd decided to . . ."

The cuckoo in the kitchen clock called twice. Two o'clock in the morning.

"Pyotr, I'll never run away secretly. If I leave, I'll tell you first. Believe me?"

He smiled tentatively. "*Da*. Yes. But where were you? In the forest?"

Sofia threw the slug of vodka down her throat and felt it kick life into her exhausted body. "Not the forest, but somewhere just as dark."

Without comment he refilled her glass, wiped a drip from the neck of the bottle with a grubby finger, and licked it off with his tongue, and Sofia experienced such a sense of relief at the normality of the boy's action that she almost told him what had happened to her tonight. The words wanted to spill from her mouth so that she could hear Pyotr say, *No, Sofia, don't be silly, you fell asleep in a field and had a bad dream.* And then they'd laugh together and everything would be back to normal inside her brain.

She drank the vodka.

"I was with Rafik. We were . . . trying to find out more about what's happening to Mikhail."

"I've been helping too. Look, I made the key." He extracted from his pajama pocket a large iron key that was a rich purple-black metal, shiny and new. He held it out to her. "And I took the old one back to the office, like you said."

Sofia dragged herself out of the comfort of the chair and hugged the boy close.

"Thank you, Pyotr. You are as clever as you are brave. We can't search the hall now in the dark, as any candle would show at the windows and attract attention. So we'll start on it tomorrow." She grimaced. "Today, I mean. It's not far off morning already."

Pyotr nodded, but she spotted the flicker of unease in his eyes.

"Pyotr, what is it?"

"Nothing."

"Tell me."

"Chairman Fomenko came here."

"What did he want?"

"He was looking for you."

Sofia froze. *Not now. Don't let him take me now.* "What did you tell him?"

"That I didn't know where you were. It was the truth."

"I'm glad you didn't have to lie to him. Don't worry, I'll speak to him tomorrow. Now go and get some sleep or you'll be dead on your feet in the morning."

He continued to stand there for a moment, his face in shadow, half boy, half man. "You too," he said at last and left.

Sofia collapsed into Mikhail's chair and rested her head back on the place where his head had rested. But she didn't sleep.

FORTY-SIX

Davinsky Camp
July 1933

THE next day Anna wasn't any better, but with the help of Nina and Tasha and even young Lara, she got herself out to the Work Zone again and back to shoveling grit. Her work rate was pathetically slow, but at least it would earn her a bare scrap of a *paiok* to eat without robbing others of theirs.

Her own weakness made her mind wander to the image of Sofia's weakness during that bad shuddering time when Sofia almost died. Slowly the injury to her hand had healed, but even now all this time later the memory of what it had cost made Anna spit blood on the ground, as though the shame still gathered in her mouth and she had to rid herself of it or suffocate.

In August of that bad year the old *babushka* died, the one who slept next to Anna on the bedboard, and the first thing Anna did was steal her coat now that Crazy Sara had taken hers. When the early snows came she had no intention of dying. In October typhus raged through the camp, sweeping up lives as indescriminately as a fox chokes chickens in a henhouse, but both Anna and Sofia had escaped its teeth. In fact it made life a fraction easier for them because the hut became less overcrowded and Anna was able to move up to a middle bunk near a window. She also stole a second, thicker coat from a dead body.

Work on the road was brutal as the temperatures dropped in November. Ice broke hammers and froze fingers to rocks. The snow drifted down out of a misleadingly soft pink sky, settling on the road and the bent backs of the laborers, its sugar coating transforming the scene into one of stark beauty. Except nobody could acknowledge beauty any more. They'd forgotten what it looked like. The nearest thing to beauty they ever saw was an extra bowl of *kasha* when the cook pocketed a bribe.

When the long line of prisoners finally trudged back into the Zone after a two-hour march through the snow in the dark, even the searchlights looked welcoming, great moons of yellow warmth. But as Anna shuffled numbly toward the hut, head lowered against the wind, a hand pulled her out of the line and a pair of eager lips that stank of cheap beer sought hers. It was the guard, the one with the surplus of pork fat and *pelmeni*. Mishenko was his name, Ilya Mishenko. She tugged away from him.

"What the fuck is wrong with you?" His hand strayed to her head, brushed snow from her headscarf, touched her cheek. "You aren't very friendly anymore, are you? Not long ago you couldn't get enough of me and all that good food I gave you, but for weeks now you've been as cold as this fucking weather. How about an extra blanket? Or a bowl of good meat stew to keep out the—"

"You bastard." She jerked herself free. "I don't want anything. I've told you to leave me alone." She gave him a bitter stare and hurried across the trodden snow toward the hut door.

"I won't leave you alone, you hot little cunt," he shouted after her. "Not till you say yes again. And you will, I know you will. One day when you're sick or hurt, you'll say yes again." He rammed his fur *shapka* tighter on his head and laughed. "It's just a matter of time."

Anna's hands blocked her ears, disgust sharp as copper on her tongue. He was dirty. She was dirty. So what was the difference between them, both exploiting what they had? But as she joined the crush to squeeze through the door into the hut, she suddenly saw

Sofia standing off to one side, oblivious of the snow. Watching Ilya Mishenko.

$\int$OFIA avoided Anna after that, as if she too were disgusted and could not bear to be anywhere close to her. For two days she hardly came near her and it was like a knife wound, gut-ripping and unexpected. Even when Anna offered a story about Vasily as a lure, all she got was a shake of the head and "I'm too tired."

Anna lay on her new bedboard, the air in the hut heavy with kerosene fumes. She was fully dressed in her work clothes and padded coat because, like everyone else in the winter, you took off your clothes only for the *banya*, the monthly bath. The smell meant nothing, but warmth meant everything.

She placed her mittened hands over her face and buried her nose in them, smelled all the filth and rank rotten fibers of them, felt the grit and thorns embedded in them scrape across her skin. They were disgusting. No human being should ever have to wear such foul rags. Yet she loved them. They protected her, got dirty and ragged and repulsive instead of herself. Gently she kissed the palm of each mitten.

Couldn't Sofia see that?

$\mathcal{E}$VENING head count was quick for once. The numbers all tallied and the commandant was sober, so the prisoners didn't have to stand out in the freezing cold for more than forty minutes. The night sky above them was a vast black blanket speckled with what looked like fireflies they seemed so close and so bright, but in fact were stars. It hadn't snowed today, but the previous day's fall lay a meter thick on the ground, so that two envied brigades had remained back in the camp to shovel paths and brush the roof of the commandant's house.

It was almost time for the prisoners to be locked into the huts for the night, and Anna was on her bunk. The woman beside her was picking at the scabs on her legs and smiling as though it gave her pleasure, while others were shuffling around the hut or collapsed on bedboards. But out of the corner of Anna's eye she saw a figure slide toward the door, and despite the scarf wound around her face, Anna knew it was Sofia.

She carried her right arm as always slung across her chest, resting the damaged hand on her collarbone. It had started to heal remarkably well in the beginning as the infection was drawn out of the flesh by the herbal potions, and the extra food had fed strength into her body, but now it had stopped. At this level of cold, nothing healed. Only the spring warmth would continue the process, so until then Sofia protected her hand with every scrap of cloth she could beg, borrow, or steal. She opened the door only a fraction and slipped out.

Anna scrambled for her shoes and pulled them on still wet, but she snapped one of the strings that tied them on her feet, so she had to fiddle with their fixings. By the time she'd wrapped her scarf around her head and hurried outside into the freezing night, Sofia was nowhere in sight. The central compound was a large floodlit square, deserted now except for a couple of guards deep in conversation as they patrolled the perimeter. They were smoking cigarettes and stamping their feet as they walked to keep warm.

What was Sofia up to?

Lockup was any moment, and if she was locked out of the hut she'd die of hypothermia overnight. The cookhouse? The dump? The *banya*? The laundry? Anna skimmed past them all, keeping to the shadows, but there was no sign of her friend. Her breath came in painfully short gasps and she told herself it was the cold, not fear, but she *was* frightened. Ever since that moment when the guard had tried to kiss her lips yesterday evening, Sofia had changed.

As she ducked her head against the wind, a sound caught her ears. It was a man's voice and he was growling. There was no other word for the animal noises he was making, and Anna recognized the sound at once, a sound she knew far too well, a sound that made her feel sick. She ran. Nobody ever ran in Davinsky camp, but she ran behind the tool hut and in the dense shadows, she found them, Sofia and Mishenko. They were almost knee-deep in snow and jammed up against the hut wall, Sofia's skirt up around her waist, his hands clutching her pale white buttocks as he thrust into her again and again. The animal growls sounded as though they were tearing her insides out, like wolves at a deer's tender belly.

Anna loathed the man for what he'd done to her and now for what he was doing to Sofia. She opened her mouth to scream at him, but at that exact moment, with head thrown back and his face in a rictus that looked like agony, he finished the job and instantly with-drew. The sudden silence came as a shock.

He turned away to adjust his clothing for only a split second, but it was a split second when the Four Horsemen galloped down on him with a vengeance. Quick as a rat Sofia drew a rock from her jacket and brought it down on the back of his skull with all her strength. He collapsed forward, face in the snow, with no more than a soft grunt, but Sofia threw herself on his back and kept pounding till Anna caught her by the wrist.

"Enough, Sofia, that's enough. You must stop now."

"It'll never be enough."

"He's dead."

A sigh rose up from somewhere deep in Sofia's chest and she stood up, her whole body shaking and her eyes unrecognizable. They gleamed white in the shadows, and she was breathing hard.

"Yes," she said harshly. "He's dead. He won't be bothering you again."

"He won't be bothering either of us."

Anna took her trembling friend into her arms and held her close, rocking her gently. They stood like that for a long time despite the subzero temperature, listening to each other's heartbeat.

"Lockup," Anna whispered. "We must be quick."

It was the work of two minutes to scoop out a man-size hole in the deep snowdrift against the rear of the hut and bundle the dead meat inside it. The snowdrift would not melt until spring, and by then who would care? They kicked fresh snow over the mound, prayed for a blizzard overnight, and then ran back to their hut before the door was locked. The knowledge that in their pockets they carried a pack of Belomor cigarettes, a steel lighter, a penknife, half a bar of chocolate, and a wristwatch gave them a wild energy that made them laugh out loud. A haul like that would feed them most of the winter.

FORTY-SEVEN

SOFIA waited in the dark, tense and breathing hard. She was standing by the tree at the gateway to Tivil. He would come, she was certain he'd come. The night sky was overcast, dark and damp, with a spit of rain in the wind, and when her limbs started to shiver, she was glad because it meant the scorching heat within her was leaking out. In the silence, in the cold, she heard Rafik's words again: *Reach deep into yourself. You are strong.*

Strong?

She didn't feel strong, she felt battered and exhausted. She wanted to weep with need. Questions crashed around her brain: what exactly was it that Rafik could see inside her and what happened inside that chamber? Who were those silver-haired people and why had the bats come for her? And would Mikhail come, would he? She had to believe he would, whether as a result of Rafik's weird ceremony or simply because Fomenko had responded to her veiled threat and decided to throw his weight around in the right places. She took a deep slow breath to calm her quivering mind and felt the night breeze wash through her lungs, flushing out the panic.

Mikhail, my Mikhail. Come to me.

She murmured the words aloud and heard a flutter of wings for a second, but when she looked up it was gone, and she wondered if her tired mind had imagined it. On the edge of Tivil she could sense the air somehow growing thinner, the danger sharper. The scars on her fingers ached the way they only did when she was nervous.

Reach deep.

Her eyes scoured the blackness for a long time and saw nothing. And then a tingling sensation started in the soles of her feet and spread to the palms of her hands, and suddenly her heart tightened in her chest. Her legs started to move, and at first she was aware of the ruts under her feet, of stones and potholes, of stumbling awkwardly in the darkness and then she was flying down the road, racing toward him, arms outstretched, raindrops brushing her cheek.

Mikhail was in her arms, warm and safe and alive. For a second she was frightened that her senses were betraying her. Perhaps this wasn't real, just another version of her desire unfolding inside her head. But his clothes stank, and dried blood lay stiff on his collar, and his unshaven jaw felt rough against her skin. His poor lips were swollen. But not too swollen to press hard on hers, or to whisper into her mouth over and over, "Sofia, my love, Sofia."

*H*E washed in the yard at the back of the house. A dim pool of light spilled from the room's oil lamp, but most of the yard lay in shadows. She watched him from inside as he stripped off every filthy scrap of clothing, threw it in a pile on the ground, and set light to it. The flames were small and smoldering in the damp air, but they sent golden fingers of light shimmering up his long naked thigh and gleaming over the strong curve of his buttock. Sofia felt a surge of desire, but as the shadows shifted and draped themselves over him like a cloak, she moved away from the window to give him his privacy.

When he eventually entered the room he was wearing a clean black shirt and trousers, and at the sight of her tucked into his big wingback chair his face broke into a smile of relief, as though he feared she might have gone. His eyes were a dull and damaged gray that bruised her heart. One eye and his lips were swollen, a tooth chipped, and he was moving awkwardly, something hurting inside, but when she started to ask he dismissed it as nothing.

She rose and kissed his mouth, gently soothing it with her tongue, and eased him into the chair. She curled up at his feet with her chin resting on his knee, and her hands began to stroke the calves of his legs, drawing the anger from his muscles, willing her strength into him. The familiar masculine scent of him at last silenced the trembling in her chest.

"You look wonderful," he said, and he tenderly touched her cheek as if it were the finest fragile porcelain. His finger traced the line of her lips. "You shine."

She kissed the tip of his finger. "I missed you."

He ruffled her blond hair and twisted a lock of it around his forefinger as though attaching her to himself. The silence between their words dropped away. He cupped his hand around the back of her head, cradling it.

"You were with me," he whispered, his gaze intent on her face. "All the time you were with me."

*H*E'S still asleep."

It was the second time Mikhail had checked on Pyotr, anxiety for the boy driving him out of his chair despite his exhaustion.

"He was worried about you," Sofia said as she poured out two vodkas and handed one to him when he was settled again. "But he's fine. He's strong."

"Thank you for caring for him."

"I did very little except take him to Dagorsk to hunt for you. We looked after each other."

"Come here, Sofia."

He held out a hand to her and when she slipped hers into it, he drew her to him onto his lap. He rested his head against hers, holding her so close she could feel the beat of his heart, and slowly the rise and fall of their inhalation and exhalation fell into step until they were breathing as one.

"Sofia," he whispered into her hair, "tell me what the hell is going on."

She was silent.

He lifted a hand and tipped her chin up to look at him, and his eyes lingered on her face. "You were waiting for me. How did you know I was coming?"

"I didn't, not for certain."

"Sofia, I was in prison being bounced from interrogation to beating and back to interrogation, over and over, no food, no water, no sleep. I count myself lucky that I hadn't yet had the Cupboard inflicted on me but—"

"What's the Cupboard?"

"You don't want to know."

She kissed the bruised eye. "Tell me."

"It's something the other prisoners in my cell whispered about. It's a space one meter by half a meter and the height of a man. The Cupboard, they call it. The bastards throw you in there with four or five or even six other poor devils crammed together, all unable to move, barely able to breathe. You could be in there hours or even days with no one able to turn or sit. Most suffocate to death in it."

Sofia buried her face in his neck.

"I'd have ended up in there if I hadn't been freed, no doubt of that," he said. His voice was savage. "Yet suddenly in the middle of the interrogation an OGPU officer marched into the room, waved around a signed release order, and I was out on the street in the rain in the middle of the night before I could say *Chto za chyort!*" He knocked back the shot of vodka and shuddered.

"And then I found you waiting for me." He kissed her hair and gently rubbed his cheek over its silky strands.

"You're safe," she whispered. "That's all that matters."

"Sofia, I need to know."

Tenderly she took his face in her hands. "Mikhail, my dearest Mikhail, I honestly don't know what happened. Your release could have been caused by Rafik—the gypsy has amazing powers to move thoughts—or by . . . someone else. Let's leave it until tomorrow, my love. You've been through enough." She brushed her fingers down the line of his smooth straight nose, still wonderfully unbroken, and along the curve of his broad brow.

Mikhail frowned. His dark gaze searched her face, and their eyes held fast on each other until suddenly something deep within him seemed to open and some emotion shook his strong frame so violently that his limbs trembled under her. He groaned, and Sofia hungrily pressed her lips to his throat. When Mikhail rose from the chair with her in his arms and bore her from the room, she shut her ears to the accusing voice in her head, the one that said she was stealing.

*T*HE world had stopped spinning on its axis, Mikhail was sure of it. How else could he have been jerked from one indelible moment of hell to such abundance of perfection? Her naked skin was a pearl. Not *like* a pearl. It *was* a pearl. A creamy translucent paleness that somehow glowed from within. It made even the tips of his fingers ache with desire for her.

They lay limbs entwined together on his bed in semidarkness, with only the faint gleam from the living room's kerosene lamp creeping into the room, where it lay like a dog on the rag rug. Mikhail didn't want Sofia to see his own body. It was a mess, covered in bruises and cuts and black swellings. It disgusted him, so what would it do to her? He had always taken a certain pride in his body, in its strength and its invincibility. He'd always been able to depend on it, but now his rage at those who had caused such damage to it and humiliation to him in the name of justice writhed, snakelike, in his guts.

She seemed to sense it. Her hand slid tentatively to his stomach, where it started to circle, gently at first, then firmer, harder, fingers splayed out, and he could feel the heat build up under them, see a delicate vein pulsing at her temple as she leaned close. She was driving the hate out of his body, but just as fiercely the heat flared deep in his groin.

His lips seized hers and his hand cradled her naked breast, small and firm and perfect in his palm. She moaned, a soft sobbing sound, and his fingers teased, stroked, and explored each delicate rise and fall of her undernourished body, the angular edge of her hip bone and the fall of her silken stomach to the dense mound of blond curls. He inhaled the exquisite scent of her, breathing it deep within himself.

His lips caressed her eyes, her ears, the tempting hollow of her throat while his fingers searched out the moist secret places that brought forth whimpers of desire from her open mouth. His lips kissed that mouth. He adored the way she growled low in her throat when he rippled his fingers down the soft inside of her thigh and the way her whole body shuddered when he took her erect nipple in his mouth. She tasted like a clean wild creature. Not dirty like himself. However hard he'd scrubbed himself with the brush in the yard tonight, he still felt the dirt of the cells and the beatings lodged under the layers of his skin.

It was as if she could see the thoughts form in his head.

"My beloved," she crooned, and she pressed him back onto the pillow.

She trailed her tongue up his cheek, then down the other. Its pliant warmth seemed to envelop him, soft and enticing, as it flicked across his forehead and along the line of his nose, a touch on his lips and a nudge on his teeth and down to his chin. He knew what she was doing, and his heart melted. She was cleansing him.

Her breath was coming fast as she lowered her head to his chest, and he gasped when her tongue flicked out once more as slowly, sensuously, in unbearable circles she started to lick the beatings and the humiliations out of his body. He buried his hands in her hair that rippled like moonlight, squeezing it tight in his fists, and he let out a howl that tore everything out of him but his feelings for this woman.

"I love you, Sofia."

"My Mikhail."

Their words were hoarse with need, and her skin exuded a musk that swept through his blood, as her skin became his skin. Her blood became his blood. When he lay above the length of her shining pearl body he held himself back, lovingly brushed a tangle of hair from her face, and looked close into her huge wild eyes.

"Sofia, sweetest heart," he murmured, "Sofia, is this . . . ?"

Her lips opened in spasm and her face turned away from his. "Is this my first time?" she moaned.

"If it is, I—"

"No, Mikhail. Don't worry, this isn't my first time."

The bitterness in her voice was harsh. Gently he turned her face back to him and kissed her lips, soothing, murmuring, whispering to her until they relaxed under his, entwined his tongue with hers and felt her naked hips rise against him.

"We'll make this the first time, my love," he breathed into her mouth. "For both of us."

*T*HIS is as it should be."

Sofia whispered the words to the darkness. No brutal fumbling behind a shed in the rain, no careless ripping open of her flesh as though she were dead meat. *This is as it should be*, a glorious outburst of joy that transformed her body into something wonderful and vibrant, something she barely recognized. She brushed her lips on Mikhail's wrist, tasting his skin once more.

"This is as it should be," she whispered.

She sighed, unable to make herself leave him. The kerosene lamp in the living room had burned out, so that the night's darkness was complete, denser now as dawn approached, and she knew she had to move. But instead she nestled closer in the crook of Mikhail's arm, rubbing her skin against his, feeling the warmth of him as he slept wrapped around her. She loved the weight of his body against hers. She listened to the rhythm of his breathing and wished sweet dreams into whatever life he was leading behind his flickering eyelids.

Her mind shut down to all else. Everything that was not love ceased to exist, and even though she knew for certain there would be a heavy price to pay, right now the price seemed nothing. Nothing. She slid a hand possessively down the length of his thigh and heard his breathing pick up as if she had slid into his dream. Her fingers sought out the bruised swelling on the side of his leg that throbbed hot as a reminder of where he had been and what had been done to him. It was all she needed. Anger drove her from his bed where love could not.

She dressed quickly and quietly, then drank the shot of vodka she had abandoned on the table last night. But before she left the house to step out into the early morning darkness, she returned soundlessly to Mikhail's bedside and bent over his sleeping form. So lightly it was barely a kiss, she brushed her lips against his forehead and even in the dark knew his mouth had curled into a smile as he slept.

She longed to keep him like this, hers forever, hers alone, to love and to cherish. To live a whole life together till they were old and gray and could look back on these days with laughter and say that magical phrase *Do you remember when . . . ?* Why not? She could. He loved her, he'd said so. Her heart tightened painfully in her chest. She could. It would be so easy to say nothing and start a new life here and now with Mikhail.

Oh Anna, I can't.

Slowly she straightened up, her bones heavy and cumbersome, lifeless things that were no use to her without his touch on them, without his kisses on them, without his arms crushing them. She stepped back from the bed and tears filled her eyes. She turned away and from her pocket drew the key Pyotr had made for her.

Today everything would change.

*P*YOTR heard movement in the house. It woke him but he buried his face in his pillow, refusing to wake up. What was happening to him and to his world? It felt as if the foundations were cracking under his feet, and it terrified him. He tried to drive himself back into the comfort of his dream, but it was no good; the dream was out of reach. Like Papa.

The noise of a saucepan banging on the stove in the kitchen reached his ears, and his heart gave a little skip behind his ribs. Sofia was still here. That cheered him and he jumped out of bed. She'd know what he should do, she'd help him . . . but Sofia was a fugitive. She'd actually confessed to him that she'd escaped from prison, so by helping her, he was making himself an enemy of the people.

That thought made him feel dizzy.

Is that how Comrade Stalin felt last year when his wife, Nadezhda Allilueva, shot herself inside the Kremlin? Sick and uncertain? Where did love weigh in the balance against the words of the Great Leader? He kicked a shoe across his tiny room in an outburst of anger. Most of all it frightened him to think what might be happening to Papa, and in a rush to escape his thoughts he hurried out of his room.

The figure at the table rose slowly from the chair, the movement awkward and ungainly, not like his father at all. Not quick and confident like Papa. Yet they were Papa's strong shoulders and Papa's voice calling his name.

"Pyotr."

Pyotr threw himself into his father's open arms, and together they tumbled back into the chair, where Pyotr clung tight and hid his face in his father's shirt. He was crying like a girl and didn't want Papa to see.

"Pyotr, my son."

Something in his voice made Pyotr look up. Papa's cheeks were wet with tears.

FORTY-EIGHT

AN unanticipated pleasure, my dear. I didn't expect to see you again so soon."

Deputy Stirkhov exhaled a gray snake of smoke that coiled around the room as he waved Sofia into a chair in his gleaming chrome office. A vodka bottle sat on his desk without its lid. It was half-empty, but the glass beside it was full.

Sofia slid onto the leather seat in front of the desk. "You underestimate me," she smiled.

"You have information for me?"

"Of course. It's what you paid me for. Didn't I promise it?"

A satisfied smile split his smooth moon face in half. "Not everyone does what they promise in this world."

"I do. If you think otherwise, you don't know me."

"I intend to get to know you much better," he said smoothly, reaching into his desk drawer. He drew out another shot glass, filled it, and pushed it across the desk to her. It had Lapland reindeer etched on its surface.

"Thank you," she said, but she didn't pick it up.

She felt his gaze on her blouse. It was one of Zenia's, of homespun cloth, a dusky rose pink with embroidered woodland flowers on the collar and cuffs.

"I am informed that a member of your village is in prison right now." He seemed to be talking to her breasts.

"If you mean Comrade Pashin, he has been released."

His eyes shot up to hers. "Indeed? When?"

"Today."

"That's a shame; I was sure they'd hold on to our wayward factory director. Dagorsk is better off without the likes of him."

"Why?"

"Because he's a troublemaker. Oh yes, I grant that he knows his stuff as an engineer and has shaken up those lazy imbeciles who work in his factory, but he's one of those arrogant bastards who think they know better than the Party line." He leaned forward on his elbows and pointed a manicured finger at her. "That one is not a man of the people like he pretends. He's hiding something, I'm certain. I tell you, I can feel it in my piss every time I see him. Just wait"—he threw the vodka down his throat and stubbed out his cigarette, still jabbing at it long after the stub was out—"he'll trip himself up one day, and I'll be there to catch him."

Sofia scooped up her drink from the desk. For a moment it seemed as though she was going to throw it in his face, but instead she raised her glass to the portrait of Stalin and drank it straight down. She made a soft noise in the back of her throat that was almost a hiss, and then she smiled at Stirkhov.

"How perceptive you are, Comrade Deputy."

"And how very beautiful you are, Comrade Morozova."

She let her eyelashes flicker and put a hand to her throat, as though to still the sudden race of her heart. "I'm glad we understand each other," she smiled. "Now we can do business."

"So what's this information you've brought me from Tivil? A *kolkhoznik* has been late to work, has he? Or did one of your ham-fisted peasants get into a drunken brawl and now is being denounced for singing obscene words to the tune of the *Internationale*?"

"No, nothing like that."

"Then what?"

"Someone in Tivil is hoarding, and I mean large amounts of potatoes, rutabagas, and grain."

It was like throwing a grenade. Comrade Stirkhov's mouth hung
open.

"Now I'll grab Tivil by the throat," he growled, "and shake it till it
begs for mercy. Who is this enemy of the people?"

SOFIA raced back to Tivil. The morning sky was a vivid splash of
blue, and a handful of crows hung on the breeze barely dipping their
wings. The street was noisy when she reached the village, because two
women and a gaggle of girls were trying to wash a goat under the
water pump and the animal was putting up a struggle. Its bristly white
coat was caked in mud from the pond, and the children were shrieking with laughter each time it butted their skinny chests. Sofia paused,
observing the scene, memorizing it, savoring the ordinariness of it.
From now on, nothing would be ordinary.

She headed over to the school where summer camp was still in full
progress. The yard was bustling with shining white Young Pioneer
shirts and shining bright eyes, young bodies all racing around and performing perfect cartwheels. Yes, she thought, Zenia was right. These
are the future of Tivil, and it astonished Sofia to realize how much
she cared. This village had in some strange way nestled tight against
her heart.

"Have you come to read to us?"

It was Anastasia, swinging on the fence with bare feet, a tendril of
her hair threaded between her lips.

"No, not today, Anastasia. Another time, I promise. I need to
speak to your head teacher, so will you do me a favor and tell her I'm
here?"

At that moment she spotted Pyotr's unruly mop of brown hair. He
was over in the shade of a clump of alder trees and was obviously
demonstrating to a circle of younger boys how to build a cantilever
bridge with logs and planks. It looked like an elaborate construction
to Sofia's untutored eye, and when a child leaped onto the central
span and bounced up and down on it, she held her breath. But it
didn't collapse, and she felt an absurd rush of pride in him. Anastasia's
eager eyes followed Sofia's to Pyotr, and her small chest heaved in a

silent sigh. Then she skipped off to the stretch of parched grass where Elizaveta Lishnikova was timing races with a large stopwatch.

For one vivid second, Sofia wanted the world to stop. Right here and now. With children at play and Mikhail safe in his bed, the sun shining and herself standing in the village street as if she belonged there. Just stop. Here and now in this small moment of happiness. But she drew in a deep shuddering breath and moved on to the next moment and the next after that. Because there was her promise to Anna.

And if Anna was already dead? If all this was for nothing? What then?

*W*HAT happened last night?"

Elizaveta gazed sternly at Sofia. "You were there," she said. "You have eyes in your head. You saw what happened yourself."

They were standing in the teacher's elegantly furnished living room. Pictures lined the walls, old photographs of men in extravagant uniforms and formidable women in large dresses, with medals and jewelry hand-tinted to shine out. Sofia wanted to spend time examining them, seeking out Elizaveta Lishnikova's strong features in their faces, but such curiosity would not be welcomed. Instead she asked the question again.

"What happened last night? You are a rational person. I don't believe you would take part in a ceremony that was . . . unhealthy."

"Is that what you think it was? Unhealthy?"

"No." Sofia shook her head. "No, I don't. But I've seen the damage it does to Rafik and the way it makes him ill."

Elizaveta frowned and ran a finger along the arch of one eyebrow, smoothing out the thoughts behind it. "Sit down," she said.

Sofia chose a seat on a fragile chaise longue, and to her surprise Elizaveta came and sat beside her, her back erect and her hands folded quietly on her lap. The pose made Sofia think immediately of the aristocratic women in the photographs.

"Comrade Lishnikova, I want to understand more about what it is the gypsies do." Sofia looked into the proud brown eyes. "Please. Help me."

The eyes didn't change, but the mouth opened a fraction and gave an involuntary smile. "I don't know you, young woman, and this is a dangerous society we are living in, riddled with informers eager to earn a cheap rouble by making up lies about—"

"I'm not an informer."

"You've been seen entering Deputy Stirkhov's office."

"Word travels fast."

"This is Soviet Russia, so what do you expect? But tell me, if not to inform, why were you there?" The older woman lifted her chin and peered down her long nose through half-closed eyes.

"To protect Tivil."

"I think you mean, to protect Comrade Pashin."

"Both."

Elizaveta nodded, and the firm lines of her face softened. "Love is not the best guide, my dear. It makes you do things that . . ." She shrugged eloquently.

Sofia laughed. ". . . That are not always wise?"

"Exactly."

"I'll take that risk."

"Rafik has taken a risk trusting you, a stranger." She held up a hand impatiently. "No, don't tell me you're his niece because I don't believe it. But . . ." She paused and studied Sofia's face. "Rafik has abilities that are beyond our understanding, and I trust his instinct."

"Thank you."

"So I will tell you what I think happened last night, if you wish."

Sofia leaned closer. "Please."

"You have to understand that Rafik has an extraordinary mind. Whether the skills he possesses are self-taught or inherited from his gypsy ancestry, who's to say?"

"Is it hypnotism?"

"It's more than that, I believe. He has a power of mind that can transcend the thoughts of others and manipulate them, but it's at a cost to himself. He once told me it causes hemorrhages inside his skull."

Sofia shivered. Outside, the sound of children's laughter belonged to a different world.

"So you help him, is that it?" Sofia said quietly. "You and the blacksmith and Zenia, to lessen the damage he does to himself."

"Yes."

"So why choose me?"

"I don't know. You must ask Rafik that question. Each night he spins what he calls a thread of protection around the village, pacing out a circle. He says if he could pace around the whole of Russia, he would."

Sofia smiled. "He's a good man, but has he really helped Tivil?"

"Good God, yes. We're still alive, aren't we? Other villages all around us have been decimated by famine and sucked dry by troops enforcing quotas, until sometimes no children at all have survived. Listen to ours." The shouts of the Young Pioneers at play made them both smile. "Tivil is still standing," Elizaveta said proudly.

"With your help."

"I have no idea whether the input of someone like myself, a dethroned tsarist, or of that godless reprobate, Pokrovsky, provides any help or not in those ceremonies. But . . ." She paused and rubbed two fingertips against her temples. "Sometimes I feel things. In here." Her long fingers traced circles on her transparent skin. "When I'm with Rafik, I do believe." She shook her head and her voice grew stronger, more certain. "I hope that helps."

"So you believe the strange ceremony last night with all five of us might have created enough power of . . . some mysterious kind . . . to cause Mikhail's release?"

"It might. Oh, call it a miracle or call it a freak coincidence if you prefer, but the point is that Comrade Pashin was released."

She rose to her feet, and Sofia understood that the conversation was over.

"One last thing," Sofia said quickly. "Tell me, please . . ." She hesitated as a roll-top desk in the corner caught her eye. It was made of exquisite satinwood, and the top wasn't quite closed. Just visible were a square inkpad, an ink stamp, and what looked like a large magnifying glass. "Tell me whether you know anything about a hut in the forest that—"

"There are many huts up there that hunters use," Elizaveta interrupted brusquely. She walked over to the desk and pushed it shut. "I know nothing about huts. Ask the blacksmith, he's the one who's often roaming around up there—when he's out hunting, I mean."

Sofia watched her and noted the teacher's unease. Was it the desk? Had she seen something she shouldn't?

"In that case, I'll speak to Pokrovsky," Sofia said as she moved toward the door. "Thank you for your time, comrade."

They smiled at each other. Enough had been said.

*T*HE smithy looked like the devil's workshop. Great sparks leaped and twisted through the air that rang with the thunder of hammer blows on metal. As Sofia entered the dim interior she felt her bones vibrate and her teeth ache with it, but the blacksmith was grinning from ear to ear, relishing every swing of his massive hammer like Thor himself. He was working on a thick iron pole that glowed scarlet at one end where it was being flattened to a point.

"Comrade Pokrovsky," she called out. She squeezed it in between blows.

He paused midswing, hammer head poised high above his shoulder in a position that would have sent most people toppling over backwards. The smith was wearing a thick leather apron over a sleeveless tunic, and his naked shaven scalp glistened with sweat. The sight of him made Sofia smile. Here was a man who loved his work. Now that the reverberations had stopped, she realized he was singing an old army marching song and wielding his hammer to its rhythm.

He lowered it easily onto the anvil and stared at Sofia with surprise. "To what do I owe this pleasure?" He wiped the sweat from his upper lip with the back of his beefy hand. His teeth were as big as the rest of him, but so white that Sofia wondered if they might be false.

"Comrade Lishnikova suggested I speak with you."

His dark eyes sparked with interest. "About last night?"

"No. About a hut."

The change in him was instant and the easy manner vanished. "What hut?"

"A hut I found up in the forest." She added cautiously, "In a clearing a few versts northwest of here. I was—"

"Stay away from huts, comrade." He stepped toward her, his treetrunk arms swinging loose. "I'm warning you."

"Warning me of what?"

"Of not sticking your nose in places that—"

"Comrade Pokrovsky, I already know what's in that hut and who goes there."

He dragged air noisily through his teeth and his barrel chest swelled. She took a step, away from him. His intimidating presence acted like a physical pressure on her, even though he hadn't actually touched her.

"Stay away from the hut," he growled.

"Chairman Fomenko goes up there to—"

"Stay away from our Comrade Chairman."

"I thought you were trying to help this village, part of Rafik's circle. So why . . . ?"

Riddled with informers eager to earn a cheap rouble. Elizaveta's words slid like slime into her mind, and she felt suddenly sick with disappointment as she realized what this man was up to.

"You're working for both sides, aren't you, Comrade Pokrovsky?"

He moved so close she had to tip her head right back to look him in the eyes, and this time she didn't step away.

"Leave Fomenko alone," he warned.

"Why? What is he to you?"

He lowered his bull neck till his eyes were on a level with hers. The sparks were there inside them now. "Leave Fomenko alone. Because I say so."

She spun on her heel and strode out of the forge.

COMRADE Morozova, shouldn't you be out with your brigade in the fields?"

Sofia would have ignored him if she could, but Aleksei Fomenko and his lean-limbed hound had stepped right into her path before she was aware of them. Her mind was churning with fears about what Pokrovsky would say to his rouble paymasters, and all she wanted was to reach Mikhil's *izba* as quickly as possible. Now this rebuke. She couldn't bring herself to look at the chairman, so she stared at the gentle brown eyes of his dog.

"Did you tell them?" she demanded.

"Tell who?"

"Tell the interrogators to release Comrade Pashin."

He laughed, a harsh bark that could almost have come from the dog. "Don't be absurd, comrade. I don't have that kind of power."

She looked up at him for the first time. His jaw was set in a stern line, but today his eyes were as gentle as his dog's. She'd learned not to trust gentle eyes.

"Don't you?" she asked.

"No."

"I see."

She did see. She saw that Rafik's binding together of Tivil's strengths last night produced some kind of force. Unless Fomenko was lying to her, and he was the one who had organized Mikhail's release. But why would he do that?

His gaze fixed on her, and the strong sunlight bleached the creases from his skin, so that for a moment his face looked as smooth as that of a boy. Sofia could picture him, rifle in his hand, the boy who shot Anna's father.

"Don't miss your shift in the fields," he reminded her.

She shook her head and walked on.

SHE slipped into the bedroom where Mikhail was sleeping. One arm was thrown out in a wide gesture of abandon as if letting go in his sleep of what he couldn't release when awake. Sofia moved silently to the bed. There were signs of his having been up and about: an empty cup by the bed and his shirt hanging on the rack of hooks in the corner instead of thrown on the floor when she slid it from his shoulders last night.

She stood there quietly and studied him, watched him breathe: the slow even rhythm, the soft tiny movements of his lips. She absorbed every detail of him, not just into her mind but into her body, deep into her blood and her bones: the fineness of him, the line of his cheekbone, the thick fan of his dark lashes, even the black and swollen bruise around his eye. His chin was dark with stubble that she longed to kiss. She imagined him laughing in the snow, building a sleigh of ice. Skating on the lake and smiling with contentment as he roasted potatoes on the fire. All these things she knew he'd done, and many more when he was Vasily. But then he stuck a knife in the throat of his father's killer and Vasily died. Mikhail was born. It made no difference to her.

Vasily.

Mikhail.

She loved them both. Softly, so as not to break the rhythm of his dreams, Sofia dropped her clothes to the floor and slid in beside him between the sheets. His naked body smelled warm and musky. Her lips touched his skin. She curled her body around his and lay like that for an hour, maybe two, and when eventually his hand found her in his sleep, she smiled. Slowly, without opening his eyes, he started to caress her breasts till a moan crept from between her lips and she heard his breath quicken.

"Ssh," she whispered, "you need sleep."

"No, I need you."

He opened his eyes and grinned at her on the pillow. Gently she kissed his split lip and drew it into her own mouth, where her tongue soothed it. His groan vibrated through her own lungs, and together they started to explore each other's bodies once more. It was leisurely this time as their hands moved or lingered, and teased desire to breaking point until he was inside her.

And suddenly the terrible ache and the fear left Sofia. The ache of loving. The fear of losing. There was just this, just him, just her. Together.

FORTY-NINE

I'VE been waiting for you."

Rafik was seated at the table in his *izba*, his hands flat on its rough planks. He was wearing the white band around his head, stark against his thick black hair, and a soft white shirt with loose sleeves and a strange geometric design picked out in intricate white embroidery on the front of it. He indicated the two chairs opposite him.

Sofia and Mikhail sat down. Sofia's eyes focused immediately on the white stone that lay on the surface of the table.

"Sofia," Rafik said and smiled at her. "It is time for you to know more. But first"—his gaze shifted to Mikhail—"what is it you want of me, Comrade Pashin?"

Mikhail gave the stone no more than a cursory glance, but he draped a protective arm along the back of Sofia's chair. "Rafik," he said, "yesterday I was incarcerated in a filthy cell looking at a future in a labor camp at best. Today I am here in Tivil, a free man." He leaned forward, searching the gypsy's face. "It's a miracle, and I don't believe in miracles."

"No, it's not a miracle. You were saved by Sofia."

Mikhail thumped a hand on the table, making the stone leap from its place. Rafik flinched but didn't touch it.

"Rafik, you say Sofia saved me, but she claims that you did. I need to know what is going on here. People have always whispered that you have strange mystic powers, but I dismissed it as village tittle-tattle, the fantasies of idle minds, but now . . ." He drew a deep breath, and Sofia could see a pulse beating below his ear.

"Mikhail," Rafik said in a soothing tone, "I'm going to tell you a history." With his words, the thoughts in Sofia's head seemed to grow heavy. "For centuries," he continued, "generations of my family were advisers and astronomers to the kings of Persia. Their knowledge and intimacy with the spirits made them a force that guided one of the greatest empires in history through times of war and times of peace. But nothing"—he brushed a finger over the stone and eased it back into its position—"nothing lasts forever—not even Communism."

He frowned, drawing his heavy black brows together. "My ances-tors were driven from their land of honey and fled throughout the known world, some escaping to Europe, others to India and farther into the Orient, as the empire crumbled."

Sofia closed her eyes for a moment. "I feel it," she murmured.

Mikhail's solemn gaze scrutinized her face, and then he passed a hand in a gentle caress over her forehead and through the silky threads of her white-blond hair.

"What does she mean?"

Rafik took Sofia's hands between his own, palms together as in prayer.

"She is like me," he said.

"She's not a gypsy."

"No. I am the seventh son of a seventh son, going back through generations of seventh sons all the way to Persia. That's where my power comes from, passed on in a mystic connection of blood. Sofia is the same."

"What do you mean? Is she the daughter of a seventh son?"

"No. She is the seventh daughter of a seventh daughter, going back through generations. Because her mother died when Sofia was so young, she never learned from her mother what she should have

been told about the power that is centered in her, drawn from the
strength and the knowledge of others before her." He pressed Sofia's
hands tight together. "My will is strong, and so is hers. But together,"
Rafik said, his black eyes searching hers, "we are stronger."

"But my father was a priest of the Russian Orthodox church,"
she pointed out. "Surely his faith would have clashed with my
mother's . . . if what you say is true."

"Faiths can work together. The bond they create can be a powerful force."

She nodded. "Have you ever spoken to Priest Logvinov here in
Tivil? About working together?"

"He's not ready. Until he is, I protect him."

Mikhail leaned forward, intent on Rafik. "That explains why the
crazy fool still has his life in one piece. I've never been able to understand why he wasn't shot or exiled long ago by the authorities. He
takes risks, big risks."

Rafik looked at Mikhail. "So do you."

Mikhail's mouth closed into a hard line and he sat back in his
chair, eyes narrowed. "What is it you know, Rafik?"

"I know you bring a saddlebag of food home from your factory
canteen each day for the Tushkov family."

Mikhail said firmly, "That would be illegal. The canteen food is
meant for the Levitsky workers only."

"Please be careful, my love," Sofia whispered.

A shout in the street shattered the moment. They heard the sound
of boots pounding outside, the growl of a truck engine revving
impatiently. Children were bounding like hares up from the school;
voices were raised in dispute, and Rafik and Mikhail hurried to the
door. Only Sofia remained where she was. She was staring at the
white pebble. She touched it, and it was ice cold.

"Sofia," Rafik demanded harshly behind her. "What have you
done?"

ALEKSEI Fomenko, chairman of the Red Arrow *kolkhoz*, stood
in the grip of two burly soldiers outside his house, and around them
swarmed the *kolkhozniki*. News traveled fast in the fields.

Sofia forced herself to watch. The way the uniformed soldiers manhandled him as though he were dirt. The erect manner with which he carried himself in his check shirt and work trousers as though proud of them, the straight back, the accusing gray eyes that swept the crowd. The black Russian soil ingrained in the leather of his boots. At his feet lay three sacks, each one packed with secret plunder.

"Hoarder!"

"Thief!"

"Filthy scum!"

"You disgusting hypocrite, after all the food you took from us . . ."

"Liar! All the time you were stealing for yourself."

"Bastard!"

A stone flew from a woman's hand and then another that hit its target. Sofia could see the blood trickle along Fomenko's scalp. She made herself watch, but where was the sense of satisfaction she had expected? Why wasn't she enjoying the gloating and the triumph? This was what she'd wanted, wasn't it? This was what she'd sworn to do. Why did revenge taste so sour?

*W*E were all shocked," Mikhail said, and he shook his head, his wet hair scattering water. "I'd never have believed it of Fomenko."

Sofia was very quiet.

Mikhail lifted another ladle of water out of the enamel jug and tipped it over the hot stones until steam rose in a great hiss and he almost lost sight of her. They were in his *banya*, the bath hut at the back of his yard. It was a small dark building constructed of wood with a slatted bench to sit on, a stove, and one tiny window high up to let in a sliver of light. In the hot moist air they had scraped each other's skin in turn with the *veniki*, the birch twigs, and in the gloom she had massaged oils into the cuts and bruises that crisscrossed his body, kissing each one with such tenderness that he could barely keep from scooping her into his arms.

But she wouldn't let him. All afternoon she'd been subdued. She'd walked away from Rafik after Fomenko's arrest, but instead of being annoyed the gypsy had seized Mikhail's arm.

"Go to her, Mikhail. Don't leave her side."

Mikhail had felt a thin trickle of fear.

"What is it? Is she in danger?"

"I see dark shadows gathering around her and . . ." He stopped.

"And what?"

Rafik rubbed his eyes hard. "Just stay at her side."

When Mikhail suggested the *banya* to Sofia, it had elicited her glorious smile and her blue eyes had lit up with delight.

"As long as I get to clean you and you get to clean me," she'd teased.

"Agreed."

For a while it had worked. He'd lit the stove and ladled the water over the heated stones until the steam opened every pore in their bodies. Their muscles relaxed to the point that their flesh seemed to melt into each other's. Mikhail longed to feed her thick greasy morsels of fat and cheese, to watch soft flesh grow over the hard angles of her bones, to see her small undernourished breasts blossom like sweet-smelling flowers. As they stood entwined together, his hands caressed her slender buttocks and he trailed kisses along the delicate line of her shoulder.

"Sofia, Sofia," he whispered over and over.

She had changed everything for him, transformed his world to something clean and worthwhile. This woman was so different from any other he'd known. But when he placed her on the steam-hazed bench, she put a finger to his lips and shook her head.

"Sofia, what is it, my love?"

She took a deep breath, quivering under his touch, but said firmly, "I want us to talk."

"To talk? Is that all? You frightened me for a moment with your coolness." He laughed and sat on the bench beside her. He let just his arm touch hers, no more. "So what is it you want to talk about?"

"I want to talk about . . . the Dyuzheyevs."

He stopped breathing.

"You know the name?" she asked.

"Yes."

"When I asked before, you claimed you didn't."

"I lied."

"Why would you lie about it?"

"Because . . . oh Sofia, I don't want to think back to those times.

They're . . . over, locked in the past. Nothing can change what happened back then."

In the silence that followed in the damp hut, Mikhail had a sudden sense of things slipping away. Just the same as that day so long ago in the snow when his life slipped out of his icy fingers. Not this time, not again, he refused to let it happen again. He stood up quickly and faced her, and was shocked to see that despite the heat, her skin was bone white.

"Why are you doing this, Sofia? What are you trying to get out of me? Yes, I knew the Dyuzheyevs. Yes, I saw them die. A day etched into my brain in every detail, however hard I try to forget it. So I've answered you; now leave it, my love, leave it alone. Whatever your connection is with that dreadful day, don't drag it in here."

He dropped to his knees on the wooden floor in front of her. The mound of blond curls at the base of her stomach was barely a breath away, but he gazed only at her blue eyes that looked so wretched.

"Sofia," he whispered, "my Sofia. Don't do this."

"I must."

He sat back on his heels and stared up at her.

"I love you, Sofia."

"I love you, Mikhail." Her eyes shimmered in the narrow shaft of light.

He gently brushed a thread of moisture from her lip. "Very well, my sweetest, what is it you want?"

She didn't speak. Her throat attempted to swallow but failed, and he waited. Only when she dragged her eyes away from his face toward the small square of daylight outside did the words come.

"Anna Fedorina is still alive."

*T*HEY were dressed and in the house. Mikhail had lit a cigarette but had forgotten it as it burned fitfully in his fingers. He was angry, not with Sofia, but with himself. Something that had happened sixteen years ago should not still have this power over him. They'd said little more after Sofia's announcement.

"Where is she?" he'd asked.

"In a labor camp in Siberia."

He'd sunk his head in his hands and uttered a long moan, but when eventually he looked up, she was gone. He pulled on his clothes and hurried to the house, fearful that she had left, but no, she was sitting in his chair, face composed, eyes calm. Only her skin was the color of rain, a strange translucent gray that held no life in it.

He stood in the middle of the room and stared down at the half-built model of the bridge on the table. "It's the Brooklyn Bridge," he said flatly. "In America. It spans the East River between New York and Brooklyn."

"I thought it was the Forth Bridge."

"No." He frowned. Why was he talking about bridges? "The Forth Bridge is cantilevered; this one is a suspension bridge." He ran a finger along the top of one of the towers, picking out the intricate woodwork. "An amazing feat of construction in the 1870s. Fourteen thousand miles of wire holds it together, and each cable has a breaking strain of twelve thousand tons. Its main span is five hundred meters and . . ." Slowly he shook his head from side to side. "What was I thinking? That one day I could become an engineer again instead of a miserable factory manager? I was a fool."

With a sudden jab he brought his fist down on top of the bridge, bringing it crashing down in a thousand pieces as each miniature girder sprang apart.

"Mikhail!"

"I've been living in a dream world," he said sourly, sweeping the mess onto the floor. "I thought that I could rebuild the past, I could create a new family with Pyotr and you, and one day my dedication to the state's demands would win me the reward of a job that I could love again." He placed his foot on one of the replica masonry anchorages lying on the floor and crushed it. "No more dreams."

"Why should knowing that Anna is alive destroy your dreams? Is your life so unbearable without her?" Her eyes were fierce. "She still loves you."

"Loves me! She should loathe me."

"Why? Because you never came for her? Don't worry, she knows you tried. Maria told her when she went to the apartment in Leningrad."

"She saw Maria?"

"Yes. That was where she was captured. But Maria showed her the name and address you'd written down, so that's why I came here to Tivil, to find you." She paused, her voice briefly unsteady. She studied her hands and tapped the two scarred fingers against her knee as if reminding herself of something. "Anna loves you . . . Vasily. She always will, till her dying breath."

Mikhail strode across the room, seized her wrists, and yanked her to her feet. The hairs on his neck and his arms were alive and quivering, and as he stood there holding her he knew he'd lost her. Something deep inside him started to hemorrhage.

"I'm not Vasily," he said coldly.

He felt her go rigid, but he couldn't stop now.

"Vasily Dyuzheyev knifed my father to death that winter's day in 1917 on the Dyuzheyev estate. My father was the soldier in charge of the patrol, but my contribution to the massacre was twice Vasily's. I shot his mother and I shot Anna Fedorina's father in cold blood." He shook Sofia, shook her hard. "Now tell me," he demanded, "that she loves me. Now tell me . . . that you love me."

$\mathcal{I}$T took them time, knot by knot, to untangle the truth. Again and again they came back to Maria to discover that she lay at the heart of the confusion. Mikhail was pacing back and forth across the room, hands dragging through his hair, trying to rip his skull apart, and he could scarcely bear to look at Sofia. She was hunched in his chair, knees up under her chin, arms wrapped around her shins, eyes dark and impenetrable.

"You say Maria told Anna that Vasily visited her twice. That he wrote down the name Mikhail Pashin with an address in Tivil and the Levitsky factory. But that wasn't Vasily. That person was me. And according to your talk with Maria's sister-in-law, the second man was Fomenko. You see, I only went to see her once." Mikhail recalled the day. The tiny apartment, stiflingly hot, and the white-haired woman so eager to please and so painfully damaged by the stroke. "I had no idea she believed I was Vasily Dyuzheyev. I'd been searching for her for years."

"Why?"

Mikhail stopped pacing. "Isn't it obvious? Because I killed the child's father. I wanted to find Anna Fedorina and do what I could to make amends for what I'd done to her family. I discovered that her mother had died years earlier and that the woman with her was her governess. But"—he spread out his arms in a gesture of despair—"both vanished off the face of the earth. It was a time of chaos, and disappearances were common. The civil war started and normal life became . . . impossible."

"Mikhail," Sofia asked quietly, "how old were you when you shot Svetlana Dyuzheyev and *Doktor* Fedorin?"

"Fourteen."

"Only three years older than Pyotr."

Mikhail shuddered. "I was so like him at that age. So totally convinced that Bolshevism was the universal truth that would cleanse the world. All else was lies."

"Tell me what happened."

"I stood shoulder to shoulder with my father that day and mowed down the idle bourgeoisie like rats in a barrel." He turned his back on Sofia. "Why torment ourselves? You cannot despise me more than I despise myself for what I did. And the ultimate irony is"—he gave a bitter laugh—"that all this time the boy who cut my own father's throat that day has been living right here beside me in Tivil. Aleksei Fomenko turns out to be Vasily Dyuzheyev under another name."

He slumped down in a chair at the table. "Neither he nor I recognized each other after all these years, but I hated him anyway for being the kind of person I used to be. And he hated me for having lost my faith. I was a threat. It didn't matter how many quotas I exceeded at the factory, my mind wasn't a Bolshevik mind, and Fomenko wanted me to relearn the faith. He is a blind idealist."

"Don't," Sofia said.

Mikhail looked at her, and something wrenched in his chest. She was perched forward on the edge of his big armchair, her hair bright in a splash of sunlight, her eyes huge and sunken in her skull as though they could only look inward.

"Sofia," he said gently, "until you came into my life I was incapable of loving anyone. I didn't trust anyone. I despised myself and believed that others would despise me too, so I was wary in relationships. I went through the motions but nothing more. Instead I gave my love to an aircraft or a well-turned piece of machinery or . . ." He gestured at the mess of wooden struts on the floor.

"And to Pyotr."

"Yes, and to Pyotr." The hard muscles around his mouth softened. "When I came to this village six years ago, riding up the muddy street into my exile from Tupolev, and spotted this scrap of a child being tossed into a truck about to be carted off to some godforsaken orphanage, I saw Anna Fedorina in him. As she was on the doorstep all those years before. The same passion, the same fury at the world. So I carried the fierce little runt into my house and I petted and protected him the way I couldn't protect her. I grew to love him as my own flesh and blood."

"But you still kept trying to find her."

"Yes." He cleared a space on the table in front of him, making room for his thoughts. "One day I did a favor for an officer in OGPU, and in return he tracked down Maria for me. But I swear I only went there once, Sofia."

Sofia nodded. "Maria muddled the two of you up in her head. She even told Irina the wrong names." Her words were heavy and lifeless. "Both tall with brown hair and gray eyes. She got it"—she clenched her teeth—"all wrong." Her gaze fixed on his face. "Like I did," she whispered.

"No matter what happens now," he said fiercely, "I want you to know I love you and will always love you."

She leaped to her feet, shaking her head violently. "No, Mikhail. I came here because I swore an oath to Anna. To find Vasily and to destroy the killer of her father if I could. Instead I've destroyed Vasily."

FIFTY

SOFIA begged. It pained Mikhail to see it, this wild independent spirit abasing itself.

"Please, Rafik, please. I implore you."

She was on her knees on the wooden floor before the gypsy, clutching his wiry brown hands in her pale ones, her lips pressed to his knuckles, her eyes unwavering on his face.

"Please, Rafik, I beg you to do for Aleksei Fomenko what you did for Mikhail."

The gypsy again shook his head. "No."

The bedroom was small and gloomy. Mikhail found it acutely uncomfortable with six people crowded in it and candles that thickened the air they breathed. Standing stiffly beside the bed were Pokrovsky, Elizaveta Lishnikova, and the gypsy daughter, Zenia. None of them smiled a welcome.

What the hell was going on here?

The row of candles on the shelf sent out a twisting, shifting light that coated faces with touches of gold, while above them a giant eye on the ceiling stared down at a crimson cloth spread out on the bed. A white stone lay in the center of it like a milky eye. Mikhail had the disturbing sense of having stepped into another universe, one that sent shivers down his spine. He wanted to laugh at it, to scoff at these grim faces, but something stopped him. That something was Sofia.

She knelt on the floor in supplication.

"Help her, Rafik." He let his anger show. "You alter reality, well, alter hers."

"No, Mikhail," Rafik said, his black eyes intent on Sofia's face. "I don't alter reality. All I do is alter people's perception of it."

"Please," Sofia whispered into the silence.

"No." It came from Pokrovsky. His huge hands were still blackened from the forge, but his presence in the room altered its balance in some important way. The bullet-shaped crown of his shaven head almost touched the eye on the ceiling, and whatever the force was that beamed down from that strange symbol, it made Pokrovsky a different man from the friend Mikhail had many times laughed with over a glass or two of vodka.

"No," Pokrovsky repeated.

"No," Elizaveta said in her clear precise voice.

"No," Zenia echoed.

The silence shivered. Shadows tilted up and down the lengths of green curtain around the rough-timbered walls, and the stone gleamed white on the bed. Sofia dragged a breath through her teeth.

"Why, Rafik?" she demanded. "It was my mistake, not Fomenko's. I was the one who stole the sacks of food from the secret store in the church and hid them under his bed when he was out in the fields. You know no one locks their doors during the day here in Tivil. I broke that trust and I denounced him to Stirkhov. It wasn't his dishonesty, Rafik, it was mine, I swear it." She pressed her forehead to his hands.

Rafik stepped back, removing his fingers from her grasp. His slight figure stood stiff and stern.

"Sofia, I will tell you this. Chairman Aleksei Fomenko has taken from Tivil everything that belonged to the village by right, and he has left us gaunt and naked. He has stripped the food from the mouths of our children to feed the voracious maw that resides in the Kremlin in

Moscow. Above all else on this earth, it is my task to protect this village of ours, and that's why I never leave it. If that means protecting it
from Aleksei Fomenko at the cost of his life, so be it."

"So be it," intoned the others. The candle flames flared higher.

Sofia rose to her feet. She begged no more. Instead she moved to
the door, and Mikhail loved her for the proud way she walked.

"Rafik," he said fiercely. "She needs help."

The deep lines on Rafik's face were etched white. He shook his
head.

Mikhail strode to the bed and seized the stone. "Give her this."

"Put it back," Pokrovsky growled, taking a threatening step
toward Mikhail.

Rafik held up a hand. "Peace," he murmured. For a long moment
the gypsy scrutinized the stone in Mikhail's hand, and then slowly he
nodded. "Give it to her, Mikhail."

Sofia watched as Mikhail took her hand and placed the white
stone cautiously on her palm, as if it might burn her. The moment it
touched her skin, something in Sofia's eyes changed. Mikhail saw it
happen—something of the wildness vanished and in its place came a
calm determination.

Please God, Mikhail prayed to the deity he didn't believe in, *don't
let her be harmed by it.*

*P*YOTR was halfway through scraping burned clinker off a big flat
shovel when he saw his father in the street. Pokrovsky had left him at
the smithy with instructions to clean all the tools.

"Papa," he called out.

A line of blue shadows was sliding down from the forest and
slowly swallowing the village, so for a moment Pyotr missed the slight
figure pacing beside his father, but the last rays of sun painted her hair
almost red as she turned her face toward the forge. She waited in the
middle of the road, still and silent in the dust, while his father came
over. Somewhere a woman's voice was raised in scolding a child. A
dog barked. The wind stilled. An odd feeling crept over Pyotr, a sense
of stepping over a line.

"Papa," he said, throwing down the spade. "I've been thinking."

His father smiled, but it wasn't a happy smile. "About what?"

"About Chairman Fomenko."

"Don't concern yourself, Pyotr. Finish up here and come home."

"I've worked it out, Papa. Chairman Fomenko would never steal from the *kolkhoz*, you know he wouldn't. He's innocent. Someone else must have put those sacks under his bed, someone vicious who wanted to—"

"Leave it, Pyotr. The interrogators will have thought of that, I assure you. So forget it."

Just then Sofia came over to them. "Pyotr," she said, "you and I have work to do."

She put her hand in her pocket and drew out the iron key.

ALL three of them searched the hall, but something was wrong, Pyotr could feel it. He scuttled around between the benches, scraping at the floorboards with one of Pokrovsky's knives, seeking another piece of string that would lead to a new hiding place. But all the time he was aware of the odd silences. They filled the hall, banging into the roof timbers and rattling the windows.

"Have you searched in that corner, Papa?"

"Sofia, look at this. The plank looks uneven here."

"What about that brick patched with cement?"

He kept up the chatter, filling the gaps, not letting the silences settle. Why didn't they speak to each other? What had happened? But his words weren't enough, and the gaps were growing longer. As soon as they'd entered the hall and Sofia locked the door behind them, he noticed the way she and Papa wouldn't look at each other. Had they quarreled? He didn't want them to quarrel, because that might mean Sofia would leave.

"What are we searching for?" Papa had asked.

"A box of jewelry."

"Whose jewels?"

Pyotr shrugged and looked across at Sofia. She was examining a wall with her back to them, standing in a patch of soft lilac light that filtered through the window.

"Whose jewels?" Pyotr echoed.

"Svetlana Dyuzheyeva's," she answered without turning.

Papa stiffened.

"We're not stealing," Pyotr said quickly.

"If they belong to someone else, then it's stealing."

"No, Papa, not if we use them to do good." Pyotr could feel his cheeks burning, and he knew that what he'd said wasn't quite right. "We searched before. Sofia tried to find them to use them to rescue you when—"

"Did she indeed?"

"And now we have to find them to use them for Chairman Fomenko. That's right, isn't it?" He aimed the question at Sofia's back.

"Yes."

That was when the pool of silence started to flow under the door into the hall, and Pyotr had to keep throwing words into it to stop it drowning them. They explored even the faintest nook or hint of a crevice, trailing fingers around bricks and behind beams. His father searched in a brisk methodical manner at one end of the hall, Sofia at the other, but her shoulders were hunched, her skin almost blue in the strangely discolored light. Pyotr kept talking.

"I think this looks a good place. The plaster is loose."

"Papa, that board creaked when you stood on it, try it again. Look at this, Sofia, it—"

A fist banged outside on the oak door. Pyotr's tongue tingled with fear. Soldiers? He swallowed hard and knew in his heart that what they were doing in the hall was wrong.

"Pyotr," his father whispered urgently. "Come here."

Pyotr scampered over a bench and was seized by his father's strong hands. Immediately he felt better. Sofia appeared at Papa's side, though Pyotr hadn't heard or seen her move. And for the first time the two of them looked at each other, really looked, speaking only with their eyes in a language Pyotr couldn't understand. Sofia pointed to Pyotr and then to a spot by the entrance. Mikhail nodded, whisked Pyotr over there, and pressed him against the wall behind the heavy door, its rough surface cold on his bare arms. The knock came again, rattling the iron hinges. Pyotr watched in astonishment as his father took Sofia's face between his hands and kissed her lips. For half a second she swayed against him and Pyotr heard her murmur something, and then just as suddenly they were apart again and Sofia was reaching for the key.

"Who is it?" his father demanded in the big voice he used for his factory workers.

*I*T was Priest Logvinov. He'd come straight from the stables and stank of horse oil and leather. Pyotr had his eye to a knothole in the door as it stood open.

"What is it you want, Priest?" Mikhail asked curtly.

Pyotr saw the priest clutch at the large wooden cross at his throat. His gaunt cheeks were gray. "Mikhail, my friend, I'm looking for the girl."

"Which girl?"

Sofia stepped into view. "This girl?"

The priest nodded, his expression uneasy. "You asked me before about a statue of St. Peter."

"I did."

Pyotr heard the rise of hope in her voice.

"I've come here because . . ." Logvinov paused, looked wistfully out into the street. ". . . because . . ." He sighed deeply. "Dear Lord in heaven, I don't know why I've come. Just that I felt . . . drawn here."

Pyotr noticed the pebble then. He couldn't see Sofia's face on the other side of the door but he could see her hand at her side, and in it she held a smooth white stone.

She spoke softly. "Tell me, Priest, what have you come to say?"

"I told you of the statue of St. Peter inside the church."

"Yes."

"But there used to be another."

"Where?"

"Outside, at the back of the church. It was a magnificent marble statue that the Komsomol devils smashed to pieces and used as hardcore under the *kolkhoz* office building." His arms were jerking like a puppet's while he pointed a stick finger out into the gloom that had enveloped the village. "Around the rear of the church beside the buttress, you'll see the old plinth where it used to stand, covered in moss now."

"Thank you, Priest."

"Go now," Pyotr heard his father say kindly, "before you become too involved."

Logvinov hesitated, then carved the sign of the cross in the air and left.

Pyotr squirmed around the door and raced down the path that led around the building, the damp evening air cool in his lungs. The plinth was there, just where the priest had said.

"You dig," Sofia urged.

Pyotr scrabbled like a dog in the dry crumbling earth, using his hands and Papa's knife to make a hole a meter deep. His breath came fast with excitement.

"I feel it," he cried when the blade touched something solid.

It was a box made of rough pine and wrapped up in sacking. Inside it, enveloped in a sheet of leather that had gone stiff with age, lay a small enameled casket. It was the most beautiful object Pyotr had ever set eyes on, its surface embedded with ivory peacocks and green dragons that Papa said were made of malachite. He lifted it carefully and placed it in Sofia's hands.

"*Spasibo*, Pyotr."

She slid open the gold catch and lifted the lid. Pyotr gasped as he caught sight of colors he'd never seen before, molten glowing stones.

"Sofia," he whispered, "these could buy you the world."

FIFTY-ONE

*T*HE pearls hung from Sofia's hand like a string of snowflakes, each unique in itself, yet perfectly matched to its fellows.

"Comrade Deputy Stirkhov, I think these might help you decide."

She dangled the triple strand of pearls over his desk and set them swaying slightly, wafting the sweet smell of money in the direction of his wide nostrils. Behind his spectacles his eyes had grown as round as the pearls themselves, and his lips had parted as if preparing to swallow them. He held out a hand.

"Let me see them. They may be fake."

Sofia laughed. "Do they look fake?"

The creamy translucence of the pearls lit up the office.

"I want to check them over."

He tried to take the necklace from her, but she stepped back and lifted them out of his reach. He was seated behind his desk and half-rose from his chair, but one look at her face made him change his mind. In front of him on a soft square of white cotton lay a brooch. It was made of silver gilt in the shape of a long-legged borzoi hound, and in its mouth it carried a dead pheasant studded with emeralds. Stirkhov's eyes slid from the pearls to the brooch and back again. Sofia could see the greed grow the more it fed on them.

"Half now," she said, "and half when the job is done."

Stirkhov puckered his smooth forehead, not understanding.

"I'll make it easy for you," she smiled and drew a small pair of sewing scissors from her pocket.

Comprehension dawned.

"No."

"Yes," she said, snipping through the strands. Pearls cascaded onto the desk, bouncing and skidding off its glossy black surface like hailstones. Stirkhov scrambled to collect them.

"You stupid bitch."

"Half now," she repeated, "and half when the job is done."

She walked to the door, a section of the necklace still in her hand.

"I could have you arrested," he snarled.

"But then you'd lose these, wouldn't you?" she smiled coolly.

She slipped the pearls into her pocket and was out of the building before he could change his mind.

*P*ATIENCE."

She was inside Aleksei Fomenko's house. The *izba* that was so bare inside, it scarcely looked lived in. She saw no reason not to be here, as she'd invaded his privacy once already, more than invaded it when she'd stuffed sacks under his bed. She'd violated it. So it was easy to break the trust of an unlocked door a second time and walk into the chairman's house.

"He'll come," she told herself, curling her fingers around the stone in her pocket. It lay there, cold and stubborn. She was staring out the back window over the neat rows of beetroot and rutabagas and turnips in his plot of land, all regimented and weed-free. Like his house.

Vasily, oh Vasily. How could I have gotten it so wrong? You gave me no sign, no warning. How could I love someone who doesn't exist? Something hurt in her chest, a real physical pain. It felt as though her heart were spilling hot blood into her chest cavity with each beat of its muscle.

Vasily, how did you become Fomenko? What happened to you?

She touched the board where he cut his bread, the skillet in which he fried his food, the towel where he dried his hands, searching for him. She walked into his bedroom, but it was like coming into a dead person's room. A bed, a stool, hooks on the wall for his clothes. She brushed her fingers over the three checked work shirts that hung there, and they felt soft and worn. She scooped a handful of cloth up to her face, inhaled the scent of it. It smelled clean and fresh, of pine needles. No scent of him, of Aleksei Fomenko. He hid even that.

On a shelf stood a mirror and a dark wooden hairbrush. She picked up the brush and ran it through her own hair as she gazed into the glass that was speckled with black age spots. No sign of him there, only her own reflection, and that was the face of a stranger. She went over to his plain pinewood bed. It was covered by a patchwork quilt over coarse white sheets but when she lifted the top one, there was no imprint of his body underneath. She touched his pillow and it felt soft. That surprised her. She had expected it to be hard and unyielding, like his ideas. She bent over and placed her cheek on it, sank into its feathers and closed her eyes. What dreams came to him at night, what thoughts? Did he ever dream of Anna? Her hand slid under the pillow, feeling for any secret talisman but found nothing, and when she stood upright she felt a dull kind of anger rise to her throat.

"You've killed him," she shouted into the dead air of this dead house. "You've killed Vasily." She felt hollow and bereft.

She picked up the pillow and shook it violently. "You had no right," she moaned, "no right to kill him. He was Anna's. I know I borrowed him, but he was always Anna's and now you've killed her as surely as you killed him."

She hurled the pillow across the room. It hit the log wall and slithered to the floor, and as it did so something tumbled out of the white pillowcase. Something small and metal rattled into a corner as though trying to hide. Sofia leaped on it. She picked it up, placed it on the palm of her hand, and studied her find. It was a pillbox fashioned out of pewter, small and round and gray. A dent on one side. It reminded her of the pebble in her pocket. She opened it and inside lay a lock of blond hair, bright as sunshine.

★ ★ ★

SHE waited, her skin prickling with impatience as she watched the sun march across the room from one side to the other. At some point she drank a glass of water. And all the time she brooded about Mikhail Pashin and about who he really was. About what he'd done. About what she, Sofia, had sworn to do to him.

She peeled back each layer of pain, like stripping bark, and looked at what lay underneath. It was a mass of confusion and error that encased a ferocious belief in ideas at the cost of all else. Mixed up in it all was such passion and hatred, yet at the same time she could see the black shadow of a desperate remorse and repentance. She forced herself to look at them, to pick through them all one by one and face up to what she found.

Oh my Mikhail, you made yourself suffer for what you did. You scourged yourself like the penitents of the Church, but found no divine forgiveness at the end of it. Instead you constructed a life for yourself that tried to atone, and you did it with as much care as you built your bridge. I don't want to smash my fist on it and bring it crashing down now. But . . . you killed Anna's father.

Again and again darkness descended on Sofia as she sat there alone. What kind of mind? What kind of person? What kind of boy shoots human beings in cold blood? She took out the pebble and placed it on her lap but it lay lifeless, a dull white. Yet as she stroked its cold surface, she felt herself change. A vibration rippled through her body and she almost heard the stone hum, high-pitched and faint inside her head. Its color seemed to gain a sheen, just like a pearl.

Was she imagining this? Was Rafik imagining it all? The seventh daughter of a seventh daughter. Was it true? And if it was, did it mean anything at all? Vasily was gone. That knowledge, that the Vasily she had loved in the camp no longer existed, had torn an important part of her away, and it left a terrible hollowness inside, like hunger. But worse. It gnawed at her with sharp rodent teeth. Now Vasily was gone and she was mourning the loss of him. She moaned and rocked herself in Vasily's chair, but finally she sat up and wrapped her fingers tight around the stone.

"Anna," she said firmly, "wait for me. I'm coming."

FIFTY-TWO

"WHAT are you doing in my house?"

Sofia felt a wave of sorrow for the tall arrogant man whom she had wronged. He stood in the doorway with no marks on him—none that showed anyway—but something about him looked bruised, something in his dark eyes.

She remained seated. "Comrade Fomenko, I am here to tell you something important."

"Not now."

He walked over to the enamel jug of water on the table and drank greedily from the glass beside it, as if to flush away something inside himself. For a long moment he closed his eyes, his lashes dark on his cheek, and she knew she was intruding unforgivably.

He turned to her, his voice cold. "Please leave."

"I've been here all day, waiting for you."

"Why on earth did you assume I would return from prison today?"

"Because of these."

She held up the remains of the pearl necklace. They

shimmered in the last of the evening light that tumbled through the window, and his mouth seemed to spasm. He drew in a breath, then fixed his gaze on her face.

"Who are you? You come to this village and I try to help you because . . . you remind me so much of someone I once knew, but you look at me with such anger in your eyes and now invade my house when all I want is to be alone. Who are you? What are you doing here?"

"I am a friend."

"You are no friend to me." He put down the glass, leaned against the edge of the table, and shook his head, his arms folded across his broad chest. "So why the pearls?"

"I used half of them to bribe an official to set you free. These"— she cradled the pale beads in the palm of her hand where they chittered softly against each other—"are promised to him now that you are home again."

He stood staring at the pearls. She thought she could see recognition of them in his eyes, of the necklace and its distinctive gold clasp, but maybe she was wrong. Maybe it was something else. He was hard to decipher.

"Who are you?" he asked again in a low voice.

"I told you, I am a friend."

Abruptly he walked to the front door and held it open. Outside, the wolfhound lazed in the sun. "Get out before I throw you out." He didn't shout. Just quiet words.

Sofia rose and moved closer. She noticed a rip in the collar of his shirt, a rust-colored smear on one cuff that looked like dried blood. He was in need of a shave. Her heart went out to him, this man she'd both loved and hated.

"Vasily, I am a friend of Anna Fedorina."

She saw the shock hit him. A shudder. Then so still, not even his pupils moved.

"You are mistaken, comrade."

"Are you telling me that you are not Vasily Dyuzheyev, only son of Svetlana and Grigori Dyuzheyev of Petrograd? Killer of the Bolshevik soldier who murdered your father, protector of Anna Fedorina who hid under a chaise longue, builder of snow sleighs and agitator for the Bolsheviks. That Vasily. Is that not you?"

He turned away from her, his back as straight as one of his field furrows. For a long period neither spoke.

"Who sent you here?" he asked at last without looking at her. "Are you an agent for OGPU, here to entrap me? I believe it was you who placed the sacks under my bed. I could see the hate in your eyes when the soldiers came for me." He breathed deeply. "Tell me why."

"I thought you were someone else. I am not with OGPU, have no fear of that, but I did make a terrible mistake and for that I do apologize. I was wrong."

Still he gazed out at the soft evening clouds, at a skein of geese that arrowed across them. "Who did you think I was?"

"The boy soldier who shot both Anna's father and Svetlana Dyuzheyeva."

No response. Her heart pounded. "Vasily, speak to me. She's alive, Vasily, Anna Fedorina is alive."

It was like watching an earth tremor, a quake from somewhere deep below the world's surface. His broad shoulder blades shifted out of alignment and his muscular neck jerked in spasm but he didn't turn. He just tightened his folded arms around himself as though holding something inside.

"Where?"

"In a labor camp. I was there with her."

"Which one?" Barely a whisper.

"Davinsky camp in Siberia."

"Why?"

"For nothing more than being the daughter of *Doktor* Nikolai Fedorin, who was declared an enemy of the people."

No more words. Neither of them could find any. The black shadow of Vasily lay across the wooden floor between them like a corpse.

THEY drank vodka. They drank till the pain was blunted and they could look at each other. Sofia sat in the chair, upright and tense, while Fomenko fetched a stubby stool from the bedroom and folded himself onto it, his lean limbs orderly and controlled once more. She wanted him to shout at her, to bellow and scream and accuse her of false betrayal. She wanted to be made to suffer the way she'd made him suffer.

But he did none of these things. After the initial shock, he snapped back from the edge of whatever abyss had opened up, and his strength astounded her. How could he hold so much turmoil within himself, yet seem so calm? His self-control was ironclad, so strong that he even smiled at her, a dry sorrowful smile, and ran a steady hand over the head of the dog now stretched out at his feet. Its brown eyes watched his face as attentively as Sofia did.

"Comrade," he said, "I am glad Anna has a friend."

"Help me, Vasily, to be a true friend to her."

"Help you how?"

"By rescuing her."

For the first time the firm line of his mouth faltered. "I have no authority to order any kind of release in—"

"Not with orders. I mean together, you and I, we could go up there. You could authorize travel permits and we—"

"No."

"She's sick."

"I'm very sorry," he said quietly.

"Sorry means nothing. She's going to die. She's spitting blood and another winter up there will kill her."

A dull mist seemed to settle behind his eyes, blurring them. "Anna," he whispered.

"Help her."

He shook his head slowly, full of regret.

"What happened to you?" she demanded. "When did you lose your ability to care for another human being? When your parents were shot, was that it? Did that moment smother all feelings in you for the rest of your life?"

In the gathering gloom he stared at her in silence.

"You don't understand, comrade."

"Make me, Vasily, make me understand. How can you abandon someone you loved, someone who still loves you and believes in you and needs you? How does that happen?" She leaned forward, hands clasped. "Go on, tell me. Make me understand."

"I traced Maria, her governess. I wanted to . . ." Suddenly words failed him.

With a groan he rose to his feet, walked over to the vodka on the table, and took a swig straight from the bottle.

"Comrade Morozova, my feelings are my own business, not yours. Now please leave."

"No, Vasily, not until you tell me—"

"Listen to me, comrade, and listen well. Vasily Dyuzheyev is dead and gone. Do not call me by that name ever again. Russia is a stubborn country; its people are hardheaded and determined. To transform this Soviet system into a world economy—which is what Stalin is attempting to do by opening up our immense mineral wealth in the wastelands of Siberia—we must put aside personal loyalties and accept only loyalty to the state. This is the way forward, the *only* way forward."

"The labor camps are inhuman."

"Why were you sent there?"

"Because my uncle was too good at farming and acquired the label *kulak*. They thought I was 'contaminated.'"

"Do you still not see that the labor camps are essential because they provide a workforce for the roads and railways, for the mines and the timber yards, as well as teaching people that they must—"

"Stop it, stop it!"

He stopped. They stared hard at each other and the air between them quivered as Sofia released her breath.

"You'd be proud of her," she murmured. "So proud of Anna."

Those simple words did what all her arguments and her pleading had failed to do. They broke his control. This tall powerful man sank to his knees on the hard floor like a tree being felled, all strength gone. He placed his hands over his face and released a low stifled moan. It was harsh and raw, as though something was ripping open. But it gave Sofia hope. She could just make out the murmur of words repeated over and over again. "My Anna, my Anna, my Anna . . ." The dog stood at his side and licked one of his hands with a gentle whine.

Sofia rose from her chair and went over to him. Tentatively her fingertips stroked his soft cropped hair, and a sweet image of it longer with young Anna's fingers entwined in its depths arose in her head.

He had cut off Vasily's hair as effectively as he'd cut off his heartbeat. Time alone was what he needed now, time to breathe. So she walked into his tiny kitchen to give him a moment, filled a glass with water, and when she returned she found him sitting in the chair, his limbs loose and awkward. She wrapped his hand around the glass. At first he stared at it, uncomprehending, but when she said, "Drink," he drank.

Then she squatted down on the board floor in front of him and in a quiet voice started to tell him about Anna. What made her laugh, what made her cry, how she raised one eyebrow and tipped her head at you when she was teasing, how she worked harder than any of his *kolkhozniks*, how she could tell a story that kept you spellbound and carried you far away from the damp miserable barrack hut into a bright shining world.

"She saved my life," Sofia added at one point, but she didn't elaborate and he didn't ask for details.

Gradually Aleksei Fomenko's head came up and his eyes found their focus once more; his limbs remade their connection and his mind regained control. As Sofia talked, a fragile smile crept onto his face. When finally the talking ceased, he took a deep breath, as though to inhale the words she had released into the air, and nodded.

"Anna always made me laugh," he said in a low voice. "She was always funny, always infuriating." The smile spread, wide and affectionate. "She drove me mad and I adored her."

"So help me rescue her."

The smile died. "No."

"Why not?"

He stood up, towering over her where she still crouched on the floor, and he spoke quietly, the turmoil hidden away, concealed deep inside. His wolfhound leaned against his thigh, and he rested a hand unconsciously on the wiry head.

"You have to understand, comrade," he said. "Sixteen years ago, to satisfy my own anger and lust for vengeance, I slit a man's throat. As a result Anna's father was shot and her life destroyed. That taught me a lesson I will carry to my grave."

His gray eyes were intent on Sofia's face, and she could feel the force of his need to make her understand.

"I learned," he continued, "that the individual need doesn't matter.

The individual is selfish and unpredictable, driven by uncontrolled emotions that bring nothing but destruction. It is only the need of the whole that counts, the need of the state. So however much I want to rescue Anna from her . . . misery"—he closed his eyes for a second as he said the word—"I know that if I do so . . ."

He broke off. She could see the struggle inside him for a moment as it rose to the surface, and his voice rose with it.

"You must see, comrade that I would lose my position as chairman of the *kolkhoz*, and everything that I have achieved here—or will achieve in the future—would be destroyed because they would revert back to old ways; I know these people. Tell me which counts for more? Tivil's continued contribution to the progress of Russia and the feeding of many mouths, or my and Anna's . . . ?" He paused.

"Happiness?"

He nodded and looked away.

"Need you even ask? You're blind," Sofia said bitterly. "You help no one, nor do you think for yourself anymore."

Something seemed to snap inside him, because without warning he bent down and yanked her to her feet, his fingers hard on her arms.

"Thought," he said, his face close to hers, "is the one thing that will carry this country forward. At the moment Stalin is pushing us to great achievements in industry and farming, but he is at the same time destroying one of our greatest assets—our intellectuals, our men and women of ideas and vision. Those are the ones I help to . . ." He stopped and she saw him fighting for control.

His hands released her.

"The radio in the forest," she said in a whisper. "It's not to report to your OGPU masters. It's to help—"

"It's part of a network," he said curtly, angry with her and angry with himself.

"The previous teacher here who spoke out of turn?"

He nodded. "Yes."

"And others? You help them escape."

"Yes."

"Does anybody else in Tivil know?"

He drew in a harsh breath. "Only Pokrovsky, and he is sworn to secrecy. No one in the network knows more than one other person within it. That way no one can betray more than one name. Pokrovsky provides . . . 'packages' and forged papers for them—where he gets them, I don't ask."

Sofia recalled the ink stamp and magnifying glass on Elizaveta Lishnikova's desk. She could guess. She also recalled Pokrovsky's hard face when she accused him of working for both sides. She was angered at her own blindness and walked over to the open door, where she stood looking out at the village.

"Chairman Fomenko," she said softly, "I feel sorry for you. You have hidden from yourself and from your pain so deeply, you cannot—"

"I do not need or want your sorrow."

But he came up behind her, and she could feel him struggling with something; a faint hissing sound seemed to emanate from him. She could hear it clearly though the room was silent.

"What is it?"

She turned and looked into his eyes and for a moment caught him unawares. The need in them was naked.

"What is it?" she asked again, more gently.

"Tell her I love her. Take my mother's jewels, all of them, and use them for her."

She slid the damaged necklace from her pocket and slipped a single perfect pearl off its strand, took his strong hand in hers and placed inside it the pale sphere that had lain next to his mother's skin. He closed his fingers over it. His mouth softened, and she felt the shudder that passed through him. In the same moment she replaced the necklace in her pocket and removed the white pebble. With her other hand she rested her fingers on Fomenko's wrist and pressed deep into his flesh as she'd seen Rafik do, touching the hard edges of his bones, his tendons, his powerful pulse, seeking him out.

"Vasily," she said firmly, fixing her gaze on his, "help me to help Anna. I can't do it alone."

Something seemed to shift under her fingers, she felt it, as though his blood thickened or his bones realigned. A tiny *snick* sounded in her head and a thin point of pain kicked into life behind her right eye.

"Vasily," she said again, "help Anna."

His eyes grew dark, but his lips started to curl into a soft acquiescent smile. Her heart beat faster.

"Chairman Fomenko." A boy's voice shouted out from the street and a scurry of footsteps came hurtling up to the doorway. It was a clutch of seal-haired youths still wet from the pond. "Is it all arranged for tomorrow?"

Fomenko jerked himself back to the present by force of will and wrenched his wrist from her hold. His eyes blinked again to refocus on the world outside his head.

Sofia stepped out into the street. She'd lost him.

"Is what arranged for tomorrow?" he demanded.

"The wagons to take everyone to Dagorsk. Like you promised last week." The boy's face was eager.

"A holiday," chirped a blond snippet of a child. "To see the *Krokodil* airplane and hear our Great Leader's speech."

Fomenko straightened his shoulders and gave a harsh cough as though trying to spit something out. "Yes, of course, it's all arranged." With a brisk nod of his head he moved back into the house and shut the door.

Sofia stood there while the boys raced away down the road, skipping over the ruts and yelling their excitement. The sky had darkened, and a solitary bat swooped low overhead. She watched a yellow glow spring to life in Fomenko's *izba* as he lit the oil lamp inside, but outside, Sofia felt no glow. Just the pain behind her right eye.

FIFTY-THREE

THE night was unbearable without her. Mikhail spent the dark hours with his own demons and wrestled with the knowledge Sofia had given him.

Aleksei Fomenko. The name was branded into his brain. Fomenko was Vasily Dyuzheyev, the killer of his father. Yet at the same time Fomenko was the son of Svetlana Dyuzheyev, the woman Mikhail himself had killed in cold blood.

They were bound together, Fomenko and himself, bound in some macabre dance of death. Both servants of the state and both sent to the same peasant *raion* to drag it into the twentieth century, where on both of them the burden of responsibility weighed heavy each day as they wrestled with the need to lead others out of the past and into a brighter firmer future. So similar, yet so different.

Mikhail hated him as much as he hated himself. And he hated the hold that Fomenko—as Vasily—seemed to have on Sofia. The image of her beautiful lithe body and proud mind, with its unshakable loyalty to those she loved, swamped his thoughts as he paced through the hours of the night.

"Sofia," he said to the moon when it slipped out from behind the clouds and trickled into his bedroom, "don't think I will let you go so easily."

His decisions started to harden. He owed Fomenko, an eye for an eye. He owed Anna, a life for a life. But most of all, he owed himself.

*J*UST before dawn she came to him. Slid into his bed, her feet chill on his and her heart beating as fast as a bird's.

She smelled so strongly of forest secrets that he almost asked her where she'd been and what she'd been doing, but he remembered Rafik and said nothing. Instead he enfolded her in his arms. They lay like that, bodies molded to each other, silent and still, until the first fingers of daylight touched her hair and painted a blush on her cheek. She kissed his throat, a soft possessive brush of her lips.

"You're not Anna's," she whispered.

"No," he said firmly, "I'm not Anna's."

*W*AKE up, you lazy toad. Rise and shine."

Pyotr burrowed deeper into his pillow and ignored his father's urging, but the bedcover was whisked away and a hand lifted him bodily from the bed.

"Papa!" he moaned. "It's *vikhodnoy*, a holiday."

"We have a busy day ahead of us. Get dressed," his father said and strode from the room. "Don't forget, your friend Yuri will be here soon."

Of course. Pyotr started to hurry, but suddenly he remembered the jewels they'd found yesterday and his heart gave a kind of hiccup inside his chest. He wanted desperately to tell Yuri about them but knew he couldn't. It was a secret, not even to be shared with his best friend. When he'd stared into the casket at the fiery jewels behind the assembly hall he'd felt their power in a way he never expected, so strong it made him nervous. He'd cradled an emerald ring in his hand, unwilling to let it go, and it shocked him, that feeling. Because he truly believed in sharing, really he did, an equal portion for everyone, no selfish bourgeois elitist values.

So where had it come from, this greed squirming inside him? Chairman Fomenko had been released, and Pyotr knew for certain it was because of the power of the pearls. That meant corruption. So he should speak out, loud and clear. It was his duty. Speak out about the existence of these corrupting jewels, that was what Yuri would say.

But how could he without denouncing Papa and Sofia? And without putting Chairman Fomenko's freedom at risk? What was right and what was wrong?

He pulled on his shorts roughly. Life was too confusing. He shook his head and in a flash his thoughts shifted to the arrival of the *Krokòdil* airplane today. Instantly his mood changed and excitement surged through him, whooshing up from his toes and setting his scalp tingling. Quickly he yanked on his shirt. He'd worry about the jewels tomorrow.

THE wide green meadow stretched out, lazy in the sunshine on the far side of Dagorsk, and from every direction carts and wagons and rattling bicycles were descending on it. Tents had sprung up all over its surface like mushrooms, and men in red armbands were running around blowing whistles, shouting orders, and waving batons, but nothing could subdue the spirit and energy of the crowd that surged onto it.

Pyotr loved every single second of it. Even the journey in the ramshackle old wagon had been fun. It was packed with villagers from Tivil, and he'd sat squashed close to Yuri at the back, legs dangling over the tailboard. Dust swirled up from the track into their mouths, coating their tongues, but everyone sang to the playing of an accordion, loud and boisterous. It was like going to a party. Somewhere up ahead in the first wagon were Papa and Sofia and Zenia, but the children of the village were bundled into the second one with their teacher, and even Comrade Lishnikova was laughing and wearing a bright red flowered shawl instead of her usual gray one. Today was going to be special. At the meadow they tumbled from the wagon in a flurry of pushing and shoving and high-pitched squeals.

"The aircraft isn't due for another half hour," Elizaveta Lishnikova announced.

"Can we look inside the film tent?" Pyotr asked.

"Yes, you may go and explore first, but when I blow my whistle I expect you all to line up just the way we practiced."

"A guard of honor," Yuri whooped.

She smiled, and her long face creased in amusement. "That's right." She seized the hand of a tiny child who was about to wander off. "And I'm relying on you Young Pioneers to do it right and show the little ones the way. In front of all the other brigades from the *raion,* I want you to make me proud of you."

"We will! For our Great Leader," Pyotr shouted and everyone gave the Pioneer salute, eyes shining. "*Bud gotov, vsegda gotov!* Be ready, always ready!"

The schoolteacher looked fondly down at her thin-faced flock but didn't join in the salute. "Here," she said, drawing a leather purse from her bag. "Line up."

The twenty-two children shuffled quickly into an obedient single file, and into each eager hand she placed a rouble. Never before had she done such a thing.

"*Spasibo.*"

"Go and buy yourselves some treats."

They were off and running like mice in a cornfield, skipping and skittering between the groups of women in flower-printed dresses and the *kolkhoznik* men from other villages in their flat caps, as well as the older, more disdainful youths from Dagorsk's factories.

"This way," Pyotr yelled.

He dragged Yuri over to a stall that sold *konfetki,* and they spent a delicious ten minutes deciding which sweets to buy. Yuri chose a sugar chicken on a stick, but Pyotr bought one of the *petushki,* a boiled pine cone, and started to pop the seeds into his mouth. Scattered among the crowds were other Young Pioneers from other brigades, also in white shirts and scarlet triangular scarves, and they eyed each other with interested rivalry. Later there would be races.

"You'll beat them," Yuri said confidently. "Easy."

"*Da,* of course I will," Pyotr agreed, and he put a swagger in his step, though in his heart he was far from certain.

Together they headed for the largest of the tents. "Come on," Yuri yelled as he broke into a run.

★ ★ ★

"I'M going to be a fighter pilot," Pyotr announced as he and Yuri emerged from the film show. They had just sat wide-eyed through the footage of the May Day Parade in Red Square for the third time, and their pulses were still beating to the powerful rhythm of the martial music. Pyotr began to swing his arms in imitation of the soldiers on screen, his legs striding out in a stiff-kneed goosestep.

Yuri giggled and copied his military bearing, puffing out his chest and grinning. "I want to become a tank driver when I leave school. Did you see those machines? Aren't they massive? They'll stomp all over Germany in no time if they give us any more trouble."

The boys marched around the field in unison, swerving to avoid a bald man with a tattoo on his arm rolling a wooden cask over to one of the tents. Yuri was clutching a pamphlet in his hand, and on the front of it was printed in big red letters, BEWARE OF ENEMIES OF THE PEOPLE AMONG YOU.

"I wonder," Yuri said, flapping the pamphlet as he marched, "who are the enemies in Tivil?"

Pyotr missed his step. His cheek flushed. "Maybe there aren't any," he said quickly.

"Of course there are. Have you forgotten that our Great Comrade Stalin tells us they are everywhere, hiding among us. Most of them employed by foreign powers to—"

"Why on earth would a foreign power be interested in what goes on in our village?"

"Because we provide the food to feed the factory workers, stupid," Yuri scoffed.

Pyotr was stung. "I bet I know more about enemies in Tivil than you do."

"You don't."

"Yes, I do."

They stopped in the middle of the field and glared at each other. Not far away the band struck up a marching tune, but neither boy wished to set off again.

"Name one," Yuri challenged.

"I could if I wanted."

"You're lying."

"No, I'm not."

"Tell me."

Pyotr shook his head firmly. "No."

"I knew it. You don't know . . ." He gave Pyotr's shoulder a scornful shove.

It was the shove that did it, as if Pyotr were a stupid child to be pushed around. His cheeks darkened and he gave Yuri's chest a thump with his fist, not hard, but hard enough to show he was serious.

"I'll tell you only if you promise to keep it secret."

Yuri's eyes gleamed. "Go on, tell me," he urged. But he didn't promise.

*P*YOTR was desperate to find Sofia. He had to talk to her, to warn her. His heart was squeezed tight inside his chest as he scoured the field, trying to catch a glimpse of white-blond hair and a cornflower dress. He zigzagged behind the tents, and with every step he swallowed hard, attempting to swallow the shame.

How could he have done it? Betrayed her just because he was annoyed with Yuri. He scuffed his shoe furiously in the dusty soil and wanted to burrow down into a hole under the ground and stay there. His skin was sticky with sweat because he knew he had to face her. And quickly.

He raced past a group of men tossing iron horseshoes onto pegs, and was relieved to spot Yuri among them. Maybe he wouldn't actually tell . . . Then Pyotr saw her down the side of one of the large tents, easy to recognize in that dress because it was the prettiest on the field. She'd know what was best to do. He started to run toward her but skidded to a halt when he saw she was talking to someone. With a funny twist in his stomach he recognized her companion. It was Deputy Stirkhov, the one who had given the address at the meeting, deputy chairman of the whole *raion*. Deputy Stirkhov was a man of the Party, a man who knew right from wrong.

Sofia was handing him something small wrapped in material, and Pyotr's heart skipped a beat because he knew without even looking what was inside it. It would be the diamond ring or maybe the pearls. It didn't matter which, but definitely it would be a piece of jewelry.

Stirkhov stuffed it deep in his trouser pocket, then leaned forward and tried to kiss Sofia's mouth. Pyotr was shocked. What had Sofia done to the man? She was corrupting Stirkhov too.

Up in the bright blue sky a thin speck of noise like a distant buzz saw started to drill into his mind, and he recognized it as the *Krokodil* approaching. He wiped his palms on his shorts, his mind spinning. He'd been right all along. Sofia wasn't just a fugitive, she really was an enemy of the people, and that realization sent a dart of sorrow into his heart because he loved her now and, more important, Papa loved her.

Papa, he must find Papa and speak with him. He started to run.

FIFTY-FOUR

SHE'S beautiful."

Mikhail's eyes shone with pleasure as he squinted up at the airplane's wings glinting in the midday sun. "Just the sight of her so close makes my hands itch to touch her."

"It's a brilliant propaganda weapon," Sofia admitted, shielding her eyes with her hand.

The high-winged silver-skinned airplane swooped down from the sky like a giant bird of prey, and on each side of the makeshift runway Sofia could see the Young Pioneers lining up, backs stiff as soldiers. Behind them stood the real soldiers, the ones with rifles to keep the spectators away from the plane.

"The *Krokodil* is one of the Maksim Gorky Agitprop Squadron," Mikhail informed her, "designed to fly from town to town across Russia. It distributes pamphlets and gives film shows to demonstrate what great strides Communism is making. It shows off Stalin's grandest projects like the building of the White Sea Canal."

"You've already told me all that. Tell me something new."

"Have I mentioned that it was named after the *Krokodil* magazine and differs from other ANT-9s by having aerodynamic fairings over the wheels and struts?"

"Interesting. But what about its engines?"

"Well, it has two M-17 engines instead of the original three *Gnome et Rhone* Titans, which gave it . . ." He dragged his gaze away from the plane, looked at her, and grinned. She loved his grin. "You're making fun of me, aren't you?"

"Yes."

"So what else shall I tell you? That Stalin intends that Russia will soon outstrip the West or"—his mouth twitched with mischief—"that you have the most beautiful eyes on earth and that I want to kiss your lips?"

"Hmm, let me think. That's a hard one to choose."

She stepped closer, leaning in toward him, but at that moment the guttural growl of the twin engines roared across the field.

"Look!" He pointed over the heads of the crowd. "Look at its teeth!"

Sofia would rather look at Mikhail's strong white teeth with their small telltale chip, but she wasn't going to argue. The plane dropped down onto the grass, where, as it rolled and bounced to a stop, the crowd broke into cheers, the Young Pioneers saluted, and the brass band struck up the *Internationale*.

"It's smiling," Sofia laughed in astonishment.

Painted on the long reptilian plywood nose that the designer Vadim Shavrov had specially added were the jaws and sharp teeth of a crocodile, curved into a disarming smile. Down the spine of the fuselage a row of bumps rose like the scaly ridges of a crocodile's back.

"It's inspired," Mikhail exclaimed. "The most famous airplane in the country."

"It makes me proud to be Russian," Sofia said solemnly.

"You're teasing me again."

"No, Mikhail. I mean it. I am proud of Russia and I am proud of being Russian."

He gave her a wide smile. "Then let's go and inspect the *Krokodil*."

He took her hand in his and led her across the field through the milling throng with a long energetic stride, but the look in his eyes was so serious and so determined, it didn't match the smile on his lips. It made her uneasy.

*S*OFIA, have you seen Yuri?" Mikhail asked.

The afternoon was measured by how many times the propellers swung into action. They were watching the *Krokodil* take off once more, and a collective intake of breath from the crowd whispered on the hot summer breeze as the aircraft shook off its lumbering attachment to the ground. It soared up into the air, and once in its natural element it possessed all the grace of a dancer. It dipped one wing and banked smoothly into a circle above the field, climbing higher and higher with each circuit.

"Yes, I saw him in the film projection tent earlier."

"Not since?"

"No. The races are about to start, so he's probably over there by the flags."

Mikhail's gaze scanned the sea of faces on the field. "I can't see him."

Sofia rested a hand lightly on his forearm. The sleeves of his white shirt were rolled well back because of the heat of the day, and she could feel that the muscle underneath was tense.

"What is it, Mikhail? What's the matter?"

"Pyotr came to see me." He released a harsh breath. "He said things about you to Yuri that he shouldn't have said, and he's frightened that Yuri will go to Stirkhov with it."

Despite the warmth of the sun, Sofia's face froze.

The voices and the laughter all around them, the band's incessant drumming, and the throb of the heavy M-17 engines all faded to nothing. Silence seemed to fill the whole wide arc of sky.

Mikhail stared at her grim-faced. "It's time to leave."

*Z*ENIA, wait a minute."

The gypsy girl was emerging from a tent. Each tent contained a different machine or process on display to indicate the modernization of industry, but the most popular by far was the one full of the latest shiny sewing machines. Every woman in the field coveted one. Sofia caught the gypsy girl's arm and drew her aside behind a heavy GAZ truck that had transported the benches and chairs. It smelled of oil and warm paintwork.

"What is it, Sofia? You look . . . unhappy."

"I saw you with your friend Vanya earlier. He isn't in OGPU uniform today."

"No, he's off-duty." Zenia couldn't stop herself smiling as she talked of him.

"But he'd hear what's going on, wouldn't he? He'd know if there's any trouble today."

"What kind of trouble?"

"A search for someone."

Zenia's features became still and she studied Sofia hard. "Wait here and stay behind the truck. I'll be back as quickly as I can. Don't move." She hurried away.

Sofia didn't move.

*S*HE remained behind the truck and knew this was the end. The end of everything. The choice was already made.

The hot breeze that blew through the silver birches bordering the meadow sounded as sad as the wind that sighed over the empty flats of the taiga, and all around her the air was delicate and clear as glass. She could taste its sparkle on her tongue in a way she never had before because now she was losing it.

It was a straight choice.

And at that moment she hated Anna with a hatred that took her breath away.

*B*ISTRO!" Zenia was back, her eyes huge. "We must swap clothes."

She was already yanking off her skirt to reveal thin childish legs and untying the red scarf from her neck. Sofia didn't ask why. It was obvious they were searching for her and had her description.

"*Spasibo*, Zenia," she said as she stepped into Zenia's black skirt with felt flowers in bright colors around the hem and buttoned up the white gypsy blouse. But the words *thank you* were nowhere near enough.

"I asked Vanya. You are to be arrested as an escaped fugitive the moment they find you."

Sofia tied Zenia's triangular scarf over her head to disguise her blond hair and knotted it at the back, while Zenia pulled on the cornflower dress. Then Sofia drew from the small pouch she wore at her waist three objects. They lay on her outstretched palm, their perfection at odds with her scarred fingers.

"Zenia, I'm leaving, but I would like you to have one of these. Take whichever you wish."

One was the round white pebble Rafik had given her. The second was a wolf's long curved tooth from her time in the forest. It hung on a rawhide cord. The third was a diamond ring, so big and so bright it looked like it had swallowed the sun. The gypsy girl took a long time deciding, her black eyelashes darting shadows on her cheeks. Her hand hovered over Sofia's and she eventually lifted up the amulet of the wolf's canine tooth, which she tied around her neck by the cord. Neither commented on the gift or the choice.

"There is a packet for you in my skirt pocket," Zenia said. "From Rafik."

Sofia rummaged in the black skirt's patch pocket and found a small twist of brown paper that contained a handful of strong-smelling herbs.

"What is it?"

"A painkiller," Zenia said and looked away.

A painkiller? What did Rafik know that she didn't?

"Thank you, Zenia."

"Take care."

Sofia's hand closed tightly over the pebble and the ring. She would need much more than care.

ZENIA told me you were here," Mikhail said as he stepped around the rear flap of the GAZ truck and gathered her into his arms. He caressed the nape of her neck, and she wanted to stay on that spot with him for the rest of her life. She laid her forehead against his chest and listened to the rapid beat of his heart.

"I thought you weren't coming back," she whispered.

He took her face in his hands and tipped it up to look into his eyes.

"I'll always come back, my love," he promised. "Always."

He kissed her mouth. Soft and tender, her tongue darting hungrily to his. She clung to him, imprinting the feel of him into her muscles, and then she stepped out of his arms and kept her voice steady.

"Did you find Yuri? Or Pyotr?"

"No. Pyotr seems to have vanished, but I learned that Yuri is up in the plane."

"What?"

The *Krokodil* had been carrying a lucky few up into the air for short flights all afternoon, but it had seats for only nine passengers at a time. Most were for the Party hierarchy, but some were reserved for workers nominated for special dedication and achievement.

"Yuri is up in the plane," Mikhail repeated flatly.

"It's Stirkhov's reward to him," Sofia moaned. "For information."

Mikhail nodded, silent and severe. "I'm so sorry, Sofia."

The aircraft was coming in for its final landing of the day, its engines drowning out the chorus of cheers hailing its return.

"They're hunting for you, my love. The perimeters are well guarded, identity papers are being checked. Our best chance of hiding you safely is in the middle of the crowd where you can keep on the move, until you—"

"Mikhail, Pyotr idealizes the Party. Don't blame him."

"I do, Sofia. I blame him, and I blame myself." He looked at her, noticed her change of clothes, and the anger in his eyes softened. Gently he cupped her cheek in his palm, and she tipped her head sideways into it.

"Well, what have we here?" An officer in khaki uniform was standing beside the front wing of the truck, staring at them. He looked just as surprised as they were.

"Comrade," Sofia smiled as she slid an arm around Mikhail's waist, "you wouldn't deny us five minutes away from the sharp eyes of my friend's wife, would you?"

The soldier laughed. His trousers were already half unbuttoned, and it was obvious he'd come to relieve himself behind the truck. His face was broad and good-natured, but his nose ran in a crooked line as though involved in one fight too many.

"Don't mind me, comrades," he said easily. But just as easily the Tokarev pistol flew from the holster on his hip into his hand, its business end pointed straight at Sofia. "Just show me your papers first." He said it with a grin to emphasize that he intended no harm, just being cautious.

"Of course, comrade."

Sofia made a show of rummaging in her pocket for her papers, but instead her hand touched the cool surface of the stone and instantly she cleared her mind, stilled her breath. She moved forward toward the *soldat*, her eyes locked tight on his, and she saw him frown and glance down at the gun in his hand with sudden confusion.

That was when Mikhail struck. Two strides and the edge of his hand to the man's throat, followed by a sharp blow to his jaw that sent the soldier's head snapping back against the side of the truck with a loud metallic *thud*. The body crumpled onto the grass. They took no chances. In seconds Sofia had the soldier's belt off and Mikhail had used it to truss his hands and feet together behind his back, and then they stuffed his handkerchief in his mouth and pocketed his gun.

"Now," Mikhail said. "Time to leave."

As soon as the *Krokodil* touched down, everything happened fast. The two crewmen and their two assistants bundled projection equipment and cardboard boxes back onto the plane, while final but mercifully brief speeches were made and the band struck up the *Internationale* for the last time. White clouds began to drift across the sun like curtains drawing a performance to a close, and the mood in the field was one of exhilaration, as noisy huddles of men started to gather around bottles of *kvass* and vodka.

But none of it stopped those in uniform going about their job efficiently, and every blond young woman was ordered to show identity papers. Sofia dodged several, but time was running out. Any moment now the soldier behind the truck would be found, but Mikhail had gone once more in search of Pyotr.

"Don't attempt to leave until I return," he'd said.

She'd kissed him farewell, a light brush of the lips, and with it everything cracked inside her. She breathed, but only because she had to, not because she wanted to. She stood in the middle of a dense gathering close to the airplane and became aware of the tall figure of the blacksmith, Pokrovsky, on her right, and Elizaveta Lishnikova over to her left. They were keeping watch, extra eyes seeking out danger, and Sofia was certain it was Rafik who had told them to guard her. She was just edging in Pokrovsky's direction to apologize for her outburst in the smithy, when the teacher shouted a warning and the next second a hand fell on Sofia's shoulder. She spun around.

It was a khaki uniform but not the one from the truck. This man was older, with alert eyes under heavy bristled brows.

"*Dokumenti,*" he ordered.

Four men in uniform stood around her, like wolves circling a sheep, and from the corner of her eye she saw Pokrovsky pushing his way through the crowd toward her. *No, don't come near;* she willed him to keep away because she didn't want him hurt too. It would be a bullet in the back for her if she ran, but a bullet in the brain if they saw the name they were searching for on her papers. Back or brain, the choice wasn't hard. Time slowed down as she reached into her pocket and slid out her residency permit. *Anna, forgive me. Forgive me, my friend, forgive me for failing.*

"Ah, there you are." Mikhail's hand suddenly slotted under her elbow, almost jerking her off her feet. Pyotr was pressed close to her other side, his brown eyes dark with misery.

"I'm sorry," he whispered.

"It's all right, Pyotr, you did what you believed was right." Gently she touched his hand and felt his fingers cling to hers.

"Your papers?" The soldier raised his voice.

"Comrade," Mikhail said sharply, "this woman is with the crew of the—"

But already the soldier was reaching forward to pull her from Mikhail's grasp, and rifles rattled around her.

"Stop that at once."

Sofia swung around and was astonished to find herself staring into the face of Aleksei Fomenko. He gave her no more than a fleeting nod, then flashed some identity in front of the uniformed officer. A space immediately cleared around her.

"I can vouch for this woman," he said brusquely. "What the hell are you and your men doing wasting your time here when you should be out there"—he flung a dismissive arm toward the rest of the field—"searching for the fugitive?"

The space around Sofia grew even larger as the soldiers backed off, and she felt Mikhail's grip tighten on her arm.

"This woman and I are to leave with the airplane crew," Mikhail protested angrily.

"I'll need to see proof of that," the officer responded, but already the aggression had waned and his manner was hesitant.

Fomenko put himself between Sofia and the uniform, his authority taking easy control. "Don't be bloody foolish, *soldat*. The cloud base is lowering every minute, so they need to leave right now, or shall I report you for causing delays to . . . ?"

"No, Comrade Chairman, that won't be necessary."

Sofia felt Mikhail jerk her into action. Her feet remembered to move as, heart hammering, she was propelled forward and into the airplane. The flimsy corrugated door closed behind her and the body of the *Krokodil* shuddered and rumbled, making noises that sounded like contentment.

Sofia breathed. Because she wanted to.

FIFTY-FIVE

RIVERS meandered lazily below as the aircraft flew due north. The threads crisscrossed through a vast water-filled landscape emptied of all color by mists that shrouded them in secrecy. The M-17 engines throbbed, and as Mikhail sat in the passenger cabin he could feel every beat of the pistons driving his blood through his veins. They powered a wonderful sense of being cut free from the earth.

It was a long time since he'd felt like this, as good as this. Which was crazy because he knew he was in serious trouble whichever way he looked, but somehow that all faded into insignificance up here. He was with Sofia and he was flying again, and he was determined to find Anna Fedorina. Reality on the ground seemed a long way down.

ARE you all right?"

Sofia turned her face from the window and gave him a smile, that crooked little curve of her lips that he loved.

"I'm fine."

"Not nervous on your first flight?"

"No, I love it. How high are we?"

"Around three thousand meters."

She nodded but looked tense. He put out a hand across the narrow aisle that divided them and stroked her arm, soothing her.

"It's the continuous juddering," he said. "It sets your nerves on edge if you're not accustomed to it."

She nodded again, a little dip of her chin. They hadn't spoken much on the plane because in the small cabin every word could be overheard. Nine seats were set out in pairs, one on each side of a narrow central aisle and one at the back. The two passenger members of the squadron whose job it was to arrange the films and distribute the pamphlets were seated at the front, but even so they were close and conversations were far from private.

"How far will we fly?" she asked in a low tone.

"The *Krokodil*'s range without refueling is seven hundred kilometers."

"We'll go that distance?"

"Yes."

Her eyes changed as they stared at him in disbelief, and then she tipped back her long throat and released a silent shout of joy.

"I thought," she said in a voice that struggled to sound casual, "that we would just be taken . . . out of that field and put down somewhere nearby."

"No," he laughed for the benefit of listening ears, "the captain is taking us on quite a little jaunt. He wants me to give my professional assessment of how these propaganda trips are working out. As my secretary, you must take notes."

"Of course," she responded in a demure secretarial kind of voice, but she rolled her eyes dramatically and mimed typing in the air, so that Mikhail had to bite his tongue to stop a laugh. As the shadows of the clouds chased each other over the flatlands below them, she asked, "Did you arrange this?"

"Yes."

She nodded and was silent for a while, gazing intently out the small window, but eventually she turned to him again. "Mikhail, what about Pyotr?"

"He'll be all right. Zenia is going to take care of him while I'm away."

Her eyelids flickered, but he couldn't tell why. Was it anger at the boy?

"I didn't expect that from Fomenko," she murmured.

He gave her a long look. *Chyort!* Was that man still in her mind? He put his head back and shut his eyes. *Concentrate on Anna Fedorina,* he told himself, *this is your one chance. Concentrate on her.*

*T*HE *Krokodil* touched down. The surface of the landing field gave them a bumpy ride, but the plane rolled quickly to a stop and they climbed out. From the air the town of Novgorki was an unpleasant black scab on the landscape, but on the ground it looked worse, drabber and darker. After hours of almost nothing but forests of massed pine trees and silver shimmering waterways with an occasional fragile village clinging to the banks, the dirt and squalor of the streets of the northern town of Novgorki came as a sharp reminder of how easily people could make a place ugly.

It was a purpose-built town dedicated to minerals, with belching chimney stacks that soared into the gray sky, thickening the air with chemicals. Yet oddly Mikhail liked it. It was a place of no pretense, and he could sense an undercurrent of wildness as strong as the stink of the sulfur, a town on the very edge of civilization. That suited him just fine.

He thanked the pilot of the *Krokodil*; a handshake was enough. Sofia observed them with a thoughtful expression but passed no comment, just kissed the pilot's cheek, which made him blush to the roots of his gingery hair.

Mikhail was glad of the walk into town as it gave them time to discuss what lay ahead. It was evening when they reached the center of Novgorki but in July the days were long and the nights no more than a darker shade of white. The main road was called Lenin Street as usual and held a crush of shabby concrete buildings, all the same monotonous tone of gray alongside squat wooden shops that seemed more permanent than the concrete. Rain-filled potholes littered the road, and even at this hour it was busy with trucks and cars making the most of daylight hours.

"What now?" Sofia was looking around warily.

"A bed and a meal."

Groups of men hung around on street corners with cigarettes dangling from their lips and bottles in their pockets. Mikhail approached one man with a thick Stalin mustache who leered at Sofia but directed them politely enough to a workers' dormitory, a bleak building where they showed their identity papers and paid a few roubles in advance. They were allotted a couple of camp beds and soiled quilts in separate communal sleeping areas.

"It's better than nothing," Mikhail pointed out.

Sofia raised a doubtful eyebrow at him.

"Have you noticed," she asked when they walked back out onto the street, "how few women are here?"

"That's why we have to take extra care of you."

They walked up the main street, aware of eyes watching them.

"More of Stalin's economic boom times," Sofia muttered under her breath with an ironic nod toward the empty shop windows.

Even at this hour many of them were still open, and they chose a prosperous-looking hardware shop for their purpose. It smelled of pine resin and dust inside, where a short man with a broad northern face and well-padded cheeks greeted them from behind the counter. His eyes crawled over Sofia.

"Good evening," Mikhail said, letting his gaze roam the shop. "Busy, I see."

The place was empty of other customers but did at least have a few goods on display. A sack of nails and screws, a box of hinges, some kerosene cans and paint brushes, but no paint, of course. Lengths of matting and a range of secondhand tools lay in a jumble around the walls, while zinc pans hung from the roof beams, low enough to crack a careless skull. But behind the shopkeeper's head were shelves holding a row of cardboard boxes, unlabeled, and Mikhail suspected they contained the better stuff for the better customers. He picked up a roll of canvas and tossed it onto the counter. Beside him Sofia stood silent.

"Is that all?" the shopkeeper asked, scratching his armpit with relish.

"No."

"What else?"

"I have something to sell."

The storeman's eyes brightened and slid to Sofia.

"Not me," she said fiercely.

The man shrugged. "It happens sometimes."

Mikhail placed a fist on the counter between them. "Who in this town might want to buy an object of value?"

"What kind of object?"

"One that is worth real money, not"—he gazed disdainfully around the shop—"not Novgorki kopecks."

The man squinted at Mikhail, his tobacco-stained teeth chewing on his lower lip. "Very well," he said, and he pointed to a curtained doorway at the back of the shop. "You, comrade, come with me. You," he pointed at Sofia, "wait here."

Before the storekeeper could draw breath, Mikhail had leaped over the counter and pinned him against his boxes, a hand crushing his throat. He could feel the man's windpipe fighting for air.

"Don't mistake me, comrade," Mikhail hissed in his face. "I am not one of your peasant fools. I do not walk blindly into your back room to be ambushed and robbed while my woman is stolen. Understand me?"

"*Da.*" The man's voice was a gasp, his eyes popping in his head.

Mikhail removed his hand and let him breathe. The harsh rasping scrape of it sounded loud in the silence of the musty store.

"Now," Mikhail said, keeping the man jammed against his shelves, "tomorrow morning I will return here at eight o'clock for no more than five minutes. If you know a buyer for a jewel worth more than you'll earn in ten lifetimes, bring him here. Got that?"

The man blinked his understanding.

"*Do zavtra.* Till tomorrow," Mikhail snapped and picked up the roll of canvas and the candles. He gripped Sofia by her upper arm and strode out of the shop.

So you're not just a handsome face after all," Sofia said.

She was teasing him, he knew that, but her smile didn't reach her eyes.

"I had to do it, Sofia. It was the only way of showing that man I'm serious. This is a hard town, my love; danger is what they breathe out here. Don't look so reproachful."

"He might have pulled a gun on you."

Mikhail patted the loaded pistol hidden under her slender waist-band, the one he'd stolen from the officer behind the GAZ truck. "Then you'd have shot him," he said, and he kissed her nose.

She shivered nevertheless, and he wrapped an arm around her to keep her warm, as neither of them were dressed for a cool northern evening, but she pulled away.

"Don't," she said angrily. "Don't take risks."

He burst out laughing and felt her fist smack into his chest. He caught it in his hand and pulled her tight to him. "This is all one huge risk, my sweet love, so what's an extra little one or two along the way?"

"Don't die," she whispered.

"I intend to live till I'm a hundred, as long as you promise to live to a hundred with me."

"To darn your socks and cook your meals?" she teased.

"No, my precious, to warm my bed and let me kiss your sweet neck."

She nestled her lips in the hollow of his throat. "I'll warm your bed and let you kiss my neck," she crooned, "if you darn my socks and cook my meals for a hundred years."

"Agreed." He laughed.

FIFTY-SIX

N O, Mikhail, we do this together. We agreed."

They were standing in the street and heavy rain was lashing down, soaking them to the skin and turning the road into a muddy torrent. A yellow stray hound crouched shivering in the gutter, its mournful eyes following their every move.

Mikhail pushed open the door to the hardware store, and Sofia positioned herself silently just inside the entrance, leaning against the timber wall where she casually laid one hand on the gun at her waistband. Her eyes followed Mikhail as he approached the stranger who was waiting next to the counter with folded arms. The man was built like a series of boxes balanced on top of each other: square hat, square head, square shoulders, a sharp square suit. His face possessed the broken veins of a drinker and the shrewd eyes of a man in authority who knows how to use it. The shopkeeper hovered in the background, as brown and dusty as his boxes.

"So, comrade, what have you brought for me to

see?" the square man said without preliminaries. "It had better not be shit. No *gavno*."

Mikhail took his time eyeing the stranger up and down in a manner that was meant to insult and which brought Sofia's heart to her throat. He didn't speak, just took a small piece of green material from his back pocket and opened it on his palm. The man's eyes widened, then narrowed to half-shut like a lizard's because even in the dim light of the hardware shop the diamond on the green cloth winked at him. He drew a loud intake of breath.

For the first time Mikhail spoke. "It's worth more than you possess."

"Comrade, there's something you need to learn. A jewel like that is only worth what someone will pay."

"And"—Mikhail gave him a hard smile—"how quickly they will pay for it."

The man nodded his square head, took out a handkerchief, and blew his veined nose into it. This seemed to be a signal of some kind, because another man stepped out from behind the curtain to the back room, a great bearded ox of a man with a badly scarred face. Instantly Sofia pulled the gun out of her waistband and, clutching it with two hands, pointed it directly at the square stranger. His lizard eyes stared at her for a second, assessing the danger, and then he waved a hand dismissively and his scarred henchman lumbered back into his curtained den.

Nothing was said, no mention was made of the short-lived intrusion, but Sofia didn't lower the gun. Mikhail took a slow and deliberate step forward, then spoke in a voice that crowded the dismal room.

"Now that we understand each other, . . . comrade"—he made the word sound like something he'd scraped off the bottom of his shoe—"let's get down to business. My time is short."

"By all means"—the man's gaze focused on the diamond, his words as smooth as oil—"let's talk money."

"No, comrade. Let's talk horses."

SOFIA waited alone in the rain. Zenia's scarf on her head was soaked, but a few meters of canvas with a hole cut in it for her head was keeping the worst of the downpour off her body. The black earth beneath her feet had turned to a quagmire, but she barely noticed the squelch of mud as she prowled soft-footed among the trees and her eyes scanned the road that ran straight as a rifle barrel into Novgorki.

Where was he?

He should be here by now.

Was he safe?

Should she race back into town?

Her head swarmed with fears for Mikhail. Her fingers played incessantly with the Tokarev pistol clutched under her canvas shroud, and she drew some comfort from it because the weight of the weapon, its hard metallic edges, its lethal simplicity, all gave her a grain of reassurance. *But Mikhail should have his fist tight around this gun right now. He's the one in danger.*

He'd forced her to wait. The square man with the smile that stretched too tight had insisted on a one-to-one deal with no guns and no henchmen. So Mikhail had kissed her, a light touch of lips that she committed to memory, and left the hardware store. Sofia had watched them disappear up the street, the yellow dog trailing behind them through the rain, and then she retreated to the spot on the edge of town where he'd told her to meet him.

Hidden from curious eyes, she waited for him. She felt as if she'd been waiting for him all her life.

*T*WO hours later Mikhail finally emerged through the gray curtain of rain. Sofia wanted to throw herself into his arms and yell at him for putting her through such hell, but instead she stood quietly under a dripping poplar tree and let him come to her. He was riding a big chestnut horse and leading two others, one of which was carrying quite a load on its back, strapped down under a canvas sheet. Mikhail slid to the ground in one easy movement, placed his hands on her shoulders, and looked carefully into her face.

"You were a long time," she said simply.

"I'm sorry. Were you worried?"

"No."

"Good. You must trust me."

"I do."

He smiled, the wide smile she loved, the one that he kept just for her, and she wrapped her fist into his sodden shirt in an effort to hold on to that smile.

"I hope one of those horses is for me."

"Always thinking of taking it easy, aren't you?"

She laughed, and the unexpected relief of it doused her fears. "Did you get a good deal?" she asked and released his shirt.

"Svetlana Dyuzheyeva would turn in her grave if she knew how cheaply her diamond ring had changed hands, but yes, for us it was a good deal."

From inside his wet shirt he pulled out a fistful of large-rouble notes, lifted the front of her canvas cape, and slipped the money into the pocket of her black skirt.

"That'll keep you safe," he smiled, and suddenly he took her in his arms as though frightened of losing her.

They stood like that, Sofia had no idea how long, heads together. But when their hearts had finally stilled, they swung up onto the horses and headed off through the forest. Behind them the yellow dog skulked in their tracks.

*I*T was the dog that warned her with a low throaty growl that raised the hackles on her own neck. They were riding through the forest with just the pattering of the rain for company and the soft shuffle of horses' hooves through the undergrowth. Mikhail was leading the way, Sofia close behind, but her horse had a shorter stride and kept hanging back. They had been weaving their way through the trees for more than an hour when the attack came.

But the dog had warned her, so the gun was ready in her hand.

Two bulky figures leaped out from the trees at Sofia with a great roar as they launched themselves toward her, and a rifle shot rang out, ricocheting off the trunks. Her horse screamed a shrill shriek of fear that split the air, and the dog snarled, loud and menacing. A man's face appeared next to her horse's head, gaunt skin stretched over sharp bones, hair black and matted, a ragged length to his shoulders. His mouth was open and bellowing words at her, threats and insults and crude curses. Sofia yelled back at him with rage as one filthy hand seized her horse's bridle, the other her ankle.

She raised the gun and shouted a warning. Her attacker's eyes grew round as coins and he yanked hard on the horse's mouth, drawing blood. In terror the animal jinked sideways and reared up, its front hooves slicing through the rain, its wet head thrashing violently from side to side, tumbling Sofia from its back.

As she fell to the ground, she pulled the trigger.

*S*OFIA."

Mikhail's voice was drifting in and out of her head. Sometimes near and sometimes so far away she could barely hear it. Other noises came and went, strange sounds she couldn't place, but through them all snagged the low whining of a dog. She fought to open her eyes but her eyelids refused to obey, so instead she called Mikhail's name, but it came out as no more than a breath.

"Sofia, wake up."

She listened to the voice she loved, to the way he made her name sound like something precious, and when she felt his cool hand brush over her forehead, she sighed. Something let go inside her and she started to float into a dream where silver-haired women stretched out their arms around her.

*S*OFIA flicked open her eyes. Her head hurt like hell. As though a splinter of iron were stuck in her brain. The air seemed as gray and warm as squirrel's fur, and for a moment she couldn't make out where she was.

"Mikhail," she murmured.

At once his head bent over her and his lips touched her temple. "Don't move, my love. You've taken a bad knock on the head."

Slowly things came to her, thought by thought, and she realized she was lying on her side, her head on Mikhail's lap. He was sitting with his back against a pine tree, one hand holding her, the other holding the gun. Above them he'd rigged up a canopy of canvas, and under it he'd lit a small fire that hissed and popped when a splash of rain blew into it. She rolled onto her back, and gazed up at him. His eyes were full of concern.

"Help me up," she said.

"No, my sweet, you must stay where you are. You have to rest."

"I've rested enough."

He didn't argue further. Just sat her up and held her steady while the world swooped and danced around her. He placed a metal cup of hot tea in her hands and sat quietly while she sipped it.

"Where are they?" she asked at last, leaning against him.

"Over there." He gestured off to the left.

"Who were they?"

"His henchmen. Come to retrieve the money and the horses."

"You're not hurt?"

"A bruise or two, nothing much."

He spoke in short bursts, barely in control of his anger. "They're dead. Both of them."

She nodded, chilled by her own indifference.

When she was ready, he helped her stand, and she insisted on going over to check on the bodies of their attackers because only seeing them with her own eyes would convince her that she and Mikhail were safe. For now, anyway. With Mikhail's arm around her waist she stared down at the two corpses in the mud. The one with the ragged hair had a hole in the center of his chest and stared back at her with sightless eyes; the other was the ox-man with the scarred face from the hardware store. His throat had been cut in a livid slash and the rain was washing his clothes pink.

She nodded, satisfied. Together they threw a few branches over the bodies and left them to the wolves, and then they struck camp, mounted their horses, and rode on.

FIFTY-SEVEN

*T*HEY rode the rest of that day and most of the night. At times they walked, allowing the horses a break, ears alert for sounds of pursuit and of the wild creatures that rustled and scampered among the trees just out of sight in the dusky gloom of twilight. Throughout the night the sky never grew totally dark above them, but under the canopy of the forest the path they picked over the pine needles was barely visible.

They talked, but not much, careful of secrecy. To navigate, Mikhail used a small hand compass, but most of the time the terrain forced them to travel in single file with the packhorse trailing behind Mikhail's mount, which meant they were too far apart to whisper any conversation, so they slid into silence and into their own thoughts. But just before dawn when the new morning was nothing more than a blush of gold on the topmost branches of the trees, Mikhail called a halt.

Sofia looked reluctant to stop.

"Enough," he insisted, and he started to unsaddle his

horse. It whickered softly when he lifted the weight from its back and nuzzled his shoulder.

"Is it safe?" she asked.

"We have to sleep, my love, and the horses need rest. We'll do best to hole up here for two or three hours."

"No longer."

Her impatience to keep moving was always there. Mikhail walked over to her and slipped an arm around her waist, and he loved the way her immediate response was to lean the whole length of her body against him. What was it that gave this extraordinary woman such strength? He recalled what Rafik had said about her ancestry and wondered whether that was where she drew her inner core from. Gently he stroked her hair, but later, when they were stretched out on a blanket under the tall columns of the trees, there was nothing gentle about their lovemaking.

It had a wildness to it, a fury that drove them to clutch at each other's bodies. Her kisses came with teeth, his caresses came with a crushing force. When she finally threw back her head with a shout, and a deep moan tore from his throat, they collapsed into each other's arms and lay like that, limbs entwined, exhausted and breathing hard. Both knew the anger was not meant for each other. It was meant for the world out there.

*M*IKHAIL."

They had both slept.

"What is it, Sofia?"

He respected her instinct for danger and lifted his head quickly from the blanket but could see nothing but a haze of insects hanging lazily in the warm air. He flicked away a *komar* that was gorging itself on Sofia's naked shoulder. Her eyes were half-closed.

"Did you know," she asked, "when we set off for the *Krokodil* display, that we would fly north in the airplane?"

"I intended to try, but I wasn't certain it would happen. That's why I said nothing to you."

She rested her head on his bare chest. "Did the captain agree to help us for money?"

"No."

"Why then?"

"I used to work with his brother Stanislav at the aircraft factory in Moscow. He got into trouble once and I helped him. That's all."

She nodded, a lock of her hair tickling his chin.

"Thank you," she whispered and set herself astride him.

*W*HAT kind of man would do this? Risk his life for someone he didn't know.

Sofia sat on the riverbank, her feet trailing in the strong current, and watched Mikhail splash water over himself as fiercely as if he believed it could wash away his sins. She was naked and letting her skin dry in the sunshine. They had traveled relentlessly for ten days and were stealing an hour of rest before moving on. The yellow dog ambled past her on the grass, brushing its wet pelt against her shoulder, and went to lie in the shade.

"What kind of man are you, Mikhail?"

He looked over his shoulder at her, surprised. He smiled at her.

"A fortunate man," he said at last.

"Really? Is that what you believe?"

"Yes, with all my heart."

"Mikhail, for heaven's sake, think straight! Here you are in the middle of a forest, no home, no job, no travel permit, with your life in danger every moment. So why say a *fortunate* man?"

He scooped up a double handful of sparkling river water and emptied it over his head. To Sofia, with his hair slicked back and his muscular figure waist-deep in the water, naked and powerful, he looked like a sea god who had taken a wrong turn and swum up the River Ob by mistake. His whole body gleamed and glistened in the sunlight, the bruises muted now.

"Fortunate because I have you, my angel. You've granted me a second chance."

"What kind of second chance?"

"A chance to right a wrong."

"You mean . . . when you killed Anna's father."

She'd said it. She had finally dragged the words from their hiding place and shaken them loose in the bright golden air.

"Yes. That's exactly what I mean."

"And Fomenko? What about your killing of his mother? Is that a wrong you intend to right as well?"

A pulse ticked in Mikhail's jaw and he smacked his palm on the surface of the water sending up a rainbow of droplets, but when he spoke, his single word was calm.

"No."

"Why not?"

"Because he put a knife in my father's throat. Tell me how I forgive that."

"I see. So when I asked what kind of man you are, maybe you should have answered *a vengeful one.*"

He looked at her solemnly. "How can I be vengeful, my love, when Fomenko allowed us to take his mother's diamond ring to rescue Anna?"

Sofia buried her toes in the grass. "So when we've done this"—she tossed him a blueberry from the clutch in her hand, and he snatched it from the air with ease—"will you stop hating yourself?"

She watched the intake of breath rather than heard it, saw his stomach muscles tighten and his chest expand.

"You know me too well, Sofia."

She laughed, and before she knew it he was charging at her through the river, sweeping sun-bleached waves in every direction as he rushed at her in a roar. She shrieked with astonishment and leaped to her feet, but he was too fast. His hand caught her wrist, sending the last of the blueberries skittering down the bank, and he pulled her to him. His wet body pressed hard against hers, his lips finding her mouth.

Behind her the dog barked, two sharp high-pitched notes.

"Quickly." She threw herself into the water, dragging Mikhail with her.

"What is it?"

"Danger."

"Wolves?"

"I'm not sure."

Together they let the current sweep them rapidly downstream, and then they struck out for the shore at a spot where bushes reached down to the river. They crouched there, listening.

"Our horses," Sofia grimaced.

"I tethered them for shade where the trees are thickest. If it's a wolf, they'd already be panicking." Mikhail brushed a strand of wet hair from her face. "What warned you of danger?"

"It was the dog . . ."

Suddenly the sound of men's voices reached them and the whinny of thirsty horses sighting water. Upstream, exactly on the stretch of beach where Sofia and Mikhail had been standing, a patrol of soldiers tumbled out of the forest.

*T*HEY rode hard the rest of the day. The pine trunks whipped past as slender shadows and the blades of sunlight sliced between them like knives. They had waited in the undergrowth by the river until their shadows had lengthened and they were certain the patrol was long gone. The soldiers missed Mikhail's horses tucked away deep among the trees, but their clothes lying at the water's edge must have caused some comment. Sofia and Mikhail rode in silence, wary of further patrols, but they kept up a good speed and the horses' flanks were flecked with foam. It was almost dusk when Mikhail spotted the silver thread of another river through the trees ahead of them.

"We'll stop here," he said. "The horses need a drink."

"My canteen is nearly empty too."

"I'll keep watch."

They dismounted and stood still, listening hard, but there was no sound except the bickering of crows, so with Mikhail in the lead they emerged from the ragged edge of the forest, but instantly he stopped dead. A groan escaped his lips.

"What is it?" Sofia asked from behind. Then the smell hit her and she vomited.

It was the patrol of soldiers. They lay like rag dolls that a child had tired of playing with and tossed aside, their khaki uniforms spoiled by holes and rust-colored stains. They were dead, all nine of them. Wild animals had been gorging on their carcasses, bellies torn open by wolverines, but worse were the faces. The eyes had been pecked into black holes by crows that still perched with a stiff-legged challenge on the chests of the young soldiers. Everywhere was encrusted with a shiny moving crust of flies.

"Stay here," Mikhail said and handed Sofia the reins.

The horses were stamping their hooves and rolling their eyes with nostrils flared, spooked by the odor of blood. Mikhail tore off his shirt, bunched it over his nose and mouth, and moved down the grassy slope. The soldiers were young, none more than twenty, and each body bore a bullet hole, sometimes two or three. Whoever did this, did an efficient job.

Without hope or expectation Mikhail examined each one, but none showed any sign of life. At one point he dropped to his knees on the soiled grass beside one boy's body and held his hand. It felt warm to the touch, and for one insane second he believed the soldier's heart must still be beating, but it was only the sun warming from the outside what could never again be warmed from the inside. These poor young men were Russia's lifeblood, like Pyotr would one day be, and the sight of them sickened Mikhail. He lowered his head in his hands, but after a moment was taken by surprise when a hand stroked the back of his neck with a tender touch.

"Who would have done such a thing. Mikhail? Bandits? Subversives?"

"No, it's almost certainly horse thieves out here in this wild region." He shook his head in disgust. "Nine lives in exchange for nine horses and maybe a couple of pack animals as well. But they'll have to move fast if they hope to get away with their miserable lives."

"Come, quickly my love, we must go."

She stooped to pick up a rifle that was lying at her feet.

"No," Mikhail said. "Don't take anything. When these bodies are found, the army will sweep through this whole region like the plague, and if you possess a single item belonging to this troop you'll be . . ."

He didn't say the word. He didn't need to.

FIFTY-EIGHT

"Is she there?"

Rafik shook his head. "No."

"Is she close?"

"She's close to death."

"Can you save her?"

"No."

A sigh like the moon's breath whispered around the walls of the chamber. Three faces grew pale.

"Save her."

"Save her."

"Save her."

"I cannot. I am losing her down a labyrinth."

Blood, like wine, was poured into a copper bowl.

"She is too far from me. I cannot disentangle the shadows."

White flesh, like bread, was crumbled into the blood.

"She is alone and beyond my reach."

Herbs, bitter as pain, were scattered on the glistening surface.

"How can we protect her? Tell us how."

"I need greater power."

"Drink the blood."

"Eat the flesh."

"Swallow the herbs."

Rafik drank and looked at the faces gazing at him. "It's not enough."

*Y*OU'VE come."

The priest swept into the room, red hair ablaze, eyes rough as sackcloth. His beard gleamed like a breastplate of fire.

"I've come."

"Your strength is needed."

"My strength is the strength of the Lord God Almighty."

Rafik rose to his feet, ghostly in his white robe. "The girl is in an abyss."

"All are in peril of the Bottomless Pit, all who worship the image of the Beast. It is written in God's Word."

"Help us, Priest."

"Gypsy, if what you are doing provides food for the devil, the smoke of your torment will be never-ending and you shall have no rest by day or by night."

"We need her, I tell you this. She is rich in power."

"What are riches? God in his infinite wisdom tells us that it is when we think we are rich that we are at our most wretched and miserable and poor and blind and naked. And as surely as night follows day, his wrath shall come to smite the scorpions of this earth."

"Priest." Rafik's voice rang out clearly. "This village knows too well that it is poor and wretched. Will you join with us?"

"God will curse you, Rafik."

"Will you watch Tivil bleed to death?"

"Sorcerers are condemned to dwell outside the City of God, and you are a sorcerer."

"Rafik." It was the blacksmith, his blackened fingers pointing at the gypsy's chest. "Tell the priest."

"Tell me what?"

The light seemed to flicker and dart across the copper bowl as

Rafik spoke slowly. "The girl has a stone, a White Stone. It has drawn help to her side already."

Priest Logvinov's face grew pale as his long fingers sought the cross that hung on his chest and clung to it. "Do not blaspheme."

"I do not."

The priest shook his fiery locks. "The Lord says in the last book of his Holy Word, 'To him that overcometh will I give to eat of the hidden manna and will give him a white stone and in the stone a new name is written which no man knoweth saving he that receiveth it.'"

"She has the stone."

FIFTY-NINE

THE light was so clear and so white that at times the land looked made of bone. As they journeyed north through the taiga, the forest of pine and spruce thinned, giving way to open marshland that left Sofia feeling exposed. They were waiting for the creeping gloom of night before they crossed the flat wetland that stretched ahead, but every delay drove Sofia to distraction.

"Patience," Mikhail cautioned.

He was adjusting the packs on the horses and picking burrs from their manes. The chestnut's head hung low, its eyes half-shut, and Sofia was shocked by how weary it looked and how its ribs poked through its hide. It that how she and Mikhail looked too? She studied Mikhail as he tended the animals because she loved to see the skill with which his hands moved over them, soothing their twitchy skins the way he soothed hers. They didn't talk much now; images of the dead patrol ousted words from their heads, and in silence her fingers ruffled the ears of the yellow dog that was resting its head against her thigh.

"I'm not good at patience," she said.

Mikhail's gray eyes skimmed over the marshland. "You're good at other things."

"Anna's out there."

"So are the soldiers who are searching for that patrol."

A thickset old man sat half asleep in the afternoon sun, leaning back against the timber wall of his solitary *izba*, a picture of contentment in the middle of nowhere. He wore patched trousers and a threadbare shirt, a twist of smoke rising from the carved pipe in his mouth, keeping the mosquitoes at bay.

Mikhail greeted him pleasantly. "*Zdravstvuitye*, comrade."

"What can I do for you, comrade?"

"My saddle girth has snapped and I need—"

"In there." The old man jerked a thumb at the barn beside the house, which was well built but slowly turning green with moss. "You'll find plenty of tack hanging on the hooks. I've not much use for it now. Old Ivan is all I've got left to pull a plow." He scratched his beard, a long gray mat that looked much older than his blue eyes. "Who's she?" He smiled a welcome at Sofia.

"My wife."

The man blew out an appreciative billow of fragrant smoke. "She can talk to me while you fix your girth. I don't get much conversation these days, not since my Yulia died."

Mikhail took the reins from Sofia's hand and headed for the barn.

"What would you like to talk about?" Sofia smiled and sat down on the bench beside him, stretching her legs out in the sunshine. The word *wife* had taken her by surprise, and to her ears it sounded good. She laughed as a tiny kitten with spiky white fur and bright blue eyes scurried to safety under the man's ankles when it saw the dog trailing across the clearing. Several scrawny chickens paused in their dustbaths to bob their heads at the intruders.

"Do you know Moscow?" the old man asked.

"I've never been there, I'm afraid," she said.

"Is it true Stalin dynamited the sacred Cathedral of Christ the Redeemer and is planning to build a Palace of the Soviets in its place?"

"So I believe."

"And what about that Dutch Communist burning down the Reichstag in Germany?" He chuckled into his beard and slapped his thigh with glee. "That's one up the ass for that goose-stepping fascist monkey who has seized power over there."

"You're very well informed."

"*Da*. I read *Pravda*. My son comes to see me every three months and brings me all the newspapers I need." He nodded his head proudly and chewed at his tobacco-stained mustache. "He's a good son to me."

They talked further, about bread rationing and the high prices in shops and the increase in educational places for girls and Kirov's plans for Leningrad. None of it could touch the old man out here in the wilderness, yet he was passionate about seeing the rebirth of Russia. Alongside a steady flow of chatter, he provided a welcome meal of chicken, boiled potatoes, salted cabbage, and cucumber with *smetana*, and in return Mikhail took an hour to split logs while Sofia stacked them up against the wall. It was almost like normal living again. Even the dog lay in a patch of shade and snored contentedly, its stomach rumbling with chicken scraps.

"Time for us to leave," Mikhail finally announced. "Thank you for your hospitality. *Spasibo*."

"I've enjoyed the company." He smiled at Sofia and patted her hand, pulling a face at the scars on her two fingers. "Been in the wars, have you, girl?"

"Something like that."

"You should take better care of your wife in future, young man."

Mikhail gave Sofia a pointed look. "She's not the easiest of women to take care of."

Their gaze met, and Sofia suddenly saw for the first time his fear for her, deep down, sharp and painful as a bayonet inside him, and a sense of longing hit her. She wanted to rid this man she loved of those dark tense shadows, to make him as content and relaxed as the dog in the dust.

"When this is over," she promised, and tipped him a crooked smile.

He nodded and returned the smile. It was only a moment, but it was a moment she would keep safe.

She thanked the old man, and Mikhail started to lead the horses forward, reins loose in his fingers, and that was when she slid her hand into her pocket to tuck a couple of cookies in there that their host had provided for the journey. One of her damaged fingers brushed against the white stone where it lay, warm from the heat of her body, and she felt something change. Startled, she looked around her, expecting to see something different, but still the silver birch branches shimmered gently in the breeze and a magpie spiraled down into the clearing to steal a chicken bone from the dirt. The *izba* looked as peaceful as ever, its windows blinking in the sun.

But something had definitely changed. She didn't know what, but she could sense it. Then slowly, like the echo of distant thunder, in the soles of her feet she felt the vibration of horses' hooves. She stood totally still, listening. She could hear the nervous beating of hearts and whispers rustling the leaves. With a sudden roar her pulse pounded in her ears, blocking out the sound.

"Mikhail," she called, her voice louder than she intended. "They're here."

"Who?"

"The soldiers."

*T*HEY prepared quickly, dismantling their packs and turning the horses into a field down by the river. Mikhail would be splitting logs in the front yard and the old man was to remain seated on his bench outside the house, this time with a wooden chess set at his side. Sofia was banished with a hoe to the vegetable patch on the other side of the barn.

"Sofia, take no chances, do nothing . . . foolish. Promise me." Mikhail took her face between his hands. "Promise me," he said again.

"We're a happy peasant family just going about our chores." She smiled at him and touched her hand to his chest, but he didn't smile back.

His eyes were serious.

"I promise," she said.

"Don't get involved," Mikhail told her fiercely. "I'll deal with them. Just keep your head down and get on with weeding." He gave her a small shake that clicked her teeth together. "You're not listening to me."

"Yes, I am."

But he knew her too well.

*T*HE rattle of rifle bolts surrounded the house. Sofia felt the hairs rise on her neck.

"Who's in charge here?"

The demand came from the soldier at the head of the troop, a lean figure with dark hair swept off his face and quick intelligent eyes. Around him the troop fanned out, nervous and trigger-fingered, memories of the murdered patrol vivid in their minds.

"This is my home," Mikhail said, polite but unwelcoming. He hung the ax in one hand and stood with legs wide and thumb tucked into his belt.

"And who are you?"

"Mikhail Pashin."

"The others?"

"My father-in-law and my wife. Why the interest in us?"

"We're searching for the killers who murdered a patrol."

"We've seen no strangers here."

"No one?"

"No, but when I was out hunting a day or two back, I caught sight of a couple of men in soft hats and carrying rifles. Too far away to see anything more."

"Where?"

"About twenty versts west of here in the forest. Near the river bend."

From where she stood beside the barn Sofia held her breath. Mikhail looked and sounded so convincing. The way his hand gripped the ax with familiar ease, his muscular frame containing just the right hint of territorial challenge, the manner in which his eyes returned a direct stare. Surely the soldiers would go and leave them in peace. Surely.

A brush of fur on her leg made her look down. The yellow hound was pushing its shoulder against her knee, a faint whine in its throat. What was the matter with it?

"Look what I've found."

The words came from one of the soldiers, a short well-built man with a neck almost too thick for his shirt collar. He was leading the three horses into the yard and grinning broadly.

"They were down by the river, and there's another old wheezer in the barn but he's not worth bothering with."

"Four horses," the officer said sourly. "That makes you a rich *kulak*."

Sofia's throat closed.

Mikhail laughed easily. "No, Comrade, I'm no *kulak*." He waved a dismissive hand around the primitive home and barn. "Do I look like one of the wealthy bourgeoisie?"

Sofia's fingers found the white pebble and drew it from her pocket. In her head she pictured the officer's thoughts as grains of sand, and then she left the barn and the hoe and stepped forward. Immediately came the metallic ring of the ax as Mikhail barked it against a log in warning, but she fixed her eyes on the officer.

"Comrade, my husband is no *kulak*."

"We shoot *kulaks*."

"So there is no reason to shoot my husband."

She kept moving closer till she was only two paces from where the officer was leaning forward in the saddle, and she tightened her grip on the pebble. She took a breath, reached out her hand, and touched his boot in the stirrup. She shifted the sand.

"No reason at all, is there?" she said in a soft persuasive voice.

His eyelids quivered, thick and greasy, then settled. "No," he muttered. "I'm not here to hunt out *kulaks* anyway, but the horses will come in useful. We need them to replace the ones that were stolen."

"Not this one." Sofia entwined her hand in the gray's thick mane. Without a horse, Anna could not travel.

"Get your hand off it."

"No."

The soldier leading the horses raised his rifle. "You heard. Let go."

From nowhere a fist slammed into the side of Sofia's face, sending her sprawling to the ground.

"How many times have I told you to do as you're told?"

It was Mikhail's voice. He was standing over her, silhouetted against the pale sky. For a moment she couldn't believe Mikhail had hit her, and she stared up at him in dismay, but his eyes were harsh. Abruptly the heat drained from the day.

"Mikhail . . . ," she whispered.

"Get in the house."

She gave a moan, and a soft warm tongue licked her cheek. She shivered, struggled to her knees and onto her feet, her head stinging. As she touched the dog's coat, she had an odd sense of Rafik being at her side and thought she heard his voice whispering in the clearing.

Don't die for nothing, Sofia. You are needed.

She hesitated.

You are needed.

The gray horse was moving away, its tail twitching.

Needed.

The word pounded in her mind.

Anna needed her. Anna needed the horse.

She reached out and seized the tail. The horse reared, the metal edge of its forehoof clipping the soldier's shoulder, and he cursed fiercely. Without hesitation the officer aimed his rifle straight at Sofia and fired.

SIXTY

NNA'S lungs were worse today. She breathed carefully and coughed carefully, and made a point of swinging her hand ax carefully, but still the blade bit into the green wood and stuck.

"You're useless."

It was a guard, the older one with curly gray hair that was thinning on his scalp but thickening in his ears. Anna nodded agreement; she had no intention of wasting precious breath on words. She tugged at the ax, but this time she couldn't release it.

Sofia, where are you?

A hand reached over and yanked it out of the wood for her with ease. It was Lara, the young fair-haired girl who was working the next felled tree, and she put the haft back in Anna's hand just as the morning smoke break was called. "*Spasibo*," Anna whispered, and she slithered to her knees on the bark-strewn earth without the energy to join the others. She leaned against the rough russet trunk for support and scanned the tree-line of the forest.

"She won't come," Lara said.

"She will."

Lara shrugged and walked off to find a light for her *makhorka*, but Anna was glad to be left alone. A hollow feeling crept up on her as she sat among the flakes of bark, a sense of something going wrong. At first she thought it might be the beginning of death creeping up on her, but now that Lara had gone and she could examine the emptiness of the feeling, she thought otherwise. It was the beginning of someone else's death. How she knew this, she had no idea. It was all too strange and set cold fingers trailing up her spine and into her skull.

"What are you crying for?" It was the guard.

"I'm not."

"So stop making those whining noises."

Whining noises? Was she whining? She put a hand over her mouth and became aware of the sounds now trapped in her head. Shrill whines, like a dog. Her heart started to quiver.

Who was dead?

Vasily?

Sofia?

THE work day was finally over. The grate of saw and the bite of axes ceased, backs were flexed and muscles coaxed back into life as daylight trickled away behind the trees. It was at that time of day that the forest began to change, its black depths wreathed in mist and edging closer, its earthy breath more rank and menacing. Prisoners averted their eyes and guards didn't turn their backs on it because it made them nervous. That was when the rifle shots shattered the silence of the Work Zone and two guards dropped dead among the wood chippings.

The crack of another shot rang out, then three more in quick succession. Another uniformed body crumpled and a brigade of women prisoners started to scream. Panic flared like a forest fire because no one knew where the shots were coming from, and people started to flee for cover in all directions. Guards fired wildly into the trees, but four more grew scarlet flowers on their chests. Voices shrieked orders, heads ducked, arms flailed.

Anna stood and stared into the forest. Using all her strength, she started to shuffle toward it.

★　★　★

*Y*OU!"

Anna took no notice and pushed herself through the trees.

"You!" The voice came again. "Stop!"

Only death would make her stop. All around her, prisoners were taking advantage of the chaos and seizing their chance at freedom, their skeletal figures flitting into the forest like fleeing ghosts into the gray mist that enveloped it. She caught sight of Nina and Tasha disappearing far ahead of her, and she envied them their speed. A hand yanked her almost off her feet and she lashed out, but her blows were weak. Her captor was the gray-haired guard, his face a mixture of fury and terror, his mouth working in an effort at control. Without hesitation Anna pointed a finger at the sinister depths of the forest and screamed.

"He's there!"

That was all it took, one brief second. The guard turned his head and she swung the hand ax that was still in her grasp. The flat of the blade connected with his skull. His fingers slid from her arm and she hurried on into the mist.

*A*NNA had no idea how he found her when there were so many fleeing women in rags. So little visibility among the trees and so much panic. She could barely breathe and in her haste she stumbled and fell, but was forcing herself to her feet when he called her name.

"Anna Fedorina?"

She peered through the dank curtain of mist, and a tall man in dark clothes rose out of it. His long-fingered hand was extended toward her, and she saw a white stone balanced on its palm. It was Death drawing her into its embrace.

"Anna Fedorina? I've been shouting for you. Someone told me you were back here."

"Yes. I'm Anna Fedorina."

"Come with me."

"No."

"Sofia sent me."

Anna started to shake. "Sofia!" she shouted.

She looked frantically among the shadowy trunks. Was Sofia dead? Had she sent Death's Messenger to fetch her, too?

"Come quickly," Death's Messenger whispered in her ear.

Without knowing how, she found herself on his broad back being transported at speed through the shadows. She rested her head on the Messenger's damp head, and it occurred to her how like a human's was the hair of an angel.

SOFIA was waiting for her. She was so beautiful. Anna didn't remember her being so bewitchingly beautiful. She was propped up against a small gray horse, a pistol in her hand and on her face a look of grim determination to defend the animal against all would-be thieves. So Sofia wasn't dead. Thank God, she wasn't dead. Sofia opened her arms and Anna fell into them.

Neither spoke. They clung together, inhaling each other's breath and letting their hearts hammer against each other's. Dimly Anna was aware of voices shouting in the distance, but she took no notice, just held Sofia tight and felt tears hot on her skin.

"You're free now," Sofia whispered.

The familiar sound of her voice gave Anna a sudden surge of strength that cleared her mind. She lifted her head and, without releasing her hold on Sofia, asked eagerly, "Where's Vasily?"

DEATH'S Messenger was called Mikhail. Even so, Anna would always think of him as Death's Messenger in her own mind because he'd killed her father. Mikhail confessed that fact to her himself at their first stop for rest in the forest, and she wanted to tear out his heart there and then. To slice it into forty-one ragged pieces, one for each year of Papa's life, but she couldn't because it was clear he'd given it to Sofia, and Anna would steal nothing from Sofia.

"Thank you for rescuing me, Mikhail," she said with cool politeness. "The debt is repaid. A life for a life."

But she was glad to see the Messenger's gray eyes remain tormented and that he felt the need to ask, "How many guards were killed back there?"

"A handful compared to the number of prisoners you released."

"Still too many."

"No, Anna's right," Sofia said, brushing her hand against his in a gesture of comfort. "You've given those women a chance at life."

"If they make it to freedom."

"Some will, some won't. We will."

Mikhail nodded stiffly. He lifted both women onto the gray horse's back once more and set off with a long loping stride.

*W*HAT does Vasily look like?"

They were lying on a blanket together, but Anna couldn't sleep. Her thoughts wouldn't stop. The moon was a giant disc in the sky, bigger than any moon she'd ever seen in the camp, and the night breeze was full of secrets instead of stale and fetid. The fresh smell of forest creatures made her giddy. It swamped her senses. She muffled her cough in her scarf and kept her eyes wide open. To miss even a single minute of her freedom would be a sin. They had traveled all night and hidden unseen among the trees by day under a green canopy of branches. They heard tracker dogs in the distance, but none came near.

"Is he still as I described to you?" Anna asked.

"He's tall," Sofia said gently. "He stands very upright and swings his shoulders when he walks as if he knows exactly where he's going. You feel he's in control. Not just of the *kolkhoz* but of himself."

"Is he still handsome?"

"Yes, he's still handsome."

"Tell me more."

"Well . . ." Sofia smiled, and Anna could hear her picking her words carefully as she gazed up at the stars. "His eyes are the kind of gray that changes shade with his mood, and they are always observant. He's watching and thinking all the time." Sofia laughed softly, and something in the laugh made Anna wonder if it was Vasily she was talking about. "He can be quite unnerving sometimes. But he gleams, Anna."

"Gleams?"

"With belief. His certainty of the future he's building gleams like gold."

"Tell me again what he said."

"Oh, Anna."

"Tell me."

"Why? It only hurts. Just remember that he gave the jewels for me to use to help you."

"I want to hear it again, what he said."

"He said Vasily is dead and gone . . . We must put aside personal loyalties . . . This is the way forward, the only way forward."

Anna closed her eyes. "He's right. You know he is."

Anna"—Mikhail spoke in a low voice so as not to wake Sofia—"she is not as strong as she pretends."

"You mean the wound in her stomach."

"Yes."

"She won't tell me how it happened."

Mikhail sighed. "It was a group of soldiers. They were taking our horses and she . . . tried to stop them."

A soft rain was falling, muffling their voices as it pattered on the canvas stretched over their heads. Anna was sitting upright in her effort to breathe quietly beside Sofia, who was fretful and restless in her dreams. Mikhail stroked her shoulder, a gentle touch so tender that it made Anna want to cry.

"Sofia mentioned a dog," she prompted.

Mikhail nodded. "Yes, there was one, an unwanted stray that she adopted and fed. It was extraordinary. When the shot was fired, it leaped in front of her and died from the bullet."

"Maybe it just jumped up with excitement."

"Maybe."

"But she was hit in the stomach anyway."

"Yes, but only a shallow wound. The bullet went through the dog first and then into her. An old man we were with at the time—the one who let us take one of his rifles—removed it and stitched her up. He said she was very lucky because at that range the bullet should have ripped holes through her vital organs, but . . ." He brushed the tangle of pale hair off Sofia's sleeping face, and the lines of his mouth curved and softened.

"But what?"

"But I don't believe it was luck."

"So what was it?"

"Something more than luck."

For a while they were silent, watching the rain, and then Anna whispered, "Mikhail, where are we going?"

A shadow crossed his features. "To Tivil, because I have a son there. Sofia and I have it all planned . . . we'll collect him and after that we'll use the remaining jewels to buy tickets for all four of us, as well as travel documents and new identities. And medicines for you. We'll go somewhere safe and start a whole new life down by the Black Sea where it's warm and your lungs can heal."

"My father had a dacha down there."

The mention of her father silenced him, and she regretted it. They sat for a long time listening to the wind in the forest and Sofia's murmurs in her sleep.

"Will we make it, Mikhail? To Tivil."

"The truth is"—he paused and leaned closer—"it's unlikely, Anna. But don't tell that to Sofia. She is so determined to make it, and I'll do everything in my power to get us there, I swear. But we're fugitives, so our chances are . . ." He didn't finish.

"Poor?"

"I have only four shells left for the rifle."

"And the pistol?"

"Two bullets." Something seemed to loosen inside him and he shuddered. "I'm saving them." He looked at Anna and then at Sofia, and it was obvious what he meant. "Just in case," he murmured, and he lowered his head to kiss Sofia's hair.

No wonder Sofia was beautiful. To be loved like that would make anyone beautiful.

"Thank you, Mikhail," Anna whispered.

*C*AN you taste the air, Anna?"

It was night. A three-quarter moon lit their path through the forest and Mikhail walked ahead with the rifle while the two women rode the horse. For hours Sofia had walked stride for stride at his side, but now she was seated behind Anna, holding her firmly in place. Anna couldn't recall how or when that had happened. Dimly she had a memory of falling off.

"Yes, I can taste it."

"What does it taste of?"

"Of wild animals and wild birds and wild berries. Of nothing in cages."

"Wrong."

"Of clean water and soap and scrubbed fingernails."

Sofia laughed. "Wrong."

"It tastes of hope." Anna took in a great mouthful of air, then leaned back weakly against Sofia's warmth behind her. "Sweeter than honey on my tongue."

"Better."

Anna sighed. She didn't mean to, but the sight of a sliver of moonlight fingering the soft brown hair that rippled in the shadows ahead of them sent a shiver of longing through her for another head of brown hair. She loved Vasily so fiercely. Would she ever stop missing him? Even though he'd made it plain he didn't want her, didn't yearn for her the way she yearned for him, she knew she could never let him go.

"Shall I tell you what the air tastes of, Anna?"

In the dark Anna nodded, and the muffled sounds of the horse's tread faded to nothing. Sofia's breath was hot on her ear, and Anna could smell excitement in it.

"The best taste in the world and the worst. Sweet and sour in the mouth at the same time. It's the taste of choosing. You can choose, Anna. Do you remember how? I had to relearn after all those years without it. It was frightening at first but now"—Anna could sense her friend's gaze seeking out Mikhail in the dark—"I'm not frightened to choose any more."

Anna tipped her head back on a bony collarbone.

"There's something else," Sofia said, as if the contact had triggered the words, "something I wasn't going to tell you but now I feel I have to."

"What?"

"Something I kept to myself because I didn't want it to hurt you by raising your hopes."

"Tell me."

A pause, during which somewhere nearby an animal snapped a twig and made their heart rate jump.

"Vasily keeps a lock of your hair under his pillow."

Anna's breath stopped. She coughed, wiped blood from her mouth with her sleeve, and felt something roar into life inside her. She stuck out her tongue to savor the cool night air and it tasted of happiness.

*T*HE nights merged together. Anna could no longer separate them from days, as darkness settled in her mind and refused to lift. She could feel her body shutting down, and she fought it every breath of the way.

"She can't travel any farther, Sofia. It's killing her."

"Mikhail, my love, we can't stop. It's too dangerous."

"Dangerous to stop and dangerous to go on. You choose."

Sofia's voice dropped to a fierce whisper, but Anna heard the words as she lay strapped to the horse's back.

"She's dying, Mikhail. I swear on my love for you that I won't let her go without seeing him one last time."

The horse walked on, and each step jarred Anna's lungs, but she didn't care. She was going to see Vasily. Sofia had sworn.

SIXTY-ONE

"A horse is coming."

Pyotr stamped his *valenki* in the snow. "I can't see any horses," he complained, screwing up his eyes to peer into the white fog that lay like a sheet over the valley.

"They're coming," Rafik repeated.

"Is it Papa?"

Rafik frowned, his black eyebrows twitching under his *shapka*. "It's him and he's not alone."

"How do you know, Rafik?" Pyotr asked.

But Rafik didn't answer. Rafik and Zenia were standing with hands linked and muttering strange words that made no sense to Pyotr. But he had an odd feeling that the words turned into something solid in the cold damp air and rose like his breath to merge with the fog over Tivil. He didn't like the feeling. He began to throw snowballs to warm himself up.

They'd been waiting there an hour and his fingers had frozen, but that didn't worry him. What worried him much more was that his hopes had frozen. He could feel them in a hard icy lump inside his chest. He'd been curled up at home in front of the warm *pechka*, the stove, when Zenia had come bounding in, cheeks glowing, bundled him up into his *shuba* coat, and dragged him out into the snow. Over recent months he'd never quite grown used to the gypsy girl's sudden bursts of energy, and often he wondered if it had anything to do with all the strange herbs she ate.

"Pyotr, come on, he's waiting for us."

"Who?" He trotted alongside her, pulling on his *varezhki*, woolen mittens, his boots crunching through the snow.

"Rafik."

"Zenia, wait a minute." Pyotr was baffled. "What does he want with me?"

"Hurry up."

"I am hurrying."

"Your father is coming home."

Pyotr sobbed, a strange animal sound he'd never heard before. Around him Tivil looked the same, the roofs edged with blue icicles, the woodpiles stacked high, the picket fences hibernating under their coating of snow. Still the same dull old village, but suddenly it had changed. Now in Pyotr's wild joy everything shone bright and dazzling to welcome Papa home.

*H*IS excitement had cooled. The wind and the snow and the sound of ice cracking on the river had stolen its heat. They'd been waiting on the road into the village for so long now, but nobody had come and he'd started to believe they were wrong. Though Rafik had given him a smile of welcome when he'd first arrived, now the gypsies paid him little heed. They talked in intense low voices in a tight huddle that excluded him.

"When's Papa coming?" he asked again.

"Soon."

Soon had come and gone.

But now Rafik had said urgently, "A horse is coming."

*P*YOTR was the first to hear the whinny of the horse. He straightened up and stared out past Zenia, wrapped in her thick coat and headscarf, into the shifting banks of fog where the road should be, but it was like floating into another world, unfamiliar and unpredictable.

"Pyotr."

The word drifted, swirling and swaying in the air.

"Papa," Pyotr yelled, "Papa."

Out of the wall of white loomed a tall figure in a filthy coat, and at his side hobbled a small gray horse.

"Papa," Pyotr tried to shout again, but this time the word choked in his throat.

He flew into his father's arms, burrowed his face into the icy jacket, and listened to his heart. It was real. Beating fast. The cloth of the jacket smelled strange, and the beard on his face felt prickly, but it was his Papa. The big strong familiar hands gripped him hard, held him so close Pyotr couldn't speak.

"What's going on here?" his father demanded over Pyotr's head.

"We've been expecting you," the gypsy responded.

Mikhail gently disentangled one hand from his son and held it out to Rafik. The gypsy grasped it with a fervor that took Pyotr by surprise.

"Thank you, Mikhail," Rafik murmured. Not even the chill moan of the wind could conceal the joy in his voice.

Then for the first time Pyotr noticed the person behind his father, and the blood rushed to his face.

"Sofia!" he gasped.

"Hello, Pyotr." She smiled at him.

Her face was painfully thin, and her eyes were different somehow. Was she furious with him for what he had done?

"You look well," she said.

He could hear no trace of anger in her voice, just a warmth that defied the cold around them. She was grinning at him.

"Did you miss us?" she asked.

"I missed your jokes."

She laughed, and his father ruffled his hair under the fur hat, but his look was serious. "Pyotr, we've brought Sofia's friend back with us."

He gestured at a dark shape lying on the horse. It was strapped on the animal's back, skin as gray as the horse's coat, but the figure moved and struggled to sit up. At once Pyotr saw it was a young woman.

"We have to get her out of the cold," Papa said quickly.

Sofia moved close to the horse's side and placed a hand firmly on the rider's leg. It looked to Pyotr more like a wispy stick than a leg.

"Hold on, Anna, just a few minutes more. We're here now, here in Tivil, and soon you'll be . . ."

The young woman's eyes were glazed, and Pyotr wasn't sure she was even hearing Sofia's words. She attempted to nod but failed and slumped forward once more on the horse's neck. Sofia draped an arm around her thin shoulders.

"Quickly, *bistro.*"

Rafik and Zenia led the way, heads ducked against the swirling snowflakes that stung the eyes. Pyotr and Mikhail started to follow as fast as they could, with Mikhail leading the little gray mare, Sofia at its side, holding the sick young woman on its back. Pyotr could hear his father's labored breathing, felt the effort each step took, so he seized the reins from his hand and tucked himself under Papa's arm, bearing some of his weight. The horse dragged at every forward pace, and Pyotr was suddenly frightened for it. *Please, don't let it collapse right here in the snow.*

The sky was darkening and Pyotr could sense the village huddling deep in its valley, shutting out the world beyond. Something stirred inside him, something strong and possessive, and he tightened his grip on his father, but instead of stopping at his own house, the little procession continued right past it. The snow underfoot was loose and slippery.

"Where are we going, Papa?"

But his father didn't speak until they stood outside the *izba* that belonged to the chairman, which stood hunched under its coat of snow, shutters closed and smoke billowing from its chimney.

"Aleksei Fomenko!" Mikhail bellowed against the wind. He didn't bother knocking on the black door. "Aleksei Fomenko, get out here."

Pyotr jumped when the door slammed open and the tall figure of the chairman strode out into the snow in no more than his shirt-sleeves, the wolfhound a shadow behind him.

"Comrade Pashin, so you've decided to return. I didn't expect to see—"

His stern eyes skimmed over Mikhail and Pyotr, past the gypsies, and came to an abrupt halt on Sofia. His jaw seemed to jerk as if he'd been hit. Then his gaze shifted to the wretched horse. No one spoke.

Fomenko was the first to move. Hurriedly he opened the small gate, ran over to the horse, and, working fast but with great care, he untied the straps.

"Anna?" he whispered.

She raised her head. For a moment her eyes were blank and glazed, but snowflakes settled on her lashes, forcing her to blink.

"Anna," he said again.

Gradually life trickled back into her eyes. She pushed herself to sit up and stared at Fomenko, as though uncertain whether her mind was confusing her.

"Vasily, are you real? Or another ghost of the storm?"

He took her mittened hand in his and pressed it to his cold cheek. "I'm real enough, as real as the sleigh I built for you and as real as the songs you sang for me. I still hear them when the wind blows through the valley."

"Vasily," she sobbed, "Vasily."

She struggled to climb off the horse, but Fomenko lifted her from the saddle as gently as if he were handling a kitten, and cradled her in his arms away from the driving snow. Her head lay on his chest and he kissed her dull lifeless hair, then turned to face Sofia and Mikhail.

"I'll care for her," he said. "I'll buy the best medicines and make her well again."

"Why?" Sofia asked. "Why now and not before?"

Fomenko looked down at the pale woman in his arms, and his whole face softened. He spoke so quietly that the wind almost snatched his words away.

"Because she's here."

Sofia's cheeks were wet, and Pyotr didn't know if it was snow or tears.

Fomenko turned away from the watching group. At a steady pace, so as not to jar her fragile bones, with the dog walking ahead of him over the snow, he carried Anna into his house in Tivil.

*T*HE air was warm. That was the first thing Anna absorbed. Her bones had lost that agonizing ache and seemed to be melting from inside, they felt so soft and comfortable. She opened her eyes.

She'd forgotten what it was like to feel like this, so warm, so cosseted, a downy pillow under her head, a clean-smelling sheet pulled up to her neck. No brittle ice like jagged glass in her lungs. She tried breathing, a swift swallow of the warm air.

Bearable.

Her gaze explored the room, sliding with slow consideration over the curtains, the chair, the carpet, the shirts hanging on hooks, all full of color. Color. She hadn't realized how much she'd missed it. In the gulag everything was gray. A small sigh of exquisite pleasure escaped her, a faint sound, but it was enough. Instantly a whining started up outside the bedroom door and brought her back to reality.

Whose house was she in?

Mikhail's? Or . . . No. She shook her head and felt a pain like acid etch into her brain. No, it wasn't Mikhail's. Only dimly did she recall being carried in a pair of strong arms, but she knew exactly whose bed she was lying in and whose dog was whining at the door.

*T*HE latch lifted quietly. Anna's heart stopped, but her eyes hungrily sought out the figure standing in the shadow of the door. He was tall and very still, holding himself stiffly, and in a flash of nerves she wondered whether the stiffness was mental or physical. His shirt fitted closely across his wide chest but hung loose at the hips, and his hair was cropped hard to his head.

Vasily. It was Vasily, with the Dyuzheyev forehead, the same long aristocratic nose, but the once-generous mouth was now held tight in a firm line. The same eyes, she remembered those gray swirling eyes. At his heel stood a large rough-coated wolfhound, and Anna recalled Sofia telling her its name.

"Hope," she breathed. It was easier than saying *Vasily*.

The dog loped toward her, its claws clipping the wooden floor, and nuzzled her hand, and that simple display of affection seemed to persuade Vasily at last to walk into the room. But there was something deliberately formal in his step, and he came no nearer than the end of the bed.

He spoke first. "How are you feeling?"

His voice was controlled, and deeper than it used to be, but she could still hear the young Vasily in it, and it sent a shiver of pleasure through her.

"I'm fine."

"Are you cold? Do you need another quilt?"

"No. I'm warm, thank you."

Another awkward silence.

"Are you hungry?"

She smiled. "Ravenous."

He nodded and though he didn't move away, his eyes did. They looked at the dog's shaggy head now resting on the quilt, at the round wooden knobs at each corner of the bed, at the white-painted wall, at the window and a gust of snowflakes careening across the yard outside. Anywhere but at her.

"You look well, Vasily," she said softly.

He studied his own strong hands, but said nothing.

This time she let the silence stay. She didn't know what was happening, and her mind felt too weak to struggle with it. Was he angry at her for coming here? For risking his position as chairman of the *kolkhoz*? Who could blame him? She didn't want him to be angry, of course she didn't, but at the same time in an odd way it didn't matter if he was. *This* was what mattered. *Being here.* Gazing at the way his gray eyes had sparked—was it anger or delight?—as he stepped into the room.

She reveled in the long lean lines of his body and the familiar set of his head on the broad shoulders. The only thing she missed was his hair, the way a soft tumble of brown straw used to fall across his high forehead and make him look . . . look what? She smiled. Lovable. These shorn hard spikes of hair belonged to a different Vasily.

He saw the smile. Even though he wasn't looking at her, he still was aware of the smile and she saw him move closer. She felt choked by the intensity of the pleasure of breathing the same air he was breathing and by the wave of love that engulfed her. So much was unsaid. And she felt no need to say it. Just looking at him was enough.

Abruptly, when she least expected it, he turned and disappeared from the room. She had no idea whether he was gone five minutes or five hours, but when she again opened her eyes he was sitting in a chair beside her bed, so close she could see the shadows that lined his eyes and a tiny web of lines beginning at the tight corners of his mouth.

"Here, time to eat."

In his hands lay a bowl of soup. Steam rose from it and brushed his chin, and she couldn't take her eyes from that strong square underpinning of his face.

"Eat," he said again.

She tried to sit up and failed, so she struggled at least to lift her head higher on the pillow. She was shocked to find herself so weak. Everything ached. Even that little movement of her head set off more coughing, and when she'd finished gasping for breath he wiped a damp cloth across her lips, studied the red smear on it with a frown, and put the cloth aside. He looked at her intently.

"How are you feeling?"

"Fine," she whispered.

For a brief moment a faint ironic smile tilted one side of his mouth.

"Fine," he repeated, "just fine."

He lifted the spoon from the bowl and raised it to her lips. Willingly she parted them and felt the thick aromatic liquid flow down into her starved stomach.

"It's wonderful," she murmured.

"Only a few mouthfuls now. More later."

"But I'm—"

"No, your body can't take much yet, Anna."

Anna.

It was the first time he'd spoken her name. She badly wanted him to say it again.

"Thank you . . . Vasily."

His eyes sought and held hers. "My name is no longer Vasily. I am called Aleksei Fomenko now. It's important that you call me that. I'm putting it about in the village that you are . . ."

But he stopped, unable to finish. His eyes were fixed on her face and she could see a thousand thoughts and questions racing through their dark gray depths, but none that she could decipher. Suddenly she was acutely conscious of what she must look like to him, a skeletal jumble of bones in a nightdress, with skin as lifeless as ash and weeping sores on . . .

Nightdress?

Who had taken her out of her filthy rags? Who had clothed her in this virginal white nightdress? Instantly she was sure it was Vasily himself. He'd undressed her and bathed her and seen the sickening state of her, and the thought sent a hot surge of shame through her. He seemed to read the thoughts in her head and he put down the bowl, reached out a hand, and rested the tips of his fingers on· her bare throat.

"Anna," he said in a low voice, "I can feel your heart pumping. You—" His breath caught, and for a long moment there was only the wind rattling the window pane and Vasily's finger brushing her throat. "You are even more beautiful than I remembered."

"Vasily!"

As his name burst out of her mouth she saw something break inside him. And suddenly his arms were around her and he was sitting on the bed holding her to his chest, rocking her, crushing her tight against himself, as though he would press her deep inside his bones.

"Anna," he whispered over and over again, "Anna, my Anna." He kissed her hot forehead and caressed her filthy lank hair. "Forgive me."

"For what?"

"For not coming."

She touched the hard line of his jaw with her lips. "You're here now."

"I made a promise," Vasily explained.

"To whom?"

"To Lenin." He shook his head. "Not in person, of course, but to the bronze statue of him in Leningrad. After I came back from the civil war"—he shuddered at the memory, and Anna felt his heart thud behind his ribs—"and couldn't find you, though I scoured the city endlessly for news of you, I swore I would become the perfect Soviet citizen, dedicating my life to Lenin's ideals, if—"

She lifted a finger and touched his lips. She could feel the blood pulsing inside them. "Hush, Vasily, there's no need to explain."

"Yes, I want you to understand. I dedicated my life to Communism. I even spilled some of my blood and wrote the promise in red to seal the bargain, in return for . . ."

"For what?"

"In return for Lenin's spirit keeping you safe."

Anna gasped. He stroked her gaunt cheek.

"I kept my word," he murmured into her hair, "all these years. When I did help people escape from the authorities, it was because they were the intellectual building blocks who would be needed to strengthen Russia." He drew a deep breath and said fiercely, "I kept my word."

"Even when Sofia came and begged."

"Yes, even then."

"To make sure my heart kept beating?"

"Yes."

"Oh, Vasily."

They clung to each other, motionless, his arms cradling her. Neither spoke for a long time.

ANNA slept. She had no sense of time. Just moments slotted into her feverish mind. At intervals she woke and Vasily was there, always there, feeding her spoonfuls of soup and finely shredded red meat, or dosing her with foul-tasting medicines. He talked to her by the hour, and she listened.

"Wake up."

Anna had dozed off again into a disturbed world of nightmares, but opened her eyes swiftly the instant she heard the sound of Sofia's voice.

"Wake up," Sofia said again. "Every time I come to see you, you're fast asleep."

She was perched on the side of the bed, wearing a wool dress the color of dark lavender, and there was a wide smile on her beautiful face.

"I can't believe how much better you look already," Sofia announced. "And you've only been here a week. How's the coughing?"

Anna pulled a face. "Give me time. I know you planned for us to move somewhere safer, but . . ."

Sofia took her friend's hand in hers and gently chafed it. "You have all the time in the world now."

"Thanks to you."

"And to Mikhail. I couldn't have done it without him."

"Yes. And to your Mikhail. Thank you both."

Their eyes met, two differing blues, and something passed between them at that moment, a knowledge of what Sofia had done but also an agreement never to talk of it again. Words were too small to voice what lay deep inside them both.

Instead Anna asked, "Has Mikhail spoken to Vas—I mean Aleksei about the killing of his father and Aleksei's mother that day at the Dyuzheyevs' villa?"

"Yes. They'll never be friends, but now they're prepared not to be enemies. It's a first step."

"That's wonderful."

Sofia nodded and smiled. "Give me a hug, you skinny lazybones."

Anna struggled to sit up, and immediately a spasm of coughing racked her brittle chest. Sofia held her safely until the shuddering ceased, and Anna could smell the clean soapy fragrance of her blond hair and the freshness of her skin. When the spasm was finally over she insisted on sitting up.

"Wash my hair, Sofia."

"It'll exhaust you."

"Please, Sofia. For me."

"For him, you mean," Sofia said with a ripple of laughter that set her eyes alight.

"Yes," Anna whispered, as she entwined her arms around the tall young woman on her bed. "For Vasily."

SIXTY-TWO

SOFIA was in the icy backyard of Mikhail's *izba* when Priest Logvinov arrived. It was just as she was stacking logs from the woodpile into her arms that he lurched around the corner of the cottage and called her name.

"Sofia."

Then again, louder.

"Sofia!"

She'd always known this day would come. That this man would somehow be involved in the disaster that she could sense breathing, snuffling and snarling, circling around the village of Tivil. The way a wolf nips and nudges at the heels of a moose before bringing it down, blood-streaked, in the snow.

She dropped the logs to the ground and turned to face him.

"What is it, Priest?"

He was draped in a threadbare coat that reached down to his ankles and a black *shapka* with earflaps, but his green eyes and flame-colored hair flashed like summer lightning. He was breathless, and Sofia realized he'd been running.

"They're coming," he shouted, though she was no more than a few feet from him.

"Who are *they?*"

"Ask Rafik."

"Where is he?"

He waved a long scarecrow arm. "Out there."

"Show me."

She ran into the house and pulled on the thick coat the gypsy girl had made for her return.

"Mikhail," she called urgently, "someone is coming. Rafik is waiting outside."

He lifted his head from the intricate work of rebuilding the model bridge, and his calm gaze immediately steadied her. One look at her and he rose to his feet; two strides and his arms were around her.

"You don't have to go, Sofia."

"I do."

"You have a choice."

She nodded her head with a quick intake of breath. "Yes, we could leave instead. You, me, and Pyotr. Right now. We could grab a few things and escape into the forest and head south like we planned and—"

"Is that what you want, my love? Is it really what you came back for?"

Their eyes held, a long, sweet, complicated moment. She leaned against him, her whole body molding itself to his, her forehead resting on his cheekbone, and she felt the fear and panic drain from where they had been squeezing her lungs.

"Hurry, Sofia." It was the priest's voice outside.

She tilted back her head to look up into Mikhail's face, her arms still looped around his waist. It felt thinner than it used to be but still strong.

"Will you come?" she asked.

"You don't have to ask."

He kissed her, hard and possessive, then released her, and she trailed a soft finger along the line of his mouth.

"We'll do this together," she whispered.

A figure in a padded coat appeared at her side.

"And me." It was Pyotr.

* * *

*M*ORE horses are coming," Rafik said, his black eyes closed as he searched for them inside his mind. "Four of them."

The group was gathered on the packed snow. Above them spread the large cedar tree at the start of the village where the valley began to widen. Fingers of white fog wreathed its branches and slithered down to clutch at the eight figures beneath it, brushing their chill cheeks and soaking their hair until it glistened. By the time Priest Logvinov led Sofia and Mikhail, with Pyotr determinedly rushing ahead of them, to where Rafik and his daughter were staring out into the shapeless distance, the sky had slid down from the ridge and closed in around them; the fog had claimed the valley for itself.

Sofia was surprised to find Elizaveta Lishnikova and the blacksmith standing shoulder to shoulder beside the gypsies, Elizaveta in stern gray, Pokrovsky in menacing black. Their silent presence here meant only one thing: Rafik was going to need help. She slid her hand into her pocket and let her fingers fret at the cold white stone that lay there. The priest raised his arm and painted the sign of the cross in the cold white air.

"Four horsemen," he announced. "May God have mercy on our souls. You understand what that means?"

"What does it mean, Sofia?" Pyotr asked impatiently. "What does it mean? Who are the four horsemen?"

"Hush, Pyotr," Zenia hissed.

"They're soldiers," Rafik said.

"Why are soldiers coming to Tivil?" Pyotr asked.

But instead of replying, Rafik suddenly fixed his gaze on Zenia, and he asked her softly, "Is it you who brings them here?"

"No, Rafik," she cried out. "I didn't, I swear I didn't." Her black eyes glittered, and her hands stretched out to her father.

Gently he enfolded them in his.

"I always knew it would happen." The sorrow in Rafik's quiet voice seemed to melt the frigid air around him. "I knew that betrayal would come, but"—his lips smiled at her tenderly, and he raised her hands to them—"but I could not see it would be you, my daughter. My love for you stood in the way of my Sight."

"Rafik, no, no."

He pressed his lips to her cold forehead just as the jangle of horses' bridles and the creak of stiff leather came upon them.

"Rafik, forgive me. I meant no harm." Zenia clung to him. "A careless word to Vanya, that's all it was, I didn't mean it. You know how I love you. I even torched the barn last summer to distract the troops from ransacking Tivil and causing you pain. Please forgive me, I—"

"Hush, my beloved daughter. There's nothing to forgive." He opened his arms to her.

She kissed his cheek.

Priest Logvinov lifted his stricken face to the heavens, stretched out his arms like a cross, and roared, "See her give the kiss, oh Lord. See, here among us is the sign of Judas."

*F*OUR shapes emerged from the white confusion of the fog. Men on horseback, bulky in their greatcoats and high leather boots, determined men who knew their own power. They were OGPU. The officer in the lead was scanning the group standing in the snow, a hard arrogant scrutiny, his collar turned up against the cold and a calming hand laid on the neck of his pale-coated horse. Sofia didn't like the horse. It had small wild eyes.

"Do any of you know the man named Rafik Ilyan?" the officer demanded.

"I am Rafik Ilyan."

The other three horsemen dismounted. Sofia saw the teacher immediately link hands with the blacksmith and the priest. Zenia joined them, and they stood facing outward in a circle around Rafik.

"We are here to arrest you, Rafik Ilyan."

"No." The word tore out of Pyotr's mouth before Mikhail could stop him.

The officer glanced at him with irritation. "Get home to your mother, boy, if you don't want a thrashing."

"I have no mother."

"You have Mother Russia."

"Comrade," Elizaveta spoke in her calm, reasonable voice, "I think there has been some mistake. Rafik Ilyan is a loyal member of our village."

"Why is he under arrest?" Pokrovsky demanded.

"No mistake."

"My father has done nothing wrong." Tears were running down Zenia's cheeks.

The priest glared at the intruders, his lips moving in silent prayer.

The officer smiled, satisfied, and nodded at his men. "Arrest the gypsy, then search his house."

They came for him, and it was Zenia who broke the circle first. She threw herself toward the officer, clung to his horse's bridle, and begged.

"Please don't. This is all wrong, a mistake. I didn't mean to tell Vanya anything . . ."

The horse tossed its head viciously, sending Zenia flying on the trampled snow. Sofia ran to her, crouched down, and put an arm around her shoulders, though the sharp hooves danced close.

"This isn't right," she said accusingly.

"Not right?" The officer chuckled, his expression so amiable she thought for a moment he was agreeing with her, but the chuckle ceased abruptly. "We have information that Rafik Ilyan has been conducting anti-Soviet activities. Arrest him."

"What exactly is he accused of?" Mikhail demanded.

"I have already said. Anti-Soviet activities."

"That's nonsense," Sofia said sharply. But she turned with an abrupt movement away from the officer and closed the gap between herself and the gypsy. Her eyes pleaded with him.

"Rafik, help yourself," she murmured.

He shook his head. "I have no power to help myself, child of the stone. I can only help others."

Sofia reached quickly into her coat and drew out the plain white pebble.

"Help me to help you," she begged.

His eyes locked on the pebble. Its milky surface seemed to pull at him, so that he stumbled toward it, but suddenly the uniforms surrounded him. With a bellow of rage the big blacksmith charged forward, Zenia at his side.

"If you take one more step, it will be your last." The officer's voice rang out through the bleak landscape. A solitary crow drifted overhead, folded its wings, and sank down on to the white fields in silence.

Rafik shook his head. He laid a gentle hand on each of his

companions in turn, on Pokrovsky's barrel chest, on Elizaveta Lishnikova's proud shoulder, on Zenia's pale damp cheek. He caught hold of the priest's hand for a moment, staring deep into his eyes, and then released him in mute farewell. When finally he stepped away from them, the three uniforms moved with him.

"Comrade," he called to the officer, "leave my friends in peace. I am the one you—"

Before he'd finished speaking Sofia stepped forward, and her hands were on the wrists of two of the OGPU men. She was pressing their flesh and murmuring to them. Time hung lifeless in the white fog. The metallic click of a rifle bolt sounded loud in the silence. "Get away from her. Come over here."

The officer was gazing fixedly at Sofia, but he was speaking to Rafik.

"Sofia, don't." It was Mikhail speaking. "I love you, Sofia." His voice was urgent. "Don't risk it all. You are needed."

The two men she had been murmuring to were standing oddly, their jaws slack, their spines soft, and Rafik was smiling strangely at Sofia.

"Mikhail is right," Rafik said. "You are needed." He placed his thumb in the center of her forehead. "I have faith in you, daughter of my soul."

"I'll say it only once more. Come here," the officer snapped.

Instead of obeying the order, Rafik turned and walked in the opposite direction toward the village.

"Rafik!" It was Zenia's desolate cry.

"I cannot leave Tivil."

His voice carried to them through the fog and Sofia heard his words echo, rebounding in her head, a split second before the shot rang out in the still air. The gypsy's wiry frame jerked. His arms flew out like wings, and then he crumpled to the snow and a stain spread from under him. The air suddenly seemed heavy.

"Run, Pyotr, run! Fetch Chairman Fomenko." It was Mikhail's voice, quick and decisive.

Pyotr ran. Sofia couldn't feel the ice freezing her cheeks or the snow treacherous under her feet; all she could feel was a huge hole in her heart.

SIXTY-THREE

*T*HE pebble crouched in Sofia's hand and she didn't move, didn't breathe.

"Rafik, don't leave me."

The words trailed out of her in a long low cry of despair, but Rafik was gone. The pain of it pooled in her chest and she closed her eyes, but dark places started to open up in her mind, lonely places she didn't want to visit. She shivered uncontrollably, and abruptly warm arms were around her and air rushed back into her lungs. Mikhail was speaking to her. She didn't hear the words but she heard the love in them, felt the strength of them banish the loneliness.

"Come," he said.

He led her to where Rafik lay in the snow. Zenia had turned over her father's body so that his black eyes gazed sightlessly up at a crow that hovered overhead, its ragged wings whispering words that only he could hear. The gypsy girl lay across Rafik's chest, her wild tangle of black hair writhing, dry sobs shaking her. Around her stood the teacher, blacksmith, and priest, faces gray with shock. Snowflakes had started to come spinning down in great white spirals, the first icy blast of a *purga*, a sudden snowstorm blowing up, and dimly Sofia became aware of angry voices behind her. She turned to see Aleksei Fomenko, a tall and broad figure in his *fufaika* coat, arguing with the OGPU officer, with the wolfhound as always at his side.

"You had no right to come into my village to arrest a *kolkhoz* member without informing me first."

"I am not answerable to a village chairman."

"It looks like you've more than done your job," Fomenko growled with fury. "Now leave."

"My men will search his house first."

"No," Sofia whispered. The strange mystical contents that lay in Rafik's house would condemn the whole village.

Mikhail stepped forward to stand beside Fomenko, eyes narrowed against the falling snow. "Look, he was just a gypsy who was good with horses, nothing more, a man who understood their moods and could get a solid day's work out of them. And now he's dead. You'll find nothing in his house except a few pots of stinking grease for softening bridles."

"So you knew this enemy of the people?" the officer demanded with interest.

Sofia's heart slid somewhere cold.

But Mikhail was careful. "I knew him only as someone who lived in Tivil. We didn't share a glass of vodka together, if that's what you mean." He nodded at the officer and banged his hands on his arms in a noisy show of the shivers. "It's cold, comrade. The coming storm will trap you here in Tivil if you don't hurry. Get back to Dagorsk with your men; this business is finished."

Sofia could feel an uneasy suspension of breath around her, and barely noticeable in the darkening of the light she moved close and touched the officer's pale horse on its big shoulder muscle. It bared its teeth but didn't bite, though the white threads of its tail twitched like serpents. *Leave. Just leave.* After a long thoughtful moment the officer shrugged and said no more but swung his horse's head and, hunched against the wind, cantered off through the snow at the head of his troop. The *purga* swallowed them.

★ ★ ★

*T*HE figures stood motionless in a moment of shock, and then Mikhail quickly wrapped one arm around Sofia, the other around Pyotr. "We must get Rafik's body out of the storm."

But before they could move, Elizaveta spoke out in a voice that was astonishingly powerful against the rising wind.

"Listen to us, Sofia."

Four figures stood in a line, blocking the path into the village. Priest Logvinov, Elizaveta Lishnikova, Pokrovsky, and the weeping gypsy girl. The blacksmith had lifted Rafik's limp body into his arms, and Zenia's hand rested on her father's dark head.

"Sofia," Elizaveta said, "we ask you to take Rafik's place."

"No."

"Sofia," Pokrovsky said, "you are needed."

You are needed. Rafik's words.

Sofia recoiled. "No."

A rustling of sound seemed to brush against her mind. She shook her head sharply. "No."

"Sofia." It was the priest. He raised a hand into the snow-laden air between them but carved no cross this time. "God will grant you strength. You are the one who can help care for our village. Rafik knew it, he believed in you."

I have faith in you. His final words to her.

"*Nyet.* No." She inhaled deeply, ice stinging her lungs. "Mikhail, it's dangerous. Tell them."

Fomenko was standing to one side, observing them in silence, his eyes intensely curious. But Sofia's eyes were drawn to the road into Tivil and she felt it pull at her, as powerfully as the moon pulls the tide. Through the snow that was now falling fast, the village drifted into view, the *izbas* waiting.

Mikhail took her hand in his. "My love, it has to be your decision, yours alone."

"I don't have the strength. Not like Rafik."

"We will help you."

Sofia looked at the circle of people around her and knew that the life she'd been pretending she and Mikhail could lead elsewhere was never destined to happen.

"I'll be with you," Mikhail said and his hand tightened on hers.

The sound of Tivil breathing came to her. She didn't want it to die, and somehow she sensed that the decision had been made long ago, before she was born. Was there any truth in what Rafik had told her, that she had inherited a special gift as the seventh daughter of a seventh daughter? She knew only that from him she had started to learn a way of applying her mind, a way of shifting sand. She looked around her in the swirling snow, at these people who believed in her and who cared so passionately for their village, and she experienced a huge sense of belonging. Here was a place that pulled at her heart, a place that was home. And she owed it to Anna. *My dear Anna, grow well and strong again. It's because of you that I'm here, with this man at my side.* Spasibo.

"I'll stay," she said simply.

SIXTY-FOUR

Tivil
Spring 1934

THE air was crystal clear, and high above Tivil the wispy trail of an airplane skimmed across a pale blue sky. Mikhail gazed up at it, shading his eyes.

"It's an ANT-9," Pyotr said confidently. "The same as the *Krokodil*."

"You're right," Mikhail grinned. "You'll be a pilot yet."

They were in the graveyard at the back of what was once the church, the grass still fragile with frost where the building's shadow lay, but the spring sunshine was tempting out the first buds. Sofia was kneeling beside Rafik's grave. In her hand she held a bunch of *podnezhniki*, snowdrops, their delicate heads softly swaying as she placed them in a jar on the grave.

"Where did you find the flowers so early?" Mikhail asked.

She smiled up at him. "Where do you think?"

"Beneath the cedar tree."

"Of course."

She and Anna had picked them together. It was there that Anna had shyly whispered the news that she was pregnant.

"It's a secret," Anna laughed, "but I can't keep it from you. Now that I'm so much better, it'll be safe."

"Have you told your husband yet?"

"Yes."

"And?"

Anna touched her stomach. "We're naming him Vasily."

"Let's hope it's a boy then," Sofia had laughed.

Now she took the white stone from her pocket and rested it on Rafik's grave.

"Why do you always do that?" Pyotr asked.

He'd grown taller in the winter months, his shoulders suddenly broader and his eyes more thoughtful, and Sofia had found herself watching him and wondering.

"I do it because this stone connects Tivil to Rafik."

She picked it up. Neither Communism nor the Church had brought peace to Tivil, but this was something different, a strength that seemed to rise from the heart of the earth itself. She looked into the boy's eyes.

"Hold the stone," she said.

Pyotr didn't hesitate, as if he'd been waiting a long time for this moment. His hand grasped the stone, and immediately his young eyes filled with light in the bright spring morning.

"Pyotr, before your papa adopted you, did you have brothers?"

"Yes, but when I was three," his eyes were studying the milky stone, "they all died in the typhus epidemic."

"Six older brothers? Making you the seventh son."

"Yes. How do you know that?"

She didn't answer his question.

"Pyotr, would you like to come for walks with me sometimes when it's dark? And learn to shape the thoughts that form in your mind?"

Pyotr looked to his father. Mikhail gazed at his son with gentle regret and nodded. "Take care of my son, Sofia."

"I will, I promise."

Pyotr stood, still fingering the stone. "When will we start?" he asked.

Sofia gazed around at the village that was her home, at the houses so sturdy and yet so fragile in the sunshine.

"Tonight," she murmured. "We'll start tonight."

Max Danby

Kate Furnivall was born in Wales and now lives by the sea in the beautiful county of Devon in England with her husband. She has worked in publishing and television advertising. Her love for all things Russian stems from her family history in pre-revolution St. Petersburg. Her previous book, the bestselling *The Russian Concubine*, is also published by Berkley. Visit her website at www.KateFurnivall.com.